SCEPTER
OF
FLINT

A LORD HANI MYSTERY

N.L.   HOLMES

WayBack Press
P.O.Box 16066
Tampa, FL
⚜

Dedicated to my husband.

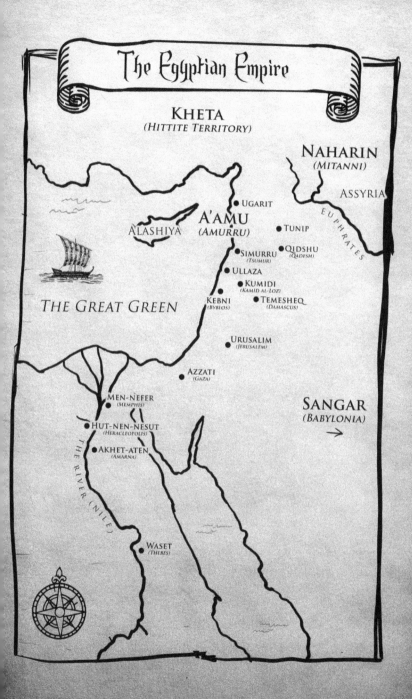

The Egyptian Empire

KHETA
(HITTITE TERRITORY)

NAHARIN
(MITANNI)

ASSYRIA

EUPHRATES

• UGARIT

A'AMU
(AMURRU)

• TUNIP

ALASHIYA

• SIMURRU
(TSUMUR)

• QIDSHU
(QADESH)

• ULLAZA

• KUMIDI
(KAMID AL-LOZ)

KEBNI
(BYBLOS)

• TEMESHEQ
(DAMASCUS)

THE GREAT GREEN

• URUSALIM
(JERUSALEM)

• AZZATI
(GAZA)

• MEN-NEFER
(MEMPHIS)

SANGAR
(BABYLONIA)
→

• HUT-NEN-NESUT
(HERACLEOPOLIS)

• AKHET-ATEN
(AMARNA)

THE RIVER (NILE)

• WASET
(THEBES)

HISTORICAL NOTES

T HIS STORY TAKES PLACE DURING the period of Egypt's history known as the New Kingdom, when the country had become an empire with holdings in Nubia to the south and throughout the Levant to the north. It begins around 1343 BCE, the approximate date of the so-called Great Jubilee of the Aten held by Akhenaten in his twelfth regnal year. Although authorities are divided about this, the author has accepted a five-year coregency between Akhenaten and his father, during which his regnal years would have begun to be counted.

The reign of Akhenaten marked a nearly unimaginable overturning of values and customs millennia old, a testimony to the absolute power of the king. But judging by the speed with which his "reforms" were reversed after his death, we must assume that relatively few people really bought into them. We may imagine that those whose livelihood was interrupted by the reforms would have bided their time impatiently and maybe hastened along the fall of Akhenaten's support.

Many scholars accept that the mysterious "Greatly Beloved Wife" Kiya was the Mitannian princess Taduhepa, originally sent to Akhenaten's father Amenhotep III. Her name suddenly ceases to be seen at a certain point, and all her monuments had her name chiseled out and that of one of the king's daughters put in its place. Baket-aten is thought by some to have been her child; others make her a late daughter of Tiyi. Less controversial is the fact that a plague did indeed sweep through Egypt, brought to the capital by northern vassals at the time of the Great Jubilee. Since many of the royal family died at that time, some think they may have been victims of the epidemic. Although the tomb robberies described in this book are fictitious, the exchange of hostages with Naharin—Mane for Pirissi and Tulubri—is real.

The Egyptian concept of the soul involved five parts, which were thought to reunite in the afterworld to form a single perfected being, the *akh*.

While we know the names of many Egyptian sculptors, the names of painters are unknown— probably because wall painting was done in teams, with many people being responsible for the final product. Among painters, as elsewhere in society, those who were literate enjoyed more prestige than those who were not.

And finally, a note about Egyptian time-keeping: they had a ten-day week with a two-day "weekend" embedded. In addition, there were so many festivals that a third of the year was non-work time!

CHARACTERS

(Persons marked with an * are purely fictitious)

HANI'S FAMILY

A'a*: the doorkeeper of Hani's family.

Amen-em-hut: Nub-nefer's brother, Third Prophet of Amen.

Amen-em-ope known as **Pa-kiki*** (The Monkey)**:** Hani and Nub-nefer's second son.

Amen-hotep known as **Hani:** a diplomat.

Amen-hotep known as **Aha*:** Hani and Nub-nefer's eldest son. Later takes the name **Hesy-en-aten**.

Amen-hotep known as **Anuia:** wife of Amen-em-hut, a chantress of Amen.

Amen-mes known as **Maya*:** Hani's dwarf secretary and son-in-law, married to Sat-hut-haru.

Baket-iset*: their eldest daughter.

Bener-ib*: Neferet's friend and fellow student.

In-hapy*: royal goldsmith and mother of Maya.

Iuty*: a gardener of Hani's family.

Khentet-ka*: Aha's wife.

Meryet-amen*: Mery-ra's lady friend.

Mery-ra: Hani's father.

Mut-nodjmet*: Pipi's eldest daughter, wife of Pa-kiki.

Nedjem-ib*: Pipi's wife.

Pa-kiki*: Hani's younger son.

Pa-ra-em-heb known as **Pipi*:** Hani's brother.

Pen-amen*: son of Amen-em-hut, Hani's nephew.

Neferet*: Hani and Nub-nefer's youngest daughter.

Nub-nefer*: Hani's wife, a chantress of Amen.

Sat-hut-haru*: Hani and Nub-nefer's second daughter.

OTHER CHARACTERS

Ah-mes: chief of the Hall of Justice under Amenhotep III and Akhenaten.

Akh-en-aten (Amen-hotep IV): known by his throne name **Nefer-khepru-ra Wa-en-ra.**

Ankh-reshet*: overseer of the right hand corps of workmen on the Theban tombs.

Apeny: wife of Ptah-mes and, in this story, *weret khener* of Amen-Ra.

Aper-el: vizier of Lower Egypt.

Ay: father-in-law and probably uncle of Akhenaten, who held considerable power under Akhenaten's reign and that of his successors, eventually becoming king.

Bebi-ankh*: "black-line man" on the Theban tombs.

Djau*: chief draftsman on the Theban tombs.

Djefat-nebty*: woman physician in attendance on the royal harem.

Heqa-nakht*: stonecutter on the Theban Tombs.

Keliya: Mitannian diplomat.

Khawy*: nephew of Djau.

Kiya: Mitannian princess originally named Taduhepa, married first to Amenhotep III then to his son, who made her his Greatly Beloved Wife.

Mahu: chief of police under Akhenaten.

Mane: diplomat assigned to Naharin (Mitanni).

Menna*: An infantry officer, whose life Hani had saved.

Nefert-iti Nefer-nefru-aten: queen and later possible coregent of Akhenaten. She was probably his cousin on the maternal side. Her name means "the beautiful one has come."

Pa-aten-em-heb (Har-em-heb): An infantry officer who becomes Pa-kiki's employer. Historically, it is

unclear whether these two names belonged to the same person.

Pa-ren-nefer: Steward of Akhenaten.

Pentju: Chief physician of Akh-en-aten, priest of the Aten.

Pirissi and **Tulubri:** Mitannian diplomats.

Ptah-mes: former vizier of Upper Egypt, First Prophet of Amen-Ra, and mayor of Thebes, current high commissioner of northern vassals (this last office fictitiously ascribed to him).

Sa-tau: Keeper of the Double House of Silver and Gold (treasurer) under Akhenaten.

Talpu-sharri*: Mitannian chamberlain of Lady Kiya.

GLOSSARY OF GODS

Amen-Ra: Amen, the Hidden One, was a local god of Thebes. When a Theban dynasty came to power in Egypt, Amen became the high god of the entire country and was merged with the all-important sun god **Ra**.

Ammit: "The Devourer", a monster who consumed the souls that proved unworthy in the judgment that followed death.

Aten: The Aten was originally just the visible disk of the sun in the sky. Amen-hotep III claimed to be himself the Aten, that is, the *manifestation* of the sun god. His son took it a step further and worshiped his father as a kind of purely spiritual high god, not to be depicted or approached except through Akh-en-aten himself, the sole mediator.

Bes: An ugly, lion-like dwarf god, protector of children.

Djehuty: Thoth, the god of scribes and judge of souls, often associated with ibises or baboons.

Hapy: God/goddess of the Nile inundation. Because he/she represented the totality of fertility, Hapy was thought of as hermaphroditic.

Haru: The solar hawk god Horus, the One on High. The king, while alive, was considered to be his avatar, except under Akh-en-aten.

Hut-haru: Hathor, a multi-purpose feminine deity—goddess of beauty, joy, music, and sex, welcomer of the dead, and personification of the gentler aspects of the sun. Her name means "mansion of Horus."

Inpu: Anubis, the god of embalming.

Khonsu: God of the moon, a son of Amen-Ra, seen as the protector of travelers.

Ma'at: Both the goddess and the concept (with a lower-case *m*) of truth, cosmic order, and right.

Meret-seger: "The lover of silence", goddess of the desert where the dead are buried on the west bank of the Nile.

Mut: The consort of the god Amen-Ra, considered a motherly protector.

Ptah: The creator god of Memphis.

Sekhmet: The Powerful One, lion-headed goddess of plague and hence of healing. She also represented the murderous power of the sun, a kind of malicious alter-ego of Hut-haru.

Serqet: The scorpion goddess who protected from poisonous stings and from illness generally.

Seshat: The goddess who personified writing.

Shu and Tefnut: The male and female principles, twins and spouses, first of all the gods to split off from the primal All. They represented Air or Light and Moisture.

Ta-weret: "The Great One," the hippopotamus goddess who protected women and children.

GLOSSARY OF TERMS AND PLACES

A'amu: Called **Amurru** by its inhabitants, this was a kingdom on the Mediterranean coast north of Byblos and south of Ugarit.

Akhet-aten: Horizon of the Aten, the new capital city built by Akhenaten.

Book of Going Forth by Day: the so-called Book of the Dead, a collection of spells, prayers, and protestations of virtue that guided the soul successfully through the judgment and into the Field of Reeds. In earlier times, many of these were written on the coffin itself, but by the New Kingdom, a real book (scroll) was buried with the deceased.

bulti: Tilapia.

deben: A unit of weight, equal to 91 grams.

dja: A unit of volume, equal to about 1/3 liter.

djed **pillar**: A pillar erected in a summer festival and also during the *heb-sed*, thought to represent the spine of Osiris. It symbolized stability.

Djahy: The southern part of the Levant, more or less Roman Palestina.

Double House of Silver and Gold: The royal treasury, although much of the wealth of the kingdom was not in the form of precious metals but of commodities.

doum palm: A type of palm tree bearing large edible fruit.

electrum: A naturally occurring alloy of gold and silver much prized by the Egyptians as white gold.

Field of Reeds: The pleasant land of the blessed dead.

Great Green: The Mediterranean Sea.

heb-sed: Festival of the Bull's Tail, celebrated as a jubilee in the king's thirtieth regnal year in the hopes of rejuvenating his vitality. It was often celebrated at shorter intervals thereafter.

Hut-nen-nesut: The city of Herakleopolis, at the mouth of the Fayyum oasis. It was sacred to Horus.

Ipet: "Shrine," a Theban festival held yearly at Luxor which renewed the divine soul of the king and reaffirmed his affiliation to Amen.

Ipet-isut: The great temple of Amen-Ra at Thebes (Karnak).

iteru: A unit of distance, equal to about a mile.

Iunu: Heliopolis, a city in Lower Egypt sacred to Ra.

ka: One of the elements of the soul, which survived death. It seemed to be the vital essence and determined the nature of the person, human or divine. The king was thought to have a divine *ka*, renewed annually in the Ipet Festival.

Kebni: The Egyptian name for Byblos, a large city on the Mediterranean coast. The natives called it **Gubla**.

Kemet: What the Egyptians called their country. It meant the Black Land, because of the rich black alluvial soil of the Nile Valley. They also referred to Egypt as the **Two Lands**.

kha: a unit of area equaling approximately 276 square meters.

Kharu: The area represented today by Syria. The name refers to the Hurrian (Mitannian)population, but most people of Kharu were Semitic speaking.

khat: the physical body of the person, which was needed in the afterlife, hence the custom of mummification.

Kheta: Hatti Land, the kingdom of the Hittites, an increasingly powerful empire in Asia Minor.

medjay: Originally a Nubian tribe used as policemen, it came to indicate the police in general.

Men-nefer: The city of Memphis, capital of Lower (Northern) Egypt.

moringa: A tree bearing beans that were pressed for oil.

Naharin: An empire in inland Syria and northern Mesopotamia which had been very powerful but was falling apart at the time of our story. Also known as **Mitanni**.

nebet per: mistress of the house, a title used for any married woman, regardless of class.

Ta-nehesy: Nubia, today's Sudan.

Nekhen: A town sacred to Horus in Upper Egypt.

pehrer: an auxiliary soldier, usually of a lesser class, who ran alongside a chariot in battle to clear a path.

Per-ankh: The House of Life, scribal school run by the priests of Amen-Ra at Thebes.

Peret: The four-month winter season, or season of "growth."

Per-hay: The House of Rejoicing, one of Akhenaten's palaces in Akhet-aten, named after his father's palace at Thebes.

The River: The Nile, which had no name nor any personification as a god.

Sangar: Babylonia.

Sau: Saïs, a town in the Nile Delta sacred to Sekhmet.

senet: A board game for two people similar to checkers.

shebyu **necklace**: A special gold necklace granted to favored servants of the king which marked an elevation of their social status.

shenu: a ring or cartridge shape tangent to a crossbar. It symbolized a loop of rope and meant "eternity." Kings' names were written in *shen* rings.

Simurru: Tsumur, a city in Kharu that became the capital of the new kingdom of Amurru.

Speech of the Gods: Writing; in our story, used to distinguish hieroglyphics from script.

sycomore: Not the *sycamore* or plane tree, but a species of very large fig with edible fruit.

sunu (m.), ***sunet*** (f.): A physician of a scientific sort, as opposed to priestly or magical practitioners of medicine.

Ta-abet: second month of the season of Peret.

Tunip: A city on the Orontes River, vassal first of Egypt, then of Hatti.

Tushratta: King of Naharin.

Wag Festival: An annual feast of Osiris, during which the dead of the family were honored.

Waset: "City of the Scepter," the city of Thebes, the capital of Upper (Southern) Egypt and seat of Amen-Ra's worship.

weru: "great ones"; high aristocrats.

CHAPTER 1

Hemmed in by an enormous crowd, Hani stood between the lion-bodied images of the king that flanked the main street of Akhet-aten. He was waiting—as it seemed he had so often in the last seven years—for the king and his family to make their appearance. This occasion was the opening ceremony of the Great Jubilee of the Aten. More splendid than even the two previous jubilees Nefer-khepru-ra had held since he'd come to the throne alone, this one had been two years in the making. All the ambassadors of foreign lands, all the mayors of Kemet's vassal states to the north, and all the princes of Ta-nehesy to the south were there to render homage—because Nefer-khepru-ra *was* the Aten. Officially, he was the son and the only priest of the Shining Sun Disk, but Hani had realized long ago that, in fact, the king in his person was intended to be the revelation of the Aten.

One god, one priest, one revelation: him.

Hani ground his teeth at the very thought of Nefer-khepru-ra's theology. Had the king no idea of the havoc his decrees had wrought? The Ipet-isut, the Greatest of Shrines, consecrated to Amen-ra, had been closed, the cult statues desecrated, the priests expelled. The Hidden One's estates had been confiscated, and tens of thousands of priests and workers had found themselves without jobs. Had the king held his celebration in the old capital, Waset, this crowd would have been dangerously hostile.

But the inhabitants of Akhet-aten were handpicked. They were the bureaucrats and tradespeople for whom the king's continued favor had been more important than conscience, and they would applaud him as he demanded.

Yet here I am too, Hani thought with a twinge of cynicism. *And here is my father, and here are my sons and daughter and son-in-law.* Nub-nefer, his wife, had been obdurate enough in her faith to refuse to attend. Sat-hut-haru, Hani's middle girl, had yielded to her mother's stern orders and declined to participate as well.

Hani mopped his forehead. The temperature wasn't extreme in this second month of the winter season. Still, packed in with a dense crowd of perspiring bodies, he was none too comfortable as sweat dampened his armpits and then chilled. The men around him were, like him, scribes and emissaries in the king's foreign office. His friend Mane was at his side, bouncing on his tiptoes, trying to see over the taller heads around him.

"I should be like a crocodile," Mane shouted over the rumble of the crowd. "They keep growing as long as they live. I'd be taller than Keliya by now." Keliya was their mutual friend, the ambassador from Naharin.

Hani laughed. He was of average height and still could see nothing more than the white-clad backs of his colleagues, the linen shirts growing transparent with perspiration. Everyone's big court wigs blocked even more of his view. He wondered if Maya, his son-in-law and secretary, could see anything at all.

Hani eyed the bright, clear sky overhead, blue as turquoise, soft and smooth as the breast of a heron. *Great Ra*, he prayed silently, *put an end to this madness*. A hawk sailed overhead far, far into the cloudless azure distance, and Hani followed it admiringly with squinted eyes. Perhaps it was a magnificent bird... or perhaps it was the god Haru, watching the Two Lands with an all-seeing and protective gaze. *Lord Haru, show us the way of truth*. Hani sighed.

He heard a scuffling noise ahead of him, and suddenly, two men lurched back into the crowd, one of them looking blanched and unwell, leaning on his anxious companion's arm. They forced their way through the throng, and Hani and Mane found themselves pressed forward into the front rank of the spectators.

"We can breathe at last," he said to Mane with a grin.

The great processional way stretched off before him in either direction, the crowd of bureaucrats a bright white-and-black fringe bordering the tall, whitewashed walls of temple and palace and sparking with festive gold jewelry. Banners rippled lazily in the scant wind. The sun-scorched street had been swept and the dust held back by a sprinkling of water, but still, it reflected the glare until it was almost impossible to see without a visoring hand. Somewhere to Hani's right, toward the palace, were the viziers and upper-level functionaries like his own superior, Lord Ptah-mes, high commissioner of northern foreign relations. To his left stood the lower-rank royal scribes and military scribes, including his sons and father.

All at once, trumpets began to bray, chiming in one after the other in a joyous ascending chord. The crowd rustled and murmured excitedly. Around the north wall of the palace, the royal procession came into view, first several army units marching in step to the beat of drums and then the royal family. The king and queen were borne high in their golden carrying chairs on the shoulders of stalwarts decked in plumes and leopard skins. Nefer-khepru-ra gazed straight ahead of him, a slight smile on his lips, and so did the beautiful Nefert-iti Nefer-nefru-aten. They were a splendid couple, Hani had to admit—and things had reached such a pass in his soul that even that admission was painful. But they were young and good-looking, although the king had begun to grow fat like his father. Decked with jewels, their crossed arms bearing the crook and flail of kingship, they sparkled like the pair of gods they were. Behind them, the royal daughters were borne aloft, pretty girls with shaved heads and the lock of childhood, several of them already adolescent. The crown prince—the Haru in the nest—who was only two, was carried in his nurse's arms, and other members of the dynasty—the queen mother and more of her children—followed. Clouds of flower petals and bits of fine gold leaf fountained into the air as they passed, tossed by enthusiastic naked children with baskets. The crowd roared its approval, and many spectators lunged forward to collect the falling gold, but soldiers stationed every few cubits held them back with lowered spears.

"Our king does love a spectacle," Mane shouted at Hani, grinning broadly.

Two magnificently dressed servants waved dyed-ostrich-plume flabella at either side of the king and queen, and behind the royal carrying chairs marched the king's special friends, the Fan Bearers, each with a single plume on a golden handle. *If real public servants were rewarded as they should be, Ptah-mes would be among them*, thought Hani bitterly. But in fact, his superior had been stripped of his high offices and even of his status of royal friend because he had dared to stand up to the young king when Nefer-khepru-ra had been his father's coregent.

And now the viziers were passing. Lord Aper-el, Hani's higher superior, with his chiseled pale northern face, and his southern counterpart, Lord Nakht-pa-aten, whom Hani knew but slightly. The higher echelon of bureaucrats was peeling off from the crowd to join the procession, and Ptah-mes was in there somewhere—Hani thought he saw his head rising taller than the others at the far edge of the group. Before long, Hani and Mane took their places in line.

The cadence of the drums pounded in his viscera as he began to walk. *I can't wait till this is over*, Hani thought glumly.

❖

Five days after the opening ceremony of the Great Jubilee, Hani reached Waset, where he defiantly maintained his residence.

"Well, my love? How did it go?" Nub-nefer asked her husband as they embraced.

"Spectacular, as always," he said, bending to smell the

25

perfume rising from her warm natural hair. "I don't know how he has time to do anything but parade around."

She sneered and gave a snort. Nub-nefer was violently opposed to Nefer-khepru-ra, who was the sworn enemy of the Hidden One, Amen-Ra. The king had cost her family their positions as hereditary priests. "There are no longer any festivals of the gods to preside over. What else has he to do?" She looked up at Hani wistfully. "Do you have to go back?"

"Not until the end of the jubilee, really. I want to see the tribute the vassals have brought. It might tell us something about the state of their loyalty. But that won't be for a month or more."

She sighed. "I wish you had nothing to do with that man. And notice I say *man*."

Man, not god. If the king refused to celebrate the feast of Ipet and receive a divine *ka* from the hand of Amen-Ra... for Nub-nefer, he was just a mortal like any other. Hani scratched his head dubiously. He wasn't sure what he thought about the king's divinity. It had never passed through his mind to question the late king's claims that he was Haru and Atum and Amen and even the Aten. But Nefer-khepru-ra had crossed an irrevocable line in that regard. Hani was no longer sure how to address him.

Eventually, Nub-nefer drew back from Hani's arms. "Where are the others?"

"They must be lingering outside. They were right on my heels."

Sure enough, he heard voices and laughter in the vestibule, and in a moment, his father, Mery-ra, burst in, followed by Maya and—guffawing and taunting each other—his second son, Pa-kiki, and his youngest girl, Neferet. The children were currently living in Akhet-aten with their elder brother, Aha, but they came home for every holiday long enough for them to make the trip and back.

Nub-nefer opened her arms to embrace the youngsters, beaming with love. Pa-kiki hugged his mother, and Neferet threw herself on Nub-nefer with her usual bruising enthusiasm.

"How are your lessons going?" Nub-nefer asked, running her fingers through Neferet's bangs. The sixteen-year-old was studying medicine with the woman physician of the royal harem.

"It's so-o-o interesting, Mama!" the girl cried. "We set a broken leg before I left. That's what I like—the hands-on sort of thing. Not all the testing for evil spirits or what angry ancestor is causing a disease."

"You should be a military doctor," Mery-ra declared. "Nobody has to figure out where that hole in a soldier's middle came from."

"I can't imagine a *sunet* would be welcome on the battlefield, Father," Nub-nefer said dryly. "Aren't military doctors all men?"

"I think they are, but if you ask me, a woman would be more than welcomed by wounded soldiers."

"Not *my* daughter," Nub-nefer said firmly.

"Speaking of the military, tell your mother your good news, Pa-kiki," Hani said, smiling.

"I got a post with the army right here in Waset!" the boy cried.

Hani thought of him as a boy even though he was twenty-one and married with a small child. Pa-kiki's cousin

27

and wife, Mut-nodjmet, had borne him a son only the year before. Pa-kiki had been working in the Hall of Royal Correspondence, but he'd hankered for the more exciting life of a military scribe, as had his father and grandfather at that age.

"That's wonderful, my dear." His mother hugged him again proudly. "It will be so nice to have you back in the city. You can start a real household now."

"If I may point out, I had something to do with that post. I claimed right of succession when I retired, and since Hani didn't want the spot, I inscribed Pa-kiki for it." Mery-ra crossed his arms smugly over his broad chest.

"I'm grateful, Grandfather," Pa-kiki assured him with exuberant sincerity. "Mut-nodjmet is happy to have me back in Waset. Where *are* the girls?" He looked around hopefully.

"Yes, where are they?" Maya echoed. His wife, Hani's daughter Sat-hut-haru, was among those missing.

"They've gone to Sat-hut-haru's. They didn't expect you back this early," Nub-nefer said.

"Then I'm off, everyone," Maya said, turning on his heel. "Pa-kiki, I can send Mut-nodjmet back."

"I'll go with you," Hani's son decided. "We'll probably go straight home from there. Mother, we'll see you tomorrow." The two young men strode off together toward the door, Maya's short steps pattering to catch up to Pa-kiki's. In a moment, their clatter faded into the garden.

Nub-nefer smiled at her husband with fond warmth. "They're grown-up and have their own families now."

"Not me," Neferet said, throwing her arms around her mother.

28

"It won't be long, my duckling," Hani told her affectionately. "You'll meet a nice young man and set up housekeeping like Sat-hut-haru, and before long, you'll have children too. Won't that be wonderful?"

But Neferet's face fell, and she began to rock uneasily, like a guilty child. She took on that stubborn look she got, with her eyes shifting to the side. "Does *everybody* have to get married and have children?"

What a strange question, Hani thought, a little taken aback. He could see from Nub-nefer's wide eyes that she, too, was shocked.

"No one has to, but most people want to," he said, caressing his daughter's face. "'It is proper to make people. Happy the man whose people are plenty.' It's a joy to have a family."

"Who will tend your tomb when you're gone, my love? No, you have to marry and have children," Nub-nefer said in a tone that allowed no disagreement on the subject.

But Neferet looked skeptical, her lip stuck out. She was clearly fighting down an argument. Hani took in his daughter, really looking at her for the first time in a long while. At sixteen, she was a blocky, broad-shouldered girl who took after his side of the family—not classically pretty, with her square face and gap-toothed grin, but so full of life and heart and self-confidence that no one noticed. Her little brown eyes were always sparkling. To him, she was as attractive as Sat-hut-haru, who had inherited her mother's beauty and softly feminine figure.

Have we not presented her with an example of happy family life? he wondered, pained.

"Let's talk about that later," Neferet said brightly. "I

want to see Baket-iset." She left her baggage on the floor of the vestibule and darted into the salon to greet her oldest sister, who lay on her couch. Baket-iset had been paralyzed in a horrible accident at the age of fifteen, toppling from the deck of a boat and breaking her back on the quay.

If I'd never had children, I would never have known that strong and beautiful soul who happens to be my daughter. Hani was always moved by the thought of Baket-iset. The fact was he couldn't imagine life without Nub-nefer and the children.

As the two of them stood face-to-face, Nub-nefer shot him a disturbed and puzzled look. Then she said with a sigh, "I'll see about dinner." She turned and made her way through the salon, casting a bewildered glance at Neferet as she passed.

Across the room, Hani heard his youngest regaling her sister with extravagant tales of life in the capital. He remembered how she used to act out everything Maya gave her to read and perform the secretary's stories of his travels, to the delight of the audience. She'd grown up a little, but there was still an effervescence about her that brightened everyone's day.

Never change, little duckling, he thought tenderly.

Later, the family had only just sat down to dinner when A'a, the old gatekeeper, appeared at the door of the salon, an apologetic look on his face. "There's a messenger from Lord Ptah-mes here to see you, my lord."

Hani felt a twinge of uneasiness. *What message could be so urgent that it has to be delivered at night? And how did it reach me so fast?* Ptah-mes must have sent the messenger by his fast boat as soon as Hani had left the capital.

"Show him in," he said, rising from his seat and making his way into the vestibule.

A'a swung open the outer door, and Ptah-mes's pompous little secretary appeared in the doorway. "Lord Hani," he said with a slight bow. He comported himself like Hani's social equal, and perhaps he was, despite being a secretary. "I have an important message from Lord Ptah-mes. He bids you report to his office in the capital as soon as possible. He has a... discreet assignment for you to perform."

"Ah?" Hani murmured, reluctant. "Can't I sleep here tonight and then come? I just arrived this afternoon."

But the secretary looked scandalized. "No, no. He needs you as soon as possible. He said to make use of his yacht, which is docked at the quay."

Hani blew out a weary breath. *Ammit take it.* "All right. Let me tell my wife and pack a few things."

Soon, the two men were clopping down the quay toward Ptah-mes's magnificent boat, which Hani had already had the pleasure of boarding several times. It rocked at the water's edge, long and sleek and painted black and green with a papyrus-shaped stern. Ptah-mes kept a double crew on board so that he could travel even by night. Such nocturnal voyages seemed dangerous to a lethal degree, considering the murderous wildlife that inhabited the River, but Ptah-mes was from one of the oldest aristocratic families of Waset and was no doubt used to getting what he wanted at a snap of the fingers.

One of his haughty looks, and the hippopotamuses probably slink away in fear, Hani thought in amusement. Yet he had grown extremely fond of his superior; they'd come to be friends despite the difference in social class. And he knew that Ptah-mes carried a heavy burden of torment that even his wealth couldn't ease.

Hani made his way up the gangplank in the wake of Ptah-mes's secretary, following his pompous little buttocks as he churned up the slope. Maya would follow next day. Hani had left a message with Nub-nefer to summon him downriver, but there was no reason the boy couldn't enjoy one evening at home with his wife first. They had two small children, whom Maya missed inordinately on their long sojourns in the capital. *There's one who is happy enough to make a family for himself,* Hani thought—which reopened the mystery of Neferet's reluctance. He wondered if seeing too much childbirth among the royal ladies at too young an age had frightened her. *But surely lots of adolescent girls are at hand for the parturition of their mothers and sisters...*

Around him, the sailors were lighting their torches and hanging them low on either side of the prow. The lights of villages began to twinkle along the silhouetted banks of the River, which was enameled carnelian by the reflected setting of the winter sun. It was getting chilly, and Hani soon retreated to the cabin. In a few days, he would find out what urgent mission awaited him in Akhet-aten.

The swift yacht made a scant three days' journey of a trip that usually took at least five. Hani arrived at the capital in midmorning and set out without delay for the Hall of Royal Correspondence. It was embedded in the royal precinct between the state apartments and the central palace, two of several royal residences that rose like whitewashed fortresses among the huddle of low, mud-brick buildings around them. The banners and bouquets that had decorated the opening procession of the jubilee were still in place. The celebrations would go on for months.

He presented himself at the reception room of the high commissioner of northern vassals' office, where the sour-faced subordinate who guarded the private offices passed him through without delay. As the door opened, Lord Ptah-mes, seated on a stool within, looked up, and his face brightened. To Hani's surprise, Aper-el, the vizier of the Lower Kingdom, sat enthroned in the high commissioner's usual chair. Hani made a deep court bow, hand to his mouth, as respectfully as possible. Aper-el had been mildly hostile to him ever since Hani had stood up against a ridiculous assignment abroad.

"Ah, Hani. Here you are in the flesh," said the vizier in his nasal voice. "We were just discussing you."

A ripple of unease lifted the hairs on Hani's neck. Ptah-mes's handsome face grew utterly expressionless. Hani had no idea whether the discussion had been positive or negative.

"Ptah-mes will go into detail with you, but the substance of what he recalled you for is this: a series of tombs have been robbed over the last few days, and Our Sun, the Lord of the Two Lands—life, prosperity, and health to him—is eager to put an end to it. After all, the country is full of foreign diplomats, and we don't want to create a scandal."

Hani, still respectfully standing, nodded, confused. "Isn't this an assignment for the *medjay*, my lord? I'm not sure where I come in."

Aper-el and Ptah-mes exchanged a dark look, and the vizier said in a lower voice, "We have reason to believe one of the perpetrators may be a foreigner. Perhaps even a diplomat. Hence, the involvement of the foreign service."

"Needless to say," Ptah-mes added, his eyes shifting sideways toward Aper-el, "the greatest discretion will be required. You're one of our most experienced men."

Hani was stunned. *Foreign diplomats robbing tombs? What an appalling incident that could provoke!*

"How do we know foreigners are involved, my lord?" he asked.

Aper-el shook his head. "Ptah-mes will give you further details." He rose, martial in bearing, as befitted a former general, then he turned and withdrew to the inner office. Hani and Ptah-mes dropped into a bow.

After the vizier had departed, Ptah-mes caught Hani's eye and, holding a finger to his lips, gestured for to him to follow. They strode out the door of the reception hall and across the courtyard before Ptah-mes said in an undertone, "I'm calling my litters. I'd rather discuss this at home."

Following him through the court, Hani noticed his superior's fashionable wig, which must have cost a fortune. Ptah-mes was always turned out in unwrinkled perfection.

At the street, the high commissioner hailed his litter bearers, and they brought the two vehicles up to the edge of the court. Ptah-mes got into one and Hani the other. Hani's superior ordered, "Home."

Hani felt the bearers take off at a trot. Before too much uncomfortably jostled time had elapsed, the litters drew up within Lord Ptah-mes's garden, and the men emerged. Across the vestibule's polished gypsum floors, painted with scenes of reeds and birds, Ptah-mes led him into the salon. There he seated himself and urged Hani to do the same.

The two men sat looking at one another wordlessly. Hani was saddened to see how tired Ptah-mes appeared, his eye sockets smudged with brown.

Finally, the commissioner spoke. "This is a bad business, Hani. It's incredible to think any foreign emissary would behave so inappropriately. Unless the affair can be settled quietly, it will cause an enormous international row."

"Are these royal tombs? Is this in the Great Place or in Akhet-aten?"

"Not royal, mercifully," Ptah-mes said. "They are all very new tombs of wealthy people in Waset."

"What makes us so sure foreigners are involved?"

"One of the draftsmen came forward with suspicions about a colleague. It seems likely that the burial workers are selling their services to reenter the tombs immediately after they've been sealed. He spoke of a man with an accent who was paying them."

Hani nodded slowly. "And we think he's a diplomat why…?"

Ptah-mes lifted his eyebrows. "That's murkier. Of course, there are an inordinate number of foreign diplomats here at the moment and probably not so many civilians. And what civilian would dare to do something like this, knowing the penalty? A diplomat might count on his immunity."

"So that's someone's speculation?" Hani pressed.

"I haven't spoken to the man myself—it was the mayor of Waset who reported the witness's words to the vizier—but so it seems. It will be up to you to prove or disprove this theory. And I definitely hope it's wrong." Ptah-mes smiled thinly. He reached out and clapped Hani on the shoulder.

"I thought you'd like a mission in Waset for a change. And you really are the best man for the job."

"I'm honored, my lord," said Hani humbly, keeping his reservations to himself. *This could be dirty. These people clearly fear neither god nor man.* "Will I have the aid of any troops? I can hardly stop a gang of tomb robbers by myself."

"Whatever you need. I'll see to it a unit is at your disposal. And you have military experience; you know some of the commanders. If there is anyone you want, speak the word."

Ptah-mes rose, and Hani imitated him. "Can I offer you some of that wine from Kebni?" said Ptah-mes with his usual perfect courtesy.

"Thank you, my lord." Hani smiled broadly. "I wouldn't say no."

❦

Early the next morning, Maya was ushered into Ptah-mes's house to find Lord Hani eating alone in the salon. For several years, the high commissioner had invited Hani and his secretary to remain at his villa when they were in Akhet-aten. Ptah-mes's wife, formerly head of the musical establishment of Amen-Ra, refused to join him in the City of the Horizon, and Hani had often said he suspected that his superior was lonely. No matter how many times Maya had stayed there, he could never quite believe he was hobnobbing with a man of such wealth. Yet Lord Ptah-mes, for all his blue blood, had not once shown contempt for Maya's dwarf stature or for his working-class origins.

Hani greeted him, beaming. "You made good time,

son. I'm sorry to have to drag you away from your family so soon."

"That's the nature of the beast," Maya said lightly.

Hani eyed him, an eyebrow cocked. "Do I detect a certain eagerness to get away? No troubles between you and Sat-hut-haru, I hope?"

"No, no," Maya hastened to assure him. "It's just that little Henut-sen doesn't sleep well at night—and that means *we* don't sleep well. I actually slept better on the boat when we tied up at night."

"Poor Sat-hut-haru." Hani shook his head. "She can't get away. I remember those days of glassy-eyed exhaustion."

Maya seated himself on the floor beside his father-in-law. "What's the urgent mission, my lord?"

"Ah, Maya, my young friend. This one could be dangerous. There have been tomb robberies in Waset, and it seems a foreigner is involved, possibly even a diplomat." Hani told Maya the scant information Ptah-mes had imparted to him. "We'll need to get back to the city and interview the worker who reported his colleague. From there, I think we have to locate that man and try to get some information from him, if he's willing to talk in exchange for immunity. We must find out if any accredited diplomats are in on this and why. I mean, does their king know about it, or are they simply corrupt individuals?"

Maya gave a dubious whistle. Tomb robbers, having already forfeited all protection of the law, were notoriously violent. "You don't suppose they're henchmen of the king, trying to discourage burial at Waset?"

Hani thrust out his lip, considering. "An interesting theory. We should find out eventually."

He rose, and together, the two men headed for the Hall of Royal Correspondence. "Ptah-mes has promised us sealed letters of royal commission if anyone should refuse to cooperate. And our pick of soldiers."

What a story this will make! Maya all but rubbed his hands together in anticipation. Fatherhood had made him more cautious, but he still had a young man's eagerness for adventure. And now he had his secret project in mind—namely, to write down all the colorful episodes of his career as Lord Hani's secretary and turn them into a tale like *Sinehat* or *The Two Sailors*. He practiced them on his mother and aunts and, more recently, on Sat-hut-haru and the children. Tepy, at two years old, was a little young to react with interest, but still, the sight of his father speaking with animation seemed to rivet the adorable little fellow.

And look who had a second child only two years after the first one, while the mother was still nursing, Maya thought proudly. Fortunately, Hani had helped him hire a wet nurse for Sat-hut-haru. *Yet another cause to be grateful to Lord Hani.* Thanks to Hani's patronage, Maya had been able to continue his basic schooling at the House of Life and become a full-fledged scribe. Without it, he would have found himself keeping his mother's books at the goldsmith workshop for the rest of his days. Through Hani's generosity, Maya had entered the ruling class. He wore his pen case proudly over his shoulder at all times so all the world would know that he was not just some dwarf with calloused hands and a bent back—he was literate. He was a royal scribe, and people had better step aside for him in the street.

The two men were walking up the main avenue of the capital, heading north toward the bridge with its gates that opened into the palace precinct where the Hall of Royal Correspondence stood. Absorbed in their talk, they almost physically collided with a heavyset, well-dressed figure who was emerging from the building.

The man's scowling face grew crimson. "Hani," he said coldly, eyeing Hani and Maya with ill-concealed contempt.

"Mahu," responded Hani with no more warmth. Neither of them had employed the honorific title of the other.

Out of solidarity, Maya tried to look as haughty and menacing as he could. The animosity was real. This was the chief of the *medjay*, the police, of Akhet-aten. Two years before, the bastard had roughed Hani up, demanding to know the hiding place of his brother-in-law, Amen-em-hut, the renegade priest of Amen.

"I understand we're going to be colleagues," said Mahu with a sneer.

Maya felt confusion rising up his cheeks in a wave of heat, and he shot a glance at his father-in-law, but Hani maintained his diplomatic cool. "We'll see. I've been told the army will be helping me, not the police."

"Well, perhaps you were told wrong, because the Lord of the Two Lands ordered me in person to carry out the investigation... with your help. If needed." Mahu smiled, his mouth a smug, thin-lipped crescent.

The lying turd. Maya clenched his jaw to hold back a comment he might regret.

"We'll see." Hani's flat tone revealed nothing. The two men nodded frigidly at one another and passed, continuing on their way. As soon as Mahu had disappeared from sight, Hani said through his teeth, "If that's true—and it must be, or he wouldn't have known anything about our mission, which is highly confidential—that really complicates our lives."

"This pretty much proves the king is at the bottom of it, though, doesn't it? He wants his henchman to cover his tracks," said Maya avidly.

Hani heaved a sigh. "I don't know. Let's see what Ptah-mes has to say about this."

They made their way toward the huddle of low buildings that housed the foreign office and crossed the sun-bleached courtyard. It took an instant for Maya to regain his sight once they entered the cool darkness of the reception hall. "But our orders came from the vizier himself, you said, my lord," he persisted. "He must have been transmitting the king's will."

Hani muttered something pessimistic and presented himself at the table of the guardian. "Hani son of Mery-ra to see Lord Ptah-mes." He turned to Maya. "Wait here. This shouldn't take long. I want to get our written orders and ask if the commissioner knows anything about this mess."

❖

Hani entered Lord Ptah-mes's office to find him seated on the floor cross-legged, writing something without the aid of a secretary. He looked up and explained dryly, "I'm no longer sure I can trust my own staff." He pushed aside his implements, rose with his usual grace, and seated himself in his chair of office, motioning to Hani to take a seat on a stool. "I have your orders for you, my friend. If anyone gives you any trouble, flash these under his nose."

"A complication has arisen, my lord—a matter of jurisdiction—and I'd like to get a clarification," said Hani.

Ptah-mes lifted an eyebrow. "Jurisdiction? How so?"

"I just ran into Mahu, the chief of police. He said the king had given the *medjay* jurisdiction over the case and I was to help him."

Ptah-mes's eyes widened in surprise, then he gave a cynical snort. "My first reaction was to say 'That's false,' but in fact, who knows what the king has said to him?" His voice dropped and actually shook a little, and if Hani hadn't known how well Ptah-mes could dissemble his true emotions, he would have sworn it was with rage. "This constant undermining of orders with counterorders happens all the time in our dealings with other kingdoms. The foreign service is a knot of contradictory policy statements."

"On the practical level, what should I do?" Hani persisted, his heart heavy over the sad state of royal policy.

"Proceed according to your orders," said Ptah-mes firmly, handing Hani a scroll covered in seals. "I'll talk to Aper-el and see if he knows anything about a change in jurisdiction." He stared into space, his body tense, his lean face stretched downward in contained fury. "Do they plan to have the police arrest a foreign diplomat like a common criminal and impale him? That will certainly mean war."

"Perhaps no diplomats are involved." Hani hesitated then smiled. "Maya thinks the king himself has violated the tombs to discourage people from being buried in Waset."

But Ptah-mes didn't smile back. He looked grim in the extreme. "Who knows?"

Hani was in a dark mood of disgust as he returned to

the reception hall, where Maya sat cross-legged on the floor, awaiting him. The secretary scrambled to his feet, his eager curiosity growing anxious as he took in Hani's expression. "What is our status, my lord?" he asked hesitantly, as if afraid to receive an answer.

"That remains unclear. Ptah-mes knew nothing about Mahu's involvement, but he didn't seem to find it far-fetched that the king might, in fact, have given him jurisdiction over us." Hani shook his head cynically. "More of the usual internal politics."

Anger simmering in his gut, Hani strode out of the hall with Maya in his wake. *What game is the king playing, with me as a pawn and the safety of the kingdom as stakes?*

CHAPTER 2

"At least it's nice to have an assignment in Waset for a change. We won't have to go back and forth to that abominable City of the Horizon," said Maya optimistically. The two men were standing outside Hani's gate, waiting for his litter.

But Hani grunted, his thickety eyebrows buckling. "Why is Mahu involved? Even if the *medjay* were called in, wouldn't you think it would be the officers from Waset? There's more to this than meets the eye." He shot Maya a glance. "More and more, I'm convinced you're right. Our Sun God is involved in this business somehow."

Pleased, Maya threw his head back in a gesture that aimed at modesty. "One never knows."

The men made their way to the quays, where despite the early hour, they quickly found a ferry crossing the River. As the sun rising behind them cast its nacreous glow of rose over the sky and the waters all around, they disembarked on the western bank and began the arduous trek into the arid mountains and valleys where the workmen's village, the Place of Truth, was located. They would need a guide to find the tombs that had been robbed.

The landscape was as bleak and devoid of vegetation as some grisly pit of the underworld. This was the Red Land, the desert—the realm of Sutesh and an image of chaos. Sharp rocks strewed the path, which mounted in steep switchbacks as it climbed into the Mountains of the West. Ahead was the Great Place, the remote valley where kings of Kemet had been buried for hundreds of years—ever since a Theban dynasty had come to the throne. But Hani and Maya turned and followed the foothills to a kind of basin in a high, rolling plain, where the white enclosure wall of the village stood out brightly against the dun rocks. A hawk sailed far, far overhead, seemingly searching for little rodents in the crevices, and Hani asked himself again who this really was and why the bird kept haunting his steps. Clustered around the village were the tombs of generations of high-level workmen, some of them quite elaborate with tall pyramidal markers and impressive stone entryways. The servants in the Place of Truth might be artisans, but they clearly didn't need to envy the tombs of modest aristocrats like Hani.

"They're far away from everything," Maya commented, huffing and puffing, as they made their way between the tombs. "Can't be much fun to live out here."

"I understand the nearest wells are half a league away. But these people are paid generously, and there are always jobs. Even," Hani added darkly, "if the present administration has moved its burial place to Akhet-aten. There are still plenty of rich private tombs being built in the area." *Ptah-mes's, for one. There's one little act of defiance he has allowed himself.*

When they had reached the Place of Truth, it was lunchtime. A line of women and girls bearing baskets were departing from the gate just as the two scribes entered. "There goes lunch for the men at their work camp. And speaking of lunch, let's see if there are any beer houses," Hani said.

The village was laid out with dense military precision, row after row of blank facades and walled yards closing in the streets. Clearly, no one was wasting any space. At this hot midday hour, few people were at work on the roof terraces, and the place seemed uninhabited except for an occasional call or burst of laughter from within the whitewashed walls. At first, the houses were small and the doors closely spaced, but as the two scribes zigzagged through the village, the dwellings became more impressive.

"The overseers and scribes must live in this area. Not likely to find a beer house here. We need to ask someone directions," Hani said.

As if in response, a man emerged from a gateway not too far ahead of him. He started in the direction of the two scribes, head down, intent upon his way, but then he looked up and said in surprise, "Hello. I don't think I know you."

Does he really know everyone in the village? Hani wondered. *There must be at least some hundreds of inhabitants, although admittedly only sixty or seventy of that number are likely to be grown men.* Aloud, he said with a friendly smile, "You don't indeed. We're here on the king's

45

business, and we're looking for a place to have lunch. Is there a beer house?"

The man protested, "Oh, men of your caliber don't want to eat there. Come to my house. My wife will be happy to serve the king's men." He took Hani by the elbow and directed the two toward the handsome red gate from which he had just emerged.

"My name is Hani son of Mery-ra. This is my son-in-law, Maya. I thank you for your most hospitable offer, but we don't want to be a burden."

"Not at all. Not at all. I am Ankh-reshet, overseer of the right-hand corps. I'm one of the councilors of the Place of Truth. You would offend us all if you refused." He was a tall, angular man a little older than Hani with a wide snaggletoothed smile and a scribe's writing case dangling over his shoulder. He ushered his guests into the garden of a miniature villa, with palm trees and some sparse bushes and a tiny pool stocked with fish.

And they have to bring water from a half league's distance, Hani marveled. To his delight, a trio of geese floated in the water. The birds watched the newcomers with an outraged stare, then they began to honk in menace, their little tongues sticking out like the anther of some hostile flower. Hani laughed, and his host tipped his head in question.

"I'm very fond of birds," Hani explained, embarrassed.

"Excellent, my lord. I try to make them welcome in my garden. This is such a barren area that we don't have many except for domesticated ones like my geese. Let me set you up here in the pavilion, where it's cooler." Ankh-reshet led them to a small pergola shaded by a reed mat and offered them stools. He disappeared briefly into the house and a moment later returned with two servants. One of them set up a small table in front of each man and set out bread and braised leeks while the other positioned a beer pot beside each one.

"Forgive me for not joining you," said the overseer, "but we've already eaten."

"This is too good of you," Hani said, already tearing off a chunk of the bread and dipping it into his leeks. At his side, Maya sucked thirstily at his beer.

Ankh-reshet pulled up a stool and, smiling, watched them eat. "What brings you gentlemen to our remote village? You say you are on the king's business?"

"That's right," Hani said. "I'm here to ask some questions of a man named Djau. I believe he's a draftsman."

"He's in my corps," said their host, starting to look worried. "He hasn't done anything wrong, has he? He's a good man, takes care of his old mother and both of his late brother's children."

Hani, his mouth full, waved a hand to reassure his host. Then, having swallowed, he said, "Not at all. On the contrary, in fact. I've been told he can help us in our investigation."

"I can take you to him after you eat." Ankh-reshet watched them, bright-eyed with curiosity, but Hani said no more about their mission. There was always the chance that Ankh-reshet was involved in the robberies, no matter how genial he seemed.

The three men made small talk as the guests ate, and at last Hani stood up from his stool and heaved a sigh of contentment. "We've eaten well, my host, and I thank you. Now, could we trouble you to take us to see Djau?"

"No trouble to help Our Sun's men," Ankh-reshet said, bobbing up and down. There was something unctuous in his manner, as if he desperately hoped Hani would tell Nefer-khepru-ra how obliging his loyal servant, the overseer of the right-hand corps, had been.

Ankh-reshet led the way back into the street, which despite the winter month was starkly sun-washed where the shadows of the houses didn't empurple it. Hani found himself almost blinded by the glare. As they followed Ankh-reshet through the narrow packed-earth alleys, the man said, "You know, we haven't had so much work since the capital moved. The king—life, prosperity, and health to him—keeps us fed, but we don't earn as much as when we were making royal tombs."

He seems to think I can help him. Anger smoldered under Hani's smile. *Here are yet more people suffering from the glorious revelation of the Aten.* "I'm sure that's true," he said neutrally. "How many noble tombs do you build in a year?"

"Oh, it varies. We've only had three big ones to complete this last year, but of course, they were begun years ago." Ankh-reshet shot Hani an anxious glance, and his voice dropped. "I guess you've heard about the robberies, my lord?"

"Yes," Hani said as Maya watched with a shrewd expression on his face from the other side of Ankh-reshet.

The latter regarded Hani for a hopeful moment, then he said, "Well, here is Djau's house. Shall I leave you, or do you want me to introduce you?"

"You've done too much for us already, my friend." Hani clapped him amicably on the arm. "Please thank the mistress of the house for the excellent lunch, and we'll leave you to whatever errand took you into the street when you intercepted us."

Ankh-reshet bobbed respectfully and made his reluctant way off down the street.

Maya asked under his breath, "Do you think he has anything to do with the robberies?"

Hani shrugged. "I have no idea, Maya. I suppose Djau can shed some light on that. Or not."

They knocked on the gate of a large house almost comparable in size to the overseer's. Draftsmen—who were literate, after all—seemed to do well for themselves. An elderly maidservant answered the door, and Hani introduced himself as the royal investigator there to see her master. He thought it best not to be more precise. One never knew who was involved in the robberies.

The servant toddled off, and a moment later, a wiry little man with a thin face and popping eyes came crunching up the path through his meager garden, which was beautifully laid out, although the harsh, dry conditions had stunted the bushes.

"My lord, how can I be of service?" Djau said in a wheezy voice. He appeared to be in his mid-thirties, but there was something old looking about his gaunt cheeks and his fleshless frame, which he held stiffly.

Perhaps he isn't well, thought Hani as the man's protruding eyes fixed on him both eagerly and fearfully. "My name is Hani. The king has asked me to look into your confidential report about... misdeeds in the house of the *ka* of a number of families in the area."

"Ah, yes, my lord. Come in. Come in, please." Djau led

them with quick, nervous footsteps through the garden and into his house. It was a pleasant place, beautifully decorated. Hani wondered if the frieze of paintings above the red dado was an example of the homeowner's skill. A chief draftsman for the king had to have considerable talent.

The little man led them into his salon, where the three of them took a seat on the colorful cushions that lay about. "Can I offer you refreshments, my lord?"

"No, my friend, we just ate. But thank you." Hani settled his face into an amiable expression that he hoped would set his interlocutor at ease. "Could you please repeat for me everything you know about the robberies, including whose tombs have been targeted?"

Djau nodded, swallowing hard. "We all were aware that several tombs had been robbed in the last few weeks, since the beginning of our lord king's *heb-sed*. To be more precise, the tombs of a certain Ah-mes, the one of Pa-ren-nefer, and the one of Sa-tau. Their private guards reported it right away, and our overseers made an announcement that anyone who knew anything should come forward."

He cast worried eyes at Hani. "About a week ago—yes, it must have been a week, because I had served my eight days in the camp and was home for the weekend—I was taken with faintness in the street, and I sat down in the shade of the wall. A moment later, I heard two men speaking low together just around the corner. I recognized the voice of one of my colleagues who draws the black lines over my red sketches, a man named Bebi-ankh. He said something about 'our successful enterprise' and that he needed more gold because he was taking a huge risk by doing so many in so short a time."

"'Doing so many?' Those are the words he used?" Hani pressed.

Djau's bugging eyes blinked nervously. "I don't honestly remember the exact words, my lord. But something like that. At first, I didn't connect it to the tomb robberies, so I'm sure he didn't say anything like *rob* or *loot*."

With an understanding nod, Hani urged him to continue.

"Then the other man spoke. He had a very strong accent—"

"Could you tell what kind?"

"No, my lord. I don't hear enough foreigners to recognize how they speak. But he certainly wasn't Egyptian." Djau's brow wrinkled in anxiety as if he feared to disappoint.

"Please go on." Hani smiled. "I'll try not to interrupt."

"The man said that when they collected everything they needed, he—Bebi-ankh—would get the rest of his reward. He said not to be afraid, because he—the foreigner—had immunity, and he would see to it Bebi-ankh didn't get into trouble."

Dear gods, Hani thought with a sinking weight in the pit of his stomach. *He really is a diplomat. This could hardly be worse.* He looked at Maya, whose eyes had widened in comprehension. *Now what?*

"Anything else?" he asked Djau, watching him closely for any flicker that might signal he was lying. He observed the man's thin, clever hands clasped tensely in his lap.

"The foreigner said something about 'the others' that sounded like a question. Then their voices dropped, and I couldn't hear any more of what they were saying. I was afraid they'd come around the corner and see me listening and kill me." Sweat had started to trickle down Djau's temples from under the edges of his round wig. "And sure enough, I heard footsteps approaching, so I lay down in the street with my arms and legs out and pretended to be unconscious." He made a noise that might have been a sob of fear and wiped his nose with the back of a hand. "Bebi-ankh bent over me and said, 'Djau, are you all right?' That was natural enough, wasn't it? We work together. He sounded honestly concerned. But oh, my lord, I was so frightened." The poor man's face collapsed, and he looked away, as if embarrassed by his tears.

"I can well imagine. You must be a good actor if you could convince him you were out cold," Hani said with compassion. "What did you do then?"

The draftsman continued, openly wringing his hands, "He slapped me a little on the cheeks, and I pretended to come to. I was so scared I was genuinely shaking and, no doubt, pale. He helped me up, and I thanked him and said I could get home all right." Djau laughed nervously. "I tottered off as fast as I could. If he'd suspected me, he might have come after me, and he's a big man. He could break me in half."

"And you've both gone to work together since? Does he act suspicious?"

"In fact, I haven't seen him. I had finished laying out the paintings and text on the walls of the tomb we were both working on, and I went on to another project. He's still at that tomb."

"Whose is it, if I may ask?" Hani said.

"The one I finished? A man named Ptah-mes. He has

the most beautiful *ka* statues of him and his wife I've ever seen."

Well, well, Hani thought in surprise. He knew how magnificent Ptah-mes's statues were because he'd seen the plaster models in the workshop of the royal sculptor Djehuty-mes. Apparently, the high commissioner had bought himself a royal artist as well.

"Anything else I should know, my friend?" he said, clapping the little man on the shoulder. The draftsman's muscles felt tense, as if he might fly apart under his anxieties.

"No, my lord. I've heard nothing else."

"And you reported this to whom? Your overseer? That would be Ankh-reshet, I suppose?"

"No, in fact. I was afraid he might be involved. I mean, anyone might be, mightn't they? So I went to the mayor of Waset." Djau's frightened, protruding eyes gave him the air of a small desert animal cornered by a predator.

"Good thinking. You didn't go to the police, then?"

"The village police? No, I didn't trust anybody."

Hani rose, and Maya and Djau followed suit. "Well, I thank you for your testimony, Djau. Let me ask you one final thing—can you suggest a guide who can take us to the tombs that have been robbed?"

"I'd offer, my lord, but I have a little trouble with my lungs. I need the weekends to recover." He looked quite apologetic.

I wonder how much dust and powdered pigment he breathes in in the course of a week, poor man, thought Hani. But then he warned himself not to be too sympathetic; the draftsman might well be involved in the crime.

Djau added hastily, "Lord Hani, allow me to call my

nephew. He's a sturdy lad, and he works with the crew. He can guide you." He was on his feet and starting into the back of the house before Hani could get a chance to respond.

Hani and Maya sat in silence, exchanging a stare. Maya evidently wanted to ask something, but before he could say it, Djau returned with a short, well-built youth of about fifteen in tow.

Hani smiled at the boy, who reminded him of his own son Pa-kiki at the same age.

The youth bowed, his sidelock swinging. "My name is Khawy, my lord. Uncle said you wanted someone to lead you to the tombs that have been robbed."

"Yes, son. Can you do that?"

"I can, my lord. But they may be guarded." He turned to his uncle as if to ask his permission, and Djau nodded with his nervous bug-eyed smile.

Hani said cheerfully, "Then lead on, Khawy. And Djau, many thanks for your information. I may be back if we need clarification on anything."

Djau bobbed an obsequious acknowledgment, his thin hands clasped so tightly the knuckles were white. "Remember us to the king, my lord."

Hani assured him he would, and the two royal scribes, led by the boy, made their way out into the street.

"It's a long walk, my lord, but not too long," Khawy assured them as they strode down the alley toward the northern gate. "Once we reach the workmen's camp, it's not far at all."

"And you make this trip every week with the men, do you?"

"Yes, my lord. We stay in the camp for the work days then come back for the holiday at the end of the week." His brows contracted as if in pain. "I don't know how much longer Uncle will be able to work, and I'm the oldest."

Hani asked in concern, "Your uncle is ill?"

Khawy nodded, his lips compressed. They walked in silence. People were starting to emerge into the hot winter afternoon, and now and then, someone greeted the boy, staring with unconcealed curiosity at the two strangers in his wake.

They passed through the gate of the walled village and began the ascent of the rocky trail into the cliffs. "Why the wall, I wonder?" Maya asked, looking back. "Surely, there are no invaders out here."

"Animals, my lord. Jackals and hyenas and foxes. Wolves, maybe, or even lions."

Maya raised his eyebrows uneasily.

"I'm confident we're safe by day," Hani assured him. But he scanned with apprehension the many clefts and crevices that could conceal a dun-colored animal lusting for flesh.

After what felt like half the afternoon had passed to the rhythm of their trudging feet, Khawy pointed off to their left to a rough cluster of huts at the foot of the cliffs. "That's the work camp, my lords. That's where we live during the week. There's nobody there now."

He led them toward the right, where Hani could make out a scatter of whitewashed tombs against the ocher rock. The shadows of the Mountains of the West were already devouring the tombs. As the men drew nearer, white, black, and red spots were visible at the mouths of several of the tombs—human figures standing or squatting. Clearly, concerned families had set guards on their houses of the *ka*.

"This one is the tomb of Lord Sa-tau," the boy said, pointing at a fine-looking entryway some cubits to the fore of a tall pyramidal shrine.

"What do you know about the break-ins, son?" asked Hani.

"They told us the robbers came down from the top, where the rock is thinnest. But the thing is, what appears to be the entrance really isn't. You'd have to know how the tomb was laid out to know where to dig." The boy pointed once more. "Over there is the break-in spot. They've repaired it and put dirt on top."

"Hmm," Hani said. *Clearly an inside job. An artist working on it would be familiar with the layout of the tomb. There might even have been a plan lying in plain sight so no workers got lost at the end of the day.*

"Do you want to see inside?" asked Khawy.

But Hani noticed how low the winter sun was getting. He found he had no desire to be caught out in the desert after sundown with foxes, wolves, and lions. "Show us the other two, my young friend."

The boy clambered over increasingly rocky terrain with Hani at his heels. Maya was struggling to keep up, but Hani didn't want to embarrass his secretary by slowing Khawy down.

"There's Lord Ah-mes's tomb," said the boy, indicating another freshly whitewashed shrine and subterranean entry.

"Did they get in the same way here?"

"Pretty much," said the boy. "And the other one, too, as far as I know." He shrugged, looking apologetic. "Maybe the grown-ups know something I don't, but that's what they told us on the crew."

Hani grinned, overcome with fondness for the boy. "What's your job on the crew, Khawy?"

"I mix paints and take them up to the artists on the scaffolding, my lord." He looked as if he were going to cry, then he managed a brave smile. "My father died up there. He fell off the scaffold and hit his head on the stone floor. That's when Uncle took us in."

Hani's nose twinged with tears. "You have an artistic family, I see," he said, hoping his voice didn't betray his emotions. "Can you read and write?"

"No, my lord. I can never be a draftsman like Uncle. But I can outline or lay in color where somebody else has already written the Speech of the Gods, like my father."

Hani asked himself whether something could be done for the boy. There was no longer any House of Life where priests could train him to literacy, but perhaps Hani's own scribe father, who was now retired, might be able to teach him—if the youth wasn't already too old. Hani's daughter, Neferet, had begun at thirteen, but she'd only learned cursive writing.

"Well, Khawy, you've helped us a lot. Now I suppose we'd better be getting back." Hani slipped a faience ring with a finely cut seal off his finger and pressed it into the boy's hand.

The lad accepted it in surprise, and his eyes grew wider and wider as he stared at the ring's beautiful turquoise color and intricate figure of a seated goddess Seshat, patroness of writing. "Oh, thank you, my lord! I'm sure Uncle will thank you too."

"He's been helpful as well. He did the right thing by reporting this business," Hani said. "Your uncle seems to be a good man."

"He is, my lord. I hope he'll live forever, but... well, when he dies, I'll be the support of the family."

That was the second time the lad had made such a comment, Hani noted. The prospect of so much responsibility clearly weighed on him.

They struck out across the rocky path once more, heading back toward the River, so that the descending sun was at their backs and their shadows grew increasingly long at their feet, rippling over the rocks and gullies. The late afternoon was silent in this realm of Meret-seger, the Lover of Silence. A raven cawed high in the sky, and a string of ibises passed overhead, heading for water, the flash of their white wings turned rosy by the winter sun's long rays. The only sound was that of the three men's footsteps clopping over the stones, sending an occasional cascade of gravel rattling down the slope.

At last, they came within view of the walled white village in its shallow valley, where the Mountains of the West began to level out along the River.

"Will you come back to our house, my lord?" Khawy asked in a tone of hope.

"I think not, my young friend. We want to get to the River before the ferries stop this evening. Please thank your uncle again for us."

They parted company with the boy, and while he set off on the road to the Place of Truth, Hani and Maya took the most direct path eastward. As he turned for one last look,

Hani saw Khawy wave and then break into a run toward home.

✦

"What do you think about that Djau, my lord?" asked Maya under his breath as they balanced on the seat of the little boat bearing them back across the River to the city of the living. "He played unconscious? That seemed odd."

Hani chuckled. "I confess, I wondered at first if he was as innocent as he wanted us to think. He was so nervous and desperate seeming. But the more I thought about it, the more I realized that he must be genuinely fearful that if the perpetrators know he has reported them, they'll do away with him. And he has huge responsibilities as his family's main support."

"I can't see him making old bones anyway, frankly," Maya said with a sniff. "Maybe Djau is so desperate for gold to keep his nephew from being strapped when he dies that he's gotten mixed up in this business. I can't imagine that a paint boy makes much compared to a chief draftsman."

"Hopefully, we'll find out who's guilty and who's innocent as our investigation goes on," Hani said.

Maya recognized Hani's bland tone as an effort to try not to defend the little draftsman before the truth came out. *He likes him or feels sorry for him. But Lord Hani will remain impartial.*

They bumped at last against the quay, and while the boatman held the prow steady, Hani and Maya clambered out of the small boat and stood up on dry land. The night was coming on. Lights were appearing in windows and through high clerestories. A fluttering torch bobbed through the gathering darkness as the watchman made his rounds.

"Let's get on home before it becomes completely black," Hani said, quickening his steps. The inhabitants of Waset were all on edge after nightfall, never knowing what mischief the discontented of their city might stir up.

The two men walked briskly, Maya struggling to keep up with Lord Hani's longer stride. It occurred to him that there was hardly anyone he'd rather have at his side in a dangerous situation than his father-in-law. Hani was a broad, thick man with a rolling gait and an air of power. He'd wrestled in his youth, and Maya had seen him flip an attacker or two even recently, despite his forty-seven years. Yes, whatever malefactors Hani couldn't win over with gentleness and humor he could beat back by force. Maya always felt protected in his presence.

They arrived at Hani's home without incident. A'a let them through the gate, and the two marched up the garden path with a gravelly crunch of mismatched footsteps. At the door of the house, Nub-nefer met them, her face brightening with love at the sight of her husband, and Maya thought, *May my wife ever give me that look when I come home.*

"Here we are, my dear," called Hani. "Sorry we're so late. There were three tombs to visit." He kissed Lady Nub-nefer as he crossed the threshold.

"We were starting to worry. Sat-hut-haru is here, Maya. She's with the other girls in the salon."

The three of them entered together, and Maya melted to see his wife jump up and run toward him with all her grace and warmth. She stooped and fell on his neck, shrieking joyfully and kissing him.

"Easy, my dear. We were only gone for a day!" He laughed, wrapping his short arms around her as best he could. She stood up, and hand in hand, they went to greet her sisters. Neferet had bounded up but, for once, summoned the self-control to wait until Hani entered the room before squeezing everyone else out of the way. At last, she descended on her father in a bone-cracking hug.

"This is a more exuberant welcome than we get when we're in Kharu for months!" Hani pried Neferet off with a chuckle.

"We've heard sounds of rioting again, my love," Nub-nefer said. "I sent Iuty out to bring Pa-kiki and Mut-nodjmet and the little one, in case there was going to be trouble. Be glad your mother is in Akhet-aten, Maya."

Maya was indeed glad his goldsmith mother had moved her workshop to the new capital. At first, his heart had been broken at the thought that she would sell the old house, the link with his childhood. But she'd surprised him by giving it to Sat-hut-haru and him. They'd fixed it up until it was a cozy little family home with a nice garden and a stable and possessions collected by dint of frugality. He hated to think of a mob breaking in and taking them.

"Well, Pa-kiki and Mut-nodjmet will be here when they get here," Nub-nefer said at last with forced jollity. "Why don't we sit down at table before it gets any later?" She called to the servants to bring out the little tables, and the family took their places here and there in a rough circle.

In the silence before everyone began to talk again,

Maya could hear a distant knock on the gate. He caught Hani's eye.

"That must be the children." Hani slipped off his stool with an alacrity that suggested he had been infected with his wife's anxiety. It was true they'd been besieged in the house by a mob more than once since the new king took the throne.

Hani disappeared into the vestibule. A moment later, Pa-kiki and his wife, with their little daughter in her arms, entered to joyous greetings, but on their heels was a pair of strange men in the garb of soldiers. Hani brought up the rear. Maya froze, not sure whether this was a social visit or a requisition. But Hani cried out in pleasure, "Look who's here! Our old friend Menna son of Ibi-aw."

And then Maya recognized the young officer who had nearly died defending his commander in Djahy. Menna owed his life to Lord Hani, who had given him a powerful amulet. Four years before, he'd turned up, quite by accident, at their doorstep, leading a unit of soldiers who had come to put down a riot. They hadn't seen him since.

Lady Nub-nefer rose and greeted the man with warmth. "Welcome, Menna."

He was a dark-skinned, bucktoothed fellow with his hair in little fuzzy caterpillars all over his head. He grinned around in a friendly fashion. "Forgive us for disturbing your dinner. I just wanted to pay my respects, and my friend Pa-aten-em-heb, standard-bearer of the Pacifier of the Aten company, asked if he could come along. He said he knew some of you."

The other man, a tall, martial-looking, serious youth whose chiseled visage reminded Maya slightly of a younger

Lord Ptah-mes, bowed. His eyes slid to Mery-ra's face, which was grinning widely, and a smile broke out on his own features. "Lord Mery-ra!"

"Pa-aten-em-heb, my boy! And here I thought I'd never see you again after I retired!"

"Both of you, sit down and share our meal," Nub-nefer urged them warmly. "It's nothing fancy, I fear, but my experience tells me young men are always hungry."

The family scooted together until more stools were fit around Hani's small table. The two young officers seated themselves without further urging.

"I apologize, my lord. I thought you would have eaten by now," Menna said.

"Normally, we would have, but Maya and I were in the Mountains of the West for an investigation."

Maya, who was seated at the next table, overheard and swelled with pride. *He* and Lord Hani were investigating.

Pa-aten-em-heb nodded grimly. "I suppose it has to do with the grave robbings of late, eh? What an embarrassment, with all the foreign dignitaries around."

Hani raised his eyebrows in accord.

The officer's face took on an intent and bitter cast, and he said under his breath, "We're the laughingstock of the nations."

Menna, looking uneasy, elbowed his colleague in the ribs. "Our host is an emissary of the king." He glanced apologetically at Hani.

"And I can tell you," Hani said in a low, significant tone, "that we are the laughingstock of the nations." He and Pa-aten-em-heb stared each other in the eye, and Maya could see understanding spring up between them.

"Forgive me, my lord," said the young officer, leaning toward Hani. Their tones had dropped so low that Maya had to strain to hear them. "My family are priests of Haru at Hut-nen-nesut. My name was and always will be Har-em-heb, but my commanding officer ordered his entire staff to change their names when the king—life, prosperity, and health to him—came to the throne." He continued to stare Hani in the eye, as if willing him to comprehend.

Nub-nefer leaned forward in her turn and said quietly, "And my family are priests of the Hidden One. My brother is third prophet."

"I've heard of him, my lady," said Pa-aten-em-heb with burning intensity.

Iy, thought Maya his neck hairs rising. *Are they talking sedition right here at the table with an officer of the king's army sitting next to them?* But although Menna looked uneasy, he made no move to redirect the conversation. A tense silence settled over that table while laughter and conversation continued to swirl around those seated there.

Finally, Hani sat back and said more loudly, "My son has just been assigned to his grandfather's post as a scribe in the infantry. He's waiting to hear whose unit he'll be seconded to."

Pa-aten-em-heb smiled, relaxing. "I can tell you that, Lord Hani. My unit. That's one reason I wanted to come tonight."

Nub-nefer shot Hani a look of such delight that Maya thought she might spring up and kiss the young officer.

"You say you're from Hut-nen-nesut?" Neferet called from her table. "That's where the House of the Royal Ornaments is."

"Yes, young mistress. My mother is lady-in-waiting to the queen when Lady Nefert-iti is in residence," replied the young officer.

"How do you know about Hut-nen-nesut, my dear?" Neferet's mother asked her. Nub-nefer was flushed with happiness and very much warmer than she'd been before Pa-aten-em-heb had revealed his real name.

"Lady Djefat-nebty has talked about it. She's going to take me down there soon to examine the king's harem."

Menna and Pa-aten-em-heb looked curiously at Hani, who explained, "She's studying to be a *sunet* with the doctor of the royal ladies."

At that point, a commotion at the door announced the arrival of Pa-kiki and Mut-nodjmet. The young couple advanced, smiling, and Neferet darted over to her cousin Mut-nodjmet, who was carrying their year-old son.

"Let me see that ado-o-orable little man!" Neferet cried, pinching the baby's fat cheek. He shrieked with laughter and reached out for her. Mut-nodjmet, beaming, handed him over and unwrapped his little cloak. Maya could remember, only a few years before, how Mut-nodjmet had pined for marriage and children. She'd been a drab, shy, overweight girl with—well, memorable breasts. The latter was still true, but she'd taken on the beauty of contentment and a new sense of her own desirability under the attentions of her husband. Maya smiled to himself with the tolerance of one who knew all about the transfiguring effects of love.

"Sorry we're late, everyone," said Pa-kiki once he'd kissed his mother and sisters, "but just as we were leaving, a messenger arrived with a letter from Uncle Pipi."

"Guess what?" Mut-nodjmet cried. "He and Mother

are going to move back to Waset so they can be near their grandson!"

Lord Hani and Lord Mery-ra exchanged a look of delight and surprise. Mery-ra said with a chuckle, "Without any horses, I hope."

Pipi had nearly bankrupted himself to buy a pair of horses a few years before, only to find out they were stolen goods. Lord Hani had barely managed to sell them for him. Maya told himself to expect more eye-rolling moments once Pipi returned. Hani's younger brother was an impulsive fellow, a boy who had never grown up.

"Does he have a job in mind? If not, maybe we can inscribe him for Pa-kiki's old post in the foreign service," said Mery-ra.

Hani agreed that that was an excellent idea. "My dear," he said to Nub-nefer, "tell the servants to bring in more stools."

But Menna and his companion rose hastily, and he said with some embarrassment, "It's time for us to leave, my lord. We don't want to impose on your family get-together."

Before they turned to go, Pa-aten-em-heb smiled at Hani. "Is this your son, Pa-kiki?"

"I am, my lord," answered the boy.

"Then I welcome you to the Pacifier of the Aten company. I'm Pa-aten-em-heb. You're to be my scribe."

Pa-kiki, all eager and wreathed in smiles, directed himself toward the soldier. "It's you, my lord?" he cried.

"It is." The officer clapped fist to chest in a salute, and Pa-kiki returned it, beaming.

Good for Pa-kiki. He has a nice young officer to serve— with congenial political views. Let's hope the man doesn't get the lad in trouble. There was something intense, almost fanatical, about Pa-aten-em-heb.

"Permit me to introduce my wife, Mut-nodjmet, and my son," Pa-kiki said proudly.

The girl, pressed against her husband's arm, nodded with a shy smile.

Pa-aten-em-heb looked surprised and pleased. "That's my wife's name too."

The two soldiers took their leave, and the family settled in to the rest of their dinner. Maya couldn't help noticing the radiant grin that lit up Lady Nub-nefer's face. But Lord Hani looked thoughtful and was quieter than usual.

CHAPTER 3

THE NEXT MORNING, HANI SETTLED himself on the floor of his salon with Maya at his side, prepared to write on a big potsherd. "So far, we've spoken to Djau and learned that a certain Bebi-ankh may be the man involved in the tomb robberies."

"How is it no one went after him as soon as they had that information, my lord?" said Maya. "It's been over a week since Djau reported him, and he still seems to be at work on Lord Ptah-mes's tomb."

"I suppose they were afraid to tip him off before they found out who his collaborators were. But I'm not sure we'll get any further unless we question him." Hani's face darkened. "I just hope Mahu doesn't reach him first and torture him to talk. You can't trust what anyone says under torture. They'd incriminate their own mother to make the pain stop."

The two men sat for a moment, and Hani pondered the touchiness of their situation. Into the silence came the distant bang of the gate. A'a entered the salon, his mouth open to make an announcement, but even before he could speak, a loud, jolly voice called out from the vestibule, "Hani, my friend? Are you home?"

"It's Mane!" Hani cried, climbing to his feet. "What's he doing in Waset?"

The ambassador to Naharin entered, a jovial, round figure beaming from ear to ear. He opened his arms to Hani, and the two men embraced. Hani had to laugh—one would think that years had passed since they'd last seen one another. But that was Mane's exuberant way.

"What brings you to my humble abode? All the excitement is in the capital," Hani said, motioning his friend to a stool.

Mane sat with a puff of breath. "I'm here in Waset to pack. It's off to Wasshukanni again for me. It may be a long time before we see each other, and I just wanted to say goodbye."

"How are things up there?" Hani asked, more serious.

"Between the Hittites invading and a civil war, not good. A certain Artatama, a brother of Tushratta, is trying to take his throne." Mane's eyes were graver than his smile might suggest. "Tushratta repelled him once, but Artatama seems suddenly to have acquired vast numbers of mercenary troops."

"How's he paying them?" Hani asked.

Mane looked sly. "That is the great question, is it not? Presumably, some foreign power is paying. Kheta Land is high on my list of probabilities."

"So, you're being sent up there to look things over, are you?"

"Yes, indeed." Mane smiled more brightly. "Oh, and

Keliya is getting new attachés—a pair of young scribes named Pirissi and Tulubri. It would be appreciated if you could show them some hospitality, Hani. Other than Keliya, they don't know anybody here."

"Of course. I'll have to brush up my Hurrian."

Mane chuckled, his belly bouncing.

"How is the King's Beloved Wife doing these days?" Hani asked.

Mane's eyebrows quirked sadly. "Oh, my friend, after all the work you did to help our little Kiya, the king has lost interest in her. She's parked with all the other royal wives in Hut-nen-nesut, at the House of the Royal Ornaments."

Hani nodded his sorrowful understanding. "If only *she* had borne a son instead of the queen. And now, of course, her father, Tushratta, sits on an increasingly tottering throne. She's lost all her political value. Our king cares nothing for our treaty with Mitanni, or he would have gone to Tushratta's aid long ago."

"Well, that's the world we live in." Mane stood up with a sigh, and Hani followed suit. "My mission is to evaluate which candidate for kingship to support."

Hani was overcome with a wave of disgust and nausea. *Is it so light a thing to turn on an ally?* But he knew only too well that it was. "Thanks for stopping by before you left, Mane."

Mane looked around him conspiratorially then said in a lowered voice, twisted with anguish, "The king wants our girl to go back home to Naharin. But, Hani, that's like murdering her. The instability of the situation up there— it's as good as throwing her into a den of lions."

"When our king is finished loving someone, he's finished," said Hani caustically.

"Unless we can change Our Sun God's mind, she'll be going back home with me. Soon."

Hani eyed him skeptically. "I hope you don't expect me to do anything about it, friend. As you know, I'm so far from having influence with the king that my patronage would be likely to hurt her cause."

"She trusts and respects you, Hani. Would you at least go up to Hut-nen-nesut with me to talk to her? She's desperate to stay, because they're going to keep her daughter here when she goes."

Hani made a noise of contempt. "Gods help the woman whose father is a king."

"Say you'll come."

But Hani was firm. "I'm in the middle of a big investigation here. I don't see how I can get away. The round trip up there and back takes weeks."

Mane shrugged, looking saddened. "They'll rip her little daughter from her arms and drag her off to a ship, and she'll be sent back to a war-torn country where she'll probably be put to death—"

"Stop it, you manipulative bastard!" Hani cried, laughing in spite of himself and holding up his hands in surrender. He'd been head of the mission to claim Kiya as the barely adolescent bride of the late Neb-ma'at-ra, and she still thought of Hani as a father figure. He, in turn, felt enough affection for the girl to be too easily swayed to help her. "But all I can do is try to make her feel better about going. You know that. I can't change the king's mind if he's decided to do this." It occurred to Hani that his own

Neferet was due to go to Hut-nen-nesut soon to attend the ladies of the royal harem. "Perhaps I can accompany my daughter when she goes down there."

Mane's eyebrows rose. "Your daughter is joining the Royal Ornaments?"

"No, no. She's a *sunet*, studying under Lady Djefat-nebty. She said something about going to Hut-nen-nesut to attend the royal women."

Mane clapped his friend on the arms, beaming. "I knew you could help. I'll let you know when I take off. It will be on my way to Wasshukanni."

"I'm going to start avoiding you, Mane. You inevitably mean trouble." Despite Hani's playful attitude, he meant what he said. Mane had been stationed so long in the Mitannian capital that his loyalties were more with Naharin than with Kemet.

The two friends said their goodbyes, and Mane set off for the door with a jaunty step. As soon as Mane had left, Maya said in a dire tone, "That girl is the one who is trouble, my lord."

Hani sighed. "I know. I'm hoping our investigation into the tomb robberies will keep me too busy to go to Hut-nen-nesut."

He took a seat on the floor once more, and Maya imitated him. He dipped his pen in the ink he'd mixed before Mane's entrance.

"I think we need to visit Djau again briefly and ask where Bebi-ankh lives," Hani said. "I'd rather talk to the black-line man discreetly at home and not in front of everybody at the work site, in case any others of the workmen are in on this. We'll take soldiers with us and arrest him. But first, I want to speak to Djau and offer to have Khawy trained as a scribe."

A sour expression flickered across Maya's face. The secretary said neutrally, "Isn't he a little old to be starting? We all trained from childhood."

Hani repressed a smile. Maya tended to be jealous of Hani's affections. "He should become good enough to be a draftsman. After all, he doesn't have to be a royal scribe."

Maya gave a skeptical *hmph*.

"My father wants to come with us to meet the boy. I think I'll bring the litter for him, and we'll look up Bebi-ankh later. It would probably scare Djau to death if he saw us show up with troops."

"Whose company are you going to request, my lord?"

"Why, Menna's or Pa-aten-em-heb's." Hani smiled.

❖

Hani and Mery-ra ended up making the trek to the Place of Truth alone. Against Mery-ra's will, Hani made his father take the litter.

"I'm not so decrepit that I can't walk, son," Mery-ra said testily as he climbed into the litter. "Whatever happened to filial obedience? I told you I didn't want to ride this contraption."

"You're sixty-six years old, Father. You don't have to prove your manhood. Why, most people never reach your venerable age."

Mery-ra sniffed. "Most people never reach *your* age, Hani, but that doesn't mean we have to treat you like an invalid."

Hani laughed. His father was incorrigible. Mery-ra had

no problem taking the litter around in the city, where it was a mark of status more than anything. But here, where the going was genuinely hard, he balked. "When Pipi moves up here, we'll be two against one. Better get used to our affectionate tyranny."

"Bah," sniffed his father, but as the bearers started slipping and stumbling over the rocky path, his protests subsided.

Hani walked alongside the litter. It had occurred to him that it might be useful to have the four bearers with them, in case there should be any problem with their witnesses. As for him, he loved the sensation of walking, one leg after the other, in the mild air of a winter's afternoon. Overhead, the sky was pure, pale, cloudless—and a lone heron, far from water, winged its way majestically toward the east. Hani drew a deep breath of contentment, able to set aside his worries about the sinister errand that took them to the west bank.

They reached the walled workmen's village just after siesta hour, and Hani led the way haltingly through the narrow streets to the gate that belonged to Djau. Mery-ra dismounted, and Hani knocked. After a moment, he could hear footsteps approaching.

The little window in the panel opened, and an eye peered out at them. A wheezing voice demanded, "Who's there?"

"Djau, it's me, Hani. I came to—"

But to Hani's amazement, the draftsman cried, "Go away. I have nothing to say to you." He slammed shut the little window.

Hani and Mery-ra exchanged alarmed looks. "What's

the matter, my friend?" Hani said to the closed gate in confusion. "Has something happened?"

Through the door, Djau cried aggrievedly, "You tricked me. You said you were investigating the tomb robberies, but you lied. How do I know you aren't one of the robbers come to assassinate me?" His voice had risen and his breathing grown ragged.

"Let's talk, Djau. I think there's been a misunderstanding," said Hani in a reasonable tone. *And I think I know what that was.* A cold fury grew in him like a sandstorm unfolding. "Have you, by any chance, spoken to Lord Mahu or another of his *medjay*?"

"I have indeed. And he told me you were not legitimately on this case."

Hani flashed his father a look of simmering fury, but he made his voice remain soft and friendly. "We're supposed to be working on this case together, according to the king's orders. But I'm afraid Mahu isn't a man who likes to share credit. Can I come in and talk this out face-to-face, my friend?"

There was a long silence from behind the red gate, then Djau said in a calmer voice, "All right." Hani heard sounds of unbarring, and the panel swung open with a soft screech. The little draftsman stood before him, his popping eyes darting around, his anger giving way to bewilderment and then suspicion when he spotted Mery-ra. "Who's that?"

"He's my father, a retired scribe," Hani said with a smile. "He's willing to give young Khawy lessons in the Speech of the Gods so he can become a draftsman and make a better living for your family."

Djau stared at him, his jaw hanging. "You would do that? You don't even know us."

"Of course," Mery-ra assured him genially. Nothing in the world could have been more benevolent than his broad gap-toothed smile. "I'm always delighted to instruct youngsters in the mysteries of the lord Djehuty."

Djau gaped at them for a moment longer, then his face crumpled, and with the back of a hand, he dashed at his eyes in chagrin. "Forgive me, my lord. I felt you were a good man, but that Mahu confused me so."

"No shame to you for being prudent, Djau," said Hani kindly. He clapped the man on his bony little shoulder.

"Come in, come in. Please explain to me what's going on." Djau led them through the garden into the house. "I could have taught Khawy myself, except... I don't have much energy left once I get home at the end of the week. He liked you. I should have known a child's instincts were sound." He ushered them into his salon, where a shrunken little old woman sat stroking a cat. She looked up, her protruding eyes a rheumy, elderly version of Djau's. "My mother," he said in a sorrowful voice. "She doesn't understand what you say to her anymore, I'm afraid. My brother's death just about finished her off."

Hani and Mery-ra made a courteous nod to the woman, who stared at them, blank as a gourd.

"You see?" Djau murmured dismally. "My life is falling apart." He motioned his guests to have a seat on a plastered dais softened with two colorfully woven cushions, and he crossed his legs and sank to the floor, his shoulders slumped. "Please, Lord Hani, tell me what's going on."

Hani pondered what he dared say. "Lord Mahu and I

76

both have orders to investigate the crimes. Presumably, that means we should help one another. But I'm afraid Mahu thinks it means he pushes me out of the way. What did he say to you?"

Djau shrugged, dispirited. "He said he was the investigator and that you were pretending to be so you could get information for someone. He left that open. I guess I jumped to the worst possible conclusion—that you were part of the gang who robbed the tombs and that you wanted to... to kill me."

Mery-ra gave a disgusted snort. Hani's face was burning with anger, but he managed to sound calm and reassuring. "The 'someone' for whom I'm gathering information is the king—life, prosperity, and health to him. I'm sorry Mahu frightened you, Djau. In fact, there are only two reasons we've come today. One is to invite your nephew to train as a scribe with my father"—he nodded at Mery-ra—"and the other is to ask you where Bebi-ankh lives. I need to question him before Mahu and his men torture him."

Djau looked up with haunted eyes. "I almost wish I had never said anything, my lord. My life has become so complicated. I think Lord Mahu believes I'm part of the gang. He became almost threatening. If anything happens to me, if he carts me off to prison..."

Ammit take the heartless bastard, Hani thought with a silent growl. "Don't be afraid, my friend. You're under my protection, and that means the protection of the vizier. Now, please tell me what you said to Mahu. And could you give me Bebi-ankh's whereabouts?"

"I told him the same thing I told you, my lord." Then Djau described the route to the black-line man's house, which was close by but on a more modest street. "He has brothers, though, all as big as he is, so be careful."

"Thank you for your warning. And now, about Khawy. Is it a problem for you if we take him on weekends? That way, he won't miss any workdays. Or he could stay with us and study every day. That would be more useful to him."

Djau stared into his lap, considering, then looked up. Hani noticed the dark, unhealthy circles around his eyes. "If you can take him every day, my lord? I don't know... I don't know how long I'll be able to work, and then it will all be on him."

"Good. Don't worry about paying us. My father is retired and has nothing else to do." He shot a glance of suppressed amusement at Mery-ra, who nodded benevolently.

"How have we deserved this, Lord Hani?" the draftsman cried, clasping Hani's hands. "How could I have suspected you of being a bad man? May the Hidden One bless—I mean..." He looked suddenly frightened again. "I mean, may the Aten bless you."

Hani threw back his head and laughed. "I'll take any blessing the gods can spare me, friend." He rose, and Mery-ra did the same. "So it's settled? Send Khawy whenever you feel you can let him go. Most of my children are out of the house, so there's plenty of room."

Djau climbed laboriously to his feet, and even that slight exertion left him wheezing. "What should I do if Mahu comes back, my lord?"

"Cooperate," said Hani, "but don't believe what he tells you. And if he threatens you again, let me know. This must stop."

They took their leave with much more warmth than

their arrival had elicited. Mery-ra refused to enter the litter, so the four bearers followed them down the narrow dust-clogged way between houses.

"I wanted to go back and get soldiers before I confronted Bebi-ankh, in case he tried to escape, but I'm afraid to wait now. Mahu could come and take him at any minute, if he hasn't already." Hani chewed on his anger as he stalked along. "The unscrupulous son of a dog."

Mery-ra shook his head, his bushy brows contracting fiercely. "He's as bad as the criminals he chases. I'll never forgive him for almost killing you."

"The real worry is that he has the king's ear." Hani forced himself to let go of his rage, and he turned to the porters behind him with a pleasant expression. "Are you fellows ready for a possible fight? You can slide out the poles from the litter for clubs."

The young men, strapping and eager for a brawl, grinned and made warlike noises.

Mery-ra chuckled. "Life is never boring around you, son."

The two scribes led the way to the gate Djau had designated, and Hani rapped smartly on the panel. After a moment, he heard the bolt sliding, and a youngish woman peeked out through a crack. "Who's there?" There was no welcome in her suspicious features as she eyed Hani up and down.

"Hani son of Mery-ra, investigator for the king. Is your husband home?"

"Another investigator? Don't you ever take no for an answer?" Her voice was shrill and sharp, but what alarmed Hani was the word *another*. Mahu had already come.

79

The woman tried to close the gate, but Hani had inserted his sandaled foot in the opening, and he wrenched the panel back in spite of her. "Where is Bebi-ankh, mistress? If you try to hide him, you're guilty of complicity."

She shouted, backing up toward the house, "He's not here. I told the other men that. Get out, or I'll call the *medjay*."

"I rather doubt that," said Hani with a gently sarcastic smile. "I'd think you'd rather almost anybody but the *medjay* came in after what they did to him."

Her jaw dropped, and she wilted. "How did you know about that?"

"Will you show him to me or not?"

"What are you going to do to him?" She was still suspicious, Hani could see, and very afraid.

"I'm going to offer him protection if he talks to me honestly."

The woman was in her thirties and attractive with her long natural hair, but there was already a worn look about her. This house had no gatekeeper, Hani saw. These were people who worked hard and were never without some need for grain.

He said kindly, "I understand why he might have gotten involved in... what he got involved in, mistress. But believe me, he's in danger. The people who are using him have no scruples. If he cooperates, I'll see to it he's protected."

She gave a cynical snort. "Like that other bastard 'protected' him?" Suddenly, her bravado crumbled, and tears began to leak from her eyes. Her mouth turned down in a wobbly crescent. "Save him, my lord. Don't let them get him. One side or the other will kill him for sure." She hid her face in her hands and bawled, "I warned him, but we were so in debt…"

"May I see him?" Hani repeated in a gentle tone.

The woman sucked back her tears with a sniff and, turning, led the way into the house. Her shoulders sagged in defeat. She preceded the two men through the salon, which was decorated with exquisite taste despite its small size, and into a small dark bedchamber. At the door, she said flatly, "Bibi, more men are here to see you."

Out of the shadows, a voice cried wildly, "And you let them in? Ammit take you, woman!"

Hani could dimly make out a figure stretched out on the bed, struggling to rise. He hastened to the bedside and laid a hand on Bebi-ankh's chest. The man fell back without a fight. Hani saw now that his leg was splinted and his face was a mass of bruises and scrapes. Although he was a sturdy fellow, pain had taken the spirit out of him.

Hani squatted at his side. "Who did this to you? The *medjay*? Did they make you talk?"

"Who are you?" the artist demanded weakly, but there was defiance in his voice.

This close, Hani saw that what he had taken for scrapes were in fact burns. His anger against Mahu mounted. *The son of a dog tortured him. He must have threatened his eyes.* "I'm Hani, and this is my father, Mery-ra. We are the real investigators of this case, and believe me, if I had reached you before the chief of police, you would not have been tortured. What did he make you tell him?"

Bebi-ankh gave a creaky laugh that clearly cost him pain. "I told the bastard nothing. Nothing. And you can't make me talk either. I don't know anything." He looked up at Hani with fever-sharpened eyes. "Who gave the *medjay* my name? Was it that little rat Djau? Was it Khnum-baf, that hound-eyed wretch? I told them we should never have let him drag us into it."

You just confessed, thought Hani dryly. "I have my sources. I want to hear you confirm what I know, Bebi-ankh. If you are helpful—and truthful—I'll see to it you're hidden away someplace safe from Mahu and from the rest of the people who are going to be after you now."

"By all the gods, talk to him, Bibi," the woman cried from behind Hani. "We can't live like this. They'll come after the children next."

Bebi-ankh's head flopped back onto his headrest in resignation. "A man approached me a couple of weeks ago and asked if I wanted to get rich. He said there might be danger but the rewards would be great."

"What sort of man?" Hani asked sharply. "Was he Egyptian?"

It was impossible to tell what Bebi-ankh normally looked like, so disfigured was his face. But his eyes rolled toward Hani, white in the near darkness. "A foreigner. Tall. Light skinned. Spoke good Egyptian but with a strong accent."

"Could you recognize the accent?" asked Mery-ra.

"No. But he was from the north."

Hani said, "How was he dressed?"

The black-line man thought for a moment. "A long tunic of wool. A beautiful color you don't often see—like turquoise stone but deeper. Some dye from chrysocolla ore, I'd say."

Ah, yes, thought Hani. *He's an artist. He would notice such things.* "What else?"

"Hair dark, cut off at the shoulders. Light eyes. Bearded around the jaw but no mustache. Nice-looking fellow. He had a mole just over his mouth on the left lip."

"That's most helpful, Bebi-ankh. I think you're on your way to buying your safety," Hani said with an encouraging smile. But inside him, something dropped, leaden, into the pit of his stomach. *A Mitannian? That will really blow up Tushratta's treaty.* "What did he want of you? How did he plan to make you rich?"

Behind him, Bebi-ankh's wife gave a little sob-like noise.

"He... he wanted me to show him how to get into a tomb."

Hani and Mery-ra exchanged a triumphant look. "To rob a tomb? Did he know the penalty if you were caught?"

"*I* didn't know—I can tell you that. It was Khnum-baf who told me. The scum disappeared into thin air after that. And I always thought he was my friend. He's probably over the border into Kush by now, the rat."

If he's still alive, thought Hani uneasily. "He was involved with you and the foreigner?"

"There were maybe seven of us—artists and stonecutters. Artists to draw a plan and show on the ground where to dig and stonecutters to cut into the roof of the chamber. He had other men, too, to do the heavy work. To... to drag away the treasure we pulled out."

"Weren't the tombs guarded?" asked Mery-ra. "These were all recent burials, weren't they?"

"Yes, my lord," Bebi-ankh answered in a voice growing

dry and gritty. He licked his lips, and his wife dodged out of the room. "But the foreigner had apparently bribed the guards. They were nowhere to be seen the night we set to work."

The woman returned with a clay cup she offered to her husband, holding his head up to drink. He guzzled it down and leaned back on his headrest, his eyes glazed with pain.

Hani went on relentlessly, "And the same arrangement had been made for the other two tombs?"

"Yes. But we were just practicing, really. The plan was to rob Neb-ma'at-ra's tomb once we had our technique down."

Dear gods. A royal tomb? Probably the same craftsmen worked on it; it's only been seven years. "Can you name names for me, Bebi-ankh?"

"Swear to me you'll protect me." The whites of his eyes glittered in trepidation.

"I swear on my mother's *ka*," Hani replied solemnly. "I'll take you away to safety this very day if you want. I have a litter outside, and no neighbor will see you."

"Don't trust him," whimpered his wife.

But the artist said roughly, "Quiet, woman. This may be my only chance."

"He can't walk," she lamented.

"Name me names," Hani said.

And the artist named names. Afterward, Hani called his bearers into the house, and with Bebi-ankh's wife's help, they loaded him into the litter.

Nub-nefer's eyes grew round with surprise as Hani and

Mery-ra entered the garden with the litter behind them. A'a stood by with a torch as the bearers lifted the badly beaten and burned man from the interior. Bebi-ankh yelped in pain.

"Hani, what is this?" she cried, clinging to his arm. "Who is this man?"

"A witness to a crime," Hani said blandly. *And the victim of another crime.* "He's going to be with us for a while until I find out what Lord Ptah-mes wants me to do with him."

She looked at him in horror and confusion. "But Pipi and his family are here. Where are we going to put this fellow?"

"Pipi's here?" Hani cried. He shot his father an astonished look.

Mery-ra shrugged innocently. "I told you he was moving back to Waset."

"Today? He came while we were in the Place of Truth?"

"So it seems." Mery-ra shrugged again.

Nub-nefer added, "With Nedjem-ib and all the children."

Hani started to laugh because there was nothing else he could do. Once again, the gods had stirred his life like a pot of greens. He laughed until his eyes were full of tears.

"Can't they go to Pa-kiki and Mut-nodjmet's house?" Mery-ra asked. "What about the farm?"

"That's a wonderful idea," said Nub-nefer. "But we can hardly turn them out tonight. They may already be in bed. It was a very long trip, and they have all their baggage with them."

"Well, put this gentleman in the kitchen if there's nowhere else. He's ill and needs warmth. And his wife

85

should be showing up soon." The crazy reality of his predicament struck Hani so brutally that it just made him laugh inwardly again. He was as helpless before the divine sense of humor as a chick in the talons of an eagle.

The four bearers carried Bebi-ankh into the kitchen and set him up next to the oven, which was still warm. Hani stayed to be sure the artist was fed. Then he returned to the salon, where he ran into Pipi in the ample flesh.

His brother Pa-aten-em-heb—Pipi—was four years Hani's junior and as lovable, feckless, and full of goodwill as he'd been as a pudgy, gap-toothed boy. He held out his arms to his elder brother, delighted. "Hani! Here we are!"

"I see that." Hani grinned as they embraced. "Have you found a job? Do you have a place lined up to stay?" It would have surprised him if Pipi had had so much foresight.

Hani's brother looked sheepish. "Not yet. I thought we could stay with you until—"

"Then you need to start looking for a house, because mine seems to be full of boarders." Hani steeled himself to be firm. Pipi would act like a child forever unless one forced him to responsibility. He was forty-three years old—solidly into middle age—but still acted on every whim with no thought to the outcome.

"All right, brother," Pipi said docilely.

"And I think we may have a job for you. Pa-kiki just left the foreign office, where he was a clerk. He's gone off to be a scribe for the army. We had him inscribe you as his successor, if you want the post."

Pipi's little brown eyes opened wide in delight. "That's perfect!" He hugged Hani with all his heartfelt strength.

"Thank you, Hani. You're still looking out for your little brother!"

Which probably needs to stop, Hani thought wryly. But old habits were hard to break. "You should shop around for a house in Akhet-aten if you're going to work there every day."

Nub-nefer entered the salon, a mischievous gleam in her eye. "I see you've found Pipi," she said, leaning toward Hani for a kiss. He put his arm around her warm copper shoulders and drew her closer. *What other woman would put up with all the dangers and inconveniences I've brought down upon the household?* She was pure gold, as her name proclaimed.

"I'm going to have to go down to the capital for a few days, my love. I need to make a report to Lord Ptah-mes and get some directions," Hani said. "Father and Pipi will take good care of you and Baket-iset in my absence." He shot an amused glance at his brother, who nodded earnestly.

Nub-nefer caught at Hani's sleeve. "What about the man in the kitchen?"

"Have a doctor come take a look at him. I don't know what shape his leg is in, and those burns probably need tending."

"What on earth happened to him?" Nub-nefer asked, her brow wrinkled in compassion.

"Mahu's police questioned him." He gave his wife a significant glance. She would remember what Mahu's police had done to Hani as a mere "person of interest."

Her beautiful face grew hard. "Like master, like servant. What jurisdiction does Mahu have in the Place of Truth?"

"That, my dove, is the great mystery. Apparently, the king has given him broad powers."

She made a noise of disgust. The name of the king never failed to elicit anger and contempt from her.

Eager to avoid any further discussion of Bebi-ankh—especially in front of Pipi, who loved to hear the latest gossip and certainly couldn't be trusted to keep it secret—Hani said again, "I'm heading to Akhet-aten in the morning. Maybe I'll bring back Neferet. She must be off for the holidays. Pipi, do you want to come and talk to the chief scribe of the archives at the Hall of Royal Correspondence? He'll tell you your duties."

"Sure, Hani. It will give us time to talk."

"Nub-nefer, my dear"—Hani turned to his wife—"if a strange woman and her children show up at the door, take them in. They'll be the family of Bebi-ankh, the man in the kitchen."

"I won't even ask what's going on, my love," she said, turning with a sigh of resignation. "They can sleep in the kitchen too."

CHAPTER 4

WHILE MAYA AND PIPI WAITED in the reception hall, Hani was ushered into the office of the high commissioner of northern vassals. Lord Ptah-mes was sitting in his chair of office—immaculate, as always, in his expensive wig and gold collars of honor.

His face cracked in a humorless smile. "Hani. Good to see you, my friend. I hope the news you have for me is better than the news I have for you."

Hani raised his eyebrows. Unease crept up his neck. *What could that be?* But he launched into his report. "Well, it seems that Mahu had beaten me to the scene, my lord. He has lied to and terrorized the innocent man who reported the case and tortured the one we knew was involved. Bebi-ankh claims he told Mahu nothing."

Ptah-mes lowered his eyes, his nostrils flaring in disgust. "But Mahu didn't arrest him?"

"Apparently not. I suppose Mahu's hoping he'll lead him to the others somehow."

Ptah-mes nodded. "Did the man talk to you, Hani?"

"He did. I told him we would protect him from his fellows and from the *medjay*. He's... he's at my house with his whole family at the moment."

"You're an unusual man," said the commissioner with a softer smile. "I hope this won't bring danger down on your family."

"He traveled in a litter, my lord. I can't imagine anyone knew he left his house." Hani dropped his eyes and then looked up again with a smoldering stare. "You should have seen the shape the poor fellow was in."

"And what about the so-called foreign diplomat?"

"Well, Djau and Bebi-ankh both spoke of a tall, light-skinned foreigner who coordinated the robberies. He said something about his immunity." Ptah-mes looked grim. "They were apparently working up to a royal tomb. One of the men took fright and ran away."

"Did anyone know where this foreign fellow was from?"

Hani drew a deep breath and said reluctantly, "From the description, he sounded like a Mitannian."

Ptah-mes received this news in silence. His arched black eyebrows drew down in reflection. Finally, he said, "Tushratta and our king have been at loggerheads from the beginning, despite the deep friendship the Mitannian enjoyed with the Osir Neb-ma'at-ra. Would Tushratta do something like this? And why? What good does it do him to break the treaty irrevocably now, when he needs our help the most?"

Hani shrugged, hopelessness weighing him down like a wet cloak. "It doesn't seem like him, my lord. He's always been very much our friend. Unless he's seeking retribution for the humiliation of his daughter, who is being sent back to Mitanni."

"That's pretty much a formal repudiation of the treaty anyway. Perhaps Tushratta feels he has nothing to lose." Ptah-mes sighed. "I would have thought he had his hands full at home, between civil war and the advance of the Hittites."

As much as Hani liked Tushratta, who could be charming, he could imagine the king of Naharin making time for revenge. Some people were made compassionate by suffering, but the king seemed to have been bent toward rancor. He was a complex man. It would be difficult to say what he would and would not do.

"My lord, how should I deal with this Bebi-ankh? He's equally afraid of the foreigner and his coconspirators on the one side and Mahu's henchmen on the other."

"Keep him for now—I mean, if he isn't too much of a burden. We don't want Mahu to get him."

Hani shook his head with a rueful laugh. "It wouldn't be a burden except that my brother and his whole family are here too. He's moving back to Waset."

"Ah, Pa-ra-em-heb? A delightful man." Ptah-mes considered for a moment. "Have him stay at my house in Waset, if you like. There are just the two of us."

"Oh, my lord, that's too kind of you," Hani cried in relief. "He'll be overjoyed. He was very fond of you."

Lord Ptah-mes gave a strained little smile as if he found it difficult to believe anyone was fond of him. He stood up, brushing the flawless pleats of his kilt and caftan, and Hani rose, too, out of respect. "You say this Bebi-ankh talked to you?" Ptah-mes asked, staring up out of the high window. "Did he give you names?"

"He did. Seven members of the work crew were involved, plus a number of others who carried out the heavy labor. I suppose my next step is to arrest them."

"Yes. Have you contacted some officer to make use of his unit? I'll write you a letter with the vizier's seal."

Hani glanced at his superior in grim amusement. "I should warn you, my lord. These arrests will slow down progress on your tomb—that's where the men were all working."

Ptah-mes raised his eyebrows and pursed his lips in a dry simulacrum of a smile. "Good thing no one is buried there, or I suspect I'd be the next victim of a robbery, eh?"

Hani had to agree. He braced himself and asked, "You said you had some bad news for me, my lord?"

Ptah-mes's face grew grave, the lines between his nose and the corners of his mouth deepening. "There's plague in the palace, Hani. Some foreigner seems to have brought it down from Djahy. I heard they had it running around up there, but Aper-el didn't think it would be worth canceling the jubilee for all that." He blew a disturbed breath out his nose. "This celebration was badly timed."

Fear ran up Hani's backbone in a shivering wave. "My daughter is a *sunet* to the palace women," he murmured.

Lord Ptah-mes said in concern, "You'd better keep her home, my friend. Once one person gets it, the whole royal household is vulnerable. She might well find herself treating plague victims."

Hani nodded. Suddenly, the fate of the royal tombs seemed pale. His little girl was in danger. "I'm planning to take her home for the holidays, my lord. I'll tell her teacher she won't be coming back for a while."

"All of us who are able will leave the capital too. Of course, the government has to continue. And," he added caustically, "the Great Jubilee of the Aten has to go on, no matter how many people drop dead."

Hani took his leave, crushed with anxiety for Neferet. And Aha—Hani's firstborn—lived in Akhet-aten too. He was a lay administrator at the Great Temple of the Aten, but no one could be sure the plague wouldn't spread out of the palace into the city at large.

In the reception hall, Pipi and Maya were still sitting against the wall. They rose as Hani closed Ptah-mes's door behind him.

"Did you give him my greetings?" Pipi asked eagerly. He'd made Ptah-mes's acquaintance several years before and had even spent days on his yacht.

"I did. He said you were free to stay at his house in Waset since we have so many... boarders at ours."

Pipi's little eyes lit up with childlike excitement. "Oh, Hani! His house must be magnificent if it's anything like his yacht. What a privilege!"

"It's magnificent, all right." Hani thought of the frigid courtesy between Ptah-mes and his wife, who held her husband in contempt for collaborating with the new king. He said more seriously, "Listen, there's plague in the palace. We need to stay away from the capital as much as possible."

"But my new job..." Pipi cried in dismay.

"We'll find you something in Waset. The mayor may have a post. I'll ask."

Hani struck off directly toward the southern part of

the city, where Aha's villa stood. Maya and Pipi, their faces tense and eyes wide, as if they feared the plague might spring out at them from behind any building, trailed him. Everything looked peaceful and prosperous, but the cloud of something terrible hung over those Hani loved. Even behind their whitewashed walls, they were no longer safe from the invisible demons of sickness.

Lady Sekhmet, spare them, he prayed over and over as he stood at the gate, waiting for Aha's porter to open it.

"Lord Hani," the man cried with pleasure when he had pulled back the door. "It's been a while since you've honored us with your presence."

"Is your master home, my friend?" Hani could scarcely fix a smile on his face for the anxiety that gnawed at him.

"He's still at the temple, my lord. Lady Khentet-ka is at her mother's with the children. Can I transmit a message?"

"Please tell him that plague has begun in the palace. He would do well to get out of the city. Tell him to send his family to our farm or to her parents'. I'm taking Neferet home."

The gatekeeper's eyes grew so horrified that Hani wondered if he would run away without even delivering his message.

The three men set off next for the house of Lord Pentju and Lady Djefat-nebty, the royal physician and his wife, the *sunet* of the royal ladies. The way had never seemed so long to their magnificent estate at the edge of the city. The sun beat down with brilliance but no warmth. These were the shortest days of the year, when the mysteries of the struggle between Haru and Sutesh—between order and chaos—were enacted.

It's going on around us now, Hani thought. *The Apep serpent is sowing fear and sickness, squeezing us in his coils.*

Leaving his companions at the gate, Hani was admitted to the house. He didn't know whether Djefat-nebty and his daughter were there or somewhere in the palace, bent over the demonic breath of a plague victim. But before long, he heard footsteps coming from within the house, and the tall, mannish figure of the *sunet* appeared in the doorway.

"Lord Hani," she greeted him with her usual cold expression, which he knew concealed a much warmer heart. "Are you here to take Neferet home for the holidays?"

"My lady, forgive a father's anxiety, but I've been told that plague has begun in the palace. Can you confirm that?"

She stood silent, as if debating how honest to be, then said, "I can. One of the men of Djahy, here for the jubilee, seems to have brought it."

Hani took a deep breath that was less steady than he would have liked. "Then may I beg you to release my daughter from her duties for a while? We're terribly concerned that tending the Royal Ornaments will expose her to the disease."

The *sunet*'s mouth drew down in disapproval. "But, Hani," she said dryly, "it's when people are sick that they need a doctor."

"Please, my lady. She's only sixteen." Hani felt a disproportionate desperation. He was ready to plead with the woman on bended knee—to weep if he had to.

"Well, I certainly can't stop you from taking her away. She's your daughter after all. But I suggest you ask *her* what she wants to do."

Hani itched to retort, "Who cares what she wants? She's

a child. Her father can tell her what's best for her." But he said none of that. "Very well." Perhaps he could convince Neferet to leave, although her mulishness was legendary in the family.

Djefat-nebty disappeared into the depths of her house and shortly thereafter reappeared with Neferet in her wake. "Papa!" the girl cried with a broad smile, throwing herself on Hani with such energy that her braids lashed his chest. "Are you taking me home for the holidays?"

"Yes, my duckling." Hani was tempted to say nothing further and simply get her home and keep her there. But he caught the *sunet*'s stern eye and added hesitantly, "Perhaps it would be a good thing for you to stay home for a while, Neferet. There's plague in the palace. Your mama and I want you to stay safe."

Neferet drew back from him, shocked and suspicious. "Do I have to, Papa? Is this an order? Because, you know, it's when people are sick that they need a doctor."

"So I've heard," Hani replied with a glance at Djefat-nebty. "I think it would be good, my duckling. Afterward, you can come back if you want to."

Neferet thrust her lip out in the stubborn expression Hani knew too well. Her little brown eyes flickered with flame. "I don't want to go. I mean, I'll go home for the holidays, but I don't want to stay. Lady Djefat-nebty relies on me, and there's a new girl who needs me to help her learn our ways. No. I won't stay."

Hani was torn between admiration and vexation. He locked eyes with Djefat-nebty over the girl's head, but she remained expressionless, her arms crossed like a man. *Help me here, by all the gods*, he willed her silently. But she said nothing.

"My love, I think you need to let older and wiser heads make this decision for you—"

"I won't, Papa." Neferet crossed her arms in angry imitation of her teacher and drew away from her father. "If you try to make me stay, I won't ever come home."

Hani's voice rose in exasperation. "Neferet, think about what it would mean if you infected Baket-iset or Sat-hut-haru's or Pa-kiki's children."

"I can't abandon my post," she said, adamant. "If the plague spreads, there won't be enough doctors to take care of everyone."

Hani thought he would explode with frustration. He replied, nearly shouting, "You foolish girl. Are you putting the king's women ahead of your own family?"

A look of wavering guilt flickered over Neferet's face. Then she rallied to her cause. "I'm putting the sick over the well." There was no sign of compromise in her outthrust lip.

Hani drew in a long breath through his nose. It would be a strategic mistake to lose his temper altogether. He looked at Lady Djefat-nebty and said in a carefully controlled voice, "I don't suppose we could look to you for a helpful word, my lady?"

But she said in her stern way, "The girl is legally an adult, Lord Hani. Nothing I could say would bind her— nor anything you could say, evidently."

If I force her, we'll lose her. We have to honor her choice of life work. "Very well," Hani said flatly, hoping it didn't sound like an admission of defeat. "Lady Djefat-nebty is right. You're not a child anymore. You've chosen what you want in life, and we respect that."

"Then, if you'll let me come back, I'll go home with you." Her big grin, with the lovable space between the front teeth, opened wide again. She threw her arms around her father, and Hani embraced her hard, as if his body could defend her from the harm that crept invisibly through the halls and slipped from person to person without a sound.

We mustn't drive her away over this, he told himself again. *It's a generous and courageous thing she wants to do.*

"So I'll see you again in two weeks, Neferet?" asked the *sunet* in a neutral tone.

"Yes, my lady. Without fail. If I have to swim. And may Sekhmet turn my nose green and pull out my navel if I don't."

To Hani's surprise, Djefat-nebty burst out in a bark of laughter. "She's quite a person, your daughter, Lord Hani. Congratulations."

The two of them took their leave, Hani torn between pride in his youngest child and desperate fear for her safety. *This won't make Nub-nefer happy.*

After picking up Pipi and Maya at the gate, father and daughter tramped in uncomfortable silence toward the embarcadero, Hani afraid that anything he said might precipitate another argument. Up the gangplank they marched, the boards bouncing beneath their feet. Hani found the four of them a place to sit on the deck, and they stayed there, unspeaking, for a long time as the ferry swung out into the current and the sailors heaved up the wide sail. It caught the wind with a clack, and the boat jumped forward against the flow.

Hani shot a sideways glance at his daughter. She was sitting cross-legged, staring fixedly out at the River, sunk deep in thought. In spite of himself, Hani's heart warmed to the girl. This thoughtful, silent Neferet wasn't the little hoyden he knew. She was growing up and not just physically. *May the Great One watch over her*, he prayed with painful fervor.

At last, Neferet said in a casual tone, as if there had been no disagreement between them, "Papa, the new girl is a wonderful person. She was studying with the *wab* priests of Sekhmet at Sau until the temple was shut down. She knows a lot already. Her father is a *sunu*, too—a friend of Lord Pentju."

"Then what is it you have to help her with so urgently, little duck?" Hani said tartly. Then he regretted his tone. He wanted to support her wholeheartedly.

But she replied without rancor, "Oh, the way we do things at the palace. There's protocol, you know. And Djefat-nebty has lots of rules. And sometimes, the priests taught Bener-ib a little differently than Djefat-nebty teaches. You know." Neferet shrugged.

Hani sighed.

Maya said sourly, "Why couldn't you have wanted to train baboons or something normal?"

As she had so often done in her childhood, Neferet began immediately to imitate a baboon, squinching her mouth and eyes and hunching her shoulders. The three men burst out laughing, and Neferet joined in.

"I love you, Papa," she said, planting a big kiss on his cheek.

"And I love you, my duckling. That's why I don't want

anything to happen to you." He put his arm around her. They sat that way until it grew chilly on the deck, then they all went inside the curtained shelter where other passengers had taken refuge. Before long, the boat put in to shore to wait out the night, and father, daughter, brother, and son-in-law slept, rolled up in their cloaks.

When they finally reached Waset, Hani found he didn't have the courage to tell Nub-nefer that Neferet insisted on going back after the holidays into the teeth of the plague. *Let us enjoy these sacred days without arguments,* he told himself wearily.

Pipi's wife and three younger children, who ranged in age from eight to thirteen, were there, a jovial presence. Nedjem-ib's contagious brays of laughter broke out over the talk from time to time, and her youngest—twins—spent much of their time chasing one another in and out of the garden. Sat-hut-haru and her children were also in the house when they arrived, and Neferet immediately swooped down on her nephew and niece. She proceeded to fall on her knees and act like a cat, arching her back, rubbing the children's legs with her shoulders, and purring. The children reacted with squeals of laughter.

"That reminds me, Papa," said Baket-iset from her couch. "Ta-miu had her kittens. We shut them away so the baby wouldn't pull their tails."

"Good for her." Hani wondered again what Neferet was thinking when she said she didn't want to bear any children. She clearly loved little ones. "Anything else of interest while I was gone?"

"Your friend Keliya was here with two young men he wanted you to meet," Nub-nefer said, her arm linked through Hani's. They stood beside Baket-iset, surveying their grandchildren.

"He's in Waset?" Hani cried.

"He said he was staying with Mane's family. Mane has apparently gone back to Wasshukanni."

"Oh, he's left, has he? He wanted me to talk to Lady Kiya before he took her home, but I never got to Hut-nen-nesut. I'll tell you why later." A pall fell over his happy mood at the thought of what was going on in court. He hoped fervently that Aha had received his message and taken it to heart.

"No, no, she hasn't left yet. It's these two men who are supposed to accompany her back, Keliya said. This Tulubri and Pi... Pa..." Nub-nefer looked to Hani for rescue.

"Pirissi, I believe, my love." Hani's voice fell. "How are our guests in the kitchen?"

Nub-nefer stared at her husband, aggrieved. "Hani, those poor people need some privacy. The man can't walk yet, and he has to use a bedpan. And I'm afraid the children will hurt themselves on the hearth or the oven. Where else can we put them?"

"Ptah-mes offered to put Pipi and his family up at his house."

"How generous," Nub-nefer said in relief. "He and Lady Apeny are true grandees, deserving of the title *weru*."

"Perhaps we can send Bebi-ankh and his crew to the farm," Hani said but then remembered that he'd encouraged Aha to send his family to the country place. He couldn't see Khentet-ka—or Aha either, for that matter—willingly sharing their quarters with an artisan.

Maya came and stood beside Hani, hands on his hips, as he looked out over his family at play. "Will we be doing any work over the holidays, my lord?"

"Probably not, except to visit Keliya's friends." *I have to inform everyone sooner rather than later*, Hani urged himself firmly. "Nub-nefer, my dear, I need to tell you something. Maya already knows. But where is Father?"

"He's at his lady friend's house." Nub-nefer smiled slyly. "He took your litter."

"Ah. I'll tell him when he gets back." Hani's voice dropped. "Lord Ptah-mes said there was plague breaking out at the palace. Someone brought it from Djahy."

Her eyes widened with horror, and she clapped a hand over her mouth.

Hani cautioned her, "Try to act normal. We don't want to scare the children."

Maya managed an offhand expression, but his face was a shade paler than usual. "Do you think we're exposed, my lord? Dear gods, if I thought I'd brought it home to the little ones..."

"I doubt it. Neither of us has been to the palace recently."

"Aha," murmured Nub-nefer in a hollow voice. "He keeps company with the king and his young friends."

"I left him a message and told him to go up to the country place. Let's hope he takes me up on it."

"And Neferet." She gasped, a look of realization dawning on her face. "Why, she works at the palace. We have to keep her here."

Hani felt his face grow hot with discomfort. *There's nothing for it. I have to tell her.* "I, er... I talked to her about that. She insists she wants to keep working. She takes her duties as a *sunet* very seriously."

"You talked to her about it? You had a conversation?" Nub-nefer expostulated, her kohl-darkened eyes growing wide with outrage. She drew away from Hani as abruptly as if he himself had the plague. "You didn't just *order* her to stay here? You're her father!"

"She's legally an adult, my love," Hani murmured uneasily.

"Well, I'm going to tell her, then." She turned and moved toward the children. Neferet was crawling around on all fours with little Tepy perched on her shoulders, laughing, his feet dangling around her neck.

But Hani held her back. "Please don't. We don't want to drive her away over this. You know how stubborn she can be. 'Speak gently that you may be loved.'"

Nub-nefer turned on him, eyes flashing with scorn. "Hani, don't quote aphorisms to me. You've spoiled her appallingly. I don't care how old she is—if her father gives her an order, she should listen."

"Well," he said mildly, "her father *didn't* give her an order. And I hope her mother won't either, because then she'll run away and never see us again—unless you plan to tie her up someplace."

Nub-nefer stood, her face red and her lips compressed as if she were struggling with herself. "It's that Djefat-nebty," she muttered. "She's putting rebellious ideas in Neferet's head."

"I rather think our daughter has enough rebellious

ideas of her own, my dove. We have to respect what she's chosen to give herself to. We can't be less brave than she is."

Nub-nefer fell silent, but she clearly wasn't convinced. After a moment, she sat down on the edge of Baket-iset's couch, and her face relaxed as she began to talk to their eldest girl.

Love will win out, he thought, a wave of relief washing over him.

Maya, at Hani's side, exchanged a glance of male commiseration with him. The secretary called out to Sat-hut-haru, "My dove, perhaps we should go. It's getting late, and I don't want us to be out after dark."

She gathered the baby and a giggling Tepy, who was engaged in some kind of mock pillow battle with Pipi's younger sons, and they moved in a block toward the door. "Goodnight, Mama and Papa," Sat-hut-haru called. A moment later, the outer door closed, and their voices died away.

Hani made his way to the kitchen, where Bebi-ankh and his family were camped. The black-line man was sitting up on the edge of the cot next to the oven, watching his two older children play while his wife nursed the youngest. He looked up and, seeing Hani in the doorway, tried to rise, but Hani motioned him back down with a smile.

"I promise your living conditions will improve, my friend. My brother is moving out tomorrow, and you'll have real rooms."

"You're very good to us, my lord. I'm not sure I deserve such kindness," Bebi-ankh said humbly. He was a big man, as Djau had indicated, with a broad face—now, no doubt, scarred forever—and thick muscles. But his fingers were long and unexpectedly fine.

Hani said lightly, "You made a mistake, but you've redeemed yourself as far as I'm concerned. Tomorrow, I'm taking troops to arrest the others. They should all still be at work on Ptah-mes's tomb, shouldn't they?"

"I guess they will be," Bebi-ankh murmured. He and his wife exchanged an uneasy look. "They're not bad men, most of them. They just couldn't resist such a temptation—any more than I could. If you have any pull with the higher-ups, my lord, don't let them be impaled, I beg you."

"I don't have any control over what the judges will decide, my friend. But I'll do what I can." *Just let me get to them before Mahu does*, he thought with a stab of anger.

❋

The next morning, early, Menna showed up at the gate as arranged, a small contingent of ten men with him. They were armed with swords and bronze rods, and one or two carried bows. Hani made sure he had the vizier's letter with him in case anybody questioned his authority. Everyone on his list should be at work inside the tomb, with no possibility of escape, and they would certainly be unarmed—except, perhaps, for rocks or pots of paint. Hani wondered if young Khawy would be there even though his uncle had moved on to a new project.

As they were organizing their plan, Mery-ra arrived in Hani's litter. He dismounted and eyed the gathered troops with Menna at their head. "Hani, what's going on here? Have we declared war on the neighbors?"

"We're going to arrest the tomb robbers, or at least the

less guilty part of them," Hani said grimly. "Whether any of them know who the leader of their little game is, I couldn't say. Ironically, he may get away free."

Mery-ra shook his head. "May Ma'at guide you, son. It would be nice to think that once in a while, justice was actually done."

His father passed on up the graveled walk toward the house. Hani turned to Menna. "Ready, my friend? Let's go. To the Mountains of the West."

Menna rallied his men, and the little procession started out the gate with the measured shuffle of sandals and a clinking of weapons. *I hope we all come back alive*, Hani thought with a sigh.

⸗

The soldiers had their own boat, and they crossed the River expeditiously. Hani led the way into the arid valley in the cliffs where Lord Ptah-mes's half-finished tomb stood.

Menna was in good spirits; he didn't seem to share Hani's fears about the encounter. "A bunch of artists and stonecutters?" he scoffed. "We've had worse opponents, my lord."

They marched in their own cloud of dust through the rocky defile, and Hani saw ahead of them the dark opening of the tomb, with its whitewashed pyramidal chapel at a remove. Men were coming and going. A small fire was built just outside the opening, where something seemed to be heating in a clay pot, although it had a caustic smell that suggested it wasn't food. Hani approached the entry a little ahead of the soldiers, but the workmen in the courtyard before the door looked beyond him to the troops. Most stopped to stare; others went philosophically about their tasks. No one, Hani observed, ran away.

One older man with a club in his hand came stalking purposefully toward them. "I'm the guard here," he called out. "What's going on?"

"King's business," Hani said evasively, flashing his letter from the vizier at the man, who was undoubtedly illiterate anyway. For all Hani knew, the guard himself was complicit. The man fell back, and Menna marched his troops to the entry. Hani approached the few workmen who remained outside. "You, there—into the tomb, please." They hustled inside, dropping their tools on the ground, their eyes wide with alarm.

Within, torches bracketed to the plastered stone every few cubits provided dim, smoky illumination for the painters. Soldiers crowding in the doorway blocked the one shaft of bright sunlight, casting long sinister shadows onto the smoothed floor of the corridor. A number of men were standing high on wooden scaffolding against the walls, paintbrushes in hand, where they were laying color on the nearly finished murals.

Heads turned. A voice murmured from somewhere, "What's going on?"

"These are the king's troops. I want the following men to step forward, please." He began to call the names of the collaborators Bebi-ankh had furnished him, scanning the faces of the stunned crewmen for signs of guilt or panic.

One man staggered forward, trembling, and fell at his feet. "Spare me, my lord," he cried. "I have eleven children to feed." Another swung down from the scaffold and tried

107

to run deeper into the tomb, but Menna darted after him before he could reach the stairs and jerked him back.

"Tie them up," Hani ordered. "There must be other men down there at work on the burial chamber." He and five of the soldiers made their way down the steps, while the remainder bound and gagged the two painters.

Between the flickering cressets, the lower corridor was terrifyingly black. Hani tried not to think about the mountain over his head. He and the men debouched into the burial chamber, where stonecutters were still smoothing one corner with echoing blows of the chisel while plasterers came in just behind them. On the opposite wall, the gridded red-ocher sketches for the paintings and texts had been finished under Djau's meticulous hand and awaited Bebi-ankh's black final outlines. Scaffolding stood along both sides, and the beautiful life-sized *ka* statues of Lord Ptah-mes and his wife, Lady Apeny, sat serenely in their niche, covered with dust and soot from the torches.

The workmen, who were removed enough from the antechamber to be unaware of what had taken place there, looked around in surprise.

"Will the following men please step forward?" Hani's voice echoed hollow in the enclosed space. He could feel the tension increasing around him, the men staring at one another, wild-eyed, starting to fidget. Most of them would have no idea what this was about and had, no doubt, begun to imagine the worst.

As Hani called their names, each trembling suspect crept forward or was pushed, screaming and pleading, by his fellows. A voice shouted, "Bebi-ankh was in on it too." The soldiers apprehended each man and manacled his arms behind his back in a painful posture. A sudden reek of urine betrayed someone's fear.

"Heqa-nakht," Hani called finally. Frightened silence fell. No one stepped forward. "Where is he, people?" His voice had become a stern growl.

A quaking youth with a pot of plaster still clutched in his hand cleared his throat and said in a wavering voice, "He went outside for a leak, my lord."

Hani nodded, trying not to reveal his disappointment. If someone had gotten away, he would almost certainly alert their chief, and the mysterious foreigner would go to ground. "The rest of you are free to go on with your work," he said, but he knew it would be difficult with members of their closely coordinated team missing. Bebi-ankh's absence had already held them up.

Breathing heavily in the stale, smoke-filled air, he mounted the stairs into the entry corridor. Some of the released workmen milled about uncertainly. The soldiers had tied the uncomfortably bound culprits into a line.

"What is more despicable than a tomb robber?" Hani said to them in a loud contemptuous voice. "For a little silver, you've deprived someone of the things he'll need in the Duat. The dead can't help themselves, you wretches. They depend on the living." He thought guiltily of the artist with eleven children. He knew how poor many of these men had to be since the royal tombs had left the Great Place nearby, but he decided to act stern rather than compassionate. Perhaps when he questioned them one by one, he would change tactics.

Hani, the soldiers, and the bound men emerged, blinking, into the bright morning light. In place of the satisfaction he should have felt, Hani experienced a dull sense of gloom. He only hoped one of these poor misled sods could provide him with the name of their ringleader and that he could get the rest of them off with a mild punishment—the loss of nose or ears.

They shuffled down the sloping scree and across the rock-strewn path toward the River. Behind Hani, someone was weeping quietly. Hani walked next to Menna, who looked pleased with the day's catch.

"Well, my friend," Hani said, "I thank you for this. You've discharged any debt you had toward me."

"Never, my lord," the officer said cheerfully. "We were just doing our duty. I'm forever in your debt. A life isn't bought so easily."

Hani chuckled, but he couldn't help thinking of the artisans they had arrested, who would lose their own lives if the judge felt inclined to severity. He wondered how close to the king the men whose tombs had been violated had been and how much that would play into the culprits' sentencing. *We're none of us any better than crass sycophants*, he thought bitterly. But somehow, that thought seemed disloyal to his friend Lord Ptah-mes, whose tomb they were leaving. The commissioner had paid for his loyalty to the throne—whoever its occupant was—with the loss of respect from his wife and children. Hani knew he was suffering daily from the rent in his conscience.

Hani was in a dark mood as they mounted the little military boat and swung out into the current, heading back to the land of the living.

CHAPTER 5

H ANI REACHED HOME AROUND MIDDAY, weary but more cheerful. A trip on the River, even the short one from bank to bank, always restored his sense of proportion. He'd seen a flock of geese—lots of them—rising into the air, their powerful whistling wingbeats and joyful honking the most beautiful music to Hani's ears.

Nub-nefer greeted him calmly, although her eyes were red.

"No more arguments with Neferet, I hope?" he whispered, stroking her hair.

She shook her head. "But I can't help worrying, Hani. You'll never convince me it's safe for her to tend the sick at the palace with plague on the loose."

"No, my dear. It's not safe. But there are many things in life that are dangerous, and we can't protect her from them all."

She sighed and straightened her shoulders, saying more brightly, "Your workmen in the kitchen have now moved into Pipi's rooms. Pipi has taken his family to Lord Ptah-mes's villa, but he left his baggage and furniture here. No point in inflicting that on your friend, who is being kind enough already."

"Good, good," Hani said with a fond smile. "Things are returning to normal." He caressed Nub-nefer's face. "I don't suppose Maya showed up to work this morning?"

"Oh, he did. He's in the salon now. I think he's a little peeved that you didn't take him to the arrest." A smile twitched at the corners of her mouth.

Hand in hand, Hani and Nub-nefer made their way into the salon, where Maya sat cross-legged on the floor, writing on a roll of papyrus across his lap. He looked up and scrambled to his feet at Hani's approach. Mery-ra was seated not far away—he, too, scratching away with concentration. He called out to his son, "How did it go at the tomb?"

"Fairly successfully. We got all but one of the culprits, and then there's that Khnum-baf who had fled earlier. I'm just afraid that one of them has gone to warn their leader and now the foreigner'll hole up somewhere, out of sight."

"The jubilee will be over soon," said Maya. "Then all the diplomats will go home, and this business will surely be finished."

"Not for several weeks. There's still time for our unknown friend to gather a new group of accomplices and make an attempt on Neb-ma'at-ra's tomb. *That* would be a huge disgrace."

"Do you think he'll dare, knowing we're onto him?" asked Mery-ra.

Hani shrugged, with a wry twitch of the lips. "You'll be relieved to know I have no insights into the criminal mind,

Father." He squatted beside Mery-ra and peered over his shoulder. "What are you working on?"

Mery-ra indicated his papyrus with a spread hand. "It's my *Book of Going Forth by Day* for our tomb. Since you keep pointing out how old I am, I felt I needed to be sure I finished it quickly." He held back the curling ends of the scroll with his fingers so that Hani could see the work more clearly.

Hani bent over and read his father's sure, graceful sacred signs: *What did you find there on the shore of the pool of Two Truths?" A scepter of flint, whose name is Breath Giver. "What did you do with the firebrand and the faience column?" I lamented over them.*

He grew thoughtful. *It's all about knowing the right answers—about knowing the names of the demons who block your way, because that gives you power over them.* "Rather like being an investigator," he said aloud.

"What's that, son?"

"The interrogations in the afterworld. It's all about making *ma'at* known, despite opposition."

"I never thought of it that way," Mery-ra said.

Changing the subject, Hani said with genuine admiration, "This is a beautiful book, Father. Your eyesight must still be perfect."

"Well, I may have to rear back farther and farther to do it, but I can still see." Mery-ra looked a little smug. "I need to find an artist to illustrate the later parts of it. The man who did the earlier pages has died."

"Perhaps our little Khawy can help. He comes from a talented family." Hani looked over his shoulder at Maya.

"That reminds me—where is he? He never showed up. Do you think something has happened to him?"

Maya said offhandedly, "Maybe Djau has changed his mind."

But a little worm of concern niggled Hani in the pit of his stomach. Between Mahu and the betrayed tomb robbers, Djau was the target of too many enemies. "Maya, why don't you pay a visit to the Place of Truth and see what's going on? I told the boy how to get to the house, but maybe he didn't remember."

Maya tipped his head in acknowledgment. "I'll go right after lunch, my lord."

"I'd better go with him. He's never been to Djau's place," said Mery-ra, climbing heavily to his feet and beginning to arrange his writing tools.

"And I," said Hani, stretching, "am headed to Mane's house to meet those two young diplomats Keliya has brought in."

◈

Mane didn't live far. Since he was so frequently in distant Wasshukanni, he hadn't felt any urgency to build a place in the new capital. Hani went on foot, having no need to prove his status to an old friend like the ambassador to Naharin.

He was greeted at the door of the vestibule by Mane's wife, a round, cheerful little woman who resembled Mane to a remarkable degree. "Come in, come in, Lord Hani. My husband has spoken of you often," she cried, beaming. "What brings you to our house? Mane is in Naharin, you know."

114

"I had hoped our friend Keliya was here, since the offices of the foreign service are closed for the holidays. He wanted me to meet his new adjutants."

"Ah, yes. Delightful young men. I'll call Keliya."

She scurried out and emerged from the corridor a moment later with Hani's old friend from Naharin, who was grinning broadly. Keliya was younger than Hani by a good ten years, but—a tall, thin, stoop-shouldered fellow with a retreating hairline—he could have passed for Hani's senior. Keliya, Hani, and Mane had together brought Princess Taduhepa—now known as Kiya, the little monkey—from Naharin to be the bride of Neb-ma'at-ra. The months-long journey had forged strong brotherly bonds among the three.

Keliya and Hani embraced affectionately. Keliya said in Hurrian, "Permit me to introduce my two colleagues, Tulubri and Pirissi. They're here for the jubilee, then they'll conduct our girl back to her homeland." He shot Hani a significant look. They both knew what that meant for her.

The young men trailing Keliya stepped forward and bowed respectfully. Like all the Mitannians, they were tall and light skinned. The one who introduced himself as Pirissi was getting portly, even though he couldn't have been thirty years old. His fellow, Tulubri, was wiry and quick, smiling through his mustachioed beard, with long laughter lines scoring his cheeks. He, too, was scarcely out of his twenties.

"We're honored, my lord," Tulubri said warmly. "Keliya and Lord Mane have told us all about you. What a friend you are to our land."

Pirissi, who was clean-shaven except for a collar of beard, added eagerly, "Perhaps you can help us convince your king not to send Lady Kiya back to Wasshukanni. Things are pretty dangerous there." He and his companion exchanged a sorrowful glance.

"I wish I could promise you that, Pirissi. But I am afraid I am not exactly the confidant of Nefer-khepru-ra, whatever Mane has told you. Have you had your audience with the king yet?"

"No, my lord," said the good-humored Tulubri. "We and Lord Keliya are going to present the gifts of Naharin in the great ceremony. We're hoping the audience will happen before the end of the jubilee so we can go home."

Hani remembered only too well how the royal audience of Aziru, the vassal king of Amurru, had been delayed for over a year. "May it be so," he said neutrally. "But this I can promise you—dinner at my house tomorrow night. Can I count on you? You are invited, too, of course, Keliya, my friend."

The three Mitannians looked at one another, brightening with pleasure, and Keliya spoke for them. "We'll be there most gladly, Hani. It will be wonderful to talk again, like old times." He clapped Hani gratefully on the upper arm. "You clearly haven't forgotten your Hurrian—fluent as ever, my friend. You sound like you just stepped off the streets of Wasshukanni."

Hani's face grew hot with embarrassment. It seemed to him that the language, which he had used rarely in the last six or seven years, was rusty enough. "Well, I'll see you gentlemen tomorrow. Keliya, you know the way."

Maya trudged through the dry, dusty streets of the

workmen's village, thanking all the gods that the pleasant weather was holding. He could imagine how *un*pleasant this treeless hole must be when the summer sun baked it. At his side, Lord Mery-ra strode gamely along with his rocking gait.

"Here it is," said the older man, stopping in front of a gate in the whitewashed wall. He knocked, and Maya could hear footsteps scurrying toward them. After a moment, the gate swung open with a creak. Before them stood an elderly servant with a white mourning scarf around his head. Maya's heart dropped into his stomach. He shot a quick, concerned glance at his companion.

"How can I help you?" said the old man lugubriously.

"We're here to see if young Khawy is ready to come to Waset to study with me," said Mery-ra with his most affable, grandfatherly smile. "Is Djau home?"

The old man's face crumpled, and he said with polite outrage, "Djau has flown into the West, my lord. He is in his eternal home."

Maya's jaw dropped, and he saw the same shock on Mery-ra's face. Hani had said the man was sick, but this seemed, nonetheless, unexpected. "Was it sudden, my good man?" he cried in horror.

"That it was, my lord. He was murdered." The old man eyed them with bitter suspicion.

Maya and Mery-ra sank to their knees and, bending to the street, gathered handfuls of dust, which they strewed over their heads in respect.

"I'm so sorry to hear that. We had no idea. Is Khawy available? We'd like to offer him our condolences," Mery-ra said soberly, hauling himself to his feet with Maya's help.

The old gateman retreated into the house while Maya and Mery-ra stood staring at one another awkwardly. "This isn't good," Mery-ra murmured.

Khawy stood before them all at once, a sturdy boy but still soft muscled and smooth skinned, with only a smudge of beard, his childhood Haru lock surmounted by a mourning scarf. His tear-ravaged face had taken on a sad, set look that made him appear only too grown-up. "My lord," he said, bowing to Mery-ra. "Thank you for coming, but I don't think I'll be able to take you up on your kind offer now. My sister and my grandmother depend on me."

Dear gods, thought Maya. *On a paint boy's salary? They're going to starve.* "When did this terrible thing happen?" he asked in a compassionate tone. "Do you know who did it?"

"It was last week. Who did it, I don't know, my lord. Ankh-reshet, our overseer, found him dead on the path to the tombs. Somebody had shot him with an arrow."

"Was no one else around to see what happened? Surely all the men go up from the camp together?" Mery-ra said.

"Usually, my lord. But Uncle hadn't been well that morning, and he said he'd follow when his faintness got better. So he started off alone after everyone had gotten to the workplace." The boy fought back tears that threatened to collapse his features and, wiping his eyes, added, "He never showed up. Someone told Ankh-reshet, and he went back to look for him. And... and he found him lying on the path with an arrow in his back."

Maya didn't know what to say. He stared in damp-eyed pity at the boy until Mery-ra asked, "Did anyone keep the arrow that killed him, son?"

"Yes, my lord," Khawy said earnestly. "Do you want it? I'd rather not have it around. It's a vile thing."

"I do, my boy. It may help us find your uncle's killers."

Khawy scampered off and soon returned with a long, thin, reed-shafted arrow fletched with goose feathers. Its head, carved from flint, was shaped like a spear blade whose point had been cut off straight and the resulting edge sharpened—a head meant to inflict as large a wound as possible. The bindings were still stained with Djau's blood. Maya could feel his lunch rising in his gullet.

Mery-ra took it in his hands and turned it over and over. He murmured, "This is a military arrow. It could sever a hand or nearly decapitate someone. There's no way a direct hit in the back wouldn't kill a person."

Mucus began to run from Khawy's nose, and he dashed at it futilely with a fist. Looking both miserable and furious, he shouted, "Why? Why, my lord? Who would want to kill a draftsman?"

"That's what we need to find out. My son, Hani, will investigate and ferret the criminal out of his lair, you may be sure." Mery-ra laid a heavy hand on the lad's shoulder and gave it a squeeze. "We must believe the gods have a reason for letting this happen, my boy. Be strong for your family."

Something occurred to Maya—the houses were all government issue, allotted according to the job of each head of household. "Are they going to turn you out of your house now that there's no chief draftsman here?"

"Ankh-reshet said we could stay for a while, but eventually, we'll have to leave, when he finds a replacement for Uncle. I'm trying to find my sister a husband who has a good position," Khawy said hopelessly.

"How old is she?" Maya asked, afraid to hear the answer.

"Twelve, my lord."

Maya couldn't control a noise of disgust.

"We'll have offerings made for Djau," Mery-ra promised.

They took their leave sadly and trudged down the street and out the gate of the village in silence, Maya's thoughts all in turmoil. Finally, as they began the descent of the rocky path toward the River, he burst out, "The bloody bastard. Is there no justice in the world?"

Mery-ra shook his head. "It sometimes seems not, I fear. But we have to believe that *ma'at* will triumph. Whoever killed our friend Djau may think he's gotten away with it, but the Judge of Souls will see through him."

"How will the murderer keep a straight face at the Weighing of Hearts when he has to say, 'I have not sinned in the Place of Truth; I have not caused tears; I have not killed; I haven't taken milk from the mouths of children?'" Maya gave a bark of savage satisfaction. "He's damned for sure, whoever he is."

"Let's hope Hani can figure out who he is, because I'd like to see some justice done on earth too." Mery-ra hawked and spat.

They fell silent again as they descended the arid chert-littered path toward the River. The clatter of rolling gravel, Lord Mery-ra's heavy breathing, and the dry rustle of wind were the only sounds that broke the solitude of this realm of the Lover of Silence. As they neared the riverbank, Maya finally said, "What must it be like to work on tombs all the time? You'd suspect it would make those people think about death a lot. And yet here they go, killing one another with no concern for the eternal consequences."

Mery-ra heaved a sigh. "In all fairness, Maya, we don't know that it was one of the workmen who killed Djau. That military arrow makes me wonder. Hani will be able to figure it out. I have confidence in him."

So do I, Maya thought fervently. *If anyone under the sun can find Djau's killer, it's Lord Hani.*

✦

"Ah, here you are," Hani called from the salon as Maya and Mery-ra, huffing and puffing, entered. "What's going on with Khawy?"

"Bad news, son," said Hani's father grimly. "Young Khawy is now the head of his family. Somebody has murdered Djau."

"Oh no," Hani cried in genuine pain. He thought of the little draftsman with his protruding eyes and labored breathing. "How do they know it was murder?" Hani's father held up an arrow and laid it in the hand of his son, who gave a low whistle of appreciation. "That's an evil-looking bird." Hani looked up at Mery-ra. "Military?"

"Can't think of who else would need one. It's a man killer."

"What does that mean, I wonder?" Hani stared at the arrow's murderous broad flint blade and bloody bindings. "Do the *medjay* use such things?"

Mery-ra made a dubious noise. "I think they're more into bronze rods and baboons. But certainly, they must have archers."

121

"Some renegade soldier in the pay of the tomb robbers?"

But Maya protested, "Why would they kill him now? He's already made his report. Anyway, the malefactors are in custody. *They* didn't do it."

"Vengeance? Their leader is still on the loose." Hani put the arrow down as if it had suddenly bitten him. "Or maybe it's Mahu, the turd. I wouldn't put it past him to do something low like this."

"But why?" Maya persisted. "It's not as if Djau died under questioning. Somebody ambushed him on the trail between the camp and the tomb and put a killer arrow into his back."

"Wait, son," said Mery-ra. "The tomb robbers were *not* in custody. The murder happened a week ago, according to Khawy."

Hani pondered this blackly. "I can't eliminate any possibility, but I still don't see a motive. He'd already made his report."

"Could it have been some tomb guard? Khawy said his uncle was alone, climbing up to the tombs after everyone else had gone. Maybe they saw a lone man prowling around and thought he was up to no good." Maya crossed his legs and sat down beside Hani with a *whump*, no doubt glad enough to get off his feet after a morning spent clambering over the steep western bank.

"It's as viable as any other theory at this point," Hani said. "I'm just glad we got Bebi-ankh out before the same thing happened to him."

He climbed to his feet and heaved a sigh. Things seemed to be getting more and more complicated—as they so often did. "I hope we can find the leader of this gang before he strikes again."

✦

Nub-nefer had decorated the house for the dinner party with greens and whatever fresh flowers she could find in midwinter, but ironically, the weather was so mild that Hani had decided they should eat in the garden pavilion. Every time he went out there, he felt a pang of regret for Qenyt, the pet heron he'd raised from an egg. He kept expecting to see her stately gray form passing through the bushes or find her posed in absolute stillness by the lily pool, waiting for a frog to emerge. He entered the pavilion through the rolled-up mat over the open wall. Over the porch, the arbor was festooned with the leafless skeletons of grapevines.

Nub-nefer was already within, putting the finishing touches on the tables. "Neferet wants to eat with the grown-ups tonight," she said with a smile. "I told her she could since she's technically an adult now." She fixed Hani with a complicit little quirk of the mouth.

"Of course, my dove. It wouldn't be fair for her to be the only one who can't be at the party." He moved to her side and gave her a kiss.

"Do you know if these young men are married?"

Hani laughed. "Surely you don't want her to move to Naharin. The country is falling apart." He couldn't help thinking of poor Kiya, whose choice had been made for her by others.

"Maybe they have young friends in the diplomatic corps here," she protested vaguely.

Hani's eldest girl and the most beautiful of his

daughters, Baket-iset, lay on her couch, made up and wigged to perfection. "And how are you, my swan?" he said affectionately, seating himself at her side and resting a hand on her withered arm.

"Very well, Papa. I just hope these guests speak Egyptian."

"I'm sure they do. But thank you for reminding me not simply to take off in Hurrian so you and Mama and Neferet can't understand." Hani grew more serious—so many things were weighing on his mind—and he said in a lower voice, "I have need of your wisdom, my dear. One of my witnesses was just murdered, and we don't—"

But at that moment, A'a appeared on the porch and cleared his throat. "My lord, your guests have arrived."

Hani jumped to his feet, brushed down his kilt, and straightened his shirt, which tended to bunch up over his stomach. Nub-nefer adjusted her shawl and rearranged Hani's floral collar, and the two of them made their way to the gate to greet their guests.

"Welcome to our house, my friends," Hani called genially to the three Mitannians. The serving girls stood by with basins and towels, ready to wash the Mitannians' feet, even though the men were all wearing closed leather shoes.

"This is good of you, Hani," said Keliya as they embraced. "Tulubri and Pirissi don't know anyone in Waset yet and certainly no one in Akhet-aten."

"Well, I can't help you there. But I'll bet Lord Ptah-mes would host you when the holidays are over. He's been very generous with his house, since he's there alone."

The men took the stools they were offered, and the

servants drew off the Mitannians' shoes and began to pour warm water over their feet.

"This is civilized," said Tulubri with a sigh of pleasure. "Why don't we do this at home?" They all laughed.

Nub-nefer handed each man a long-stemmed water lily and affixed a cone of perfumed wax to the top of each head. "You don't have wigs, so I hope this won't slide. It will infuse your hair with perfume as it melts."

"All the stories we've heard about the sophistication of Kemet are true, I see," said Pirissi, beaming.

Keliya looked on benevolently. He took on an almost paternal expression of pride at this display of good manners by his young colleagues.

Hani led the guests through the salon, decked with flowers as it was, and thence into the garden. The winter night had already fallen, but Nub-nefer had set oil lamps along the path to the pavilion, and their bright flames flickered, warm and festive, in the darkness. Ahead, yet more lamps and torches lit the pavilion with a welcoming glow. Hani saw Neferet inside, smiling from ear to ear, waiting to bestow a floral collar on each guest. The mild night pulsed with crickets. He felt cheerful and at peace, despite all the problems that lurked around the edges of his life. Tonight, they would eat and drink and enjoy the company of their guests. In the morning, he would return to the world of murder and tomb robbing and Naharin's civil war.

The dinner unrolled pleasantly. The two young Mitannians were proficient in Egyptian and were witty and interested in everything—perfect guests. Hani suppressed a chuckle as he saw Neferet corner Tulubri and describe in extreme detail her work at the House of Royal Ornaments.

"Have you met our princess, Lady Kiya?" asked Pirissi, leaning across his companion.

"Not yet, my lord. But Lady Djefat-nebty said we'll be going up to Hut-nen-nesut soon to look at the king's harem—those who aren't at the palace in Akhet-aten," Neferet said enthusiastically.

She continued to bubble on about the health of the royal ladies while Hani's thoughts darkened. Only a few years before, Kiya had had her own place at the king's side. She'd been the Greatly Beloved Wife, with a *maru*—a private meditation garden—in her name and her face on every piece of official art. The Great Queen herself had seen Kiya as a rival. Now, despite Hani's efforts, Kiya was disposable, her political value annulled by her father's slipping grip on the throne of Naharin.

"I need to go to Hut-nen-nesut too," Hani said. "Mane wanted me to comfort Lady Kiya." *He wanted me to keep her from being exiled, but there's no way I can accomplish that.*

"That would be splendid, Hani," said Keliya gratefully. "I'd be happy to accompany you."

The men continued to talk about one thing and another, Neferet inserting herself, as usual, with a little more than polite frequency. Nub-nefer and Baket-iset smiled and occasionally offered a ladylike remark. The cones of wax on the diners' wigs were slumping considerably by the time Nub-nefer leaned over to Hani and whispered, "I'll get the sweets and tell the servants to refill the lamps."

She started to rise, but Hani stood up and pressed her

back with a fond hand on her shoulder. "Let me, my dear. I need to take a leak anyway."

He slipped out by way of the porch and made his way through the garden. Some of the lamps lining the path had already burned out. The sounds of laughter and conversation drifted in from the pavilion. Hani entered the salon—which was mostly dark, the lamps having consumed their moringa oil—and was heading to the kitchen and its latrine when he saw, from the corner of his eye, Bebi-ankh, standing in the doorway of his room.

He's able to walk better now with a crutch, Hani thought, pleased. But there was something about Bebi-ankh's expression that wiped the smile from his face. The man's eyes were wild with fear and disbelief. As soon as he saw Hani looking at him, he dodged back into his room and closed the door.

⁎

The next morning, the household slept late. The Mitannians had stayed nearly till dawn, enjoying the beer and the conversation that stretched on even after the delicious dinner had been picked to bones. Keliya had been grateful for the hospitality toward his young confreres and promised to host another get-together at Mane's house as soon as their old friend got home.

Hani awoke slowly and lay in bed at Nub-nefer's side, listening to the twittering of birds from the garden. Eventually, he got up, dressed quietly, and made his way to the kitchen. He was standing there, eating some leftover partridge and a stale piece of flatbread, when he heard a female voice hissing softly, "Bibi? Where are you?"

The painter's wife entered, her hair disheveled from sleep, a suckling baby latched to her breast. She saw Hani and jerked back. "Oh, my lord. Forgive me. I was looking for my husband."

"Quite all right," he assured her. "He wasn't in the room? I saw him last night standing in the doorway."

"He was gone from the bed when I woke up, my lord. He can't have gone far on his crutch. But we don't like to wander around the house and bother your family."

"No bother, mistress," he said kindly. "I'm glad he's able to get around better. I hope his burns are healing. My daughter is a doctor, if he needs anything."

"Thank you, my lord. He's doing well. But he's still afraid, you know? He's afraid those people are after him even here." She heaved a shaky sigh and fondled her baby's shaved head.

"Well, reassure him that that's unlikely. Nobody knows where he's gone."

The woman ducked a little bow and headed back off to her family's room, leaving Hani sunk in thought as he remembered the expression on Bebi-ankh's face the night before. Before long, Neferet appeared, rubbing her eyes but cheerful as ever. She gave Hani her usual rib-cracking hug and began to poke through the leftovers for something to eat.

"How was your first grown-up dinner party, my duckling?" Hani asked with a smile.

"It was fun, Papa. Those men speak good Egyptian."

"They do," he agreed. He'd hosted many foreigners over the course of his career, and some were more fluent than others. Keliya, of course, had been in the country for years. But the other two Mitannians, who'd never set foot in the Two Lands, had learned somewhere to speak effortlessly and with a passable accent. "I wish I were so good at Hurrian."

"But you speak so many languages, Papa. You can't be good in all of them," she said matter-of-factly, popping a chunk of bread into her mouth.

"I'm going to Akhet-aten later this morning and, from there, to Hut-nen-nesut. Do you want to come with me?"

"Yes, I do. Bener-ib and Lady Djefat-nebty need me."

Hani forced himself not to say anything; they'd had that conversation already. He just gave Neferet's shoulders an eloquent squeeze.

"Hani? Father? Where is everyone?" Pipi called from the vestibule. A moment later, he appeared in the kitchen door—a squat figure, like all the men in Hani's family, although fattening up in addition. He'd never been as athletic as his older brother. The sight of Pipi's square-jowled, cheerful face and honest little eyes never failed to awaken in Hani the affection and protectiveness he'd felt since childhood.

Pipi took off his wig and scratched his head vigorously.

"Don't tell me there are fleas at Lord Ptah-mes's house!" Hani protested with a snort of laughter.

"Not at all. I'm just tired of dressing up. Even his servants are better kitted out than us." He chuckled guiltily. "But oh, Hani, what a place he has! By the balls of the Hidden One! I wake up every morning thinking, 'Can I really be here? I must have died and gone to the Field of Reeds.'"

Hani laughed and scrubbed his brother's short-cropped hair with his knuckles.

Pipi laughed, too, until his belly bounced. Then he said more seriously, "Hani, old man, I've been thinking. A post with the foreign service is too good to pass up. I think I want to go up to Akhet-aten after all."

Hani eyed him in surprise. This was the first time he'd ever heard his little brother express any kind of ambition. "It's up to you, Pipi. The job is yours if you want it, just… just be careful, all right?"

Pipi, jovial again, assured him, "I won't have anything to do with the court—believe me. But it would be nice to be a royal scribe again. Enjoy a little respect." He looked up at Hani from under his eyebrows, as if ashamed to make such an admission—he, the free spirit of the family, concerned with people's respect.

Hani knew that his brother had always felt a sense of failure when comparing himself to his elder, who had made a good career for himself. Pipi had actually left the royal service and taken a lower-ranking position with the local government of Men-nefer. Perhaps Pipi's dogged refusal to mount the usual ladder of advancement was in part due to a fear of becoming engaged in a competition he couldn't win. Hani's heart clenched with tenderness for Pipi's pain, which he'd never thrown in Hani's face.

Hani clapped him on the shoulder to hide the affection he felt for him and couldn't resist goosing him in the side. Pipi twisted away, hooting, and came at Hani with a mock growl. Hani locked his leg around Pipi's, and the two of them fell, laughing and roaring, to the floor, writhing and wrestling. Neferet shrieked with laughter in the background.

At that moment, Mery-ra entered. "I see the two old men have entered a second childhood. Good thing you and I are here to be the grown-ups, Neferet."

Hani and Pipi picked themselves up from the floor, dusting off their kilts. Pipi found his wig and clapped it on his head. "Morning, Father," he said, his cheeks red with exertion and pleasure.

Mery-ra embraced him. "What brings you back to our humble abode, son? The ancestral home must look pretty poor after Ptah-mes's palace."

"I told Hani I wanted that post in the foreign service after all. I'll go down to the capital with him and Neferet."

"Is it safe?" Mery-ra shot a quick look of uncertainty at Hani, who shrugged.

"He can do whatever he wants, Father."

"Shall I examine you for injuries?" Neferet asked.

Minutes have passed without her being the center of attention, Hani thought with amusement.

"You may have strained something, Uncle Pipi. Papa is a top wrestler."

Hani had to laugh. "Better put that in the past tense, my duckling. I haven't been a wrestler since my student days. And Uncle outweighs me."

"Then *you* may have strained something, Papa."

Hani put an arm around the girl's shoulders and pressed her to him. "It's time we got you back to where you have real sick people to take care of." He tried not to think about the implications of that. "As soon as Maya gets here, we'll be off."

They passed all together into the salon, where their baskets and bags had been deposited. Hani was about to head back upstairs to the bedroom when he heard A'a's voice from the garden saying, "He'll be right here, my lords."

"Who is it, A'a?" Hani called from the foot of the stairs.

"Lord Keliya and his colleagues, my lord."

"I forgot they were accompanying us," Hani said to his brother. "We'll make quite a delegation. I guess we'll have to charter an entire ferry. You take up half the deck yourself."

Pipi gaped at him, uncomprehending, then he made clawlike hands at Hani and pretended to pounce on him in anger. "Who are you calling fat?"

Hani jumped away, laughing, and the two brothers would have fallen into another rough-and-tumble, but at that moment, A'a ushered in the three Mitannians, Maya in their wake. "Ah, my friends," Hani cried, panting. "You're prompt. Let's be on our way."

They trooped out through the garden single file while Mery-ra waved to them from the doorway. "Hani, where is your wife?" Keliya asked. "I wanted to thank her for the delightful party the other evening."

"She had errands to run this morning," Hani said vaguely. There had been quite a few such mysterious errands lately, and—from her smug, beatific expression when she returned—Hani had the suspicion that Nub-nefer was secretly meeting with her brother, the third prophet of Amen-Ra. Hani's brother-in-law was in hiding while he embarrassed the government with a barrage of anti-Atenist harangues.

The six men and Neferet moved in a block down the street, heading for the quays. There, Hani hailed a long-distance ferry of medium size, which seemed to have enough places for them all. As the group, with its three exotically dressed Mitannians, marched up the gangplank, a few heads turned to watch them but not for long. The country was crawling with foreigners during the Great Jubilee.

From the gunwales, the two young diplomats watched the loosing of the boat while Pipi and Neferet climbed up to the raised stern to see what they could see. Hani, Maya, and Keliya made themselves comfortable on the deck in the shadow of the cabin.

"Do you happen to know a countryman of yours who has a collar of beard and a mole on his left lip?" Hani asked quietly. "He may be associated with your delegation somehow."

Keliya looked up at him quickly. "I can't think of anyone, Hani. Perhaps he's a servant. Why do you ask?"

Still speaking in an undertone, Hani told him about the string of tomb robberies and the description Bebi-ankh had given him of the leader. Keliya's droopy eyebrows rose, and his face became even more lugubrious than usual.

"That's an appalling breach of good faith. We're all likely to have our credentials revoked." He looked at Hani earnestly. "I'll certainly keep my eyes open."

The conversation reminded Hani about the disappearance of Bebi-ankh. *Where can the man have gone, right from under my nose?* Perhaps something had spooked him so badly that he'd fled, leaving his family behind.

"Keliya, how much do you know about your young adjutants? How thoroughly have they been vetted?"

The Mitannian looked anxious, as if Hani's suspicions had infected him. He said in a low voice, "They were sent to me by the foreign office; their credentials were all in order. I'm sure they were checked out. But I must admit, I didn't know them personally. I've spent most of the last few years here, with only infrequent visits home, and they're part of a different generation of scribal training." He shrugged apologetically. "From what I've seen, they're good men—hardworking, taking instruction without ego, interacting well with the locals. The stuff of successful diplomats."

Hani clapped him on the shoulder to reassure him. "I just need to consider everyone, my friend. I'm sure they're fine. And for that matter, just because our mystery Mitannian spoke of immunity doesn't mean he actually has it."

They broke off as Neferet came prancing down the deck toward them. She plopped down beside her father and thrust her arm through his. "Uncle Pipi and the others are talking about irrigation and excavation and fertilizer. Bo-o-oring."

Maya quoted tartly, "Do not intrude on a man. Enter when you have been called." He was young enough to rebuke Neferet without eliciting an eye roll. But she stuck out her tongue at him then gave her irresistible gap-toothed grin to show there were no hard feelings.

Soon Pipi and his two companions approached, deep in a conversation punctuated by laughter. "I didn't know you were so well versed in agriculture, my brother," Hani called.

"Oh," said Pipi, tilting his head modestly, "I've been studying up on it. I thought that, now that I'm back, I might buy a few *kha*s of land and do a little farming." He sank into a seat on the deck, and the young Mitannians did the same.

"Not raising horses, I hope," Maya said innocently.

Hani concealed a grin and said in mock seriousness, "There seems to be unanimity on that, my brother. Better hear it as the will of the gods."

"Actually, that was an ambition of mine," said young Pirissi. "But there's been nothing but war at home for so long that I've pretty much abandoned it." He sighed, but it hardly seemed to create a ripple on his good cheer. "I applied for the foreign service instead."

Hani posed the question that had become a standard part of his friendly interrogation. "How did you gentlemen learn such good Egyptian? Have you been here before?"

"No, neither of us. We learned from one of your men, a trilingual scribe who works in our chancery," said Tulubri.

"Min-mes. Do you know him?" Keliya interjected.

Hani said with a nod, "I do."

They sat in congenial silence for a while. The rhythmic splash of the paddles propelling them down the current, the hiss of malachite waters parting around their bow, and the broad, glittering stream that slipped past them as they traveled lulled Hani into a state of pleasant drowsiness. Through a sleepy eye, he watched a heron rise with majestic grace from the marshes, but it made him a little sad because it reminded him of Qenyt. Before long, his chin dropped to his chest, and consciousness drifted pleasantly away.

CHAPTER 6

F IVE DAYS LATER, THEY ARRIVED in Akhet-aten. Pipi, Hani, and his secretary set out for the Hall of Royal Correspondence, where the former peeled off at the copying room. Hani and Maya continued to the reception hall outside Lord Ptah-mes's office, Neferet in tow.

"I might as well check in with Ptah-mes since we're here," Hani explained. "Our Mitannian friends will wait on the boat."

Maya and Neferet camped in a corner of the room while Hani was admitted to his superior's office.

Ptah-mes greeted him with a forced smile. "Hani. Did your holidays pass pleasantly?"

"They did, my lord." Dreading the answer, he added, "And yours?"

Ptah-mes tipped his head cryptically, his mouth smiling but his kohl-edged eyes bleak. "Apeny spent it with our daughter in Men-nefer." He dropped his gaze. "I have some news you won't like, my friend."

Hani's stomach clenched in expectation. He could think of many pieces of news he wouldn't like to hear.

"Mahu has arrested that Bebi-ankh."

"What? I can hardly believe it," Hani cried. "He's been at my house for weeks. How did Mahu manage to nab him so quickly? He must have been observing my gate." The thought sent a cold wave of anger flooding through Hani's middle. *The low-down bastard. May Ammit take him. He's more dangerous than the criminals.*

"It's quite possible. He has also obtained custody of the others from the army."

This absurd breach of all hierarchies of authority left Hani speechless with fury. He stared at Ptah-mes with his jaw hanging.

"I think we can assume he's acting in the king's name," said the high commissioner dryly.

"He'll torture them until they tell him what he wants to hear," Hani cried in a voice strangled with anger. "I told them they had the vizier's protection."

Ptah-mes lifted a caustic eyebrow. "Only one person outranks the viziers. Or perhaps two. Life, prosperity, and health be to them."

I have other wishes for them, Hani thought, simmering. "I suppose I'll have to tell Bebi-ankh's family."

Ptah-mes nodded, his face taking on that cool, expressionless set that—to those who knew him—indicated distress.

"Thank you for telling me, my lord." Hani forced his voice level. "And thank you again for hosting my brother's family. They'll be off your hands soon. Pipi has accepted the offer to succeed to Pa-kiki's post in our foreign service archives, and he'll find a place here in the capital."

"In spite of the plague?"

"So it seems." Hani smiled lightly, but concern tightened his throat. "I see you're staying, too, my lord."

"The government must go on, Hani. Besides," he added with an arid smile, "there is no one who much cares if I die. That relieves me of a great weight."

Hani wanted to protest, but anything he could think to say seemed somehow facile. His heart went out to his superior, all the more because he seemed so stoic about his situation. *But that's where breeding shows,* Hani thought in admiration.

Ptah-mes rose, and Hani did the same. "Are you headed back to Waset now?" the high commissioner asked.

"No, my lord. I'm accompanying the Mitannian delegates down to Hut-nen-nesut. I'm supposed to comfort Lady Kiya before her departure for her homeland."

Ptah-mes snorted. "You know the king is keeping her child?"

"I've heard that," Hani said sadly. "People under my protection don't seem to fare very well."

"Nor mine, Hani, if that's any consolation." Ptah-mes opened his door, and Hani took his leave.

In the reception hall, he found Maya and Neferet still sitting on the floor, playing some sort of miniature game scratched on the back of a potsherd. They looked up at his approach, and Neferet bounded to her feet, Maya following at a more decorous pace.

"What is it, my lord?" Maya asked hesitantly.

"Mahu has found and arrested Bebi-ankh."

Maya's eyes grew round as doum fruit. "Oh no!"

"And he has taken over custody of the rest of the tomb robbers from the army." Hani spread his lips in a grim smile. "Busy little man."

"How did he find Bebi-ankh? Purely by chance? He'd only just disappeared from your house." Maya looked so shocked he could hardly close his mouth.

"Who is Bebi-ankh?" Neferet asked.

"The man who has been staying at our house, my duckling," Hani said distractedly. He turned to Maya. "I suspect Mahu had followed him to my place and was watching the gate. What I don't understand is what made Bebi-ankh bolt. I saw him the night he disappeared, and he looked like he'd seen an ancestor's *ba*."

Maya shook his head, his lips compressed. "Mahu's letting you do his work and then swooping in for the credit, the bastard."

Hani was so disgusted he dared not speak. After a moment of breathing like a bull, he said more calmly, "We need to get back to the ferry. The Mitannians are waiting for us."

They stalked down to the embarcadero in a silent line, Neferet following, curious but—mercifully—unspeaking. The cool white sun of midwinter shone down on the gravelly slope from a sky as limpid as an aquamarine. Boats of all sizes and degrees of luxury bobbed along the bank of the River, cargo barges side by side with expensive private vessels like Lord Ptah-mes's, which Hani saw rocking in the shallow water nearer to the palace. In the distance, drawn up to its pale stone quay, lay the Dazzling Sun Disk, the royal yacht. Anger rose like bile in Hani's throat.

Keliya and the two attachés were leaning on the gunwales as Hani and his fellows approached the vessel. "We bought food for lunch," Keliya called with a wave.

Hani forced down his fury and managed an amiable smile. "Thanks, my friend. That was thoughtful." He stumped up the gangplank with Maya and Neferet in tow. "We can eat en route and not have to stop until nightfall."

"How far is Hut-nen-nesut from here, Papa?" Neferet asked.

"Not far—two or three days. It's near the lake of Pa-yom." He turned to Maya. "That's where our friend Pa-aten-em-heb is from, remember?"

"I'm going to meet Lady Djefat-nebty there. We're treating the Royal Ornaments," Neferet said to Keliya, trying to sound casual about the honor. He received her statement with grave admiration, while the two young adjutants smiled at one another. A warm glow of love and concern melted Hani's anger. *Be safe, little duckling.*

The group of travelers, smaller by the absence of Pipi's ample volume, moved up the deck in search of a shady place to spread their picnic. They'd just settled cross-legged onto the boarding and spread Keliya's purchases out before them when someone cried roughly from the embarcadero, "You there! Don't touch that rope! We're coming aboard."

Hani's senses prickled in trepidation. He knew that voice. Thunderous footsteps came barreling up the gangplank, and the sailors scattered. Hani sprang to his feet, his hackles rising. He expected the worst.

And there the worst stood—Mahu, with half a dozen burly policemen, spewing onto the deck, armed with bronze rods and wooden bats. One of their number restrained a sinister-looking leashed baboon, but it wasn't Hani's old friend, Cub.

"Well, Hani. Here you are in the dubious company of foreigners again," Mahu said with a sneer. "Makes me wonder where your loyalties lie."

"With the alliances that make the Two Lands strong," said Hani in an icy tone. *What, by all that's holy, is he up to?*

"Breathe easy. I'm not here for you this time. It's these two gentlemen." Mahu turned his scowling red face upon the Mitannian attachés, whose surprise had turned to open alarm.

Pirissi shot a confused look at his superior. "What's this about, my lord?"

For answer, Mahu flicked a hand, and his *medjay* stepped forward, surrounded the two Mitannians, and bound their arms behind their back. The foreigners made no move to defend themselves, but their horror and disbelief were writ clearly in their gaping mouths and staring eyes.

"What have we done?" Tulubri sputtered.

"I arrest you for tomb robbing," Mahu growled. Hani was sure he saw a dark gleam of triumph in the chief of police's eye. The words seemed to echo for endless heartbeats.

Then Keliya, recovering, cried indignantly, "I protest. These men have diplomatic immunity."

But Mahu said with a thin smile, "If they don't want to be treated like criminals, they shouldn't commit criminal acts. They'll have a fair trial."

"I can imagine," Hani spat. "You may just have provoked a war with a foreign power, Mahu, you ignoramus."

Mahu's face grew livid. He was a big man, powerful and

heavyset, with hard, fleshy features that revealed his savage temper. He and Hani entertained a visceral hatred for one another. Hani had heard that Mahu was a commoner born, and he knew him to be touchy in the extreme about fancied disrespect from aristocrats like Hani.

"Would you like to join your criminal friends on the end of a stake, Hani? Then keep talking."

Keliya, normally the most easygoing man in the Two Lands, had grown spiky. He cried in an outraged voice, "I'm protesting formally to your king about this. This is an insult to the kingdom of Naharin. We have a treaty—"

"A treaty with whom? Neb-ma'at-ra, if I'm not mistaken. Treaties have to be renegotiated every generation, my fine fellow. And there's not enough left of Naharin to make it worth anyone's trouble to scribble out any treaty." Mahu smirked.

Keliya swelled with rage. He towered over Mahu and said in a voice trembling with the effort to control it, "I'll see to it you suffer for this, my lord. This is behavior unacceptable among civilized nations."

"You do that... my lord." With a sarcastic little smile, Mahu turned, and his men trooped after him.

Neferet cried out in anger, "Your baboon is better than all of you."

Several of the policemen suppressed a snicker, but Hani's heart leaped into his mouth. He gestured frantically at Neferet to be quiet, not to draw attention to herself. Mahu whirled and advanced on Neferet, who confronted him, chest up, stubborn lip outthrust—a storm of righteous indignation in the body of a girl.

"Is this your bodyguard, my lord?" Mahu asked Keliya

sarcastically. He shot a sideways glance at Hani. "I'd say from the look of her this is one of Hani's spawn. Am I right? Call off your little attack bitch, my lord, or I'll take her in for obstructing justice."

Hani moved in quick menace between his daughter and the policeman. His flesh was physically tingling with the urge to throw himself upon this foul man and beat him into oblivion. "Try, Mahu."

Mahu bristled, violence building under his skin like the swelling of a blister. Hani's breath was sawing in his nose. He knew how ready Mahu would be to toss him to his henchmen or throw him overboard. He struggled to control himself and just prayed that Neferet would keep her mouth shut.

After a long, intense space during which the two men glared at each other like street dogs, Mahu turned toward the gangplank once more. His men hustled the desperate Mitannians away with unnecessary brutality and disappeared off the side of the boat, while Hani and Keliya were left staring at one another in raging consternation.

"I can't believe this," Maya cried in a stunned voice. "They're accredited diplomats."

"I hate that man," Neferet said passionately. "He's a ba-a-ad person."

Hani felt sweat break out all over him as if he had been holding it in, along with his breath, during the whole tense confrontation.

Keliya's face had drained of its already pale color. "I'm getting off, Hani. I have to deal with this."

"Of course, my friend," Hani assured him. There

would certainly be repercussions. He followed Keliya to the gangplank. "I'll see to it your baggage gets back to you."

"Thank you, Hani." Keliya took his hand and squeezed it warmly. "And thanks to you and Lady Neferet for defending us."

He'd turned to descend, but Hani said quietly to his back, "Keliya, how sure are you they're innocent?"

Keliya whipped around, and the two men stared at one another for the space of many heartbeats before the Mitannian strode off down the gangplank on his long legs.

Hut-nen-nesut was a large city located at the juncture of the Great River and a canal that carried water to the lake of Pa-yom. There, past kings had transformed a natural marsh into the vast reservoir that helped control flooding and provided a source of irrigation for the groves of palms and greengrocers' gardens that flourished around the lake. As for Hut-nen-nesut itself, it was a market town that had once been the capital of the two lands.

Maya stood with Hani and Neferet at the gunwales, watching the white cubes of the city slide into view, reflected in the glittering waters of the River. He was still trying to get his mind around what had happened at Akhet-aten. Every time he thought about it, the memory gave him cold chills.

At his side, Hani stood, silently staring out over the water and the fast-approaching bank. His normally cheerful square-jowled face was hard and unreadable. Even Neferet spoke less than normal—for once, perhaps, scared by her brush with the brutality of the world. Maya thought to himself that he should have spoken up too. *What kind of man am I to let a little girl of sixteen show more courage than I?* But he'd been so stunned, as if all ability to act had flown out of him. *Foreign diplomats arrested as common criminals—who has ever heard of such a thing?*

"Lord Hani," he said hesitantly after a while, "how sure can we be that Tulubri and Pirissi are innocent?"

Hani shot him a sharp look. "I wish I knew, my friend. Certainly Pirissi doesn't have a mole on his lip, but Tulubri's lip is concealed by his mustache. Keliya seems to trust them..."

"I'm for anybody who that Mahu is against," said Neferet, still belligerent. She looked up at her father for reinforcement. He smiled distractedly.

"Are we still going to see Lady Kiya?" Maya asked. "Should we tell her about the arrest or not?"

"I guess we'll have to. Pirissi and Tulubri were supposed to take her back to Naharin. I don't know what will happen now. Will she stay? Will some of our own take her up?" Hani blew out a breath. Then suddenly, he stiffened, his face intent.

"What is it, my lord?" Maya asked in alarm.

"Remember I told you that Bebi-ankh had looked terrified the night before he disappeared from my house?"

"Yes..."

"That was the night the Mitannians ate with us." Hani shot a significant glance at Maya. "Do you suppose he saw or heard the men? That he recognized the leader of the tomb robbers, whom he feared so much, and thought the foreigner had tracked him down?"

Maya could feel the blood rushing out of his face. "Bes

protect us! That sounds all too likely. Are we in trouble now for standing up for them? Mahu may think we're complicit."

"I'm glad I stood up for them," said Neferet stubbornly. "The only one of those policemen I like is the baboon."

She made her baboon face, and Maya pretended half-heartedly to be amused. But fear sent prickles up the back of his neck. He was avid for adventures to add to his eventual book, but a stint at the receiving end of the *medjay*s' clubs seemed a bit too much. Even worse, the thought of having his nose and ears cut off filled him with dread. Such people were shunned by everyone. Maya had worked hard enough for acceptance.

"As soon as I get back to Akhet-aten, I want to ask Ptah-mes if he knows what's going on. What sort of evidence Mahu might have found." Hani's voice grew icy. "What I'm really afraid of is that he's tortured Bebi-ankh or the others until they 'revealed' to him what he wanted to hear."

"I told you he was bad," said Neferet fiercely.

The boat slid into the bank with a thump, and the sailors began to scurry around, throwing ropes overboard to the waiting men on the shore. Maya stared at the whitewashed buildings around him, glaring under a bright sun-bleached sky. In the distance, he could see the high walls and pylon of a temple, but the flags were not flying.

Lord Hani followed his gaze. "That was the temple of Haru. Remember? Pa-aten-em-heb said his family were priests."

Maya nodded grimly. *More angry, disenfranchised priests and lay workers.* "Where is the estate of the Royal Ornaments?"

"On the edge of town. I've only ever been there once before."

"We don't want to be late, Papa. Lady Djefat-nebty is expecting me," Neferet said, a note of anxiety in her voice.

"It's not far, duckling," Hani said, smiling down at her fondly.

Once the boat had been secured, the travelers gathered their scant baggage and clumped down the bouncing boards of the gangplank. Hani negotiated with some of the longshoremen to store the Mitannians' things, and they set off for the king's harem. Or more properly, Maya thought, the house of those wives and concubines who didn't enjoy the king's special favor. Hundreds of women were housed there—foreign princesses who'd been exchanged as gages of alliance, other girls who'd seized the king's fancy at some point but whom he had tired of, and aristocratic ladies whose ambitious fathers had consigned them to this sad and boring life, which they passed in luxurious idleness, perhaps without ever seeing their husband.

As if he'd read Maya's thoughts, Hani said, "While she was the King's Beloved Wife, Kiya lived at the palace at Akhet-aten and even had her own palace. Now she's back in the kennels."

"How is it the king couldn't beget a son for so long? He has enough women for a whole village here," Maya said sourly. *I had a son ten months after my marriage.*

Hani's smile grew caustic. "When the gods turn their backs on you—"

"They give you daughters?" Neferet finished, hands on her hips. Her little eyes were wide with accusation.

"No, no, my love. Daughters are a blessing."

147

Neferet dropped her eyes, suddenly troubled. Hani exchanged a glance of concern with Maya and tipped the girl's chin up. "What is it, Neferet? What's wrong?"

"I was going to say 'The king never did have a son.'" She looked reluctant, almost frightened. "But I swore I wouldn't tell anyone."

What's this? Maya thought uneasily. He fixed Lord Hani with a questioning stare.

Hani's face had grown rigid with suspicion. He drew his daughter out of the stream of pedestrians and into the mouth of a quiet alley. He laid a hand on her shoulder and said in an undertone, "What do you mean, Neferet?"

"I swore I wouldn't tell, Papa, but... it's been worrying me ever since. I don't think it's honest, but I don't know what to do." Her eyebrows were buckled, her eyes a little shifty.

"You can tell your father, girl," said Maya sternly.

Neferet looked undecided for a moment longer, but then she heaved a huge sigh. "Remember Lady Djefat-nebty took me to the palace for the first time to help her with the childbirth of the Great Queen and Lady Kiya? The king's sister was having a baby at the same time."

"It was a good year for babies," murmured Maya, remembering. His own little Tepy had been born the same day two years before.

Hani nodded, never taking his eyes off his daughter's.

She continued in an unsteady voice, "The queen gave birth to a stillborn girl"—Maya and Hani gasped—"and as soon as Lady Djefat-nebty saw she was dead, they took the baby away from the queen, even before she could see her."

"Bes rescue us!" Maya exclaimed. "The queen didn't even know?"

Neferet shook her head. "And then they sent me into Princess Sit-pa-aten's room."

"Whose?" Maya cried, confused.

"Sit-amen," Hani said. "Nefer-khepru-ra's sister. She was her father's, er, wife. Remember?"

"Her father's wife?" Neferet's nose wrinkled in disgust. "Well, she's somebody else's wife now. And she had just given birth to an adorable baby boy. And they told me to put the dead little girl in his place and take the boy. And, and... to put him beside the queen."

"Prince Tut-ankh-aten?" cried Maya in horror. "He's his own cousin?"

Hani groaned and covered his eyes with a hand as if he couldn't bear to look another moment upon such a lying world. He opened his eyes at last and said to Neferet in a flat voice, "Who knows about this, little duckling?"

"Me, Lady Djefat-nebty, her husband, Lord Pentju, a midwife, and Princess Meryet-aten."

"Nefert-iti's eldest daughter? She knows about the switch?"

"She knows that we switched children, yes, but not whose child the little boy was." Neferet looked at her father anxiously. "Lord Pentju made me swear to tell nobody, and he had me write you a letter saying that the queen and Lady Kiya had given birth but nothing more. I had to swear to him not to tell." Suddenly, her face crumpled. "I swore on Mama's *ka*, Papa. Have I put her soul in danger?"

Hani wrapped the girl in his arms. "No, my love. A forced oath doesn't count. You did right to tell me." He kissed her on the top of the head. After a moment of throbbing silence, Hani led the way back to the main street, and they resumed their journey.

"Pentju is the king's physician," murmured Maya. "Do you think the king was behind this?"

Hani shrugged. "Maybe. But someone like Ay seems more likely. As long as his daughter bears the king his heir, her place is assured—and so is Ay's influence. Otherwise, who knows?"

"Then there's one more person who's aware of the switch—and a dangerous one."

"Say nothing to anyone, either of you. I'm not sure the witnesses are safe." Hani stared grimly into the glaring road ahead of them.

❖

A cold wave of fear and anger lapped at the edge of Hani's heart—not that he cared so very much whether the king's son or his nephew succeeded to the throne, but his daughter had been dragged into a shady and shameful bit of palace intrigue. *Nub-nefer was right*, he told himself bitterly. *We should never have let her get involved with these people.* He was disappointed to think that Lady Djefat-nebty, who seemed so adamantly honest, would have lent herself to such a thing. Either her husband had more control over her than Hani had thought, or she was more a zealot of the Aten than he had perceived. *I wish I had talked to Baket-iset about her. She has such an insight into people.*

Yet here I am, turning Neferet back into the sunet's *hands.* Hani drew a deep breath. Suddenly, he felt overwhelmed by all the things he couldn't control yet was expected to fix.

The clustered cubes of the city itself were thinning out, giving way to the fertile, Flood-watered countryside between the River and the canal of Pa-yom. Palm trees swayed, graceful in the tepid breeze, and a hawk floated lazily in the air high above the road. Hani stared upward, shading his eyes with a hand. *There he is again. Is it the Lord Haru watching over his sacred city?*

Ahead of them loomed the white walls of the House of the Royal Ornaments. The gate was swarming with Nubian soldiers in fancy uniforms, plumes in their hair.

"It's better guarded than the Double House of Silver and Gold," Maya commented.

"Because the contents are more precious." Hani turned to Neferet. "Where are you supposed to meet Djefat-nebty, my duckling?"

"At the entrance. But neither of us knew the exact hour I would arrive. I can just wait until she comes."

"Not by yourself," Maya said firmly. "Your mother would never forgive us."

"If you have to wait, we'll wait with you," Hani told her.

At the pylon gate, Hani gave his credentials and those of this daughter. The three of them were ushered into the vast courtyard shaded with rows of trees. Even this semipublic area was a place of soft luxury, with flowers and pools and walls painted with scenes of nature so convincing they seemed to exhale the perfume of real blossoms. At the back stretched a colonnaded porch patrolled by yet more soldiers in a variety of costumes. Hani and his companions mounted the broad steps, where they were met by a majordomo dressed in immaculate linen with a full, fashionable cluster of pleats hanging to his knees in front.

"My lord Hani," he said with a pompous little bow. "Lady Kiya awaits you."

Hani had just started to say, "But we can't leave my daughter here alone," when he saw, striding toward them out of the depths of the palace, the tall figure of the *sunet*. She lifted a hand in greeting and quickened her pace.

"You're very prompt, Neferet," she said approvingly as she drew up to them. "Thank you, Lord Hani, for bringing her on time."

He tipped his head in acknowledgment, biting back the reproaches that hovered on the tip of his tongue. *How could you drag my little daughter into such slippery business? She was only fourteen. How could you put her under oath with such a heavy secret?*

"Come, Neferet," Djefat-nebty said brusquely, turning. Neferet stepped out after her, shooting her father an uncertain smile.

Together they disappeared down a dark corridor through a cluster of bowing servants. Hani could hear his daughter asking eagerly, "Is Bener-ib here yet?"

He stood, wrestling with his conflicted conscience, then he said to the majordomo, "Lead on, please."

The man resumed his strut ahead of them, his staff clicking on the polished gypsum floors. They traversed broad halls, past luxurious apartments where giggling girls hung in the doorway and naked handmaids with wreaths of flowers on their lush wigs passed back and forth with platters of fruit and sweetmeats. At last, they came to a courtyard carved into a sunken garden with a covered walkway, all around, looking down into it. Various ladies in diaphanous caftans in the latest fashion strolled the sidewalk, laughing or talking. They stared up at the newcomers momentarily then continued their conversations.

Hani saw Maya craning his neck around to take in everything. Hani was surprised that they had been admitted to this seemingly private area, but perhaps it wasn't so private—soldiers stood unobtrusively at every corner of the quadrangle. The majordomo led them around the cloister and bade them wait while he disappeared through a nearby doorway.

Maya beside him, Hani took a seat on a stone bench and absorbed the fresh, fragrant air cooled by the long pool in the middle of the courtyard and perfumed by beds of flowers. He tried to imagine what he could say to Kiya that would give her any comfort. A pair of ducks came flapping in from the River and dropped with outspread wings into the water. Hani observed them with a smile. Birds never failed to warm his heart. "They're so clumsy on land yet so graceful in the air or in the water," he said fondly.

"Who's that, my lord? The Mitannians?" Maya asked, confused.

Hani laughed. "I was talking about those ducks. Sorry." Of course, Maya was still thinking about the Mitannians. Hani's mood blackened with the recollection of what had happened to them in Akhet-aten.

Footsteps clattered on the pavement, and a moment later, the majordomo reappeared with a tall, slender specter in his wake. "Lady Kiya," he announced and bowed himself away. Hani noticed that he took up a post out of earshot but not much farther off.

Hani and Maya rose and made a full court bow, hands on their knees. Kiya might be in marginal disgrace, but she was still a wife of the Great King.

"Hani," she said in a weak voice. "Thank you for coming."

Certainly Nefer-khepru-ra's loss of interest in his once-Beloved Wife could not have been due to fading physical charms—she was only twenty-two and as beautiful as ever—but all the sparkle and vivacity had gone out of her. Her kohl-edged eyes red and swollen, she seemed as transparent as her caftan, as if she were beginning to disappear already. "Can't you make them relent? They want me to leave little Baket-aten behind, and she's... she's all my life now." Her lip began to tremble, and her voice grew very high. "She's all I have left."

Hani's fatherly heart ached for the girl, but he was helpless to aid her. He said gently, "My lady, I know what you're going through. But I beg you to obey with good grace. Neither of us can prevent what's happening, so there's no point in beating yourself against the reality. It will only cause you more pain. Surely, seeing your father and mother again will be some comfort to you."

She buried her face in her hands, and her hunched shoulders began to jerk. "Why has he cast me off, Hani? What have I done wrong?" she sobbed.

His first instinct was to tell her she'd done nothing wrong and that her royal husband was a fickle, spoiled bastard. But she'd had a brief affair with a sculptor, and the queen was aware of it. Hani had managed to forestall Nefert-iti's vengeance, yet perhaps the queen had finally decided to reveal her rival's misdeed. If so, sending her away was a merciful understatement of a punishment.

Hani heaved a sorrowful sigh, and he exchanged a hopeless glance with Maya. Kiya took her hands from her face and made a valiant effort to stifle her tears. She nodded in resignation. "I'll go. What choice have I?" She faced Hani with the bravery of a true princess. "When is my father sending his men down to escort me home?"

Hani cringed. He would have to tell her what had happened. "My lady, there has been an unfortunate occurrence. The two men sent by Tushratta have been arrested."

"Arrested?" she cried, her eyes round with outrage. "Who would dare to arrest my father's emissaries?"

"The same man who is separating you from your child," Hani said in a quiet voice.

Kiya let out a howl that might have been sorrow and might have been fury. She grabbed her wig at the temples with both hands. "Why? Why? Why am I being humiliated again and again like this?" She sank to the bench, her face a twisted mask of misery. Eventually, she grew calmer and asked Hani bitterly, "What accusation have they concocted?"

Hani drew a deep breath and told her, "Tomb robbing. I'm supposedly the one conducting this investigation, but in effect, the royal police have taken it over. And they have decided that the culprits are Pirissi and Tulubri, your countrymen."

"The queen is behind this, I'm sure, Hani," Kiya said in a desolate voice. "She hates me." She dashed at her eyes with the back of a hennaed hand. "She even refused to take

Baket-aten to raise. But I thank the gods it won't be her. The queen mother has said she'll take her in."

"Why, that's good. The child should do well in the loving care of her grandmother." Hani tried to sound enthusiastic.

Kiya shot him a look full of pain. "She would do better in the loving care of her mother." She gave an ironic sniff. "So, who's taking me back, Hani? You?"

"I don't know yet, Lady Kiya."

"They'll probably just stuff me into the back of some merchant's wagon along with the rugs." She stood up, less washed-out than she had been before. The final humiliation hadn't broken her but rather had galvanized her. "Thank you for coming, my old friend. I hope it's you who takes me back. That would close the circle."

"My lady, I wish you all the good in the world. You're young; you can marry again. I hope your life will become happy once more." He tried not think about what was happening in Naharin—the wars between Tushratta and his brother and the pieces falling off the kingdom under the onslaughts of the Hittites. He wondered if she would even reach her homeland alive.

The sound of soft-soled footsteps made Hani turn. A Mitannian man was approaching the royal lady with the smooth, humble mien of a high-level servant. He bowed before her. "Forgive me, my lady. I didn't know you had visitors. You directed me to bring Lady Baket-aten's nurse to you. She's waiting in the outer vestibule."

"Thank you, Talpu-sharri." Kiya turned to Hani, and all at once she was radiant. "This is my chamberlain. He's worth his weight in gold, which perhaps I didn't realize until he was absent for a few weeks." She smiled at the chamberlain with a bit too much warmth. "The poor man was sick. I was so worried." The last statement seemed to be addressed to Talpu-sharri.

Hani tipped his head in greeting, and Talpu-sharri smiled and bowed a little, his hands clasped at his waist. The man was probably in his thirties, tall, and well-built, with dark wavy hair down to his shoulders and a collar of beard. He had fine eyes of a light golden brown.

And a mole above his left lip.

At Hani's side, Maya let out a gasp then covered it up with a cough.

Although his heart had started to hammer in his chest, Hani managed a smooth voice as he said, "We leave you in good hands, my lady. Goodbye... and perhaps farewell."

"Farewell, my dear old friend."

Hani turned and retreated down the cloister, tingling with excitement, Maya pattering in his wake. The majordomo popped up from where he was sitting to accompany them from the palace.

CHAPTER 7

"Bᴜᴛ ʜᴏᴡ ᴄᴏᴜʟᴅ Tᴀʟᴘᴜ-sʜᴀʀʀɪ ʜᴀᴠᴇ gotten down to Waset so often?" Maya exclaimed. "He's a sort of servant. He must have duties."

The two men were once again on the deck of a ferry, this time bound upstream to Akhet-aten. Maya's head was reeling with the latest complication in their case.

"Didn't you hear Lady Kiya say he'd been sick? He probably took time off from his duties, but instead of lying in bed, he hotfooted it south," Lord Hani said pensively. He stared at Maya. "Somehow, we have to get Pirissi and Tulubri out of Mahu's hands before he has them impaled."

Maya shook his head, confused and disgusted. "Too bad we don't have Bebi-ankh anymore. No doubt he could make a positive identification." He returned Hani's caustic look. "Will Mahu even listen to us if we tell him we've found the real ringleader? Knowing him, he just wants to hand the king a closed case, not find out who's genuinely at fault."

Hani snorted. "We need to talk to Ptah-mes. Perhaps

he can get the vizier to intervene. After all, we're working for him."

As soon as they reached the capital, Hani and Maya headed directly for the Hall of Royal Correspondence. But Lord Ptah-mes wasn't in his office. Maya realized then that it was the end-of-week holiday and none of the government offices were open.

"Let's track him down at home," Hani said, and with Maya scampering along behind him, he set out briskly toward the southern edge of the city.

They presented themselves at the high commissioner's gate, and the porter, who knew them well, admitted them to the garden. "Lord Ptah-mes is under the arbor, my lord."

Hani and Maya, who stayed with Ptah-mes when they had business in the capital, needed no guide. They found the high commissioner seated under the leafless grapevines with a scroll across his knees.

"Ah, Hani, Maya," he said, looking up, his somber expression relaxing. "I was just looking over a *Book of Going Forth by Day* I commissioned for my tomb." He turned it upside down and showed Hani the illustrations. Maya peeked around his father-in-law's broad body and saw text and pictures as beautiful as Maya would have expected from Ptah-mes, whose taste was impeccable and for whom no expense was prohibitive.

"'What did you find on the shore of the pool of the Two Truths?' A scepter of flint whose name is Breath Giver," Hani read aloud. He laughed nervously. "Believe it or not, that's exactly the passage I read in my father's *Book* a few weeks ago. Someone's trying to tell me something."

"What exactly is a scepter of flint?" Maya asked. "I

picture it something like those knives they use to cut the umbilical cord."

"Perhaps. That would be a 'breath giver,' in a sense," said Lord Ptah-mes, tipping his head in acknowledgment.

"But it's a scepter. Like a *was* scepter—tall? Like the king's crook, small enough to hold in your arms?" Maya found himself intrigued.

But Lord Hani said, "Let's figure this out later, Maya. We need to tell Lord Ptah-mes what has happened since we last spoke."

Ptah-mes gestured to the two men to have a seat on the stools that punctuated his garden.

Lord Hani began with a deep breath and said, "I think we've found the ringleader of the tomb robbers, my lord."

Ptah-mes's arched black eyebrows rose. "Well done, Hani. Who is it?"

"It's probably the chamberlain of Lady Kiya, a man named Talpu-sharri. At least, he matches Bebi-ankh's description. And he pretended to be sick for the last few weeks, which would have given him time to go to Waset and direct his robberies."

"Why did he speak of his immunity?" Maya asked.

"Perhaps he was just bragging to reassure his henchmen. Royal servants don't enjoy any real immunity that I'm aware of," said Ptah-mes. "Where did the man come from, anyway? He certainly wasn't sent down with Lady Kiya."

"I can confirm that, my lord. You've posed a good question." Hani caught Maya's eye. "Make a note of that, son. We need to look into it. Or better still, we'll have Neferet check him out. A good-looking man like that—I'll bet all the royal girls know everything about him." Hani blew out through his nose, which Maya recognized as an expression of discouragement. "We have to get the others out of Mahu's clutches. I'm sure Bebi-ankh could identify the man. But there's hardly a chance that Mahu will cooperate."

Ptah-mes looked grim. "Let's see what the vizier says. I don't think he likes Mahu much."

He rolled up his *Book of Going Forth* carefully and tied a ribbon around it. Then he sat up straighter, his long ringed hands crossed in his lap on top of the scroll. "I have some news too. The dowager queen has died."

"Lady Tiyi?" Hani cried. "How sad. Was it the plague?"

She's the one who was supposed to be taking care of Kiya's daughter, Maya thought.

"Yes," Ptah-mes answered. "It's spreading. It's in the city now."

Maya's stomach clenched in dread. He and Hani exchanged an uneasy look. "Perhaps you should get out, my lord," said Hani.

Ptah-mes gave an ambiguous twitch of the shoulders. His smile was as dry as the sands of the Red Land. A tense silence fell over the three men.

Maya could hardly swallow. His first thought was, *Let's flee this accursed city.* And then, *Lord Hani's brother and two of his children live here.*

"Do you want me to continue to investigate, Lord Ptah-mes? Or do we bow to Mahu's takeover?" Hani asked.

"I talked with the vizier after our last conversation. He confirmed that you are the investigator, at the king's order. He's going to speak to the king about the confusion of jurisdiction—in fact, he may already have done so. Our friend Mahu may be arrogating more authority than he was intended to. I can imagine that taking prisoners away from the army bent a few noses." Ptah-mes's smile widened, but there was no warmth in it.

"I hope he can do something. I would like to question the men a little, but Mahu may have tortured them to the limit already." Hani looked sunk in thought, then he brightened. "Perhaps Bebi-ankh's wife knows something. She seemed to be aware of what was going on."

Rising, Ptah-mes replied, "Do what you must, Hani. I hope you gentlemen will honor me with your presence tonight."

"Thank you, my lord. We accept gratefully."

Maya could feel cold sweat breaking out on his forehead. *No, let's get out of here now. Now.*

Night had fallen. Hani and Maya and their host had dined together on expensive delicacies prepared with the utmost sophistication. Afterward, they sat around with cups of wine from Djahy and made small talk. Finally, Maya excused himself and headed off to bed, leaving Hani and Ptah-mes alone.

"How are things, Hani?" Ptah-mes asked quietly.

"Well, my lord. I just dropped my daughter off with her teacher at the House of the Royal Ornaments. That's where I had the visit with Lady Kiya and was introduced to her chamberlain."

"Your family is all well?"

"Mercifully, yes. And yours?"

"They're well," Ptah-mes said vaguely. Hani knew he

rarely saw his children, who were all married. He and his wife barely spoke.

An uncomfortable silence descended.

Hani realized that his host was wearing no mourning scarf. "Is there no official mourning for Lady Tiyi? She was a great and powerful lady in her day."

Ptah-mes snorted. "Nothing public. The king doesn't want it known how seriously the ranks of the royal family and servants of the palace are dropping."

Hani felt a chill ripple up the back of his neck. "Neferet," he murmured. "She's tending the sick."

"Load her with amulets, Hani. That's all you can do." Ptah-mes's grave look was full of pity.

He rose and stretched. "Forgive me, my friend, but I'm tired. I think I'll go to bed early."

He looks tired, Hani thought. Ptah-mes's face was thinner than usual, and he'd developed bags under his eyes. *Of course, he must be fifty.*

"I'm tired too," Hani admitted, getting to his feet and brushing the accumulated crumbs from his kilt.

His host moved with his usual grace to the staircase, and Hani found his accustomed room. He heard Maya snoring loudly next door. As he removed and folded his clothes, he asked himself, *What is the motive of a man of Talpu-sharri's status for risking such an enormous punishment? Simple greed? Some political agenda?* His heart stumbled a beat. *Surely he wasn't acting on Kiya's behalf. And who is he?*

And then, there was the strange reaction of fear on Bebi-ankh's part the night of the party. Had the mere sound of a Hurrian accent frightened him—or was there more to it?

＊

As soon as Hani had reached his home in Waset and greeted Nub-nefer and Baket-iset, he knocked on the door of Bebi-ankh's room. The painter's haggard wife appeared, and when she saw Hani, she cried bitterly, "You said he would be safe here, my lord, but he's disappeared. Where is he?"

Hani drew a deep breath. "He voluntarily left my custody, mistress. And I'm afraid Mahu and the *medjay* have him again."

The woman clutched her face and screamed, "No! They'll finish him off this time!" She staggered back into the room, and Hani followed her, afraid she might faint. But she sank onto the unmade bed, oblivious to the stares of her three little children, and began to sob into her hands. "What will I do? How will I put food in the babies' mouths?"

Hani felt as if an undigested lump of lead sat in his belly. He said kindly, "Can you help me confirm the identity of the ringleader, mistress? He's the one who is really guilty, not the workmen who saw a way to feed their families."

"All I know is this." She gulped. "Bibi said the man was a foreigner, tall and fair skinned, and had light eyes and a mole on his lip. He mentioned that when we were talking about how different foreigners looked."

Hani nodded. He already knew all of that. Talpu-sharri fit the description. "Anything else?"

"He had on a beautiful blue-green tunic. Bibi was very struck by it."

"Did he mention anything else distinctive about the man? How did he meet Bebi-ankh? When did all this start?"

"Now, that I can tell you. It was the week before the Great Jubilee. Bibi said one of his colleagues, a color man named Heqa-nakht, whispered to him that he knew a way to make some silver. And that was ironic, because Bibi had lost a lot of our pay to Heqa-nakht, betting on Hounds and Jackals." The woman snorted. "He was a no-good piece of trouble, that Heqa-nakht. I told Bibi to stay away from the scum, but of course, they had to work together."

"How did the foreigner meet the men he wanted to work for him?" Hani pressed.

"There was a tomb just being excavated. The plasterers hadn't even gotten to it yet, so there was no guard. Heqa-nakht passed him the word, and he went there at night. The foreigner explained what he wanted from them and told them the enormous rewards they'd get." She blew out a sharp breath of disgust. "He *didn't* tell them what would happen to them if they got caught. But I warned Bibi..." She drew her second youngest, a girl of perhaps three, against her knees and played mechanically with the child's Haru lock. Her face was stricken.

Clearly, we need to find this Heqa-nakht, Hani thought. *He's the one who got away the day we arrested the others.* "Where did Heqa-nakht live?"

"At the Place of Truth, like all of us. They had a nice house but didn't take care of it. His wife's a complete slattern, as bad as her husband, and their children are always snot-nosed and dirty. I didn't want mine to play with them."

"Could you show me their house?"

"I can, my lord."

Hani told her to be ready to cross the River the next

afternoon, and he headed back to the salon. He said to himself, "I must remember to return the Mitannians' baggage to Mane's house."

✦

The following morning, Hani and his wife were sitting side by side, eating breakfast in the salon. Nub-nefer had been as deeply unnerved by news of the spreading plague as he was.

"Hani, we have to get Neferet out of there. I don't care what you told her," she said fiercely.

"And Pipi and Aha, too, I suppose. Perhaps we can pretend to be insurgents, stage a raid, and kidnap them all." He managed a wry smile despite the anxiety that gnawed at him.

"Don't mock me, my love. Our children's lives are at risk," she chided, giving him a baleful stare. "At least Aha has sent Khentet-ka and the children up to her mother's country place."

"While Pipi has just called his family down to the capital. I've never seen him excited about a job before. These are truly extraordinary times."

Nub-nefer clapped her hands to her temples and shook her head in frustration. "You're hopeless, Hani. How you can make jokes over a subject like this…?"

Hani reached out and caressed her coppery arm. "It's because I can do nothing about it, my dove. Lady Sekhmet chooses whom she will to afflict, and there's no place to hide. Better to smile than to weep and wring our hands, isn't it?"

Nub-nefer took his hand and kissed the knuckles. Her

eyes sparkled. "Can't I do both?" They shared a laugh, with the resignation of those whom the gods have tossed about. Her arm stealing around Hani's waist, Nub-nefer said, "Have you ever figured out who the mysterious foreigner is?"

"I think I have a good idea. Bebi-ankh's wife is taking me to the Place of Truth today so I can talk to another of the conspirators—or more likely, his family. I'm sure *he's* fled someplace far away. I'd like a confirmation of the foreigner's description before I take the man in for questioning."

"What about the murderer of that artist?" she asked.

A spearpoint of remorse pricked Hani. "I'd forgotten about him, with all the other things going on. Thank you for reminding me." He heaved a deep breath. "There were no witnesses to his murder, so I'm not really sure where to start. Maybe with the overseer Ankh-reshet. He's the one who found him."

Nub-nefer leaned in to kiss him, and Hani, suddenly fighting down a lump in his throat, thought, *This is why* ma'at *must be restored: so that innocent people like my family won't have to suffer the punishment of a lawless kingdom.*

Maya arrived, chipper and ready to work. He and Hani had just started toward the door into the vestibule when the outer panel opened, and the broad silhouette of Mery-ra appeared.

"Ah, Father," Hani said. "How would you like to join us in the Place of Truth? It occurs to me that we can divide up our interviews and get things done more quickly."

"Of course, son. I don't want my skills to get rusty now that I'm retired." Mery-ra beamed his gap-toothed smile.

"And I'm fortified by a lunch at Meryet-amen's house. Her cook is superb."

Hani and Maya exchanged a knowing grin. Meryet-amen, a rich widow, was Mery-ra's lady friend.

"I want to ask about Djau's murder too. Maybe Ankh-reshet can remember something useful," said Hani as the three men crunched down the garden path toward the gate. Bebi-ankh's wife hadn't dared to leave her children after all, despite Nub-nefer's offer to help, but she had given Hani directions to Heqa-nakht's house.

"Djau... was that the man killed with the military arrow?"

Hani nodded.

"Why don't you ask Pa-aten-em-heb about that? Maybe he could identify it in some way to narrow down your search," his father suggested.

"Excellent idea. In fact, why don't I appoint you and Maya to look into that while I start across the River? You can catch up to me in the Place of Truth if you have time."

Mery-ra agreed cheerfully. "I welcome a chance to see my old colleagues again."

He and Maya peeled off in the street heading for the quays and turned south toward the barracks. Although a huge contingent was now stationed in Akhet-aten, the main body of the army still resided at Waset and Men-nefer. For his part, Hani continued to the River, where he quickly found a ferry, and before much time had elapsed, he stepped out onto the bank of the Place of Silence.

A strong, dry wind was blowing into his face, the swirling dust stinging his eyes and making it hard to see. He had to struggle up the slope toward the Place of Truth and then down again, his feet slipping in the roll of gravel and small stones as he lurched along, almost blinded. He entered the gate of the walled village gratefully, and suddenly, the wind was cut off by the clustered houses. *What a desolate place this is. The "truth" is harsh.* Hani rubbed his eyes with his fists to clear them and felt grit on his knuckles.

He trudged through the arid streets, following the directions Bebi-ankh's wife had given him, and came to a gate with peeling paint and a few desiccated weeds trailing in the dirt around it. Hani knocked. A moment later, a naked little girl of about ten opened the panel and stood there in the crack, staring at him suspiciously. Her face and hands were grubby, and her sidelock half-unplaited. Hani gave her a friendly smile. "Hello, my girl. Are your parents home?"

She said nothing but turned and pattered off through a small yard into the house. The door was open, and only a rolled-up mat hung raggedly over the opening. The whole place reeked of poverty, despite the government-issue housing. Hani thought sadly—once again—that it was no wonder the man had been tempted by the promise of riches.

After a brief space of time, a thin, dark woman emerged from the house and marched up to the gate. "Who are you?" she demanded. "Why are you here?"

"May I speak to your husband, mistress?" Hani asked disingenuously.

She shot him a hostile look. "He's not here. Why do you want him?"

Hani said in a voice so low that no neighbor could overhear, "He's in danger. His companions will think he

169

has betrayed them on the one hand, and the *medjay* are hunting him on the other. I can protect him."

Her eyes grew wide with fear, and she made to slam the gate, but Hani forced his way inside. "You need to talk to me."

"Who are you?" she cried shrilly, backing away.

"I'm a royal investigator," he said, still speaking in a quiet, gentle voice such as one might use with a panicked animal, "but I have no interest in apprehending your husband. I only want to find the man who was paying him. There are things Heqa-nakht alone can tell me."

"Why should I believe you?" she snarled.

"My protection—the vizier's protection—is your husband's only hope. If he cooperates, he will be set free and be able to resume his work. If he doesn't, the *medjay* will track him down and torture him then impale him. Which would you prefer?"

She stared into space, her brows contracted, and Hani could almost see the thoughts galloping around in her head. At last, she grumbled, "Wait here."

The woman darted into the house, and Hani heard her shout, "Stay here, you brats, and don't budge until I come back. If anybody goes outside, I'll beat the shit out of them, do you hear me?"

She returned directly, breathless, tugging a threadbare shawl over her shoulders. Without a word, she gestured to Hani to follow her. They passed at a swift clip through the narrow streets of the workmen's village and out the north gate, where the wind hit them like a slap across the face. Hani, protecting his eyes with a hand, saw the woman draw her shawl over her nose and lean into the wind. She looked as if she might blow away. Nonetheless, her thin legs, the skirts flapping about them, propelled her up the rocky slope with the energy of a mule. Her homemade straw sandals were worn slick on the bottom, but she mounted the path at such a speed that Hani was hard put to keep up with her.

At last, they came to the mouth of a deep ravine that Hani recognized, with a shock, as the Great Place, where the kings of the Theban dynasty were buried. *Where is she taking me?* he thought uneasily. It crossed his mind that she might be leading him into a trap. Even though it was broad daylight, no one would hear a cry for help in this abandoned valley.

Eventually, she stopped in the shelter of a large fall of rocks and turned to Hani. "You stay here, facing the opening of the valley," the woman said roughly. "Don't turn around till I come back."

"Now *I* have to trust *you*," Hani said with a smile that he hoped looked more reassured than he felt.

She gave a mocking snort and took off into the valley, yelling in her shrill voice, "Turn around, or I won't come back."

"I guess she'll beat the shit out of me too," Hani said to himself, more to hear a human voice in this bleak and silent place of the dead than for any other reason. He settled himself on a low rock with his back to the wind and, squinting against the sun, stared into the stark ocher landscape. Not a living thing met his gaze. Only the swirling dust gave movement to what might have been a scene from the underworld.

After what seemed like an inordinately long time, Hani heard footsteps crunching over the gravel behind him. "Is that you, mistress?" he called out, hoping his voice didn't betray how uneasy he felt. He could only too easily picture some desperado sweeping down on him unseen, a club or dagger raised.

"It's me," she said over the wind. "You can turn around now."

He obeyed. Before him stood the woman and, at her side, a little squat man with broad shoulders and bulging, muscular arms and thin, bowed legs. His physique proclaimed him a stonecutter.

Heqa-nakht stood staring at Hani in a suspicious, considering way. "My wife tells me you're offering me protection. How do I know you're telling the truth?"

"I've been sitting out here with my back turned. You could have killed me easily," Hani said with a friendly smile. "You'll have to trust me as I trusted you."

The man drew closer. "Who are you?"

"My name is Hani son of Mery-ra. I'm the man who brought the soldiers to the worksite and arrested your fellows."

Heqa-nakht drew back a few paces. "That's not much of a recommendation," he said sarcastically.

"Had they remained in my protection, they would be back to work by now. Unfortunately, the *medjay* took them away from me. They're being tortured as we speak." Hani took a step forward. "Mahu wants a wholesale slaughter—a lot of little fry who will make him look good before the king. All I'm interested in is finding the man who is behind these robberies."

"Who cares what he wants? No one would be able to find me anyway."

"Don't think he won't," Hani said. "The police have dogs and baboons. They'll find you, all right, before you make it over the border. Talk to me now while you can still get out."

The artisan shot an edgy glance at his wife, who stood scowling at his side. While her face was broad and bony, she had extraordinary almond-shaped eyes.

"All right," Heqa-nakht finally said. "What do you want to know?"

"You were the first of the workmen this mysterious foreigner approached, right? What did he say to you?"

"He just promised us riches. He said it would be dangerous but worth our while. Things have been pretty lean since the royal tombs moved out of this valley. How are we supposed to stay alive on three noble tombs a year?"

"Did he say anything about what *he* expected to get out of it?" Hani asked. "Was he just into it for gold, or was he trying to embarrass the king or make this place look unsafe or what?"

Heqa-nakht raised his eyebrows thoughtfully. "He said something about putting the rightful man on the throne. I don't know why he'd care who was on the throne. He doesn't even live here."

"Do you know where he was from?"

"Naharin. I used to work with a man from Naharin, and a lying bugger he was too. I shoulda known this fellow wasn't on the level." Heqa-nakht snorted cynically.

Hani raised his eyebrows. "What makes you say that? Did he cheat you?"

"Not yet. But all those Mitannians are the same. We take the risks, and the chief gets the treasure."

Hani had the feeling that all this was more about the man's prejudices than about anything that could serve as a clue. "Can you give me some description that would help me identify him? Did he have any companions who might have called him by name?"

Heqa-nakht described the mysterious foreigner in pretty much the same terms as everyone else had, citing the mole on the lip and the light-colored eyes as distinctive.

"What color was his hair?" Hani asked.

"Darkish, like most people's. Not black but darkish brown."

That could be almost anyone in the world, Hani thought with a sigh. "No companions? No name?"

Heqa-nakht said caustically, "No. He was alone. He never said, 'I, so-and-so, want you to break into a tomb for me.'"

"You're going to have to be more helpful than this to earn your pardon," said Hani, beginning to tire of the stonecutter's snideness. "Tell me something I don't already know."

The man looked uneasily at his wife. "I can't tell you what I don't know. He did say once that because of his backers, he had immunity and would protect us. Frankly, I think it was a lot of ass shit."

"Backers?" Hani pressed, beginning to feel that sparkle in his gut that told him he might be onto something.

"Yes. He didn't say who they were, but they were clearly someone important, right? That was when he said that bit about putting the right man back on the throne. He said we'd be doing something good for the kingdom." Heqa-nakht gave a bark of laughter. "Just sweet talking us, if you ask me."

Hani considered this. Heqa-nakht was getting restless, starting to look around him as if fearful. His wife shot him a worried glance.

"How did the rest of that conversation go, friend? Be honest, and rack your memory. This could be what saves you."

The stonecutter spread his hands helplessly. "What more can I say? This was when he first met with me to ask me to gather a team I thought could help him. He introduced himself as someone who represented powerful people who wanted to see *ma'at* restored in the kingdom by putting the right man on the throne and said that, by helping, we could do a lot of good—that he could protect us because of who he worked for. Then I asked him what sort of workmen he wanted, and he told me painters and stonecutters. That's all I know—I swear by my mother's *ka*."

Hani smiled at him pleasantly. "I think you've been helpful, Heqa-nakht. I suggest you and your family disappear fast, because one of your colleagues is almost surely going to blame you for getting him into this, and the *medjay* will come for you."

"Yes, my lord," the man said, lapsing into politeness for the first time. "Turn around again, if it please you."

⚜

Maya and Lord Mery-ra entered the army compound south of the city, the flint-headed arrow unobtrusively under the old scribe's arm. In the distance, still farther upstream,

Maya saw the ghostly walls of the Ipet-isut, abandoned now by its dishonored god, shimmering in the wind-troubled sun of early spring. *As the power of the priesthood goes down, the power of the army rises*, Maya thought gloomily. *Nefer-khepru-ra seems to think he can count on their loyalty.* Considering men like Pa-aten-em-heb, he wondered if the king were not leaning on a rotten stick.

"We should find our friend in his office down this way, if he isn't out on maneuvers." Mery-ra led the way across a vast open court with a well and a pool for watering horses. The buildings that surrounded the court were plain, low, and serviceable with watchtowers at the outer corner. Officers and scribes passed them in one direction or another, including a fast courier jogging toward the general headquarters. Maya kept up gamely with Mery-ra's pace— for an old man, Hani's father could cover ground.

They entered the headquarters, where the dark and cool enfolded them. A row of scribes sat on the floor, writing busily by the light of the clerestories. Maya's eyes widened to see Pa-kiki among them. He reminded himself that the lad worked there now.

Pa-kiki looked up at their footsteps then brightened, crying aloud, "Grandfather! Maya! What brings you here?"

"Just checking up on you, my boy, to be sure you haven't disgraced the family name," said Mery-ra with a big grin.

Pa-kiki looked appalled then laughed as he realized it was a joke. "Do you want to talk to Lord Pa-aten-em-heb, then?"

"We do, son."

Pa-kiki set aside his writing implements and sprang nimbly to his feet. He disappeared through one of the numerous doors in the wall behind the scribes, and in a moment, the young officer appeared. He strode quickly forward to meet them, a delighted expression on his handsome face.

"Lord Mery-ra. Maya, isn't it? What can I do for you?"

Mery-ra produced the arrow. "Can you tell us anything about this?"

Pa-aten-em-heb pursed his lips and raised his eyebrows. "Let's step into my office." He led the way inside a room little bigger than a cubicle, lit by a high window, and stood carefully in the square of sunlight, examining the arrow—its gray goose fletching, its broad squared-off head, the bloody bindings. Then he looked up, curious. "Where did you get this?"

"It was used to kill a man who reported tomb robberies. I was hoping you could tell us who might use such a weapon. I suspect it isn't something just anyone would have access to."

"No. Only a soldier—and not every soldier at that. It's not a long-range weapon, not something the infantry would typically use. I'd say it probably belonged to cavalrymen. You'd be fighting at close or medium range, and you would want to be sure of your kill. A slim point can penetrate armor, but you can never be sure you'll hit a vital organ. With this, even a strike in a limb somewhere would bleed a man out pretty quickly."

Maya and Mery-ra exchanged grim looks. Djau hadn't stood a chance against such an arrow.

"In this case, a man was killed as he climbed up from the workmen's weekly camp near the Great Place to the site

177

of their labors. How close would his murderer have had to be?" Mery-ra asked.

"There's plenty of cover up there for an ambush at relatively close range. He wouldn't have had to be so close that you could see him standing right in front of you, but he wouldn't have been at the tops of the cliffs either."

Mery-ra sank into a pensive silence. Maya wasn't sure this interview was doing anything but confusing him.

"I can also tell you this. Every unit fletches its arrows differently, so if you give me a little time, I can narrow your suspects down to a handful," Pa-aten-em-heb said.

"That sounds promising." Mery-ra grinned broadly. "Thank you for your help, my friend." He clapped Pa-aten-em-heb on the shoulder. "That's worth some dinner one of these evenings, I should think."

"Sounds very attractive," said Pa-aten-em-heb with a laugh. "The two Mut-nodjmets can meet."

Mery-ra's voice dropped. "How is my grandson working out?"

"He's a fine secretary and a pleasure to work with, my lord." The officer smiled.

Mery-ra drew himself up, proud. They made their goodbyes and left the office, waving to Pa-kiki as they passed. As soon as the two men were out in the courtyard once more, Maya said under his breath, "Is the queen's father behind this, do you think? He's head of the cavalry."

"True, although it could just as easily be some archer the foreigner has suborned."

"How many Egyptian soldiers would work for a Mitannian? They were our enemy until a generation or so ago, and a lot of us still don't trust them." Maya would have put himself in that category if he hadn't met the amiable Keliya.

"Let's see what Hani has learned. It may shed some light on this business," Mery-ra said. "Although, I remind you that gold can overcome a great many patriotic scruples."

They tramped up the street in a mismatched thudding of footsteps. Maya thought, *What we need to find out is who ordered this assassination and why. Why was Djau still a threat to anyone?*

By the time Hani returned from the west bank, the others had come back and were sitting in the salon, chatting with Baket-iset. Hani greeted them and flopped down on his stool, fanning his face with a hand. "It's getting warmer every day."

"It's almost harvest season," Mery-ra said. "What do you expect?"

"Well, let's debrief one another." Hani turned to his daughter. "Pardon us, my love, while we talk business. If you have any insights, please tell us." He looked at his father and Maya once more. "Here's what I found. It isn't a lot. I talked with Heqa-nakht, the only one of the grave robbers who's still at liberty and the one who conscripted the others. He couldn't add much to what Bebi-ankh had told us except to say that the foreigner claimed to be working for someone important who could give him immunity. He claimed that his agenda had to do with putting the right man on the throne. And he claimed that by helping him, the workers would be performing a service for the kingdom."

"By robbing tombs?" Maya looked skeptical.

But Mery-ra shot his son a piercing stare. "That sounds like something your Crocodiles would say, Hani. You don't think…?"

"That this has been engineered by the former priests of the Hidden One?" Hani was disturbed by his father's words because the same thought had passed through his own mind. "They're ruthless in their way, but I don't know if they'd commit the sacrilege of robbing a tomb. And why would they do that? They can't lack for gold. They're all from old, rich families."

"And why would they use a Mitannian as their agent?" Maya said, puzzled.

"It wouldn't be the first time," Hani reminded him. Two years before, he'd discovered that the priests of Amen-Ra were systematically trying to undermine the regime of Nefer-khepru-ra—and they'd made use of Mitannian mercenaries.

The men sat staring at one another in silence. Baket-iset looked thoughtful. "Is Uncle Amen-em-hut working with them, Papa?"

"He is, my love."

The silence stretched on. The men's busy thoughts were a tangible presence in the room, a vulture circling over their heads.

"So, let me tell you what *we* found out," Mery-ra said at last. "Pa-aten-em-heb told us that the arrow was likely to be a cavalry weapon for short-range assured kills. He said that he could probably tell us which unit by looking at the feathers."

"Is Ay behind this, then?" Hani asked. In the abstract,

that wouldn't surprise him. But it didn't fit with the theory of the Crocodiles being involved.

Mery-ra shrugged. "We may know more when Pa-aten-em-heb tells us what he finds."

Maya said somberly, "If Lord Ay's part of this, we'll never be able to prosecute the case. The king will shut it right down. Ay's the king's father-in-law—and uncle."

"Or it could just be some renegade soldier or mercenary." Hani earnestly hoped that was the case.

"What's next, Lord Hani?" Maya asked.

"I suppose that, while we wait to hear from Pa-aten-em-heb, we should interview Ankh-reshet and see what he might have observed about the murder. He was the one who found Djau's body. Oh!" Hani cried suddenly, slapping his forehead. "I keep forgetting to return Keliya's clothes and those of his attachés. Let me run those down to Mane's house right now."

"As you will, son." Mery-ra shrugged. "As for me, I've been tramping around the city all morning. I think I'll stay home and work on my *Book*."

"Do you need me, Lord Hani?" asked Maya eagerly.

Hani smiled. The young man was always ready for an adventure to add to his growing *Tales*. "I think I won't need anybody to help me. I'll load the baskets onto the donkey. But thank you for offering." He turned to Baket-iset. "Tell Mama to go ahead and serve lunch, my swan. I'll be back shortly and will get something on my own."

He called Iuty, the young gardener, and told him to put the packsaddle on the donkey. Then Hani went out to the kitchen court, where he'd stored the baskets and chests of the Mitannians. Iuty hoicked one into his arms and started out for the stable yard. Hani stooped to pick up a lidded basket woven of reeds, but it was heavier than he expected, and he felt it sliding out of his grip. He gave a yelp as it fell awkwardly to the ground and opened up, spilling its contents.

"Ammit take it," he muttered crossly and began to collect the heavy woolen tunics and bits of linen smallclothes. Suddenly he stopped, sucking in his breath. Lying on the ground was a beautiful tunic the color of turquoise. His hair rose on his neck.

Hani stuffed the clothing back into the chest, heart pounding. He carried it in his arms—carefully this time— and handed it to Iuty to balance on the packsaddle with the other bundles. *I've got to talk to Keliya about this.*

Hani had intended to take the litter, but he decided he wanted to make better time. "Iuty, you know where Lord Keliya lives. I'm going ahead and will tell him you're on your way." He charged out of the gate and headed down the packed-earth lane. The neighborhood was emptied out anyway due to the moving of the capital, but at this siesta hour, it was a city of ghosts.

Under a warming sun, he strode along at a brisk pace. He would outdistance the lazy donkey in no time. His thoughts were a tangle, as chaotic as a stork's nest. *This is bad. Keliya may find himself implicated. Mahu will torture Pirissi and Tulubri to make them confess, and who knows what they'll say to defend themselves.*

The culprit had to be Tulubri.

With a mounting sense of dread, Hani reached Mane's house and sought entry. Keliya greeted him shortly, his face more lugubrious than usual. Hani was aware of his own heartbeat pounding in his throat.

"Bad news, Hani, my friend," Keliya said gravely. "I've received a copy of a letter Tushratta has sent to Nefer-khepru-ra, and he's outraged. He demands the two young emissaries be released—"

"Well, of course." Hani could understand such a reaction only too well. It was exactly what he'd predicted.

"He said that as long as your king holds Pirissi and Tulubri, he's keeping Mane hostage in Wasshukanni."

Hani's stomach leaped into his mouth as if he had been pushed off a cliff. "Oh no! Poor Mane! I hope that animal Mahu doesn't do anything to them, or Tushratta will take it out on Mane, and he's innocent of any wrongdoing." Keliya nodded, long faced. They stared at one another for a moment, then Hani added in a lower voice, "I think that, in fact, they may be guilty, my friend. I'm bringing your baggage back—it should be here any minute—and when I was loading it, someone's chest fell open. In it was a turquoise-colored tunic like the one several people have described the ringleader as wearing."

Keliya faced him with a pained expression on his face. "That's not conclusive evidence, Hani."

"Of course not," Hani assured him. "But I'd very much like to see Tulubri's upper lip. Would he submit to a shave, do you think?"

"With his life on the line? I should imagine so. The question is, will Mahu let you see him—and with a razor in your hand?"

"I'll see if Ptah-mes can't get me a pass from Aper-el.

Surely that dog turd of a police chief doesn't outrank the vizier," Hani said somberly.

Keliya took his hands and shook them. "Thank you for this, my friend. We have to show that he's innocent."

"*If* he's innocent."

The Mitannian nodded—reluctantly, it seemed to Hani.

He took his leave and set off once more for home. His thoughts were troubled. They kept doubling back to that passage from the *Book of Going Forth by Day* that had haunted him lately, and all at once, the cryptic words began to make sense. *Here I am at the pool of Two Truths*, he thought with a kind of wonder. *Truth One: if I don't pursue this, I may be letting a guilty man go free. Truth Two: if I help condemn Tulubri, I'm dooming my friend.*

CHAPTER 8

T HE NEXT MORNING, HANI LEFT for Akhet-aten with
Maya.

"I'm sorry to have to take you into the teeth of the
plague, my friend, but I need to talk to Ptah-mes," Hani
said. "I have to get permission to see the two attachés." He
told his secretary about Tushratta keeping Mane hostage.
"Even if Tulubri's guilty, we need to argue his immunity.
Let our king send him home, but he mustn't be put to
death."

Maya expelled a low whistle. "This has gotten sticky."

When they reached the capital five days later, Hani was
gloomier than ever. The painful test that lay before him
crushed him down like a sack of stones on his back. "We're
facing the Weighing of the Heart every day," he murmured,
apropos of nothing, as they marched down the gangplank.

"How so, my lord?" asked Maya.

"The choices we're constantly being forced to make—
it's like all the interrogations and confrontations of the

soul in judgment. I suspect we ought to take them more seriously."

Maya eyed him askance, as if wondering what had provoked such a state of mind. They strode up the processional street toward the Hall of Royal Correspondence in silence.

Hani had to wait awhile in the reception room while his superior dealt with other business. As he sat cross-legged on the floor, his thoughts kept circling that passage about the pool of Two Truths and the scepter of flint from the *Book*. There had to be a clue in there somewhere.

At last, the sour-faced guardian of the waiting room gestured Hani into Ptah-mes's office. "He'll see you, my lord," he said loftily.

Hani left Maya waiting and made his way to Ptah-mes's door, which was ajar. He scratched at it and entered, only to find the vizier of the Northern Kingdom sitting in Ptah-mes's chair. Hani's superior had taken a humble seat on a stool.

"My lord Aper-el," Hani cried in surprise, folding into a court bow.

"It is I indeed," said the vizier with a slight twitch of a smile. "I decided to stay and hear whatever you may have to report about your investigation, Hani."

"Here's where we stand, my lord." Hani launched into a summary of the evidence given him by the workmen, the intervention of Mahu, and his suspicions about Kiya's chamberlain. Then he added, "Just before I left to come here, however, I found in the baggage of Keliya's adjutants a distinctive tunic that matched the description everyone gave of the mysterious foreigner's dress." He saw Ptah-mes's dark eyes widen in surprise. "I came to ask for permission to interrogate the men, who are now Mahu's prisoners. I thought if we shaved Tulubri's mustachioed lip, we'd find out for certain whether he could be implicated."

"You're aware, I suppose that the Mitannians are holding hostage our ambassador in Wasshukanni?" said Aper-el. His pale, sharp face was grave.

"I am, my lord," Hani said regretfully. "Lord Mane is an old friend of mine. But we have to pursue *ma'at* in this case."

Aper-el and Ptah-mes exchanged glances. The vizier said, "The Great Jubilee of the Aten will be concluding soon—in a few days, in fact. I assume you will be present for the homage of the nations?"

"I will, my lord." Hani had certainly intended to attend, if only to observe the gifts brought by vassals and allies, but with the plague afoot in Akhet-aten, he'd pretty well changed his mind. Now that his superiors expected him to be there, he seemed to have changed it back.

"Mahu and his men will all be busy with controlling the crowds and making sure no one's house is robbed while they're watching the spectacle. That might be a good time to visit the *medjay*'s jail," Ptah-mes suggested.

Aper-el nodded. "Good idea. I'll give you a letter with my seal on it, Hani. Anyone but Mahu will honor it."

"Permit me to ask," Hani began hesitantly. "How much is the king—life, prosperity, and health to him—aware of all this? Is he supporting our investigation? Because Mahu keeps invoking some direct order from Our Sun God to push me aside. I don't think the army would have surrendered their prisoners to him without instructions from on high—especially after I promised your protection for them."

Ptah-mes lowered his eyes, expressionless, and Aper-el looked sour, his nostrils pinched. "I suspect they're both true. He supports us, *and* he has sent in Mahu."

How can that be? Hani asked himself in irritation. *Here, yet again, are two truths that cannot coexist.*

Ptah-mes's glance flickered to Hani, but he showed no emotion. Aper-el rose, and Ptah-mes followed suit. Aper-el was dressed in his long kilt of office, knotted under the armpits, his neck laden with *shebyu* collars of honor. His upper arms were clasped by priceless gold cuffs; earrings glittered at the edge of his expensive wig. Everything about him spoke of power. Yet someone had more power still.

Aper-el turned and swept off to the inner office, while Hani and Ptah-mes dropped into a bow. "We'll speak this evening," Ptah-mes murmured to Hani, and he followed the vizier.

Maya had entertained himself during his wait by mentally polishing the story he planned to tell about his foray into the City of the Dead. *A hostile ghost might spice things up some*, he thought, although he didn't want to scare the children. *Perhaps a ghost who begged for justice—yes, the* ba *of one of the victims of tomb robbery.* That would set the whole case in a moral perspective, and it was no doubt true on a spiritual level. And his hero, the Traveler—himself—would do battle with the guilty workmen, who wouldn't go quietly into the hands of the law. His stance would be implacable— for *ma'at* and against wrongdoers—even though the men crawled to his feet and begged him to be merciful toward a father of eleven. He realized he was conflating Lord Hani's recounting of the arrest with his own fact-finding mission, but his mother and aunts—not to mention the children—were more interested in entertainment than in historical accuracy.

Maya was so enthusiastically imagining the events, and even working out some wording here and there, that he was almost sorry when Lord Hani emerged from the office, his face set, his eyebrows drawn down. Maya climbed to his feet.

Hani waved a sealed packet of folded papyrus at Maya. "We have Aper-el's permission to go to the police office while Mahu himself is surveilling the closing of the Great Jubilee. If they're interested in keeping the law, they'll let us in."

"That's the day after tomorrow, isn't it?" Maya said in surprise. "The Jubilee is almost over."

"This case is dragging me down, Maya. I just hope we can clear Tulubri, because otherwise, Mane will suffer."

"Don't you think the evidence is stronger against that chamberlain of Lady Kiya?" Maya asked. "Anybody can borrow or steal a tunic, but a man's face is what it is."

"I just keep remembering how terrified Bebi-ankh became the night the Mitannians were in the house."

Maya absorbed this. The evidence was by no means univocal. They would have to do more investigating.

That evening, he and Lord Hani were still hashing over the facts of the case when Ptah-mes arrived at his house. He joined them in the garden, where they were sitting under the naked arbor, and sank wearily into his chair.

"You gentlemen have been busy," he said with a thin smile. "What's next?"

"We'll need to shave Tulubri. And we still haven't solved the mystery of Djau's murder. A young officer of our acquaintance is looking into the weapon. He thinks it's a cavalry arrow and believes he can identify the unit from which it came."

"If it was some renegade soldier our foreigner hired, that might not tell us much," Ptah-mes said. "But if the order came from higher up the official military hierarchy, we might as well stop investigating right now, because we know where that leads."

He clapped his hands, and a servant girl appeared, bowing. "Bring us a ewer of chilled wine and three cups," Ptah-mes said in a brusque voice.

That's why people think he's haughty and cold, Maya told himself.

Ptah-mes heaved a sigh and brushed his unwrinkled kilt mechanically. His eyes were fixed on some distant point, which gave him a hollow look. The wine arrived, and Ptah-mes, shaking off his gloom, poured each of them a cupful. Maya could feel his mouth watering. He remembered the exquisite wine of Kebni Ptah-mes had served them once before.

The commissioner handed out the cups and lifted his in a toast. "To the reestablishment of *ma'at*."

Whatever those cryptic words might imply, Maya and Hani seconded the wish enthusiastically. For once, they could be honest with their toast. So many of them were for the king.

"Apeny has been feeling a little under the weather,"

Ptah-mes said after they'd swallowed their wine. "I'll probably go back to Waset for a while, if you should need me. You can report on the shaving of Tulubri when you get home."

"My best wishes for her speedy recovery," Hani said graciously. But Maya was sure every man there was asking himself, *Is it the plague?*

♭

Hani stood among the diplomats of the foreign service, not far from the royal kiosk set up on the shore. Before them stretched the main street of Akhet-aten, swept and sprinkled. The foreign emissaries bringing gifts from their homelands would approach up the road, while the king received them from his shaded and flowery viewing stand. Around him stood his family and the plume-holding Fan Bearers. Hani watched the king's children more closely than the foreign bringers of tribute. The little Haru in the nest, the crown prince, was held in the arms of his eldest sister Meryet-aten, a pretty girl who had already surrendered her Haru lock for the clusters of braids of a marriageable maiden. The decorative lock that she wore over them marked her as the king's child—which she would ever be, no matter her age. At the sight of her, Hani remembered what Neferet had said about the mysterious events surrounding the birth of Prince Tut-ankh-aten and how the princess had witnessed at least half of the exchange of babies. *What must an eleven-year-old girl have thought? What must she think now of the little brother who, to her knowledge, is nothing of the sort?*

As soon as the procession of foreigners and vassals was well underway, drawing every eye, and the royal musicians filled the air with the wail of pipes and the clash of drums and cymbals, Hani edged inconspicuously out of the crowd. He'd left Maya in the audience, thinking that if anyone happened to observe his passage, the presence of a dwarf might stick in their mind more than yet another white-clad bureaucrat.

At intervals along the street, raised guard platforms stood, from the height of which the *medjay* scanned the crowds. Hani quitted the area of surveillance as quickly as he could and strode purposefully through the back alleys east of the processional way. No one was around; the presentation of exotic gifts had drawn them as relentlessly as gaudy flowers drew bees. Hani's footsteps clopped softly on the unpaved streets, the only sound except for cicadas, which had already begun their summer concert. Ahead of him stood the three-story tower that served as the headquarters of the city's police.

He entered with a firm step, even a bit of swagger, and announced himself to the scribe on duty in the reception room. "Hani son of Mery-ra, here by the vizier of the Lower Kingdom's orders, to interrogate the Mitannian prisoners."

He flashed his sealed papyrus at the man, who rose from the floor and bowed his way out, murmuring, "One minute, my lord."

A moment later, a youthful *medjay* with bronze-hard muscles approached Hani. "How can I help you, my lord? I'm afraid our chief is overseeing the security of the ceremony today, but I'll do what I can for you."

"I need to meet with the Mitannian prisoners. Their king is not happy with the way they were apprehended, and the Good God Nefer-khepru-ra wants me to interrogate them." Hani forced his voice to sound full of authority.

"Please follow me." The policeman took them to a heavy door reinforced with bronze bands and pushed up the external bar. Over his shoulder, Hani saw the two Mitannians jump to their feet nervously.

Hani pushed in and said to the guard, "That will be all. Lock us in, if you must, but these men are not desperadoes."

It was a small, ill-lit room with high, barred windows shedding the only light. Pirissi had grown a beard during his detention. Both men looked scruffy, their sleepless eyes wide with what might have been fear or hope. They smelled unwashed, and their fine woolen clothes were rumpled and dirtied as if they had been lying on the floor.

"Lord Hani!" cried Tulubri in relief, surging toward him. "Thank the gods you've come! They wouldn't let Keliya in to see us."

"I hope this means they're going to let us out," Pirissi said, clasping Hani's hands in turn.

"They haven't mistreated you, have they?" Hani drew a deep breath. How painful it would be to raise their hopes and then say, *I'm, sorry. You're guilty and have to stay.* "Before we do anything, I would like to request something of you, Tulubri. Have I your permission to shave off your mustache?"

The young man raised his eyebrows in surprise, nothing in his reaction suggesting the fearfulness of the guilty. "But of course," he said, confused. Hani perceived in the poor light that his eyes were a greenish brown—not exactly pale but not as dark as most people's.

Hani pulled the razor from the waist of his kilt. "I hope this won't scrape too badly. I have no soap."

Tulubri tilted up his head with no gesture of reluctance, and Hani began to shave his lip. He took the hair off the right side first and then, dreading what he was going to find, began to shave the other side. Tulubri didn't flinch.

He had a mole.

Hani's heart dropped. He stared at the young man, who returned his gaze innocently. Tulubri was nervous, but anxiety would be normal, given the circumstances. He seemed to have no fear of being exposed. *Perhaps he doesn't know the witnesses have described him.*

He looked up at Hani with questioning eyes. "Is that all, Lord Hani?"

Hani found breathing difficult all at once. He sat down and gestured to the two Mitannians to join him. "My friends, I must tell you this. Tulubri, you match perfectly the description given of the leader of the tomb robbers."

Tulubri looked horrified. He stared first at Pirissi, who had gone quite pale, then at Hani. "I, my lord? But Pirissi and Keliya can vouch for my whereabouts."

"You have a turquoise tunic, do you not?"

"I do, my lord."

"You have light eyes, dark brown hair, and a mole on your lip—"

"A mole?" He looked at Pirissi in confusion. He put a finger to his lip. "You mean this?" he picked the dark spot off with a nail. "It's a scab. I poked myself in the face with a stick—it sounds inane, I know—"

But Hani heard no more. Relief washed over him like a cool shower on a hot day. That same scab couldn't have been there months before, when the tomb robberies would have been organized. *Tulubri must be innocent. He can't be the only man in Naharin with a blue-green tunic.*

"Then, you *don't* match the description, and we need to get you out of here as quickly as possible, before Mahu returns."

Hani stood up and went to the door. He and the two prisoners were indeed locked in. "Guard!" he called. Sandaled footsteps came clapping up to the door, and the bar slid back with a rumble.

The wiry policeman stood before him. "Are you ready to leave, my lord?"

"Yes. And these men are leaving as well. They're unquestionably innocent."

The policeman looked startled and reluctant. He started to say something, but Hani flashed his official papyrus at the man, pointing to a line the *medjay* could, no doubt, not read. The man scratched his head uncertainly.

"I'll answer to your superiors. This order comes from Lord Aper-el."

"Very well, my lord," the policeman said, still not wholly convinced.

To the two Mitannians, Hani murmured in their language, "Get out of town as quickly as you can, and hole up in Mane's house."

They wasted no time in hustling away.

Hani turned back to the guard. "I'd like to see the prisoner Bebi-ankh now, my good man." His heart was pounding and his stomach tight at the thought that Mahu could walk in at any minute.

The policeman led him into a courtyard surrounded by

high walls, where the five incarcerated men sat or crouched along the shady side, squeezed together to stay out of the murderous sun. Hani could see from their bruised faces and tattered kilts that they had not been treated gently. Bebi-ankh had his broken leg stretched out in front of him. His broad face, which had begun to heal at Hani's, was once more swollen and purple. Hani felt a mixture of pity and guilt. "Bebi-ankh," he called.

The workmen all looked up, wide-eyed with fear. *It's my fault they're here*, Hani thought with a dull pang in his middle. *Or at least, that's how they will see it.*

Leaning on his crutch, Bebi-ankh struggled to his feet and limped over, his eyes puffy and suspicious. "You again, my lord."

Hani lowered his voice so the others couldn't hear. "Why did you flee, my friend? You were safe at my house."

"I heard... I heard men talking. It sounded like the foreigner. I was afraid you were in cahoots with him."

"Did you recognize his voice, or was it just the accent that scared you?" Hani pressed.

Bebi-ankh shrugged. "It sounded like him is all. Maybe it was just the accent; maybe it was the voice. Spooked me good."

Hani said, still speaking barely above a whisper, "I promised you protection, and I'll be faithful to my word. Get out of here and hide. Send word for your family at my house later. But hide right now, understand?"

Bebi-ankh nodded, hope beginning to come alight in his swollen eyes.

Hani turned to the policeman and said more loudly, "This man is wanted for questioning in the vizier's office. I take him into my custody." He put on his most authoritative tone, hoping the fellow wouldn't be too suspicious.

"Shall I shackle him for you, my lord?" the *medjay* asked.

"No, no," Hani said dismissively. "He can't run." With all the aplomb in the world, he turned and, taking Bebi-ankh roughly by the elbow, marched him out of the station.

The two men made their limping way just far enough down the street to be out of sight, then Hani turned to the painter. "Here is some silver for the ferry. Go now."

Still, no doubt, in a state of shock, Bebi-ankh mumbled his thanks, and he set off as fast as his splinted leg permitted.

Hani heaved a huge sigh of relief, like a man who'd just escaped death. The ebbing of his tension started to allow him to think about what he'd done. He said to himself, "You'd better hide, too, my friend. As soon as Mahu gets back, he'll know immediately who has relieved him of his prisoners."

❖

When Hani reached Waset five days later, he headed for Ptah-mes's house to report on what had happened since they last spoke. There was a heavy quiet over the estate that made a seepage of unease rise in Hani's gut—for precisely what reason, he couldn't say. The gateman was slow responding to his knock. Then Hani saw with a shock that he wore a white mourning scarf around his curly hair.

"Has there been a death in the household, my friend?" Hani asked in alarm.

"That there has, my lord," the gateman said in a quivering voice. "Lady Apeny has crossed to the West."

197

Hani's stomach clenched in horror. "May the Lady of the West have mercy on her and give her safe passage to the Field of Reeds," he cried. He sank to his knees, picked up a handful of dirt, and threw it over his head in the age-old gesture of the mortal in solidarity with the dead. "Lord Ptah-mes... how's he taking it?" He climbed heavily to his feet.

The gateman shook his head mournfully. "Hard, my lord. Very hard."

The relationship between Ptah-mes and his wife had been strange. He had decided to continue working for the present regime, while she, an employee of the Ipet-isut, had refused all cooperation whatever. But Hani appreciated that the commissioner had acted in conscience as surely as his wife. This loss had to fill Ptah-mes with guilt as well as sorrow.

"He's in the garden, my lord. He might well be glad to see you," said the gatekeeper.

With a heavy heart, Hani crunched over the gravel paths and made his way to the sheltered arbor where Ptah-mes was accustomed to sit. The new spring leaves were appearing on the grapevine, a sweet-smelling cloud of pale green. Beneath the vines, a figure was slumped over a small table, a ewer of wine at his elbow. At first, Hani didn't recognize him. Then the man looked up, fixing Hani with unfocused eyes, his thin cheeks streaked with tears and melting kohl. Hani gasped. Ptah-mes's whole face was smeared with dirt from the dust of mourning, and he wore no wig. Hani saw for the first time his balding head of short-cropped graying hair.

"Hani?" Ptah-mes said in a wavering voice. He tried to rise but fell unsteadily back into his chair.

Dear gods. He's drunk, Hani thought in pity and a kind of scalding embarrassment. Ptah-mes was always so magnificently in control of himself, so proper and elegant. It seemed almost obscene to see him this way, in his full human vulnerability—as if Hani had come upon him naked.

Hani hurried to his superior's side and laid a hand of comfort on his back "My lord, they told me at the gate. We'll make offerings for her. I'm... I'm so sorry for your loss." He could feel tears mounting to his own eyes under the onslaught of Ptah-mes's contagious grief. "Do your children know yet? I'd be happy to notify them if that would save you some trouble..."

"They know," the commissioner murmured, his speech slurred and weak. "They're in the house, seeing to things." He looked up with unfocused eyes. "But thank you." His head dropped again to his arms. "Thank you."

Hani's heart was knotted with almost unbearable pain for his superior and friend. Ptah-mes was not the cold and haughty man he seemed to many, Hani knew. And he loved his wife in spite of everything that had come between them. Her contempt had driven a dagger into his soul.

"Sit down, Hani. Have a drink," Ptah-mes mumbled, catching at Hani's arm. "Oh, there's only one cup..."

"It's all right, my friend. I'll gladly sit with you. I just wish there were something I could do for you."

"It was the plague," Ptah-mes said, his voice starting to harden. "She had a cold—that's all it was—and then suddenly, she had the plague. Where did she get the plague?

Did I bring it home to her from that accursed place we call the capital?" He looked up, his bloodshot black eyes burning through their tears. "Did *I* kill her, Hani?"

A ripple of fear made its way up Hani's spine. *Plague in Waset?* "No, my lord. Of course not. Lady Sekhmet takes whom she will, and there's nothing we can do."

A blast of hatred darkened Ptah-mes's desolate face. "Then it's him. It's *his* fault. The gods have turned their backs on Kemet because of his impiety. I can serve him no more."

Ptah-mes collapsed, his face down once more on his folded arms. Hani saw his back shaking and realized he was weeping. "I loved her, Hani. I loved her. I loved her even after she stopped loving me. And I let some stupid high-minded principle come between us. We were never reconciled. She died hating me."

Hani writhed within. He could never in a million years have imagined Ptah-mes coming unstuck like this. "She didn't hate you, my lord. She understood your struggle, and she admired you."

But Ptah-mes, for once without inhibitions, shook his head. "She was my cousin, four years older than I was. I worshiped her, even as a child. She was the perfect woman—beautiful, smart, well-bred. I was sixteen before I got up the nerve to ask for her hand in marriage. She bore me seven children, Hani." He lifted his head and repeated loudly, his voice raw. "Seven children. Doesn't anyone understand? I have seven children. If I let the king strip me of my property, what would I leave to them? I had no choice."

"You did the right thing, my lord. Nefer-khepru-ra

already had it in for you precisely because you were honest. You had no choice." Hani felt helpless before the man's self-contempt. He shook his superior's shoulder with a little grip of solidarity and wished he dared do more, but Ptah-mes wasn't a warmly demonstrative person, and even in the man's present condition, Hani wasn't sure what would be welcome and what would be seen as an intrusion.

"Shall I leave, my lord? Perhaps you want to grieve alone..."

Ptah-mes groped for the cup and ewer and tried unsuccessfully to pour himself more wine. Hani gently steadied his superior's shaking hand but couldn't keep the wine from sloshing over the front of Ptah-mes's expensive shirt. Ptah-mes managed to get some of it down, then the cup fell from his hands with a clang as he slumped bonelessly back upon the table. The commissioner was fast sinking into a drunken stupor.

"I'll go, my lord. Let me know if there's anything you need. We'll join you for the funeral, for sure. My condolences to you and your family."

Hani left Ptah-mes sprawled over the table and headed to the street as precipitously as he could, his face burning. *This is no time to bother him with work.*

⚜

When Hani arrived home, Nub-nefer greeted him with happiness written in her every gesture. He wrapped his arms around her and held her as tightly as he could, as if his body could protect her from harm. He murmured in an intense voice that reverberated with all the sweet swelling of his heart, "I love you, my dove. Whatever happens, know that that is true."

She drew back from him and smiled, curious. "What is it, Hani? Why this sudden passionate declaration? I had no doubt in my mind that you love me as I love you." She caressed his face with a slim hennaed hand.

"Lady Apeny has just died, and Ptah-mes thinks she didn't love him."

Her smile gave way to a look of grief and horror. Apeny had been her much-appreciated superior as a chantress of Amen. "Oh no! What happened?"

"Plague," Hani said grimly.

Nub-nefer's eyes grew wide in horror. "Here? We must take Baket-iset to the farm, then."

Hani remembered that his sister-in-law and her family were still living in hiding at his country estate while Nub-nefer's brother, the renegade priest, lay low. Apeny had been one of their go-betweens. "It will be a full house, but do it, my love."

Nub-nefer dropped her eyes. "If only we could get Neferet to safety too. Aha's managed to get an assignment traveling around to the various estates of the Aten." She looked up again, anger whitening the wings of her nose. "Which those thieving Aten priests have stolen from the Hidden One."

"If it keeps our firstborn safe, I'm inclined to forgive the usurping bastards," said Hani with a dry smile.

Hand in hand, they drifted toward the salon. "I'm devastated to hear about Lady Apeny," Nub-nefer murmured. "I so admired her. She was a *djed* pillar, a pillar of strength, for all those of us who—"

"Resist?" Hani finished under his breath.

Before she could answer, Mery-ra called from the inner doorway, "Ah, Hani. There you are, son. I have some information for you. Although I don't know how helpful it will be." He came toddling toward Hani, his face eager.

"What is it, Father?"

"Pa-aten-em-heb has reported back about the arrow. He says it was made for the Glory of the Horizon company of cavalry." Mery-ra raised an eyebrow. "Although that only limits the number of suspects somewhat. How many men in a company, by the face of Ra?"

"Well, better to have to examine two hundred men than an indefinite number. If only we knew who ordered the murder and why." Hani heaved a sigh and sank into his chair. "Ptah-mes's wife has died. He's come completely undone. I couldn't even tell him the latest in our investigations. Perhaps I should talk to the vizier."

"Is it that urgent, my love?" cried Nub-nefer. "You just got back."

Hani chuckled darkly. "Yes, well, I committed some pretty egregious sins against the *medjay* in Aper-el's name."

"Tell! Tell!" Mery-ra pressed avidly. He lowered himself to a stool at Hani's side.

Hani told him about the setting free of the Mitannians and the "escape" of Bebi-ankh. "Mahu will hang my hide up on his wall when he finds out. But Ammit take it, Tulubri is innocent. It wouldn't be according to *ma'at* to hold him."

Mery-ra looked uneasy. "No, it wouldn't. But I'd be careful with Mahu."

"From Akhet-aten, I'll go on up to Hut-nen-nesut and

arrest that Talpu-sharri. He's the only suspect left. Then hopefully we can wrap this case up."

"What about the murder of Djau?"

Hani stifled a curse. "I keep forgetting about the poor man. Maybe if we beard Talpu-sharri, he'll tell us why he did it. If he did it."

"How did he get hold of a cavalry arrow?"

Hani shot him a wry glance. "Someone would ask." He slapped his father companionably on the back. "That's what we have to find out."

Nub-nefer said, "If you're planning to go back to the capital tonight or tomorrow, Hani, my love, it won't do you any good. Everyone will have dispersed for the harvest festivals."

"You're right. Everything will be closed." To himself, Hani thought, *And poor Ptah-mes will have a little time to pull himself together before he's expected to be back on the job.*

"I hope Neferet will come home." Nub-nefer sighed. "Well, let's go out to the pavilion and eat. Baket-iset has been waiting out there all the while."

⬥

Hani, pleasantly stuffed after a midday meal of bread, cucumber salad, and fresh cheese, was heading to the staircase, preparing for a siesta, when he saw Bebi-ankh's wife, with her children clinging to her skirts, tiptoeing toward the vestibule.

"Mistress!" Hani called. "Has your husband called for you?"

She whipped around, wild-eyed, then relaxed when she saw Hani. "Yes, my lord. We thank you for your kindness.

He told me what you did for him." She was halfway to prostrating herself and kissing his feet, but Hani lifted her up.

"The only thanks I want is to see him one more time. I've come up with a few more questions I'd like to ask him." He patted the head of a pot-bellied toddler who clung to his mother's leg and gaped up at Hani.

She looked reluctant, her eyes shifting uneasily. But she was in Hani's debt. "Come with me, then, my lord."

He followed the family out through the garden burgeoning with spring green and ornamented by birdsong. They hastened down the packed-earth road with its empty mansions and headed north into the warren of poor little private homes and workshops that marked the less prosperous part of town. It was the hottest part of the day, and the air between the close-packed walls was suffocating, almost visible—thick and shimmering like molten glass. Hardly anyone was afoot at this hour. Hani mopped his forehead as he trailed after the woman.

She approached a door in a wall and, casting a furtive look around, knocked in a pattern that had to be a code. Almost immediately, the door opened, and Bebi-ankh, in his own short, disheveled hair, peeked out. A big grin spread across his bruised and burn-scarred face as he looked at his family—but as soon as he caught sight of Hani, his eyes widened in terror.

"It's only me, my friend, and your secret is surely safe with me," Hani said with a reassuring smile. "May I come in?"

Bebi-ankh backed away from the door to make room for his passage then, with another cautious glance around, shut the door softly behind him. "I didn't want anybody to know where I was."

Hani's smile broadened. "I *don't* know where you are. I could never find my way here again." He looked around him at the small unpaved court in which he stood. A modest house rose at his left, with a rolled-up mat hanging in the doorway.

"It's my mother's house," Bebi-ankh explained. "I came here until Iryet and the children could join me. Now we're going someplace less obvious. Maybe to Ta-nehesy. Surely, they could use artists up there."

"Then I'm glad I caught you before you got away. Is there somewhere we can talk?"

Bebi-ankh drew Hani behind the house, where a much-mended wooden pen held a goat and a few geese. He led him to the little reed goat shed, and the two men dodged inside. "We're safe here," he said with a twitch of the mouth. "The goat doesn't speak Egyptian."

"Were you aware that Djau was dead?" Hani asked point-blank.

Bebi-ankh shifted uneasily. "I suspected he would be soon if he weren't already."

"Why? He'd already made his report. What further danger was he to anyone?"

The painter eyed Hani up and down and said, incredulous, "Why, because he saw the foreigner, of course. And he wasn't up to his ears in crime, so he had nothing to lose by ratting him out."

The little bastard never told me that, Hani thought in surprise. "When did this happen?"

"I don't know when it was, my lord. Months ago. He

overheard me speaking to the foreigner on a street corner. I knew, because I saw his head peep around the corner. Then he took off. I ran after him, and when I laid hands on him, he suddenly had a coughing fit—or pretended to—and twisted away when I let him double up to cough. He ran into a nearby door, so I couldn't follow him."

Here I am again at the pool of Two Truths. Somebody's lying. "And what would have happened to him if he hadn't gotten away, Bebi-ankh?" Hani asked severely.

The painter hung his head then looked up again with a hopeless smile. "I would have bashed his self-righteous little skull against the wall, my lord."

Hani nodded slowly. Bebi-ankh wasn't a bad man, but he'd been desperate, fearing for his life. "I guess we can't indict you for something you *would* have done. Do you have any idea who *might* have finished him off?"

"The foreigner, no doubt."

"No, I mean, who pulled back the bowstring? He was shot with a cavalry arrow. Were there any soldiers involved with your plot?"

Bebi-ankh looked uncomfortable. "The workmen he brought in to dig and carry off the grave goods had that air about them. I mean, they weren't in uniform or anything, but they were all very clean-cut young men and proper. Not like some peasants he might have rounded up to do the stoop labor. You know—they were disciplined. Asked no questions. Just dug when they were told and carried all the spoil dirt off without a word."

That doesn't sound like cavalry people. They tend to be blue-blooded. I don't picture cavalry archers carrying dirt... unless orders came from high above. Although the workmen

207

might have been scouts or runners, who are usually commoners.
"I see your memory has been jogged," Hani said. "Anything else you know or suspect? Did the foreigner see Djau too? Did you tell him who the spy was?"

Bebi-ankh looked sheepish. "I did, my lord. He asked next time I saw him, and I answered. I... I was aware it probably meant Djau's days were numbered, but he knew that I was implicated."

Hani thanked the black-line man for his additional information and wished him well. Then he took his leave. It crossed his mind that Mahu might have put a tail on him as he had once before. *Get out now,* he willed Bebi-ankh silently. *Quick. Quick.*

Hani set off down the street, not knowing exactly where he was. He decided it would be best to head for the River and then south to his home by a familiar route. He turned along the broad processional way that flanked the River— the way where once the barque of Amun-Ra had passed, borne on the shoulders of the *wabu* at the time of the Ipet festival, accompanied by all the pomp and magnificence the most powerful priesthood in the world could provide. Hani thought of Nub-nefer marching along, singing hymns and shaking her sistrum rhythmically, her face alight with fervor. He remembered his brother-in-law, Amen-em-hut, in his starred leopard skin and jeweled sporran, proudly bearing the ram-headed standard of the god as the glittering procession passed from the Great Southern Temple back to the Ipet-isut. How the people had gathered on the banks and cheered!

Hani sighed. *Will the old days ever return?* Perhaps it

was a lack of faith, but sometimes he wasn't sure. *The power of the king is nearly absolute. Who can stand up against him?*

A faint, thin cry from the sky made Hani look up. High overhead, a hawk circled on graceful, deadly wings. Hani made his way to his gate and was about to knock when, from within the garden, he heard voices raised in anger.

"No, you may not search our house. How dare you. I told you, Hani isn't home," came Nub-nefer's outraged cry. A thrill of anger and fear rolled up Hani's spine.

Then a man's voice growled, "We'll see about that, mistress. Now, stand aside."

Mahu.

CHAPTER 9

H ANI BEGAN TO HAMMER WILDLY on the gate, furious as a jay defending its nest. "Open up! A'a! Open to me now!" he roared.

The gate opened a slit, and Hani burst his way in. "What's the meaning of this?" His face was burning, his heart ready to explode. He rushed to Nub-nefer's side, and she put her arms around him and hid her face against his chest.

Mahu and four of his men and their leashed baboon stood in the gravel path. The chief of police was scowling like a thundercloud. At Hani's precipitous entry, his angry expression turned to a snide smile. "Well, well. Look who's here."

"I told you he wasn't home," Nub-nefer shouted in a raw, accusing voice.

"What do you want?" Hani demanded, stepping between his wife and the policemen.

"You're under arrest for interfering with the king's justice," said Mahu, looking almost delighted.

Hani said haughtily, "I'm sorry your intelligence hasn't given you the rest of the story, Mahu. I was acting as the agent of the vizier of the Lower Kingdom and of the high commissioner. You'll have to take your grievance up with them." He was breathing hard through his nose, trying to restrain himself from the quivering violence he felt creeping along his body. His hands clenched in defiance. *Stay cool. Don't give in to a shouting match or worse.* "Go bully women somewhere else."

Mahu swaggered up to Hani, and the two men glared at one another, almost nose to nose. *Do not strike him. Do not strike him, no matter how much he deserves it.*

"I think we'll just take you in while we find out whether you're telling the truth or not," Mahu said through gritted teeth. His face had grown as crimson as a pomegranate.

"I have letters of mission, signed with the vizier's seal. You can read them for yourself."

Over Mahu's shoulder, Hani was aware of his father standing in the doorway of the house, his bristling eyebrows murderous. "Here, what's this?" Mery-ra cried as he surged into the garden. "My son has a royal commission. You have no right to apprehend him." He extended the packet of papyrus and unfolded it, holding it out toward Mahu but not relinquishing it.

Mahu ran a quick eye over the document but seemed reluctant to back down even in the face of evidence. However, his bravado had slipped a notch.

Hani said contemptuously, "Inquire of the vizier whether or not my actions are on his behalf. I had proof the Mitannians were innocent, and there was no longer any excuse to hold them. Their king has already made a complaint to Nefer-khepru-ra, and you'd better not aggravate the situation."

Mahu hung there, quivering with impotent rage, but he seemed to have doubts about crossing Aper-el. "We'll see whose commission will prevail, Hani. But I advise you to stay out of my way. You're making yourself very obnoxious."

"To whom, Mahu? To you?" Hani couldn't resist saying. "I'm trying to find out the identity of a criminal. To restore *ma'at*. To whom does that make me obnoxious?"

The apoplectic scarlet mounted in Mahu's face again, but he spun on his heel and, with his men in his wake, stormed out through the gate.

As the panels closed behind them, Hani let out his breath. "Thank you, Father. That was a timely entrance."

"Oh, Hani, I hate that man. He's abominable," Nub-nefer cried, embracing her husband. "He's just the sort of brute the king would use to do his dirty work."

"You seem to have gotten up his nose pretty badly, son," said Mery-ra, folding the papyrus.

"Yes. Mahu is never happy to see the truth come out. He's clearly protecting someone—at that someone's orders, I suspect."

"You seriously think the king is involved?" Mery-ra asked in a quieter voice.

"Or somebody close to him. Otherwise, why would Mahu be trying to obstruct my investigation? Why would he have been put on it in the first place? Why would he have any authority in Waset?"

Hani was silent, breathing in the perfume of bergamot and lilies that rose from Nub-nefer's body, while his thoughts spun. At last, he said pensively, "Where did that Talpu-sharri come from?"

"Naharin. What do you mean?" Mery-ra said.

"I mean how did he come to be Kiya's chamberlain? He certainly didn't come from Naharin with *her*. And I don't remember seeing him around two years ago." Hani blew out a breath. "I asked Neferet to ask around discreetly, but I haven't seen her since. I need to go arrest him as a suspect of tomb robbing. But it seems to me even that's not really going to solve our crime."

"Right now?" Nub-nefer asked reluctantly.

"I think I'd better, before someone tips him off. It will take nearly a week to get there." He turned to Mery-ra. "Father, send someone to tell Maya that we'll be leaving for Hut-nen-nesut tomorrow by midmorning."

"Bring Neferet back with you, Hani, if she hasn't already left." Nub-nefer pulled away and started into the house. "I need to tell Baket-iset what happened. If she heard those voices, she'll be worried. And then we'll get ready to go to the farm."

⁜

The next morning, Maya appeared at Hani's door as arranged, Sat-hut-haru with him. She and the children would be joining the other women at Hani's country place until danger of plague had lessened in the city.

"We had a little visitation from the chief of police yesterday," Hani told him with a sour smile. He described how Mahu had invaded Hani's home and bullied Nub-nefer and how Mery-ra had saved the day with Hani's written commission.

Maya swelled with outrage. "That piece of jackal shit. He never gives up."

"So now we need to take Talpu-sharri into custody before Mahu gets to him. That's why we're going up. And to fetch Neferet home for the holidays. Menna is giving us a half dozen of his soldiers."

"To bring Neferet home?" Maya said in mock surprise. "I know she's lively, but…"

Hani chuckled. "Let's hope that's the worst thing they have to face."

Hani considered and discarded the idea of trying to see Lord Aper-el, thinking he must surely be at home for the holidays. But then he decided he needed immediate confirmation of his mission—Mahu surely wouldn't wait to test him out.

As soon as the boat tied up at the capital five days later, he hurried to the Hall of Royal Correspondence. As he'd feared, Aper-el had gone. But his secretary permitted Hani to write a brief letter describing what he'd done and promised to give it to the vizier as soon as he came back to the office.

"Back to the boat and away, Maya," Hani said, feeling more cheerful now that the burden was off his back and onto Aper-el's. "The soldiers are waiting for us."

As they were crossing the courtyard toward the main road, he heard a voice cry, "Hani!" and he turned around in surprise. Pipi was hailing him from the corner of the court outside the hall of scribes. He jogged toward his elder brother in an ungainly gait, his belly bouncing and a big gap-toothed grin spread across his face. "Brother! I never see you anymore." His smile grew sly. "And I have something to tell you that you'll like."

"Is Nedjem-ib expecting?" Pipi and Nedjem-ib's youngest were eight, so that seemed unlikely, but one could never tell.

Pipi drew the two men toward the corner of the court, away from the occasional passerby. "No. Father told me about your investigation. I've been assigned to the reception hall on certain days." He lifted his chin with innocent pride. "And then yesterday, who should walk in but Lord Ay. He'd come to talk to the vizier, although Aper-el turned out not to be here. Ay is master of the king's horses, you know, and he had a soldier with him, a cavalryman. He was like a sort of aide de camp."

Hani had a suspicion he knew where this was going, and a fizz of excitement started bubbling within. "And?"

"While they were waiting in the reception hall for the vizier, they started to talk. There was hardly anybody else there, and their voices echoed more than they probably realized. And—*yahya*, Hani!" Pipi's boyish square-jowled face beamed. "What do you think they started to talk about?"

"What, man? Out with it," Hani said impatiently.

"The murder of that Djau, or at least, it sounded like it."

Sounded like it. Hani started bracing for a disappointment. "More specifics, please."

"Lord Ay said under his breath, 'Have they found the one who did it?' And the soldier said, 'No, my lord. And

215

they won't.'" Pipi looked up in delighted expectation of praise.

"That's all?" Hani didn't want to disappoint his well-meaning brother, but such a conversation could be interpreted in a number of innocuous ways.

"And then Ay said, 'Be as discreet with the next one, please.' And the soldier said, 'You can count on the son of Ah-hotep-ra.' Or something to that effect."

"Who is Ah-hotep-ra?" Hani said, pondering all this.

"Why, the soldier's father, of course."

"Or the father of someone else who is trustworthy. It does sound vaguely as if it might pertain to our case, but—"

"'But'?" cried Pipi, getting more and more excited. "It's practically an admission of guilt." He was all but jumping up and down.

"Are you going to come back to Waset for the holidays?" Hani asked, unashamedly changing the subject.

"I guess. I don't want to stick around this plague bed any longer than I have to." His little brown eyes sparkled. "Hani, let me help you investigate this case."

Hani laughed and cuffed his brother's head fondly. "What? Already bored with your new job as a royal scribe?"

Pipi made the irresistible pleading eyes of a hound.

That look must be part of our patrimony, Hani thought in amusement. *How many times have I seen it on Neferet's face?* "Take your family home, Pipi, and enjoy the holidays. We'll talk about this later."

He gave Pipi a hug to soften his disappointment, then Hani and Maya took off briskly toward the embarcadero. "Come on," said Hani, still chuckling. "We're keeping Menna's men waiting."

"Do you think there's anything to what he overheard, my lord?" asked Maya, trotting to keep up. His pen case clacked rhythmically as it bounced on his shoulder.

"Could be," Hani said. His amusement had changed to pensiveness. "Or not. We'll have to be very careful sniffing around the God's Father Ay. At least, we can try to find out who the son of Ah-hotep-ra is."

The two men clattered up the gangplank of their vessel, a fast army boat, and swung out into the current. In two or three days, they would be in Hut-nen-nesut and take Talpu-sharri into custody, charged with tomb robbing and probable murder.

But when they presented themselves at the gate of the House of the Royal Ornaments and asked for Talpu-sharri, the majordomo told them he was gone.

"Gone?" Hani exchanged a startled look with Maya. "You mean disappeared?"

"No, my lord," said the majordomo, looking shocked in his turn. "He went back to Naharin with Lady Kiya and the two diplomats."

"Well, then. I thank you for your time. Now, if I could see the Lady Neferet, the royal physician's young apprentice..."

"I'll see if she's here my, lord." The man bowed and scuttled away.

Maya was both surprised and not surprised. He shot Lord Hani a grim, knowing look. "That's practically an admission of guilt, my lord. The son of a dog has run away out of our reach."

"Perhaps," said Hani thoughtfully. "Or perhaps he simply accompanied his mistress to serve her needs, as a chamberlain might be expected to do."

"What do we do now?" Maya persisted. *He's guilty as can be, the rascal.*

"We probably go after him."

A flush of warlike eagerness spread over Maya. Life had become a little boring lately, since he and Hani had stopped traveling abroad, and his stories had begun to suffer. He was ready to see the world again and smash a few foreheads.

At that moment, a happy cry rent the air. "Papa! Maya!"

Out of the inner doorway, Neferet ran to them— oblivious to her dignity as a grown woman and a *sunet*—and threw herself exuberantly upon her father. "You came to get me! Oh, good! I want you to meet my friend Bener-ib." She gestured to a girl who had followed her in and now stood behind her in polite silence. Neferet dragged her forward by the elbow.

Bener-ib was a small, neat, delicately built young woman with a pointed, sharp-featured face and a grave expression. She made a polite bow.

Well-bred at least, Maya thought. The higher he rose in society, the less he could tolerate vulgarity.

"Bener-ib was studying medicine with the *wab* priests at Sau, but when the temple of Sekhmet was closed, she came up to Akhet-aten to study with Lady Djefat-nebty," Neferet informed the men breathlessly. "Her father is a doctor and a friend of Lord Pentju. She knows e-e-everything." Neferet put an arm around her friend's shoulders and squeezed her proudly, while the other girl blushed.

"Can she spend the holidays with us?"

"Hello, Bener-ib," Hani managed to get in. He turned back to his daughter. "I suppose so, but I must tell you that there's plague in Waset, too, now, and your mother and Baket-iset are at the farm."

"Oh, we're not afraid of plague, Papa. Are we, Bener-ib? We're around it all the time."

Lord Hani flinched. *The girl seems mighty cavalier about a deadly disease,* Maya thought dryly. *The young always think they're immortal.*

"Are Bener-ib's parents aware that she'll be with us? Where do they live, my dear—in Sau?"

"Yes, my lord," said Bener-ib in a childlike voice that seemed at odds with her serious mien.

A woman of few words, Maya thought.

Neferet had enough words for the two of them. "Papa, your friend Lady Kiya has left." Her voice dropped to a loud whisper. "Don't tell anybody, but she was pregnant." She grinned mischievously, baring the space between her front teeth that made her look even more like a female version of Hani.

Maya felt a hot wave of outrage burning its way up his cheeks. *Scandalous! The king is well off without that little she-cat.*

Hani shot Maya a resigned glance. Lord Hani had tried so hard to get Kiya to the Two Lands, had so often intervened to save her from her own folly. *And look at her. Ingrate.*

"When did she leave, my duckling?" Hani asked.

"Only yesterday, Papa."

Hani turned to Maya and said, hope brightening his voice once more, "Then we can still catch them with our fast military vessel. Maybe they haven't left the country yet."

"And," Neferet said smugly, "I found out when Lady Kiya's chamberlain came. It was not quite a year ago. He claimed to be a friend of her father's or somebody who had served him or something—everybody I asked had a different version—and she hired him on the spot. Really eager, if you follow me." She turned to Bener-ib and snickered. "Apparently, she was a bit sweet on him."

"Thank you, little duckling. Your information is very valuable," Hani said with a smile. "I just hope you didn't make yourself too conspicuous with your questions."

"No, no, Papa. I was ve-e-ery discreet. May Lady Ma'at boil my eyeballs and pull out all my hairs one by one if I wasn't!"

Hani laughed, filled with love for his daughter. Then he turned to his secretary. "We have work to do." He gestured to Maya and the girls. "Come on, my friends. Back to the boat. We're heading north."

They hustled out in a motley procession and, oblivious to the beauties of the flowering city sacred to Haru, pounded down to the quays, where their boatload of soldiers waited. Hani herded the two girls up the gangplank, and Maya followed.

Hani found the captain of the boat and told him, "There's a royal yacht a day ahead of us on the River. They're no doubt heading for Men-nefer or Iunu, and from there, they'll go overland across the desert to Naharin. We must try at all costs to overtake them before they disembark. Once they're on the road, it will be almost impossible."

The captain saluted, and Maya heard him yelling out

orders to his men, who scrambled to their benches and pulled out their paddles. The boat eased out into the current and then shot off to the rhythmic splash of its rowers.

"Where are we going, Maya?" Neferet asked her brother-in-law. "Isn't this in the opposite direction from Waset?"

"We're going after a murderous tomb robber, my girl," Maya said, throwing out his chest a little. He turned to face the wind and inhaled a deep breath with satisfaction. The air was damp and musky and cooler by far than it had been on land. "What a story this will make!"

❖

Midmorning the following day, Hani's boat overtook the small yacht that had belonged to Kiya in her days as Greatly Beloved Wife. He had one of the soldiers hail it down as they passed in front of it.

"Pull over! Pull over! Go ashore in the name of the king!" the fellow cried, waving his arms. His voice carried well over the water, and Hani saw the sailor on the prow of the yacht gesticulating to his fellows. Soon, a man who had to be the captain appeared at the gunwales and signaled his acquiescence. The boat veered toward the east bank, and the pursuing military boat followed suit, cutting the other craft off in case, for some reason, it should try to flee.

"What's this all about?" shouted the captain of the yacht.

"We're going to board you—king's orders. Anchor, and put out your gangplank," Hani called in loud voice.

He saw Kiya emerge from the cabin and heard her little voice cry, "What's going on?" Then she spied him standing on the deck of the military boat and broke out into a smile as she waved to him. "Hani! You came!"

She was going to be shocked and disappointed at the role he was preparing to play. Hani himself felt no pleasure. But he anticipated the imminent arrest of Talpu-sharri with a grim eagerness. This case had dragged on too long.

"Neferet, my duckling, I want you and Bener-ib to stay on the boat, no matter what. Do not get off. Do you understand?"

"Of course I understand, Papa. What's happening?" She stared across the increasingly narrow water between their boat and the yacht and waved at Kiya.

"We're here to arrest someone on that boat. He may be desperate and dangerous. Maya will stay here to keep an eye on you."

Maya shot him a look of disbelief from the other side of her.

"I want to go, too, Papa. What if someone is injured?"

Ammit take it, Neferet can always be counted on to make objections. "No," Hani said roughly. "Stay here. This is an army maneuver, and girls have no place in it."

She fell silent but not in defeat. The stubborn lip was set in place. "Why don't girls ever get to do anything fun?" she said accusingly. "You still treat me like a child."

"I would say the same thing to your mother, Neferet. This isn't fun; it's serious business for professionals. You can't come. It's dangerous."

The boat jerked as it struck the bank gently. The yacht had begun to slide out its gangplank, the lower end of which fell with a crash to the bank. Soon, the military boat did the same. The soldiers gathered, spears and axes in hand, and prepared to disembark, Hani at their head.

"Oh, no you don't, my girl," Maya cried out. He grabbed Neferet's arm and pulled her back as she edged toward the gangplank. "Your father said you couldn't go."

"I suppose tending plague victims isn't dangerous. Do you think I'm afraid?"

At the end of his wits and beginning to grow tense over his own impending danger, Hani roared, "Stay here, I tell you."

He felt a pang of regret when he saw her shrink back, wide-eyed. *But by the seven-headed demons, the girl won't obey an order given in a normal voice.* He turned and stomped down the gangplank, leaving his daughter watching sullenly from the deck, Maya planted wide-footed at her side, hands on his hips.

Hani strode across the gravelly bank to the gangplank of the yacht. Kiya stood at the top, beaming. Tulubri and Pirissi approached from behind the cabin, looking curious.

The soldiers marched purposefully up the plank of the yacht, their footsteps reverberating on the ribbed boards. Kiya met them at the top, surrounded by a bevy of her handmaids, with Tulubri and Pirissi standing behind her, looking uncertainly at the armed men.

"Are you going to come with me after all?" the princess cried in delight.

"No, my lady. You're in good hands with these two gentlemen. I have come... I've come for your chamberlain. Could you call him for me?"

"Of course." Her dazzling smile deepened. As soon as

she had stepped away, Pirissi said under his breath, "What is it, Lord Hani? Why the guard?"

"We may have found our tomb robber. I think it's Talpu-sharri."

The Mitannians exchanged a round-eyed look. "Does he have a mole on his lip?" asked Tulubri.

Hani stared at him. "You mean you haven't seen him?" he cried.

"No, my lord. Our countryman seems to have been under the weather. He's kept to the cabin since we embarked."

Suspicion smoldered like an unquenched ember under Hani's breastbone. "How strange," he said. He was hardly surprised when Kiya came back at a run, her skirts flying, and wailed, "He's gone! Talpu-sharri is gone!"

"Search the boat," Hani barked at the soldiers, and they dispersed to comb the deck and hold—anywhere a man might hide. "When was the last time you saw him, Lady Kiya?" Hani put on a severe face. He knew she was no more honest than she had to be.

"Right after he entered," she said, her face puckered in distress. "He said he was feeling ill and that he was afraid it might be the plague and that I'd better stay out of the cabin. The crew pitched me a little tent last night."

"The slippery bastard," muttered Hani, a huge weight of disappointment descending upon him. *So close.*

"It would have been all too easy to sneak off the boat last night in the dark," Pirissi said. "Everyone's so afraid of the plague that no one would want to get too close."

Hani was steaming with frustration. He faced the soldiers, who were starting to trickle back after turning everything on the deck upside down. "That's it, men. Our prey has escaped. Back to Akhet-aten with you." To the two diplomats, he said, "May the gods grant you a safe journey, my friends. Get our girl home safe."

"We'll never forget what you did for us, my lord," said Tulubri with feeling. "Our king will hear what a good friend you have been to Naharin."

They parted reluctantly, Kiya weeping brokenheartedly in the arms of her ladies. Before he stepped upon the gangplank to descend, she murmured to Hani through her tears, "Why is no one faithful to me, Hani? I only want somebody to love me."

He marched down, somber and filled with pity for the unhappy princess, who asked so little and so much.

⁂

Maya had watched the action aboard the yacht with incomprehension. *Why didn't they arrest Talpu-sharri as planned?*

At his side, Neferet said to her friend, "You see? They didn't even fight. We could have gone with them."

"Let's see what happened first before you get smug, my girl," Maya said in warning. They waited while Hani trudged heavily up the gangplank, his thorny eyebrows knit in dissatisfaction. "What happened, my lord?"

Hani let out a long breath through his nose. "The son of a dog has absconded. He pretended to be sick, and then he slipped off the boat, probably when they put ashore last night."

"How did he know we were coming for him?" Maya cried in disgust. "Who could have told him?"

Hani shook his head, his mouth quirking bitterly. "We may or may not ever learn that. But we have to figure out what to do next." He glanced at the two girls. "We need to get these ladies back to Waset for the holidays, then you and I will do some sniffing around. I want to know why those three tombs were targeted first—or exclusively. Because I hope to Ma'at that there will be no more."

"May that be so, my lord," Maya replied fervently. "With Talpu-sharri in flight, I can't foresee that there will be more robberies."

Hani frankly didn't know what was going on. *How did that wretch know we were coming—or was he already planning to jump ship? Surely he wants to get back to Naharin. There's a price on his head here.*

While the soldiers disembarked at the capital, Hani made a visit to Aper-el, hoping that he would be in the office still before the Hall of Royal Correspondence emptied for the holidays. He needed to be sure the vizier was aware of his actions and was ready to cover him when Mahu pounced. But again, he could only leave a message to be handed over on the vizier's return. Hani was deeply uneasy. *Who knows when my letters will be delivered?*

The rest of the trip to Waset passed without mishap, and at last, the four of them made their way up the garden path to the door. It stood open except for the matting that kept out flies. Mery-ra met them in the vestibule with outspread arms. "Hani! And look who's here—Neferet!"

"And Neferet's friend, Bener-ib," his granddaughter said enthusiastically, drawing her friend forward. Bener-ib nodded respectfully, still looking serious and uncomfortable. "She's Lady Djefat-nebty's new student. She lives in Sau, but her parents said she could spend the holidays with me. Isn't that wo-o-onderful?"

"It is, but the other women are down at the farm." Mery-ra turned to his son. "Are we all going down?"

"You can if you want to accompany the girls, Father. I think I'll stay here. There are still leads to be pursued. For one thing, I want to look into the men whose tombs were robbed—see who they were and what sort of enemies they might have had in common."

"We want to stay here, too, Papa," said Neferet. "It's boring in the country."

She used to love going out on the marshes with me to look at birds, Hani thought with a mixture of amusement and sorrow. Her childhood was over, and she had her own interests now. "Don't you want to see Mama and Baket-iset?"

"Of course. But there are going to be so many people down there if Aunt Anuia and her family are still around."

"And you don't want to be stuck babysitting your cousins," said Mery-ra with a knowing wink.

She snickered guiltily.

"You can stay here if you want, my duckling," Hani said. "But I'll be busy."

"Maybe we can help you."

"No, and that's my last word on the matter," Hani said severely.

"But what if you need medical advice? What if your best witness dies and you have to find out if he was poisoned?"

Hani only wished he knew who his best witness was. "All right," he conceded. "If that happens, I'll call on you."

Neferet looked at her companion in triumph. "I'll show Bener-ib to Sat-hut-haru's room. She can sleep there."

"Very well, my dear. You're the mistress of the house at the moment." He turned to Maya. "Do you want to go down with your family, Maya?"

"If you don't need me..." The secretary looked apologetic.

Mery-ra said to his son, "I can help you, my boy, so Maya can have the holidays with his little ones."

So it was decided. That afternoon, Maya set off for the country house, and Hani sat down with his father to bring him up-to-date on the case. "When we went on board Kiya's yacht to apprehend Talpu-sharri, he'd already gotten away. Someone must have tipped him off."

Mery-ra grunted skeptically. "I'm not surprised. Mark my words; he's more than he appears to be—a mere servant."

"Any insights hidden behind that cryptic remark, Father?" Hani said with a grin.

"Not yet. It's just a gut feeling. What else has happened?"

"I ran into Pipi, and he said he'd overheard Lord Ay talking with some soldier about how they had gotten away with it once and the soldier had better be just as careful next time." Hani raised his eyebrows. "Pipi assumed they were talking about the murder of Djau, I think, but it might as easily have been any number of other things."

"So what are you planning to do in the meantime, son?" Mery-ra asked.

"Did you know a man named Ah-mes? Someone named Pa-ren-nefer? Sa-tau?"

"I knew none of them personally, but by reputation, yes. They were all high functionaries at court—first of

Neb-ma'at-ra, then of his son. Why?" Mery-ra eased himself down on a chair, and Hani did likewise.

"Theirs were the tombs that were robbed," Hani said, reflective. "I wondered if they had anything in common— if they'd gotten on the wrong side of the king somehow. Or had dealings with Mitanni."

"Let's go ask their families. I can pretend to be a friend come to pay my respects."

"So they were men your age?"

"More or less, yes. That is to say, reverend gentlemen full of years and wisdom."

Hani pretended to swat Mery-ra, but he couldn't help laughing. "So you're reverend, are you, you old rascal? If you weren't my favorite father, I don't know what I'd do to you!"

❖

Hani and Mery-ra made a visit that very afternoon to the villa of the Osir Ah-mes. The gatekeeper showed them into the luxurious mansion, and before long, a tiny older woman entered, dragging one leg. "My name is Henut-tawy. Can I help you, my lords?" she asked hospitably in a sweet, melancholy voice.

Hani bowed respectfully. *I should do this for my own reverend father, I suppose*, he thought with amusement. "My lady, my name is Hani son of Mery-ra. I am the king's investigator in the robbery of your husband's tomb."

"And I am Mery-ra, his father. I was close to our dear departed Ah-mes." Mery-ra sighed dramatically. "How we all miss him," he said, hands piously folded over his broad belly.

The little lady's face grew bright. "Oh, bless you. Only a few people have bothered to come by since the funeral. They don't seem to realize how hard it is on those who survive—those who are left with nothing but memories. We were married for fifty-two years, my lords. Do you think it's easy finding myself alone?" Her eyes grew misty, but she took Mery-ra's hands in delight. "Tell me about him, Lord Mery-ra. You knew him. How was he at work? Did people like him?"

Mery-ra shot his son an uncomfortable look, but he said gamely and with feeling, "We all loved him, my lady. Loved and admired. He was a... a beacon to us." He cleared his throat as if to purge himself of the lie.

Hani suppressed a laugh.

"Oh, how happy that makes me. Because sometimes Ah-mes felt he wasn't appreciated." She searched both their faces for comprehension. "Under the new king, I mean—life, prosperity, and health to him, of course."

"It's hard for us of the old guard, I know," said Mery-ra, nodding.

The woman's voice dropped. "His heart was here in Waset, Lord Mery-ra. You understand what I mean. The young were willing to be buried in that new place, but Ah-mes wanted to be laid to rest near his ancestors. Wouldn't you?"

"Indeed, we would," said Hani. "Our tomb is not far from your husband's."

She took Mery-ra's hand and then Hani's and squeezed them, as if to form a bond among the three of them. "The moment I saw you, I knew you were good men. True friends."

"Yes, indeed," Hani said in his kindliest voice. "And so, as a friend and an investigator, my lady, let me ask you a few questions, if you will. We want to know if the three men whose tombs have been robbed lately had anything in common. If they were targeted or were simply random victims."

Ah-mes's widow gestured for them to be seated and took her own seat upon a splendid chair that barely let her toes touch the ground. Mery-ra bounded up and gallantly slid a footstool under her little sandals. She had to lift her left leg with both hands.

"Ask me anything, my dear friends."

"You said your husband felt unappreciated. Did he have any enemies? Rivals or political opponents?"

She gave a tinkling little laugh, brushed ever so lightly with bitterness. "Hani, my dear, he was master of the Judgment Hall. Of course he had enemies. But anyone who would do this terrible thing to him? I can't imagine, can you?"

Alas, thought Hani, *I can imagine only too well. Some people would rob their own mother's tomb for gold.*

"Did Ah-mes have anything to do with Naharin, my lady?"

She looked confused. "Naharin? Why, no. Why would he?"

"A Mitannian seems to be involved with the robberies," Hani said in a confidential tone.

Henut-tawy put a shocked hand over her mouth. "You know, now that I think of it, there was that nice young man who came to see him immediately before he died. I'm not sure he was a Mitannian, but he was a foreigner for sure.

231

It was the very evening Ah-mes died. He never told me why the man was here, because within hours, he had an apoplectic fit." Her voice trembled, and she lowered her head.

"Might Ah-mes have refused to lend him gold or something?" Mery-ra asked. "Our dear old Ah-mes was so well loved for his generosity that I can easily imagine someone coming for a loan."

"Yes, he had a heart of gold, although the face he showed to the world was often gruff," Ah-mes's widow said, the tender memories flitting across her withered little face. "It's altogether possible the man came for gold."

"Could you describe the Mitannian for me, my lady?" Hani asked gently.

But she shook her head. "Oh, I don't remember much. He was tall and nice looking. A beard, like a collar around his jaw. Very courtly."

"By any chance, a mole on his lip?"

Henut-tawy laughed ruefully. "I don't see that well, my lord. He may have had, at that. But I can't tell you for sure."

Hani rose, and Mery-ra heaved himself up too. He bent and took the little mistress of the house's hands and bowed over them. "A pleasure to meet you, my lady. Dear Ah-mes always spoke of you with such affection that we all felt we knew you."

"You're too kind, dear friend. It makes me so happy to hear that. Do come back any time. I would love to hear some of your stories about Ah-mes." She smiled at them with sorrowful sweetness.

Hani thanked her for both of them, and the two men made their exit. Once out in the street, Hani threw back his head and laughed. "'Our dear old Ah-mes'! He was probably a despicable curmudgeon who beat his poor little wife!"

"How could you say that about my friend, Hani?" Mery-ra said in mock horror. "You never knew him like I did."

"Which is to say not at all, you old fraud!" Hani shook his head, chuckling. The two men set off down the street, elbow to elbow. "What I can see is that you're the one who needs to be interviewing the widows. You could make a rock weep."

"That's a good idea, son. Pipi and I can approach the families of the victims of this fellow while you look into Djau's killer—who is almost certainly the same person. You see how your Mitannian was involved in the first victim's life?"

But Hani had lost him with the first sentence. He stopped and gaped at his father. "Pipi?" he demanded suspiciously.

"He's coming home for the long holiday, of course, and he's very eager to help you."

"Father, Pipi—for all that I love him—is the last person in the Two Lands I would want on a sensitive case. He can't hold his tongue any more than Neferet can." Hani rolled his eyes, feeling trapped. "I hope you haven't said anything to him about it."

Mery-ra shrugged. "Nothing definitive," he said vaguely.

"I thought Maya or Pa-kiki might help me."

"Pipi's not stupid, you know, Hani. He told you about

that conversation he overheard between Ay and a soldier, didn't he?"

"Yes, Father. And I have absolutely no idea if there was anything sinister in it," Hani said glumly. "Am I supposed to go to Lord Ay's wife and pretend to be his friend?" The talk of friends reminded Hani of Ptah-mes. *I ought to go see him. He needs to be filled in on what is going on, if he has recovered enough.* "Let's go home and drop you off, then I'm heading for Ptah-mes's house."

But to Hani's amazement, when they reached his home, A'a told him in a whisper, "Lord Ptah-mes is in your garden, my lord."

Mery-ra faded discreetly into the doorway while Hani made his way through the garden to the pavilion, where the family often ate on summer nights. In the shade of the vine-covered porch, he could see the gleam of white linen. He increased his pace and knocked tentatively on a column. "Lord Ptah-mes?"

The high commissioner rose from Hani's chair, slim and tall and elegantly attired in his usual fashion except for the mourning scarf around his head. Hani tried not to remember him as he'd last seen him, wigless and undone.

"Hani, my friend," Path-mes said in a low voice. "I apologize to you for the spectacle the other day. I wasn't myself."

"No apologies needed, my lord," said Hani kindly. "I compassionate your grief, believe me. If anything were to happen to Nub-nefer, I'm sure I would react just the same."

The two men seated themselves. Ptah-mes looked brittle and ravaged, his eyes circled with black. Hani had the feeling it wouldn't take much to make him lose control again.

"Can I offer you beer?"

Ptah-mes nodded, a forced smile on his lips, and Hani called out to a servant girl to bring them a pot or two of the herb-flavored brew of which Nub-nefer was the master.

The beer arrived. The two men sucked on their straws and then sat in silence. Ptah-mes stared into space, his mouth drawn down.

He looks less alive than his ka *statue*, Hani thought in pity. "I need to fill you in on what has been happening on our tomb robbery case, my lord. Whenever you feel…"

But Ptah-mes's eyes snapped back from their distant reverie, and he said acidly, "Tell me, Hani. The king's business can't wait for my feeble spine to stiffen up."

He hates himself, Hani realized with a pang. *He may never be all right again.* He told his superior what they'd learned about the arrow, Talpu-sharri's sudden appearance and disappearance and the botched arrest, and Pipi's overheard conversation. "At the moment, my lord, my father and I are interviewing the families of the victims to see if they had anything to do with each other or with Naharin. And it turns out Lord Ah-mes received a tall foreigner the very evening he died of an apoplexy. He was, as well, I think, dissatisfied with the regime. His wife was careful about what she said, but that was the sense I took."

Ptah-mes glanced at him sharply. "Well done, my friend. It will be interesting to see how the others are implicated."

"I've been unable to reach the vizier. He must be at home in Men-nefer for the holidays."

"I don't know," said Ptah-mes, who usually knew

everything about everyone. He lapsed once more into silence then finally rose and brushed down his kilt, which hung as neatly as if he'd never sat. "I leave you, Hani. Your support is appreciated."

Hani clasped his superior's arm in a gesture of solidarity. Ptah-mes started down the gravel path, his fashionable sandals with their curled-back toes crunching on the stones. Hani accompanied him to the gate and waited until he'd mounted his litter. As the bearers set off, Hani waved, sorrow a leaden lump in his belly.

Maya had found that, as much as he loved the company of his family, the quiet life of the country suited him little. The whole time he'd spent in the overcrowded quarters at Hani's modest farm, he'd been thinking longingly of all the avenues of investigation that remained to be pursued in the tomb-robbing case. And so he'd returned to Waset.

A'a admitted him to Lord Hani's garden, where voices from beyond the bushes told him that Hani and Mery-ra and Hani's brother, Pipi, were talking and laughing there somewhere. He called out, "Lord Hani?" and emerged onto the porch of the garden pavilion, where the three men sat— remarkably similar in appearance, all broad and thickset to the point of squatness with jovial square-jowled faces and humorous little eyes.

"Ah, Maya, my friend," Hani said. "Have you given up on country life?"

"I'm afraid so, my lord. Things were pretty crowded." Maya, who was an only child, had a low tolerance for familial chaos.

Hani laughed. "Well, you'll be useful here, no question. Here are the things I want to look into—"

"Interview the two remaining families—that's my job," Lord Mery-ra interposed. He put on a look of martyrdom. "It's been sad, losing so many of my friends at one time."

His two sons snickered.

Hani said, "Maya, you can go talk to Ankh-reshet, the overseer of the workmen in the Place of Truth. Find out what he saw regarding Djau's death. Pursue any leads he might give you. And I... I'll check around the cavalry for more information about that arrow."

"What about me?" asked Pipi, an edge of hurt in his cheerful face.

Hani tried to look encouraging. "Well, you can try to find out who that officer was. But do not, Pipi, *do not* sniff around Lord Ay. We can't afford to draw his wrath down on us, or the king will shut down the case. At the moment, I have a certain amount of cachet in his eyes because I helped his daughter become coregent or whatever she is. We can't squander that." He took them all in with a look. "Everyone, keep your eyes open for our mysterious Talpu-sharri. If he didn't leave the country, it's for a reason."

Maya nodded solemnly. This was his sacred commission in company with these three highborn men. He was one of them—not just a secretary but an investigator. A peer. "I'll head over to the West immediately, my lord," he said with a touch of self-satisfaction.

They dispersed then, and Maya set out toward the quay in search of a ferry. A brief while later, he found himself on the arid banks of the City of the Dead. The last time he had been there, it had been in the cool of the season of growth. Now the sun beat down even in midmorning, so that walking across the baked, stony sand was like sticking his head into the goldsmiths' forge in his childhood home. The heat radiated up through the soles of his sandals. It was hard to breathe, and sweat began to prickle on his back and dribble from beneath his round wig. He cast a squinting glance around him at the whitewashed, pyramid-roofed burial chapels of the artisan class that surrounded him. Over there somewhere was his father's tomb. Maya cast a little prayer in the direction of this father whom he barely knew.

He trudged upward and to the south, flanking the cliffs of the Western Mountains. At last, the white wall of the workman's village gleamed against the dun of the surrounding landscape. Maya wished that he'd thought to bring a gourd full of water.

The gate was open, and people thronged the streets. *Perhaps it's market day.* Certainly, all the workmen would be home and not up in their remote weekday work camp.

He followed the streets he remembered from his first visit with Lord Hani. The crowd jostled him heedlessly, an elbow in the face here, a hip in the back there. But he was used to it. He adjusted the writing case on his shoulder to remind the world that he was a royal scribe on a mission. *One will do all you say if you are versed in writing,* he reminded himself in the words of one of Lord Hani's aphorisms.

At Ankh-reshet's red gate, he rapped and was admitted. He had forgotten how prosperously decorated the garden was, despite the absence of wells. The woman who answered the gate led him into the vestibule and called, "Ankh-reshet! There's a dwarf here to see you."

Maya forced down a wave of annoyance and managed to greet Ankh-reshet with a cool, official expression. "I am Lord Hani's secretary," he said frostily. "I'm here to interrogate you about the death of your draftsman Djau."

"Ah, most unfortunate." Ankh-reshet gestured Maya into the salon, where the two men seated themselves on the floor.

Maya took out his scribal tools and prepared to write.

"He was a superb draftsman. I haven't found anyone who can really replace him." Ankh-reshet settled his angular frame and leaned toward Maya with an eager gleam in his eye. "Have you found out anything?"

"The investigation is proceeding," Maya said blandly. "Tell me how you found him."

"He didn't show up for work, and the men were waiting for him. The fellows finally said we ought to go look for him. So I did. He was lying on the trail with an arrow sticking up out of his back." Ankh-reshet shook his head. "Waste of an arrow, if you ask me. He couldn't have lived long anyway." He looked up. "Bad lungs, you know."

"In the back, you say? Straight in or from the side?" Maya was picturing the terrain and realized that if the man had been shot from the cliffs or some cleft in the rocks, the arrow would have gone in from above and to the right.

"Straight in, I'd say. Standing straight up out of his back." Ankh-reshet blew out his breath and mopped his forehead. "I hope I never have to see anything like that again."

"Hmm," Maya murmured. *The shooter must have been*

on the trail behind him, although an arrow, even a short-range one like this, can be shot from some distance. How is it Djau didn't see or hear him?

"What were the conditions? Weather? Where you found him? Time of day?"

The overseer pushed back his wig and scratched his head. "It was midmorning, right about this hour. Hot, but not as hot as it is now. There was a lot of wind blowing, I remember. I had to cover my eyes to see where I was going, the sand was so bad. It was in that rocky bit just before the trail begins to get steep, where you can start to see people's mortuary chapels against the cliff front."

Maya eyed him skeptically. "Within sight of the tombs? And no guards saw what was going on?"

"That's a good point. I hadn't thought of that. In fact, I don't remember seeing any guards. That's been a problem lately, hasn't it? Those tombs wouldn't likely have been robbed if there had been guards on duty, would they?" Ankh-reshet looked surprised at this revelation.

We've learned something that may be important, Maya told himself, elated.

After the overseer had assured him he could think of no other details, Maya struck off down the street, beaming with satisfaction. Lord Hani would surely find this information useful. He'd gotten as far as the gate when it occurred to him he should talk to the tomb guards. They might be defensive, of course, if they'd been derelict in their duties, but maybe one would rat out the others. He turned uphill instead of downhill and proceeded to trudge up the rattling scree of the trail while the midday sun crushed him. He could feel it burning like a flame on the back of his neck.

A parched wind hissed past and caught up its skirts in a swirling little cyclone full of ocher dust.

By the time he reached the now-empty workers' camp, he was crackling with thirst and his face was sand scoured. And the noble tombs were yet higher up the foothills. He saw the looming cliffs. Somewhere in there was the Great Place, where kings were buried. *Were the tomb robbers really working up to a royal tomb?*

He blew out a breath, and again, he wished he'd thought to ask Ankh-reshet for a gourd of water. Then he began his dogged climb. *How did Djau manage this every day?*

At that hour, the shadow of the cliffs had just begun to creep toward the River, and it was not until he was very close that he found himself in the shade at last. He saw Lord Ptah-mes's tomb, where a guard and other men scurried about. No doubt, it was being prepared to receive Lady Apeny's *khat*—her embalmed mortal remains. He saw guards elsewhere, too, sitting on a rock or wandering back and forth to keep from falling asleep with boredom.

Outside Lord Ah-mes's tomb sat a guard who was middle-aged, at least, but looked wiry and martial with a stave over his shoulder. Maya made his way toward him. "*Yah,* my good fellow," Maya called, waving a hand.

The fellow whipped around and hefted his weapon in menace. "This is private property, little man. Clear off."

A flush of outrage simmered under Maya's skin, but he kept calm, remembering how Lord Hani never let insult ruffle him. "I'm a royal investigator," he said loftily, a hand on his hip. "I wanted to talk to one of the guards hereabouts to see what anyone might have seen or heard when those three tombs were robbed in recent weeks."

The man looked uneasy and none too friendly. "I wasn't here when the tombs were robbed. I was sick."

You look plenty healthy now, Maya thought suspiciously. "Perhaps you heard one of the others talking. We have reason to think the guards may have been paid off to be absent the nights of the robberies."

"Well, I wouldn't know about that." He turned as if to cut off the conversation.

"You were gone all three times? They were days, if not weeks, apart."

The man seemed to swell with anger, but Maya had a suspicion it was in large part bravado. "Are you trying to call me a liar, little man? I'm a former cavalryman, a *pehrer*, a runner. I've got a spotless record in Our Sun's service, and I won't have anybody call me a liar."

"All right, all right," Maya said, piqued. He didn't want to antagonize the guard by locking horns with him. "All the more reason your insights could be useful to the good god. But if you won't cooperate..."

"I wasn't here, I tell you," the guard cried in a loud voice. "I know nothing."

"Very well. If you should hear anything from one of the other guards, send me word. I'm the secretary of the famous Lord Hani." Maya lifted his chin then added quickly, "Who am I talking to, in case a message should come?"

"Djed-ka-ra, formerly of the Glory of the Horizon company."

Maya took his leave with chilly civility and wondered if it would be worth his while to hunt down some of the other guards. Surely, they hadn't all been sick. He held up a hand in farewell, and Djed-ka-ra grudgingly did the same. Maya couldn't help noticing how hard with calluses the guard's right hand was—the inside of his fingers was downright yellow. *Is that from swinging an ax or drawing back a bow?*

⚜

Hani headed toward the southern edge of the city, well east of the Ipet-isut, which sat in melancholy splendor, liquefied by the shimmering heat and the humidity of the River. A pang of sorrow and anger twinged in Hani's heart as it did every time he saw the Greatest of Shrines with its flags down and its golden doors boarded over.

He was looking for the army garrison, where he hoped to find Pa-aten-em-heb. Hani had spent his younger years employed there, but the journey seemed longer than he remembered. *It must be that*, he told himself with a smile. *It couldn't be that I'm getting older.*

He gave his credentials at the gate and entered an immense courtyard punctuated by a broad cup-shaped well and a rectangular pond for the animals to water. The familiar tart smell of horses was in the air, and it aroused his nostalgia. A few men crossed the court in one direction or another—grooms with tack over their shoulders or soldiers striding briskly, their quilted aprons flapping against their legs. *They look so young.*

He followed the worn track across the court, past the buildings that ringed it, and into a second quadrangle where the infantry mess was located. It was lunchtime, as the clatter and gabble of men and dishes from within proclaimed. The chances were good that Pa-aten-em-heb was there if he was in Waset.

Indeed, no sooner had Hani stopped in the doorway,

243

gazing blindly into the cool, shadowy hall where men ate with gusto, seated on the packed-earth floor, than Pa-aten-em-heb rose and approached him eagerly. "Lord Hani!" he cried, fisting his chest in a salute. "I was going to come see you as soon as I had the time. I've found out some things for you." He drew Hani back out into the court and against the wall, where they had a little shade and more privacy.

"I have a friend in the cavalry who is a scribe for the Glory of the Horizon company—he's employed by the quartermaster. He told me that a few months ago there was a mysterious robbery from their depot." Pa-aten-em-heb grinned evilly. "A quiver full of arrows went missing. Broad-headed medium-range arrows, such as the scouts use for sharpshooting when a kill is imperative."

Hani's heart began to pound. "That's an important addition to our case, my friend. You've done us a huge service."

Pa-aten-em-heb held up a hand. "But that's not all, my lord. About the same time, one of their men—a scout—was honorably discharged after a disabling wound. He was hale enough, but he couldn't run anymore as a scout needs to. He was an older fellow, anyway, apparently." He paused for effect. "He was an archer. Can that be a coincidence?"

Hani threw back his head and laughed with relief. "You've outdone yourself, Pa-aten-em-heb. This is worth more than one home-cooked dinner. I can't thank you enough."

The young officer tilted his head modestly. "It's the least I can do, Lord Hani. You saved my friend Menna"— his voice dropped to a near whisper—"and your family is keeping the faith."

Hani took his leave, clapping the officer warmly on the back. "I'm serious about dinner, my friend. I'll be offended if you don't show up." He waved and crossed the bleak courtyard once more, while Pa-aten-em-heb returned to his lunch.

Hani made his way back north through the city, his thoughts tumbling. The heat made it harder than normal to think straight. *Was this retired archer the murderer? If so, why was he involved?*

It was late in the day when Hani arrived home. After he'd poured a jug of water over himself for a shower and oiled his skin, he took a seat in the empty salon to ponder. Empty indeed, he noticed, without Baket-iset's couch and Nub-nefer's gracious presence. He was thinking more about how much he missed them than about the facts of his case when he heard Maya in the vestibule, followed shortly thereafter by Mery-ra. They emerged together into the salon, surrounded by a pungent, oniony reek of sweat.

"Hello, Hani, my boy. Where's Pipi?" Mery-ra said.

"I don't know, Father. He hasn't come back yet." Hani no longer remembered what Pipi was doing. "Let's pool whatever we found. I want to try to construct some kind of shape to this case."

The three of them seated themselves on stools under the clerestory-like ventilator in the ceiling, hoping to catch a draft. Hani began by describing what he'd discovered about the missing arrows and the ex-archer. He could see Maya's eyes grow wide.

"That sheds light on what I found, my lord," the secretary cried excitedly. "First, I talked to Ankh-reshet, who said the arrow was sticking straight up out of Djau's back. That means it was fired from the trail behind him, not from the cliffs. At first, I thought it strange that Djau wouldn't have heard someone walking behind him, but there was apparently something of a sandstorm that day."

"Excellent deductive work, Maya," Hani said. "If the murderer was a trained scout, he would know how to move silently. And it must have taken some skill to shoot an arrow, even at close range, in a wind."

Maya continued breathlessly, "I interviewed the guards of the three tombs that were robbed. Two had alibis, but the third, Djed-ka-ra, the guard of Ah-mes's tomb, claimed he'd been sick—on all three nights. He said he was a retired cavalryman, a *pehrer*. He was very touchy when I questioned him—threatening almost. He must be the discharged scout!"

A warm tide of satisfaction began to rise in Hani's middle. At last, they were getting somewhere. "How did your investigations go, Father?" He turned to Mery-ra.

"I talked to the families of Pa-ren-nefer and Sa-tau. They knew of no connections to Naharin. But they were both men whose loyalties lay quietly with the old ways, despite being highly placed functionaries of Nefer-khepru-ra. And they were both very rich, like Ah-mes. If I were out to rob a tomb, I would certainly target them." Mery-ra sat back, smiling.

Before Hani could even reply, Pipi burst triumphantly into the room. He'd shed his shirt, which trailed like a tail behind him, stuck by a corner into the waist of his kilt. "*Iyi*, everybody's here already," he cried. "Am I late?"

"This is all informal," Hani assured him. "What did you find out?"

"That officer, the son of Ah-hotep-ra, is named Iby. He's Lord Ay's aide de camp in the cavalry."

"Do we have any reason to think he's involved in this business?" Hani asked in a neutral tone.

"What do you mean?" Pipi asked, confused. "He's the one who coordinated the whole thing for Lord Ay."

Mery-ra exchanged a look with Hani and said mildly, "You may be jumping to conclusions, son. We'll need some supporting evidence to make that claim conclusively. So far, all we have proved is that he's Ay's aide."

"Maybe Pa-aten-em-heb would have information on this fellow," suggested Maya.

"Perhaps," Hani said. "Let's lay out what we know so far. Maya, my friend, take notes for us, please."

Maya unhitched his writing case, mixed up some ink, shook a potsherd out, and laid it on his knee. "Ready, Lord Hani."

Hani stared blankly up at the ceiling while he gathered his thoughts. "We have a pretty good idea that Talpu-sharri was the organizer of these robberies. Why, though? And why didn't he get out of the country while he had the perfect chance? If he's still here, it's for a reason."

"And who is he?" Mery-ra said. "He claims to have immunity. He says he's acting for powerful people and that the tomb robberies are for the good of the kingdom. He speaks of regime change. Who's really behind this, by all that's holy?"

"We have three suspects," said Hani, holding up three fingers. "The king, Lord Ay, and the Crocodiles." With each name, he folded down a finger.

"What crocodiles?" Pipi asked.

"Those who hope to bring back the Hidden One and restore his priesthood."

"But we all do that," Pipi protested. "I pray for that every day."

Hani said, "Well, the Crocodiles are doing more than praying. The thing about putting the rightful king on the throne and doing good for the kingdom sounds just like them. I'm not sure they would rob tombs, but it honestly wouldn't surprise me."

"But why?" Maya looked up from his writing. "Why would they rob men who were sympathetic to their cause?"

Hani shrugged. "That's part of what we need to find out. Maya, put that question off to the side—why is this whole affair going on?"

"What else?" asked his father. "If this Djed-ka-ra is the murderer of Djau, why did he do it? The man had already reported the robberies to authorities."

"But I later found out that Djau not only heard the conversation between Bebi-ankh and the foreigner, but he saw the foreigner's face as well. He was still a danger."

Maya looked up again. "Is that why Djau lied to us, Lord Hani? He was afraid to tell anyone what he really knew?"

"I would think so. He probably didn't trust me fully, even though he seemed cooperative."

"How did Talpu-sharri know you were coming to arrest him?" asked Mery-ra, his eyes narrowing. "Maybe he already intended to jump ship, but that seems like a little too much coincidence."

"I don't know, Father. Let's think. Did Pirissi and Tulubri talk to him? Is there someone in Kiya's entourage who is part of the plan? Nobody knew where I was headed except us and Menna." Hani saw from the corner of his eye that Pipi was squirming. "What is it, brother?" Hani turned to him. "Do you know something?"

Pipi looked up guiltily from under his bangs. "I... I may have said something to the soldier I interrogated about the son of Ah-hotep-ra."

Hani felt a wave of anger rising in him, but it turned to hopelessness somewhere on its way up. Pipi was simply not to be trusted, good-hearted though he was. He couldn't hold his tongue. He wanted too hard to look important. *How ironic that the free spirit of the family is so desperate for respect.*

He blew out a breath through his nose and said blandly, "Well, that may, in fact, be where the word got out. But it confirms what we suspected—that the cavalry is somehow involved."

"And *that* tells us that it's probably the king or Lord Ay behind it all," cried Maya.

"But why?" Hani pushed back his wig and scratched his head. "How does all this help the kingdom and put the right man on the throne?"

"Wait," said Mery-ra. "Would the king be trying to put someone else on the throne? It can't be him."

"Then that leaves Ay," Hani mused. "Which supports the participation of the cavalry and maybe explains Djed-ka-ra's involvement."

"I told you so!" Pipi cried, recovering his excitement.

"Is Lord Ay plotting a coup?" Maya asked, his eyes round as plates.

"Now," Hani said, ignoring them, "why were these

three tombs targeted? Simply because they belonged to rich men? Why would Lord Ay need any more wealth? Through his daughter, he can have almost anything he wants. And that being true, why in the world would he be trying to put someone else on the throne, unless it's himself? And why would a Mitannian be involved with him?"

The men fell silent. Hani felt there was an answer just out of reach. "Lord Ah-mes seems to have met with Talpu-sharri just before he died. Is that significant?"

"But as far as we know, the others didn't meet with him," Maya said. "What they seem to have had in common was dissatisfaction with the new regime."

Mery-ra said, "And yet they continued to be loyal. They were hardly revolutionaries. Maybe there *was* no conscious selection. These were all tombs that were completed within the year, and the same work teams probably constructed and decorated them."

Hani unfolded his legs, rose, and stretched. "We're just not at the point where we can answer these questions yet, my friends. It's well past midday, and I haven't eaten. Let's see what the cook can put together for us."

CHAPTER 10

T HE NEXT MORNING, AS THEY ate milk and a chunk of bread in the kitchen, Hani said to Mery-ra, "Neferet and her friend have been suspiciously quiet. What are they up to?"

"Judging from the smells emerging from her room, they're concocting some medicinal brew," his father replied with a chuckle.

"I think they should go down to the farm with the others. I almost feel that Neferet is trying to avoid her mother." *Is she afraid Nub-nefer will badger her to get married?* he wondered.

"Or should some of the others come back here?" Mery-ra asked. "Meaning, everyone but Anuia and her family."

Suddenly, Hani thought of something that had been in the back of his mind ever since the meeting with his coinvestigators the previous afternoon. "Maybe I should talk to Amen-em-hut—"

"Not that you know where he is, of course," Mery-ra said with a sly wag of the eyebrows.

"He might be able to tell me whether the high priests have a paw in this. I've lost Lady Apeny as a go-between, but I'd be amazed if Anuia doesn't know how to reach him. Or," Hani had to admit, "Nub-nefer."

"Why don't you let her talk to him? That Mahu may be having you watched."

Hani looked up at Mery-ra. "How does he play into all this, Father? That's something we didn't talk about yesterday. I've tended to think about him as a pest, but he isn't interfering with the case on his own. He's following the king's orders—ham-handedly, perhaps, and officiously, but it suggests that someone the king is protecting wants this investigation shut down."

"If the king wants it shut down, why did he put you on it in the first place?"

Hani snorted. "I don't know. What on earth could be his motive for robbing tombs? How could he want a regime change? And threatening to rob his own father's tomb, if Talpu-sharri wasn't just trying to impress his workmen... Maybe the king has nothing to do with it."

"You'll figure it out, son. I have confidence in you." Mery-ra patted him on the shoulder. "Your mother used to say you were the devious one in the family."

"She did?" Hani cried in surprise. "Why?"

"Because you could lie with a straight face. Pipi would always blush and giggle; he couldn't convince anybody."

Hani's dismay must have shown on his face, because Mery-ra laughed and said, "That's what makes you such a good diplomat, son."

"I'm hurt that she thought I was dishonest," Hani said

with a half-hearted laugh. "I try very hard to live in *ma'at*, Father."

"Oh, you're not dishonest, Hani. You were always scrupulously honest. But you know how children can be. Occasionally, something comes up that has to be concealed from Mama and Papa."

Hani pondered this, wondering again if Neferet had something to conceal. *She* certainly couldn't lie with a straight face. And her mother was definitely the more demanding of her two parents.

Hani said to his father with a fond smile, "They say that one parent is typically the disciplinarian, but I don't remember either you or Mother being very strict. We were a wild pair."

Mery-ra chuckled. "You were both good-hearted boys. We didn't worry about youthful pranks, as long as you weren't unkind."

"May you live forever, noble Father," Hani said, his voice breaking a little, which he attempted to hide with a punch at his father's arm.

They dusted the last of the crumbs off their chests and prepared to go about their day's work. Hani's ears pricked up at the sound of girlish giggles in the salon. "There are the missing young ladies," he said with a smile.

He passed into the salon and saw Neferet, carrying a big jug in her arms, on her way to the garden. Bener-ib followed closely with a smaller vessel in either hand. They were murmuring to one another and laughing like madwomen. It reassured Hani to see his daughter's friend happy for a change, but he was more than a little curious as to what they were up to.

"What are they concocting, I wonder?" asked Mery-ra, joining his son. The two men stared after the girls as they disappeared into the bushes.

A moment later, squeals of triumph arose. Neferet cried loudly, "It worked! Lady Djefat-nebty will be so proud of us!"

Hani moved quietly away, chuckling to himself, while Mery-ra craned his neck in the effort to see what was going on. Eventually, he shrugged and followed Hani. "I'm going to see Meryet-amen. I've been so busy with my new career as an investigator that I've neglected her. And her cook," he added with a twinkle in his eye. He toddled off to the front door, pushed the mat aside, and disappeared.

Hani stood, staring pensively after his father, wondering what he should undertake first. He wanted badly to find Talpu-sharri and question him. There was always a chance that the man might reveal who was protecting him and why. But first, Hani decided to go greet the girls and ask what they'd made that elicited such excitement. He set off around the bushes with a smile and then stopped dead, his heart in his throat and his smile freezing.

Neferet and Bener-ib were sitting on the ground wrapped in each other's arms. He saw his daughter lean over and kiss the other girl on the mouth.

Hani backed up and fled the last few steps into the salon, unable to breathe. *What have I just seen? Is it some ritual that's part of making their concoction?* But he knew that it was not.

Hani dropped into a chair, his pulse throbbing in his throat. *Sweet Lady of Love, explain this to me.* Hani recognized the look on Neferet's face. It wasn't friendship.

He swallowed hard. *What do I do now? If only Nub-nefer were here.*

He tried to decide what to say to Neferet—or whether to say nothing at all and pretend he'd seen nothing. But for all that he was a master of concealment, as his mother had thought, Hani wasn't sure he could carry off *that* deceit. He swallowed again, and it barely went down. His throat seemed to be clogged.

He was still sitting there, frozen in place, when Neferet entered the room, red-faced and smiling, Bener-ib trailing her with her empty pots. "Hello, Papa," his daughter said cheerfully and made as if to continue.

"What were you girls making, my duckling?" Hani tried to smile and sound normal, but he felt as if his face were stiff with shock. He kept telling himself it wasn't what it had looked like.

"It was a very difficult recipe for treating sweating fever, Papa. Lady Djefat-nebty dared us to make it. She didn't think we could." She and her friend exchanged a grin that was a little too warm and secretive for Hani's taste.

He could think of nothing to say, so he just nodded. His heart was pounding as if he'd run a race. He wanted to talk to his youngest daughter, to say, "I saw you. Please explain it to me." He wanted ask her questions. But he found his courage failed him.

To Hani's extravagant relief, Nub-nefer came back around midmorning with a basket of vegetables from the farm. Hani was sitting in the salon, looking into space, when she appeared. He roused himself, jumped up, relieved her of the basket, then embraced her fervently.

She stared at him, a tinge of suspicion in her eyes. "What is it, my love? You look disturbed."

Should I tell her? Or is this Neferet's to tell? Hani tried to ease into the subject as if he were slipping little by little into the cold water, splashing it on his arms and legs first to accustom himself to the chill. "My doe, I saw Neferet and her friend today. They... they seemed to be more than friends."

She tilted her head in incomprehension. "What does that mean, Hani?"

He swallowed hard. "She... they were in a rather compromising act."

She gaped at him. "Like what? Plotting a murder?"

"No, no. It was... rather... amorous, if you follow me." He could feel sweat breaking out on his temples. "I don't want to make it sound worse than it was, but I think... they're in love."

Nub-nefer burst out laughing, but it wasn't a wholly amused noise. "I don't follow you. Two girls? You must have misunderstood."

Hani drew a deep breath and let it out. "I don't think so. I've known men like that, my dear. And they were fine men, good scribes. One was an army officer."

"Men like what?"

"Who preferred other men. I suspect this may be why she doesn't want to get married."

Nub-nefer faced him, wide-eyed and stunned. She opened her mouth once to speak, but nothing came out. At last, she said hotly, "Our daughter is normal."

"So were those men."

"And I'll bet they were married and had children, didn't they?"

He had to admit that that was true.

Nub-nefer turned away, staring into space. Tears had begun to well in her eyes. She murmured in a trembling voice, "Hani, this is so shameful. How have we failed? She loves you so. She loves her brothers. What has turned her?"

"I've asked myself that, my love. But I think nothing has turned her. It's just the way the gods have made her. 'Each man is led by his nature.'"

Nub-nefer was having none of it. She burst out, her voice hard, "It's that Djefat-nebty. She's corrupted our child." She began suddenly to weep and pressed herself against Hani's chest. "Why did we ever let her go down there? It's been nothing but... but ruin ever since."

Hani held her close, not knowing how to comfort her. Yet within his own heart, something was shifting. "We only want her to be happy, don't we? And she is happy. She loves being a *sunet*, and she loves her friend. She's happy, and she's doing good for people—is that so ruinous? I'd say we've done a fine job with her."

"We should arrange a marriage for her, Hani. Separate her from that strange girl."

"What makes you think she's strange?" Hani asked with a gentle smile. "You've never even met her."

"Are you on her side?" Nub-nefer demanded, pulling away.

"I'm on Neferet's side, and so are you. Why make her miserable, sticking her in a loveless marriage?"

"But, Hani..." Her objection trailed off. She stared at the floor for a long space of time. Hani could almost see the argument going on behind her smooth golden forehead. When she spoke again, it was less in outrage than in regret. "But, Hani, she won't give us grandchildren."

"Neither will Baket-iset, but you don't hold it against her. Do you love her less than the others who have children?" The more he argued with Nub-nefer, the more at peace he was about the situation. Here, at least, was a problem he didn't have to solve.

Nub-nefer stood in silence, her brow pleated in thought.

"How long will you be here, my dove?" Hani finally said. "Can you have lunch with me before you go back?"

She nodded, calm returning. That was another thing he loved about Nub-nefer—she could rally. She was passionate, and her first reactions were often explosive, but she could rally.

"I have a question for Amen-em-hut, dear one. Can you put me in touch with him?" he asked, picking up the vegetable basket as they made their way to the kitchen.

She nodded again, looking up at him. "Yes, but what if that awful Mahu is watching you?"

"Why don't you see your brother first and tell him I would like to meet him at someone's house. We'll arrive at different times. No one would have reason to expect anything subversive."

Nub-nefer said, "All right, Hani. Can I ask what it's about?"

"He may have some insight into this tomb-robbing spree. Some of what we learned makes it sound as if the high priests could be behind it, but I can't be sure without more information. He would know."

They laid the vegetables on the table for the cook and drifted, hand in hand, back out to the salon.

"I'll go ask right now," she said.

✦

Hani decided to go alone to his rendezvous with Amen-em-hut. The renegade priest had agreed to a meeting but had not yet told Hani where they were to meet—a precaution, Nub-nefer assured her husband, in case someone should overhear. This way, they wouldn't have time to mount an ambush.

The following morning, Nub-nefer set out on her habitual "errand," and when she returned, she whispered to Hani, "Lord Ptah-mes's house."

Hani's jaw dropped, but he said nothing. *Does Ptah-mes know about this?* He had reservations about intruding on a house of mourning, especially knowing how hostile Ptah-mes was to Hani's brother-in-law. But Amen-em-hut had to know what he was doing.

He walked Nub-nefer down to the quay and saw her onto a ferry heading upriver, then he directed his steps toward Lord Ptah-mes's magnificent ancestral estate, a little queasy at the prospect of intruding.

The gateman let him in and said quietly, "In the salon, my lord."

Hani half expected to see Ptah-mes waiting for him, but instead, he perceived the small, handsome figure of his brother-in-law, the deposed third prophet of Amen-Ra, rise from a chair and come toward him, beaming. "Hani! It's been too long since we've seen one another."

The two men embraced. Hani was pleased to see that

259

Amen-em-hut looked healthy and well-groomed. Two years before, he'd spent months hiding in Hani's boat shed and had come out rather the worse for wear.

"Nub-nefer said you had something you wanted to ask me." Amen-em-hut indicated a chair, and he and Hani seated themselves.

"My brother, I have to ask you this first," Hani began under his breath. "Does Ptah-mes know you're here?"

Amen-em-hut laughed. "Of course." He locked eyes with Hani and said meaningfully, "Things have changed, my friend. I think the Osir Apeny is praying for her husband."

I hope so. He needs it. Hani said, "Do you know anything about a string of tomb robberies here in Waset?"

"I may have heard something. Why?"

"I don't suppose your colleagues have anything to do with that, do they?"

Amen-em-hut's fine black eyes widened. "Not that I'm aware of. And I think I *would* be aware if it were so."

"Apparently, a Mitannian is involved. I wondered if this might be an effort to discredit the regime in the eyes of all the foreign emissaries who have been here during the Great Jubilee."

Amen-em-hut twisted his mouth in thought. "It may well be, but not on our part. I can almost swear to that. Who were the victims?"

"Ah-mes, Pa-ren-nefer, and Sa-tau."

Amen-em-hut shook his head. "They were partisans of the old ways. I can't imagine any of us would have wished them harm."

Hani nodded, both relieved and disappointed. He

would have to look elsewhere for a mastermind, then. Still, it relieved him to learn the high priests were not involved. They were ruthless in their efforts to bring down Nefer-khepru-ra and his Aten, but at least they stopped short of desecrating the house of someone's *ka*.

"What do you know about Lord Ay?" Hani asked. "How loyal is he to the king? Does he really believe in the new religion, or is it just useful for advancing his daughter?"

"I wish I knew, Hani. I can only tell you he isn't part of us. Is there anything else I can do for you?"

"How are things with Lord Mai and Lord Si-mut?" Hani said, referring to the first and second prophets.

"Well." Amen-em-hut grinned. "We're making inroads into the army."

Hani thought of Pa-aten-em-heb and could well believe it. "Then I thank you for taking this risk for me, my friend. You've helped me. Please give my regards to your colleagues."

The two men rose and clapped one another amicably on the back. Amen-em-hut retreated quietly into the back of the house, while Hani made his way through the splendidly painted vestibule toward the front door. He'd just stepped down from the porch when Ptah-mes appeared in the path before him, tall and immaculate with a face like a stone.

"My lord," cried Hani, pleased to see him but feeling a little guilty.

"Hani," Ptah-mes said with a bleak smile. "Don't worry. I know why you're here."

"Good. The choice of meeting place rather surprised me."

Ptah-mes gestured toward the arbor, and the two men

walked side by side across the garden. "I've changed my mind about some things. My loyalty to the throne is... shaken. Our king has forfeited the blessing of the gods; this plague is proof of that."

Hani shot a sideways glance at him. "You're going to resign, my lord?"

"No," said Ptah-mes grimly. "I can be of more use to those who share my viewpoint where I am."

"You've talked to the priests, then?" Hani asked under his breath. The priests had asked the same thing of Hani.

Ptah-mes met his eye, and there was a smoldering rage behind the dark irises that almost frightened Hani. "Better late than never, eh, my friend?" The commissioner's lips were thin and hard. It occurred to Hani that, much as he admired him, he would not like Ptah-mes for an enemy. "I myself should still be a priest, were it not for the forces of... politics. Perhaps that has colored my antipathy toward Mai, who was after all, my replacement. But the time for personal rancor is past."

Hani knew that his friend had been stripped of the high priesthood and the viziership by Nefer-khepru-ra, even before the latter had come to the throne on his own. "Just be careful, my lord. The king's attack dogs would like nothing better than an excuse to bring you down."

"Let them. I'll take others down with me." Ptah-mes's grim expression lightened, and he said in a different tone, "Have you anything to report on your case?"

Hani brought him up-to-date on his investigations, explaining how they seemed to have eliminated the Crocodiles from suspicion and could find no motive for the king. "That seems to leave Ay—and if he is the culprit, the investigation is over, because we can never bring him to justice. Unless, of course, he's plotting behind the king's back, in which case Nefer-khepru-ra would probably like to know about it."

"Have you any idea where that Mitannian has gone to ground?" the high commissioner asked. "If he's still around, he's probably planning something else."

"I don't know, my lord. It's one of the things we need to look into." Hani tugged thoughtfully at his chin. "And it occurs to me that if he's been selling off a lot of grave goods from wealthy tombs, we should be able to find traces of them on the market. Some must surely have names on them."

"Good idea. He may have taken them to sell elsewhere than Waset, though. Check the markets in Men-nefer and Hut-nen-nesut too. And our holy capital." His voice was slick with sarcasm.

"I'll do that," Hani said. "I need to take my daughter back to Hut-nen-nesut anyway, now that the holidays are ending." The thought of Neferet awakened all sorts of anxieties, which Hani forced down.

"Keep me posted, Hani." Ptah-mes seemed to struggle to swallow, but his voice was cool and casual as he added, "I hope to see you at the funeral."

"Absolutely, my lord."

Hani left through the splendid gateway and trudged up the street past walled estates that might or might not have been inhabited. In any case, their proprietors had the gold to hire caretakers in their absence. Hani's own less exalted neighborhood had not fared so well. He saw yet again—and with sorrow, as always—the down-at-heels emptied houses of midlevel bureaucrats who had once been his neighbors. Overhead, he spied a hawk planing high in the burning faience-blue sky.

As soon as Hani had reached his own gate, A'a told him that Maya was within. Hani entered, slipped off his sandals, and savored the cool smoothness of the polished plaster floor under his feet as he padded into the salon.

"Maya, my boy," he said in greeting. "Are you ready to work? We have some new lines of inquiry to pursue."

"Ready, my lord," the young man said brightly, adjusting his writing case over his shoulder.

"We need Father too. I want him to revisit the families of the victims and find out what sort of objects were missing from the tombs. That will help us track them down."

"Did I hear my name? Or rather, my title?" Mery-ra came toddling in from his apartments at the rear of the house. "That's 'reverend Father' to you, Hani. I'll also put up with 'noble Father' or 'august Father.'"

"Ah, just in time." Hani outlined what he wanted Mery-ra to do. "Maya and I will go up to Hut-nen-nesut with Neferet, checking bazaars and shops on our way back. Talpu-sharri must have sold the goods, or why would he have stolen them? And, everyone—keep your eyes open for him."

"You're leaving Neferet home by herself for weeks?" Mery-ra said dubiously. "She'll have burned the house down."

Or worse, thought Hani. "You'll be here, august Father. Your assignment won't take more than an afternoon." He and Maya headed out to the quay. "Downriver we go again, my friend."

They decided to return the girls first and make their visits to shops on the way back. Hani wasn't altogether sure the stolen items would be out in the open market, but they had to check. It would be easier to do when Mery-ra got a list of the purloined objects from the families of the victims. They combed every bazaar and hole-in-the-wall dealing in precious items at Hut-nen-nesut, but with no luck.

At Men-nefer, Hani drew Maya aside. "Let's split up. We'll make better time that way. You take the north side of the city, and I'll take the south. We'll meet at the boat whenever we both have covered the territory. All right?"

"Right you are, my lord," Maya replied, rubbing his hands together eagerly.

As it turned out, many of the chicer shops had closed, following their wealthy clientele to the new capital. Maya found himself with only a handful to consider, and they were all clustered on one street opening into the market place. The first was extremely modest in size—mostly an awning extended over the narrow front of a building, with collapsible shelves upon which were ranged an assortment of old or used vessels of faience, bronze, and pottery. Under the suspicious eye of the proprietor, he glanced over the merchandise, but it was hard to imagine anything priceless showing up there.

The second store had even fewer select products outside, but within, there were a few pieces of nice furniture. *Yes*, Maya thought as he drew closer, *very nice furniture*. Made of precious woods, inlaid with ebony and ivory, carved with birds' heads and lion paws... they were the sort of thing

265

a very rich man might have seen fit to put in his tomb. Maya had a better view of the chairs and stools than most shoppers would have without stooping, and he liked what he saw. *We just need to compare this with Lord Mery-ra's list, when he gets it.*

The third and final shop seemed to be that of a dealer in old jewelry. A massive servant sat at the door to discourage anyone who might want to dodge in and help himself. He gave Maya a withering look as he entered. Maya adjusted his writing case over his shoulder conspicuously and went strolling in, looking as proud and affluent as possible.

A little old man emerged from invisibility in the corner of the shop and approached Maya, bowing and clasping his hands obsequiously. "And what can I interest the young gentleman in today?" he chirruped.

"A gift for my patron," Maya said, imitating the upper-class drawl of Lord Ptah-mes. "Something rich but not flashy. Something... something suitable for an older man who can buy anything he wants. For his *ka* house, let's say."

"Ah," said the merchant. "You'll want something unique, then." He returned to his corner and came back with a bundle wrapped in discolored linen. He folded back the wrappings reverently, and Maya looked down at a beautiful masculine bracelet of gold and silver. It was ornamented by two bands of chased writing filled in with blue frit. Among the symbols, Maya saw the word "Sa-tau." His heart began to thunder until he feared the merchant could hear it.

"How much is this piece?" Maya asked casually—as if he would ever in his life possess so much wealth.

"The metal alone weighs more than a *deben*, my lord,

and it's pure gold, with silver from Kheta Land." The merchant smiled a toothless grin of pure complaisance. "The workmanship is exquisite, and in addition, it's very old. Let's say for you, a man of discrimination, five gold *shenas*?"

Maya, who hadn't grown up in a goldsmith's studio for nothing, recognized this as a ridiculously low figure. The man clearly wanted to unload it. *He probably knows it's stolen, even if he can't read the inscription.*

"I'm interested," Maya said, "but I don't have that sum on me. I'll have to come back for it. Can you show me something else old while I'm here?"

The old man trundled back into his corner once more—*the contraband corner*, Maya thought caustically— and pulled out a lovely pair of hoop earrings made of a hollow tubelike sheet of beaten gold. They were perfectly simple and elegant in a manly way. *What do you bet my mother made them? Very old indeed.*

"Good, good," Maya said airily at last. "I'll make a decision and come back."

"Shall I hold them for my lord?"

"No, no. I'm not sure when I'll return to the city."

"Oh, my lord," cried the merchant in warning. "Pieces this beautiful may not be here when you get back."

"I'll take my chances. Who knows? I may find something more beautiful still," said Maya, moving toward the door.

"Wait, my lord. Will you give me five for the bracelet *and* the earrings?"

"Sorry," Maya said with a nonchalant little wave of the fingers, and he strolled toward the door.

267

Once out of sight of the doorman, he took off running. *Wait till Lord Hani hears about this!*

✦

Hani, mopping the sweat out of his eyes as he sat on the deck of the ferry, was starting to get discouraged by what had turned into a fruitless quest. *We probably should have waited for Father's report on the missing items before we bothered to go looking.* He'd encountered nothing he judged to be of a caliber for a rich man's tomb furnishings, although he'd probed many a faience kohl tube and gilded bronze jug. Either the goods had not been put on the open market, or they hadn't reached as far as Men-nefer.

Hani had just emptied his gourd of water, pouring the last few drops over his head, when he saw Maya running as hard as he could toward the boat on his short legs. Hani suppressed the twitch of amusement that tickled at him and jumped up to stand at the gunwales. "What luck, my friend?" he called.

As he ran up the gangplank, Maya pumped his fists jubilantly. "I found some! One piece even had a name on it!" He dropped, panting, into the shade and stretched his legs out in front of him. Hani took a seat at his side and waited until the secretary had regained his breath. Red-faced and triumphant, his chest still heaving, Maya grinned. "I'm sure I saw some furniture from a rich tomb, and next door, they had several pieces of expensive gold jewelry, which they were selling for nothing. And one bracelet actually had the name Sa-tau on it!"

Hani laughed with pleasure. "Good for you, my boy. I think we need to steer Sa-tau's family up here with some soldiers to make an identification and let them regain their lost treasure." He sat pondering the implications of this find. "I wonder if the merchant innocently bought contraband or if he's part of the gang."

"I don't know, my lord. It's altogether possible that Mother could tell us who the pieces were made for, if she had anything to do with making them."

"Something to consider. We know now that our mysterious foreigner sold off the treasures, probably to put them into a more portable form than furniture. And less identifiable than jewelry."

But gradually Hani fell silent, his exultation starting to cool. The discovery didn't really prove anything, except that tombs had been robbed. "Get off the boat, Maya," he said, rising to his feet. "We're going back to that shop."

They clattered back down the gangplank, Maya flashing a look of confusion at his father-in-law.

"I want to ask those merchants who sold them the goods. Our foreign friend may have colleagues."

As quickly as either of them had the energy for, they walked back up through the center of town and into the northern marketplace. Maya pointed out to Hani the two shops where he'd found what seemed to be grave goods. They entered the first under the suspicious eye of the big servant. When the little old merchant rose from his corner, Hani put on an easygoing smile. "Hello, my friend. My colleague here said he saw some jewelry in your shop that may be heirlooms of my family. I've been trying to trace them for a long time."

"I... I don't know, my lord. People bring things to me and I resell it. I suppose they're all heirlooms if you go back far enough." His filmy eyes flicked from one face to the other, uneasy. Perhaps guilty.

"Let me ask you, do you remember who sold the gold-and-silver bracelet to you? He probably had other pieces as well."

The merchant hesitated, and Hani saw him trying to attract the eye of the guardian at the door.

"Don't be afraid," Hani said reassuringly, but he stepped between the old man and the sight line of the servant. "I just want to find whoever sold my family's goods."

"He was, he was… a foreigner, my lord. From Naharin, I think."

Now we're getting somewhere, Hani thought triumphantly. "Do you remember what he looked like, my good man?"

The little old merchant hunched his fleshless shoulders in ignorance. "I can't see well, my lord. He was… tall. Dressed in blue-green. I can't see much more than that."

"Thin? Fat?"

The old man shrugged again.

"You seem to see jewelry well enough to evaluate it," said Hani with a smile. "Can't you give us a few more details? Distinguishing marks? Any moles?"

"Dark hair."

"Oh, that's distinctive," Maya said dismissively.

The little man pleaded, "It's all I can see."

Hani exchanged a skeptical look with Maya. "Very well. I was going to buy the pieces if they were my family's, but if you don't know where they came from, maybe they're copies."

"Uh, uh…" the merchant stammered. "He was fat, my lord."

"Thanks, friend," said Hani dryly. "You at least have an imagination, if not eyes."

He and Maya made their way out of the shop under the baleful gaze of the servant and headed back to the quay.

Once they'd settled themselves once more on the deck, they fell silent. Hani eyed the sky, which was nearly white with the heat of early summer. They'd entered the season of waiting for the Flood. Far off over the bank, a flock of ducks rose heavily then found their rhythm and took to the air with powerful beats of their wings.

They're like young people, Hani thought, a little melancholy. *It takes them a while to settle into what their nature has equipped them to do.* He could remember his own adolescence, which had been permeated with a generic sense of unhappiness—not because anything untoward had ever happened to him. His life had been good, and he'd had the most sympathetic of parents. But the simple fact of turning from a child into an adult was a painful process. A young person tried on so many identities before the true one descended, unsought, upon him. *Maybe that's what Neferet is groping toward. Maybe she'll move past this stage at some point.* But it didn't matter, as long as she found happiness. Because that was surely the touchstone of having found oneself.

"Do you believe him, my lord? I mean, that he couldn't see the man who sold him those things?" Maya asked.

Hani snapped his thoughts back to the present. "I doubt it. But at least he connected the sales with a Mitannian in a turquoise tunic. Our friend has been busy."

"What do we do next, then?" asked Maya as the ferry slid upstream with its broad sail bellying.

271

"We urgently need to find Talpu-sharri, but I'm not sure how to go about that. A more manageable task is to see if one of our military friends can tell us anything about Lord Ay that we don't already know."

"All our friends and relatives are in the infantry, unfortunately." Maya shook his head.

"And Ay is chief of the cavalry. Ah, but Pa-aten-em-heb has a friend in the cavalry, doesn't he? There must be scuttlebutt about what sort of commander Ay is and that sort of thing. Wouldn't you think?"

"Yes, although soldiers may not feel free to tattle on their commanding officer." Maya looked doubtful.

"We'll see," Hani said with amusement, because he could imagine that scribes would be only too eager to tattle on *their* superiors.

The River was at its low point, and marshes and sand bars had appeared where normally there were none. *A good place to go bird watching*, Hani told himself as they slid past reed-choked shallows. But that meant slow and cautious sailing, and it took them a full ten-day week to get home.

The first thing Hani saw as he crunched up the garden path with Maya in his wake was Ta-miu sprawled luxuriously in a patch of sunlight on the porch, her two half-grown kittens gamboling at her feet. "Hello, little bird eaters," Hani said affectionately.

Then he realized that where Ta-miu was, Baket-iset must be found. The women had come back from the farm. Although that put them in danger, he was inordinately glad.

"Baket-iset, my dear! Nub-nefer! We're back," he called. He and Maya dropped their baggage in the vestibule and headed for the salon, where Sat-hut-haru came running out to them with a squeal.

She headed straight for her husband—with a cry of "Papa!" on the side—and bending, began to pinch Maya's cheek, cooing and making over him as one would a baby. "How's my little husband? It's been so long since I've seen you!"

Hani had to laugh. Maya, far from being offended, lapped it up with the all the pleasure of Ta- miu at a bowl of cream. Hani knelt at Baket-iset's couch and kissed her cheek. "How is my favorite eldest daughter?" he said tenderly.

"Well, Papa, it was lovely in the country but, with all Uncle Amen-em-hut's family, a bit crowded. We decided to come home. Mama brought a pig back, and she was directing the butchering. She must be in the courtyard."

"Ah, that's the girl I married. Not only a polished and beautiful lady but a woman who can butcher a pig." Hani laughed. He remembered Ptah-mes saying Apeny was the perfect woman, and he thought, *No, I've married the perfect woman.*

While Maya and Sat-hut-haru billed and cooed, Hani made his way through the kitchen and into the little work court behind, half-shaded with reed matting. Nub-nefer was standing with her hands on her hips and her skirts tucked up while two naked servants carved the bloody carcass, packed it in salt, and prepared to hang strips on lines for smoking. The reek of blood and offal was horrific.

"May all your enemies end up thus," Hani said to her back.

She spun around and cried, "Hani!" He put his arm

273

around her shoulders, and they kissed. "Here you are at last, my love."

"Baket-iset told me you were out here being the mistress of the house," he said with a smile. "I've missed you more than I can say."

"We came back for Lady Apeny's funeral. And it was crowded at the farm. Anuia tends to fill up the space around her."

"I hope you're not running any risk here in the city," he said uncertainly.

She looked suddenly sober. "There were cases of the plague out there, too, Hani. There's no place to go where we're really safe. We just have to trust and make offerings to Sekhmet."

"I'll ask Maya's mother to cast us all amulets," he assured her.

They stood together, watching the butchers at work. At last, Nub-nefer said quietly, "I told Baket-iset about her sister."

"And?"

"She already knew somehow. And was only happy for her that she had found someone to love."

"That's altogether like Baket." He felt proud of his eldest daughter, but within him, a sad little voice said, *She will never find someone to love, alas.*

"She said of all the people we have to worry about, Neferet was the least in need of our anxiety. It gave me comfort."

"The girl is a divine oracle, my dove. We've seen this before. Somehow, in taking one thing away from her, the gods have supplied her with other gifts."

"It was costly," said Nub-nefer, her voice suddenly unsteady.

Hani gave her shoulders a squeeze. His nose burned. "How is Father doing?"

She gave a snort of laughter. "You mean *reverend* Father? He has some news for you he's bursting to share. And Pipi's here. I told him you were gone, but he said he'd just come for the funeral."

"When exactly is the funeral?"

Nub-nefer stared at Hani disbelievingly. "Why, tomorrow. You didn't know? You just arrived today by accident? It would have been terrible if you'd missed it, Hani. All we owe that family…"

"The gods directed my step, my dove. Khonsu the Traveler guided me back."

◈

Hani and his entire family—except for Aha, making his rounds of the temples of the Aten, and Neferet, in distant Hut-nen-nefer—had come to the chapel of Lady Apeny's tomb to pay their respects to her. Lady Apeny had been an admired *weret khener* and a staunch resister of the new cult. They stood at the outskirts of the crowd, behind Ptah-mes's large family and the more eminent guests, including the two viziers and the high prophets of Amen.

Ptah-mes's firstborn, a tall, handsome younger replica of his father, opened the mouth of his mother's coffin with a ceremonial adze. All the daughters tore their garments and poured dust on their heads and wailed as effectively as a troop of professional mourners, and Hani remembered that the whole lot of them were chantresses of the Hidden One.

The children looked genuinely distraught, leaning on each other and taking one another in their arms along with a handful of older people whom Hani assumed to be relatives of Apeny. But Hani noticed with a pang that not one of them stood by their father or put an arm around him or tried to comfort him in any way. Ptah-mes stood all alone like a beautiful, elegant stone statue before the mouth of the tomb, pale faced, dry-eyed, and expressionless, with his mouth drawn down, thin as a slit. Hani's heart ached for him.

Portraying the ancestors of the Osir who was being laid in the house of her *ka*, the Muu dancers swayed and lifted their arms. Shaven-headed priests, in their leopard skins, chanted and bowed and swung their incense bowls. Then scores of servants began to carry in the grave goods, all that Lady Apeny would need in the afterlife—furniture, jewelry, golden vessels, as well as food in abundance. Ptah-mes had spared no expense for the woman he'd worshiped. At the end, Apeny's lavishly decorated coffin, draped with wreathes, was sledged inside the tomb, into the darkness that would dawn upon the reunion of her souls. And the tomb was sealed. Silence reigned once more in the realm of the Lover of Silence.

Nub-nefer was weeping openly as the family made its way down the rocky slope among the guests. Hani turned back at one point and saw Ptah-mes still standing there alone, as if he'd been petrified on the spot, staring at the stone-plugged doorway. Something broke in Hani's heart, and he debated going back to put an arm around his superior's shoulders so the man would know he wasn't completely alone. But it seemed too intimate a moment to interrupt.

"She was a strong woman," Hani murmured, and Nubnefer nodded, trying to stop her tears with the corner of her shawl.

"A wonderful person. An example of faith to us all," she agreed, gulping.

Mery-ra looked back at the tomb, where Ptah-mes lingered. "I'm not sure he'll recover. Trees that won't bend will break."

His heart leaden, Hani shook his head sadly, unable to find words.

After a moment during which their crunching footsteps were the only sound, Maya said, "I'll bet this is the next tomb that's robbed."

Hani and Mery-ra both jerked around to stare at him. "Don't put the evil eye on her, boy," cried Mery-ra with an apotropaic gesture. "Whatever makes you say that?"

Maya spread his hands at the obviousness of it. "It's the latest tomb here, the same work crew built and decorated it, and it's as rich as they come. And she was known to be opposed to the king's policies."

Dread sank like a rock into Hani's stomach. "You're right. We must warn Ptah-mes to put a guard on it."

"All the robbed tombs had guards, Hani," said his father.

"Reliable guards. I'll offer to take the night watch myself."

Mery-ra and Maya exchanged a look. Mery-ra said,

"Then I'm coming to keep you company. Things could get dangerous."

"Count me in, too, my lord," Maya added stoutly.

Hani turned to his father. "You and Pa-kiki and Maya take the women back. I need to talk to Ptah-mes."

The others left as part of the throng that flowed down to the riverside. Hani saw below him Lord Ptah-mes's yacht drawn up against the muddy slope where the water of the River was low. It had borne Lady Apeny's *khat* from the land of the living to the Mountains of the West, but it would go back without her. He turned and began the rocky ascent to the cliffs once more.

The wind had come up in the late afternoon, lifting little clouds of ocher dust that trailed Hani's footsteps like an ostrich tail. The servants, priests, and dancers had departed. Only a watchman and Ptah-mes stood beside the sealed tomb, the latter unmoving as a statue.

"My lord," Hani called tentatively, and Ptah-mes turned, his kohl-rimmed eyes as dead as those painted on the coffin. "My lord, it's Hani." He wasn't sure if his superior had even registered who was approaching him. "I think you should be aware that Lady Apeny's tomb may be targeted by the robbers. I would like to keep guard personally over it at night for a while, if you approve."

"I'll stay with you," said Ptah-mes dully.

"Then I'll be here at nightfall." Hani dared to clasp Ptah-mes's forearm. "Don't forget to eat something," he said in a quieter voice, full of concern.

He descended the slope again. Hani looked back once to see if Ptah-mes was coming, but he saw no one. *He'll probably stand right there until dusk*, he thought with a sigh.

Maya was ready when Lord Hani called out, "Come on, men." Lord Mery-ra emerged from the kitchen with his rocking gait and heavy shoulders, looking downright menacing with a club in his hand, and the four sturdy litter bearers stood to attention. Hani had pressed them into service as a safety measure, and it made Maya feel better. Hani was a stout comrade in arms; however, Maya had his doubts about Hani's sixty-seven-year-old father, no matter how formidable he appeared. And Maya—well, his courage left nothing to be desired, but he wasn't very big.

Carrying torches and tallow lanterns, they trooped down to the River, and to the astonishment of their ferryman, the body of armed men set off for the West just as the sun was setting in their faces.

Maya tapped his bronze rod against his leg. He meant business.

They disembarked with a clatter and a clang, holding up the torches, which suddenly seemed small against the immensity of the night sky. Navigating the trail, with its rocks rolling underfoot, was hard going, and Hani took his father's arm and steadied him on the steep ground. Maya thought that they all would probably make better progress on hands and knees; the path, which was taxing in daylight, was positively perilous in darkness.

Somehow, they found themselves at last at the foot of the cliffs and turned south toward Lady Apeny's tomb. A lone torch was flickering at the mouth, a brave little star of orange light against the devouring velvet night. Maya could see Lord Ptah-mes in a short kilt and serviceable shirt—none of the usual floating caftans and full sleeves and fashionable gathering of pleats—with a wicked-looking battle-ax in his hand.

Hani greeted him. "My lord, we have here enough men to scare any band of robbers away. I suggest we extinguish our torches and cover the lanterns. I would rather the criminals come and we catch them than that they not come."

The flickering light transmogrified Ptah-mes's eye sockets into the deep black pools of a skull's eyes. He tipped his head in acquiescence and ground out his torch on the soil but said nothing.

"How do you want us grouped, Hani?" asked Mery-ra. "All at the mouth of the tomb or scattered around to surprise anyone who comes?"

"Why don't our stalwarts stay here in front, and the rest of us can hide here and there? The last tombs to be robbed were broken into from ground level, over the passageways, but here we have the cliff overhead, so I'm not sure where they'll strike. If you see anything at all, men, give a whistle. The rest of us will uncover our lanterns and come running." He reached out and took his father's arm, drawing him to one side. "You to the left here, Father. Maya—same side but farther up. Lord Ptah-mes, with your permission, you and I will take this side."

"As you see fit," Ptah-mes said expressionlessly. "You're directing this maneuver."

Groping his way up the rocky slope on all fours, Maya followed Lord Mery-ra. As Maya's eyes adjusted, the starshine began to shed a pale half-light over the landscape, ghostly and surreal. That reminded him of all the dead who surrounded them. *Are the* bas *of the men who were robbed angry? Vengeful?* A shiver ran up his back that had nothing to do with the fast-descending chill of night in the desert.

He cleared himself a flat spot free of stones and settled there with a big rock at his back—the area was too exposed to hunker down out in the open where anyone could sneak quietly up from behind. He sat, and time passed. The familiar sounds of night on the banks of the River were absent—no frogs, no crickets, only the dry, scurrying footsteps of the wind and its eerie moan among the cliffs. Maya heard an occasional scuffle that he hoped was Lord Mery-ra changing positions. His imagination began to people the darkness with lions and jackals that stealthily drew closer, and he gripped his bronze rod in both fists. His senses seemed superhumanly alert. His heart pounded with expectation, and even the hair on his arms stood to attention. He felt that something was going to happen at any moment...

But when he awoke, stiff and dry mouthed, the sun was coming up in his eyes, and the chill of night was ebbing fast. He saw Lords Ptah-mes and Hani standing below near the mouth of the tomb, talking head to head. The soldiers were gathering the torches. Next to Maya, Mery-ra lay on his side, snoring.

Maya scrambled to his feet and dusted off the sand that had gathered on him. "Lord Mery-ra," he called. "Everyone's up. Our watch is over for the night."

While Hani's father heaved himself to a sitting position, Maya descended the slope to the others.

Hani looked up and smiled wearily. "No tomb robbers

last night. But we won't let up. We'll be back tomorrow night, Lord Ptah-mes."

Ptah-mes, who looked a hundred years older than he had only days before, nodded somberly. "I'll stay here until the day guards arrive. Thank you, Hani."

They left him staring pensively out over the desert. Mery-ra had joined them, and they scuffed down the rocky pathway toward the River.

"I feel as if I've been beaten," groaned Mery-ra. "It couldn't have been worse if we'd actually had to fight off the tomb robbers."

Hani chuckled. "Nobody's making you do this, Father."

"Well, as long as I can get some sleep during the day, I'm still in."

"One thing I'd like to do today is find out more about Ay. And also that soldier Pipi told about our intent to arrest Talpu-sharri. Whoever he is, he seems to be in with them. Maybe we can follow him and learn our Mitannian's whereabouts."

Scratching his head skeptically, Maya said, "Lord Hani, didn't we arrest all of the artisans who broke into those tombs? Who does Talpu-sharri intend to use if he's aiming at Lady Apeny's? A whole new group of the men who worked on it?"

"There aren't many of them left, I grant you," Hani said as they approached the bank of the River. "And you'd think they'd be a little skittish, since they saw us drag away their colleagues."

They were tramping up the gangplank of their ferry when Mery-ra cried, "Oh, Hani, I've never told you about my second visit with families of the victims."

"That's right. We've been so busy I forget what needs to be done. How did they go?"

Mery-ra struggled unsuccessfully to conceal a grin. "They were ve-e-ery fruitful, as our girl would say. I did get a list of the stolen goods for you, and I found out how the other two men died. Sa-tau had an apoplectic fit, like Ah-mes. Pa-ren-nefer died of the plague. But the most interesting information came from the servants."

Hani crowed. "We should have thought of that sooner. What did you find out?"

"Well, Pa-ren-nefer, too, received more than one visit from our foreign friend." Hani and Maya exchanged a triumphal glance, and Mery-ra continued. "And Sa-tau held secret meetings at his house from time to time. And who do you think was one of his guests?" He waited until the others' baffled looks and impatient murmurs had mounted sufficiently before he said with a smirk, "Pirissi."

"You've got be joking!" cried Lord Hani, his jaw hanging open.

Maya was so shocked he could hardly find his words. "If... if they were in cahoots with Sa-tau, why did they rob his tomb?"

But Hani held up a hand. "We don't know this had anything to do with the tomb robberies."

"Hani." His father snorted. "What else could it have been? Why should a Mitannian attaché pay a visit to a private citizen?" They lurched as the boat cast off from the shore and slipped into the stream.

Maya was confused. "Why were Mitannians involved at all in Ay's scheming? What did Pirissi have to do with

283

Talpu-sharri? He seemed not even to know what he looked like."

"Of course, surprise can be counterfeited," Hani said thoughtfully. "What role did the Osir Sa-tau play in the government, Father?"

"He was the keeper of the Double House of Silver and Gold. The treasurer."

Maya whistled, impressed. *This business involves the cream of the elite. But what* is *this business?* "I can't tell the good side from the bad," he said, pushing back his wig and scratching his head.

Mery-ra smiled. "Wait, boys. I've saved the best for last. One of Sa-tau's servants gave me a little clay cup with some liquid inside that he said didn't belong to the household. He said he saw it for the first time the night Lord Sa-tau died."

"You know, my friends," said Hani in a serious tone, "this is beginning to sound like more than tomb robbing. I think we have a case of serial murder."

CHAPTER 11

"I HAVE TO SPEAK TO PTAH-MES right away. His wife's tomb may not be the only thing in danger—he may be too," Hani added after the long space during which the others had absorbed his words in shocked silence.

"But surely, he has had nothing to do with the Mitannians. He would certainly have said so, son," Mery-ra objected, looking befuddled.

Hani shrugged, feeling just as confused as his father. "He's had a lot on his mind in the last seventy days. Perhaps he forgot or didn't think it was important."

"Hmm," said Mery-ra skeptically.

But Hani was already leaning over to tap the steersman on the knee. "Turn around, please."

The man gave him a look that suggested Hani was touched by the sun, but he leaned on his steering oar, and the boat began to turn ponderously in midstream, rocking them around as the sail emptied and then refilled. The day was well underway, the pearly sunrise yielding to the staggering brightness of midmorning. Ibises rose in an explosion of flashing white and black from the marshes. *How I'd like to be out watching that peaceful race of shore birds,* Hani thought with a sigh. *Instead I'm tracking our own murderous kind.*

He stepped ashore on the west bank once more, and Maya and Mery-ra pushed off for Waset, leaving Hani to engage another ferry for when he should finish. Hani trudged the arduous way back up the slope to the base of the cliffs, where he saw Ptah-mes still standing at the doorway of his wife's tomb, leaning his head on his forearm against the sealing stones. The day watchman sat on a rock in the shade of an outcropping, a gourd of water at his side.

"My lord," cried Hani. "I have some more information for you."

Ptah-mes raised his head and stood up straight. He shaded his eyes against the sun and said uncertainly, "Hani? Is that you?"

Hani mounted the last of the slope in long strides and presented himself to his superior, panting. "It is. My father just told me some new facts, and I need you to illuminate them for me."

"Don't look to me for much light, my friend," said Ptah-mes aridly.

"Did you ever meet the Mitannian adjutant named Pirissi? A young man, tall and corpulent. A pleasant, well-spoken fellow. Clean-shaven."

"I did, Hani." He looked desolate. "Forgive me my faulty memory. That was right before... he actually came to see Apeny, to talk about music."

"He must have come immediately after I freed them

from jail. I sent them back to Waset, where they were staying with Mane."

"That sounds about right. I didn't hear the whole conversation, of course—she had her life, and I had mine—but the part I heard was definitely about music. I actually congratulated him on his liberty. He said he would like to talk to me too."

Hani thought in anguish, *How can I tell him Pirissi might have been the cause of his wife's death?* But Apeny had died of sickness, not from a wound. Just as had the other three men whose tombs were robbed. The grandees in particular were old, and a plague was raging. No one had to have murdered them for them to drop dead. Yet still... there was that mysterious cup.

"That's all you heard, my lord?"

"I'm almost sure, Hani," he said, untying his mourning scarf for the first time, as if he'd forgotten he was still wearing it after the burial. "Although I can't trust my recollections anymore. There seems to be a black chasm surrounding her death."

That's because you were dead drunk, Hani thought in pity. He tried not to remember Ptah-mes as he had been at that meeting.

"I wanted to warn you, my lord, that I suspect the three robbing victims may have been murdered somehow, even though their deaths appeared natural. Each of them seems to have talked with Pirissi or Talpu-sharri shortly before he died suddenly—it's too much coincidence. Were they involved in some plot? Were they witnesses to something? And now it seems that Lady Apeny may have had the same involvement. Just be careful."

"It would be a favor to the world to kill me, Hani," Ptah-mes said expressionlessly.

Hani winced. "We need you, Lord Ptah-mes," he said quietly, his heart going out to his friend. "Now more than ever, we need good men."

"Good luck finding one."

⬩

"I need to talk to a doctor," Hani said.

Nub-nefer looked up at him, her kohl-edged eyes wide with sudden fright. The two of them sat together at their little table for dinner. "Dear gods, you're not sick, are you?"

"No, no, my dear. But I need to know something medical that has to do with this grave-robbing case."

"I'm sure Neferet can help you."

"She's not here."

"No, but she will be for the long holidays of midsummer." Nub-nefer laid a hand on Hani's. He was grateful that they had not confronted Neferet and driven her away.

Hani laughed. "When do we ever work in this country? Very well, my dear, I'll wait. She should be back within days. I wonder if her friend is coming with her."

Nub-nefer's face stiffened, but she managed to return her husband's smile. "Will you, too, be able to take a holiday for a change, Hani? You've worked constantly on this case with never a break." She squeezed his hand.

Hani sighed. "I fear there's a deadline on this, my dove. Apeny's tomb is likely to be robbed, and I'm afraid Ptah-mes may be a target for a killer."

Her eyebrows twisted with distress. "Why should the life of a scribe be so full of dangers? I thought it would be better when you transferred from the army. But when you're not off at the ends of the earth, someone is shooting arrows at you. You're nearly fifty, Hani."

"Too true, alas. But the men in my family live a very long time." He seized her hand and brought it to his lips. "You should have seen Father out in the Mountains of the West, sleeping rough with the best of them."

"Ah! Ah! You didn't say 'reverend Father'!" cried Mery-ra from the doorway.

"And the men of my family move quietly despite their size," Hani added loudly. He drew over a stool for Mery-ra. "Listening in on our conversation, were you?"

"Innocent of charges. I was napping all morning. That's what sleeping rough at night does to you."

"Oh, no, he wasn't listening." Nub-nefer grinned.

Mery-ra leaned over Hani's dish and extracted a slice of pickled turnip. "I love these." He crunched it down and smacked his lips while Hani and Nub-nefer watched in amusement. "What's next in our investigation?"

"I suppose we need to ask if Pa-aten-em-heb's cavalry friend can tell us anything about Ay that might be significant. I admit the thought of sniffing around the god's father gives me palpitations."

"Hmm," muttered Mery-ra, spearing a bread crust with Hani's knife.

"If you want lunch, you're welcome to it," said Nub-nefer.

Hani rose from the table and bade his wife and father good day. "I'm off to the barracks."

But Nub-nefer put a hand on his arm. "Why don't we

invite Pa-aten-em-heb for dinner? You said you were in debt to him. And Pa-kiki and Mut-nodjmet can come too."

❖

That evening, Hani was supervising the turning of the spits in the kitchen court when he heard voices from the salon. He wiped his sooty hands and made his way into the house. Oil lamps flickered, their little lights like yellow fireflies.

"Ah, Pa-aten-em-heb! Good to see you, my friend," Hani cried at the sight of the young officer. "But you're alone—we wanted to meet your wife, the other Mut-nodjmet."

"I'm as sorry as you are, my lord," Pa-aten-em-heb said with a crooked smile. "But she's pregnant and hasn't been feeling well. She's lost so many children. We just didn't want…"

"We'll meet her later, with a healthy baby in her arms," Nub-nefer said graciously, laying a wreath around his neck. "Let's go sit in the garden and enjoy some beer until Pa-kiki gets here. Our eldest daughter has eaten and gone to bed early. I do hope you'll excuse her. It was a tiring journey back yesterday."

She seated them all, and the serving girls passed the basin and towel and affixed cones of perfumed wax to their wigs. The two men sat at their ease while the mistress of the house excused herself to oversee preparations. Hani was mildly disappointed that Baket-iset wasn't present. He would have liked to have heard her take on the personable young officer.

"Before the others get here, Pa-aten-em-heb, I have some questions I'd like to ask of your friend in the cavalry," Hani began quietly.

"Yes, my lord?" Pa-aten-em-heb leaned forward, all courteous attention.

"What can he tell me about Lord Ay? What is Ay's real attitude toward the… changes in our kingdom? Is there any chance he might be involved in any kind of machinations behind the king's back? Could he—would he—tell me things like that?"

Pa-aten-em-heb smiled with an unreadable expression that might have been rueful or bitter. "I doubt if he could, my lord. But I could. Lord Ay is my father-in-law."

Hani gaped. He found himself speechless, partly with shock but also with embarrassment. At last, he managed to say apologetically, "Forgive me, my friend. I didn't mean to impugn him…"

"You can impugn him all you like, as far as I'm concerned. He's an unscrupulous fox of a man who has treated his own daughters shamefully." The officer's face was flint. "I'm glad Mut-nodjmet isn't here to hear me say it, because she seems to feel obliged to defend him in spite of how he has hurt her, but that's the truth."

Hani remembered his own sole meeting with the God's Father and his firstborn, the queen. How charming—and dangerous—the man had struck him as being, quietly giving signals to Nefert-iti to guide her in her actions.

"Do you think he's loyal to the king?"

Pa-aten-em-heb snorted. "He's loyal to Ay. Everyone else he uses to advance himself. You'll ask me how much he believes in this Aten business. I can't read hearts, but I'd wager my *ka* on the fact that he'll change sides immediately when the wind blows in a different direction."

Hani nodded slowly. "That lines up with my own

observations. But of course, I don't know the man at all well."

"I do. And I tell you the truth."

Hani fixed the young officer with a hard stare. "I'm going to reveal to you something about why I have asked these questions. Needless to say, it must remain between us."

"On my honor as a standard-bearer. On my mother's *ka*," Pa-aten-em-heb said fervently.

In an undertone, Hani filled him in on the basic lines of the tomb-robbing case and his suspicions about the deaths of the four grandees. He described the involvement of Ay and his cavalrymen—what little he knew of it—and the possibility of the king's patronage, for which there was still no apparent motive.

"Ay might be plotting against the king, then," Pa-aten-em-heb said thoughtfully when Hani had finished. "But I don't understand why all these Mitannians are involved. Why should they care who's on the throne?"

"That's what we need to find out. I think the rest will fall into place after that."

"I thank you for these confidences, Lord Hani. I'll keep my ears open for anything that sounds relevant." Pa-aten-em-heb squared his shoulders, and his jaw tensed as if he were preparing for battle. But it was only the first course, which Nub-nefer brought in, smiling, dressed in her broad collar of flowers.

"We're starting without Pa-kiki and Mut-nodjmet?" Hani asked with a lift of the eyebrows.

"They're in the salon, washing their hands as we speak." Nub-nefer took her seat as the servant handed around the bowl of dates wrapped in fat smoked pork, swimming in a tangy pomegranate-juice sauce.

Before it had made the rounds, the young couple entered and greeted everyone, kissing their hostess. Pa-kiki looked surprised and a little embarrassed to see his commanding officer at table with the family. "My lord," he cried, his earnest face alight. "What an honor! I feel terrible that I've kept you waiting for me."

"Not at all." Pa-aten-em-heb's face softened with his attractive smile. "In fact, as you see, we haven't waited."

Everyone guffawed, and before long, they fell upon the savory dishes with much laughter and conversation.

❧

Less than two days later, a loud, jolly voice from the vestibule told Hani that Neferet had arrived. He braced himself to see Bener-ib in her wake and was not disappointed. The girl entered smiling broadly, but as soon as she saw Neferet's family, despite their warm greeting, she grew as solemn and closed off as before.

Why is the poor woman so uncomfortable around us? Hani wondered. *Does she have a guilty conscience?*

Mery-ra, who was sitting on the floor, working on his *Book of Going Forth by Day*, said, "Your father has some medical questions to ask you, Neferet, my child."

"You're not sick are you, Papa?" the girl asked, seating herself on his lap.

"No, no, my dear. I'm investigating a case. Can you tell me whether someone could provoke an apoplectic fit, or something that appears to be one, artificially?"

Neferet and her friend exchanged a considering look.

Neferet finally said, "Bener-ib is more advanced than I am. What do you think, Ibet?"

The girl looked as if the effort to speak were impaling her. "I think they could. There are drugs that could do that to a person. There's a flower that comes from the islands of the Great Green." She dropped her head.

"You see how smart she is?" Neferet beamed, and Hani felt a pang of tenderness for her because he knew what it was like to worship someone—although this rat-faced little slip of a female would not have been his choice. "Why, Papa? Are you wanting to kill the suspect?"

"No, my love. Some people have recently died of what appears to be natural causes, but I have my doubts." Hani hesitated. "So let me ask you this, my young oracles—could a person deliberately give someone the plague?"

"Oh, yes. If you touch the sick person's spit or the pus from their carbuncles, you could infect someone with it. You could wipe their plate or something." Seeing her mother's expression of horror, Neferet added quickly, "That's why Lady Djefat-nebty tells us to wash our hands, with special prayers to Lady Sekhmet, before and after we examine anybody—and I mean re-e-eally wash. It's like a propitiation of the demons inside the person so they don't enter us."

"Be sure you follow her directions, my love," Nub-nefer said anxiously.

"How long would it take for them to get sick?" Hani persisted.

Neferet pursed her lips pensively and stared at Bener-ib. "What do you think, Ibet?"

"A few days," mumbled the girl in her babyish voice. "You get it in less than a week. Half a week or less."

A chill ran up Hani's back. What a terrible, inhuman weapon. And completely untraceable. *Except some maladroit oaf left behind that cup.* "Thank you, my wise ladies," he said. "You have helped to reestablish *ma'at* in the world."

Neferet slid off his lap. "We're going upstairs to put our things away, Mama. We'll come back down soon."

Hani smiled distractedly, his thoughts roiling. They now had a method but no motive.

Pipi was the next one to arrive, with Nedjem-ib and the children. The house suddenly seemed very small, echoing with their cheery laughter and the thudding about of the undisciplined twins.

"Nub-nefer. Hani, my brother," cried Pipi, holding out his arms. "Here we are, back for the holidays. The children want to see the Wadjet Festival, and you can be sure no one is celebrating it in Akhet-aten."

"No, just the king parading back and forth every day. What fun," said Nub-nefer tartly.

Hani's lip drew up in a dry smile. "The rising and setting of the Shining Sun Disk, my love. You're missing the symbolism here."

Nedjem-ib laughed raucously, and the two women went off to the guest apartment to set Pipi's family up while Hani and his brother took their places under the angled ventilator in the ceiling. There they sat, enjoying the slight breeze that made its way in.

"Where's Father?" Pipi asked after a moment, staring around.

"Sleeping late. We've been keeping watch over Lady Apeny's tomb every night."

"Any action yet? How is Lord Ptah-mes holding up? He looked embalmed at the funeral."

Hani sighed. "It's hard to say. He's functioning, but I think he's only staying together by effort." He leaned forward. "I wanted to ask you, brother—who was the soldier you talked to about the 'son of Ah-hotep-ra'?"

Pipi looked up from under his eyebrows, ashamed. "I'm sorry, Hani. I didn't know he was part of the gang."

"He may not be. But he apparently told someone who is. I want to find him."

"By the balls of the Hidden One, I don't know his name," Pipi said defensively.

Hani was growing exasperated. "Where did you run into him? Is he an officer or an enlisted man? What made you pick *him*? I'm not berating you, brother, I just want to find the fellow."

"A charioteer. I saw him crossing the courtyard at the barracks and followed him into the mess."

"Someone noble, then. Do you know what company he's in?"

"The Glory of the Horizon... or something."

Hani pondered this news. *Djed-ka-ra's unit.* "I wonder who the standard-bearer is of that company. It seems his whole troop is up to no good."

"Hani," Pipi said tentatively, "can I help you and Father keep watch at the tomb?"

Hani's first instinct was to say no, but there was really no reason why Pipi couldn't. Assuming he could spend a night without talking. "I suppose so, Pipi. We'll leave just before dusk. Better bring a gourd and a blanket—we've found it gets cold at night."

Pipi's face brightened in childlike delight. "Thanks, brother." He reached across and squeezed Hani's leg. "You're the best brother ever!"

Hani laughed. "You may not thank me after you've spent a night on the rocky ground." He rose and went to pick up his father's *Book of Going Forth*, which lay on the floor where Mery-ra had been working on it. Hani unrolled it with careful fingers and held it out toward Pipi. "Look how beautiful this is. Father has a masterful hand with the Speech of the Gods. That must be where Pa-kiki gets it."

"Father's been working on it for sixty years; he *should* be good," Pipi said fondly, leaning over the book. He read aloud, "'I have witnessed acclaim in the Land of Fenkhu'— that's you, Hani, heh heh!" Hani smiled at him, and Pipi continued. "What did they give you? 'A firebrand and a column of faience.' What did you do with them? 'I buried them on the shore of the pool of Two Truths.'"

Something rattled in Hani's memory.

Pipi continued, "What did you find there on the shore of the pool of Two Truths? 'A scepter of flint whose name is Breath Giver.'"

"It's that passage again!" Hani cried. "Everywhere I go, I keep finding it. What's it supposed to mean?" *Perhaps it is finding me.*

Pipi looked alarmed at his brother's outburst. "It's magic, Hani. It's something that happens in the Duat. It doesn't mean anything here."

But Hani wasn't so sure. As far as he was concerned, a man lived out the Weighing of the Heart every day.

And sometimes the strangest, most anodyne things awoke connections in his mind. *The scepter of flint...*

◆

That evening, the little troop set out, as had become their custom, for the City of the Dead, each with a blanket and drinking gourd for the chilly watch in the desert. Fortunately, the nights were at their shortest at this time of year.

By the time Hani's party had climbed up to the tomb opening, darkness had fallen, and they'd lit their torches, which flickered and flared in the dry wind, loosing sparks into the blackness of the sky. Hani stared up at the pulsing stars, the souls of those who now rowed the Sun Barque with Ra himself. A black shadow flitted past, obliterating the stars for a moment, and its buzzing cry told him a nightjar was hunting. Ptah-mes was already there, as before. He welcomed the men grimly, and they dispersed to their posts.

Hours passed. Hani huddled in his blanket, trying to stay awake. He thought about the investigation. He thought about his children. He thought about the wrath of the gods that had fallen upon the Two Lands. He'd just begun to drift off in spite of himself when a sound came to his ears, soft but louder than anything else around it—a disorderly shuffling as of many feet making their way stealthily across the rocky scree. He stared into the darkness below him but could see nothing except the darker lumps of the litter bearers in the court of the tomb. At his side, he caught the whites of Ptah-mes's eyes. Barely visible by starlight, Ptah-mes laid a finger to his lips and got silently to his feet, hefting his ax. Hani followed suit, lifting his club quietly from the ground beside him.

This is it, he thought, his heart starting to beat harder. *We'll get them now for sure.* He wished he could signal Maya, Pipi, and his father on the other side of the tomb, but he didn't even know if they were awake. *Don't let them be caught off guard, unable to defend themselves,* he prayed.

The brighter court was filling now with shadows, and Hani concluded in dread that the four stalwarts posted there were all asleep. He longed to cry out to them and had almost made up his mind to do so when Lord Ptah-mes yelled in a loud, authoritative voice, "Who goes there?"

One of the dark figures uncovered a lantern, and Hani saw, with a sinking feeling in the pit of his stomach, that it was Mahu. As other lanterns began to be uncovered, the litter bearers sprang awake at the sudden light, and from above the tomb, Hani and his men started skidding down.

As soon as Mahu saw Hani, he chuckled without humor. "Why am I not surprised? What brings you to a rich tomb at midnight, Lord Hani? The foreign service not paying as much as it used to?"

"They are guarding my wife's burial place at my request." Ptah-mes stepped forward. He was livid, his nostrils pinched and his mouth murderous, but he maintained his haughty posture, and his gestures were controlled. "What is the meaning of this intrusion?" he demanded in a contemptuous voice.

"The police are doing their duty, my lord. We had word that a robbery was going to be committed tonight, so we came to apprehend the malefactors. And look who we found?" Mahu smirked at Hani.

299

Hani forced down the snarl of rage that had begun gurgling up within him. "You heard Lord Ptah-mes. We're here at his request. Your services are not needed."

"Nor are they welcome," Ptah-mes added pointedly. "Please be so kind as to leave my property immediately."

"Not so fast, my fine lord. Hani here has been obstructing our investigations for a long time. I think it's time *he* left"—he cast a sneering look around at Pipi, Mery-ra, and Maya—"and his toy soldiers with him. You, of course, are free to stay."

"How generous of you," the grandee said scornfully. "Off my property now. Your master will hear of this." Ptah-mes's tone had grown threatening, beyond his usual cool control. Hani thought that if Mahu realized how close to losing himself Ptah-mes had become, he might be less antagonistic. Hani just hoped that his superior wouldn't finally fly at Mahu with drawn ax.

"Have it your way, Ptah-mes. But don't be surprised if I come for all of you for obstructing the king's justice." Mahu turned and swaggered into the darkness, his men at his heels, shadows against the bobbing light of their lanterns. "Happy hunting," he called over his shoulder. Hani could hear him laughing as he disappeared.

"As if the robbers are going to come now, after that troupe of dancing cows tromped through," grumbled Mery-ra. "They've probably wakened the dead as far away as the Great Place."

Hani's anger had begun to give way to bone-deep disappointment. How close they had come to apprehending the guilty party. He had so many questions to ask them, and if Mahu got to them first, Hani would never even have a chance.

Ptah-mes pinched the bridge of his nose as if to dispel a headache and looked up at Hani. "I'm sorry about this."

"It's certainly no fault of yours, my lord," Hani replied, growing grimmer. "That Mahu has to be stopped. I'm surer than ever that he's covering up for someone."

"You think he purposely disrupted our watch?" asked Maya, looking fierce.

Hani snorted. "I find it impossible not to. Who do you suppose 'told' him that there would be an attempt tonight? If he's not openly in league with our robbers, they have a go-between."

"And who is that?" Lord Ptah-mes murmured pensively.

"Who is that indeed, my lord?" Hani said. They milled about for a bit, picking up torches and the blankets the police had kicked around, then Hani turned to his men. "We'll stay out the night, boys. There won't be any ferries till daybreak anyway."

"You don't think the robbers will still try tonight, do you?" Pipi looked both dubious and hopeful.

"I doubt it. I don't even know what time it is. Dawn may already be near."

Lord Ptah-mes stared up at the stars. "Not so late, I think. Let's go back to our posts and see if Mahu's source was telling the truth."

They took up their watch once more. Hani found he was wide-awake, his thoughts churning, throwing themselves against all the things that didn't fit together. The intervention of Mahu complicated matters even further. *I need to complain to the vizier.*

301

The noise began so softly that at first he wasn't sure he heard anything more than the usual sounds of the desert at night, but Ptah-mes reached out and put a tense hand on his shoulder. *He hears it too.*

They rose silently and tightened their grip on their weapons. The noise drew closer, a rhythmic crunching—as of feet moving quietly, Hani realized. *Is that Mahu come back to devil us?* He hoped none of the others would uncover their lanterns, and he thought to warn them. His heart had begun to pound in anticipation; he was holding his breath, straining his ears.

At last, the footsteps stopped somewhere above him. There came a scraping noise and the dull metallic sound of shovels coming out. Then came the quiet punctuation of digging—screech *bam*, screech *bam*. Ptah-mes gestured to Hani, and the men began to creep forward. Behind him, he could hear his bearers starting up the slope quietly.

With those shovels, the robbers are as good as armed, Hani thought uneasily, *and we have no long-handled weapons.*

All at once, Ptah-mes lunged forward, his battle-ax raised. Hani caught a terrifying glimpse of his face before Hani, too, fell upon the diggers in the paling darkness, swinging his club. He made contact with someone's bent back that sent a shock wave up his arm. Cries broke out. The lanterns flashed on from all sides. A shadow started to run away, and Maya went hurtling through the air after him and dragged him to the ground. Mery-ra brought his staff down on the man, and he lay still.

But the element of surprise had worn off, and now the robbers were beginning to rally. They knew how to fight, swinging their shovels in an arc to keep their attackers at bay. Hani heard one of the men pant, "Run, run! I'll hold them off." And suddenly, the melee dissolved, and dark figures tore away, heading for the cliffs.

"After them!" Hani cried to his bearers.

They took off, scrambling after the others, knocking rocks and gravel in a shower down upon the lone defender, who jabbed and slashed with the blade of the shovel, grunting with effort. Clangs and clacks marked the contact with rods or clubs. Suddenly, something flew through the air. There was a thud and a cry, and the battle stopped dead.

Hani dropped his club, panting. "Is he down?" he called.

"I hit him with a rock! Did you see that, Hani?" Pipi's proud voice came out of the darkness, which was already raveling under the rays from their lanterns.

"I'm glad someone thought of that," Ptah-mes said dryly. He was winded, and his face was streaked with perspiration.

Hani bent to tie up their victim. The man was unconscious, but apart from some blood on his scalp, he didn't seem badly hurt. Hani took from the robber's own sack a length of rope and tied his wrists to his ankles behind him so he couldn't even walk, let alone run away. Then he doused the robber with the contents of his water gourd, which brought the man abruptly to consciousness, spluttering and shaking his head. Dawn was starting to gain the eastern sky. Hani saw around them on the ground a pile of hempen sacks and the robbers' abandoned tools.

By now, the litter bearers were returning triumphantly, each pair carrying between them a trussed-up prisoner hanging from the handle of a shovel.

"Is that all there is?" Ptah-mes called out.

One of the men replied, breathing heavily, "I think there was another, my lord, but he got away into the valley."

He'll tell his leader what happened, of course. Hani eyed the miscreants. They were young, strong, and well fed and had clearly demonstrated their fighting skills and coordination. "What company are you from?"

One of them began, "The Glory of—"

"Shut up, you idiot!" The shovel man snarled at Hani, "We're not soldiers."

"No, you're cavalrymen, aren't you? Runners and charioteers and scouts. This work is a little below your dignity, I should think—robbing tombs. And now you've been defeated in battle by a bunch of scribes. Nice story to tell your grandchildren. You should have stayed with your horses."

The men were silent except for their heavy breathing. "We do what we're told," growled the spokesman.

"Tell me, Iby son of Ah-hotep-ra," Hani said, taking a chance, "what did your leader promise you to make the fine young men of your company abandon all decency?"

The prisoner said nothing.

"Tell me, like a good obedient soldier, Iby. Who is he? What did he promise you?"

"We fight for the king and the good of the Two Lands, as always," Iby cried defiantly.

Ptah-mes drew nearer and fixed the man with a cold-eyed stare. "Who is your protector? What was to be your reward for the heinous act of robbing a tomb? Did he promise you impalement? The gift of losing your nose and ears so that you can't hear the songs of the Field of Reeds or breathe in the breath of life?"

Even in the pale half-light of earliest morning, Hani could see the man's face blanch. "It was for the good of the kingdom," he stammered. "He said it would help our foreign relations better than waging war."

Ptah-mes and Hani exchanged a look. "Robbing someone's tomb will help the kingdom?" Hani said. "I'm afraid I don't follow his logic."

"They were all enemies of the Aten. Who cared whether we starved their souls? With the treasure, he said we could do good for foreign relations."

Ptah-mes's face grew as sharp as a flint blade, his teeth bared, and Hani almost feared to see his superior fall upon the man and beat him to death.

Mery-ra, who had stepped to Hani's side, said in a kindly voice, "Who is 'he,' son?"

"Lord Ay, the god's father. He is our protector, and no one can touch him."

Hani nearly jumped back, as if the man had sprouted flames. He'd both expected and not expected this. They found themselves swimming in dangerous waters—this pool of the Two Truths. "Who is the foreigner who is involved with your scheme?"

"I don't know his name. Lord Ay said we should do what he told us."

"Is he still directing you? Are you expected to do any more of this despicable business?"

The cavalryman looked reluctant to say more, but Ptah-mes, squatting at his side, pushed the blunt edge of his ax blade against Iby's throat until his head lolled back.

"Perhaps if I crush your larynx, you'll find it easier to stay silent," Ptah-mes growled in a barely controlled voice.

The man swallowed with difficulty and choked out, "Yes."

Ptah-mes stood and walked away, as if he didn't trust himself not to kill the cavalryman.

"If you take him in, Ay will probably have him released," Mery-ra said under his breath. "We know who Mahu has been protecting now." He and Hani moved downhill together in the direction of Maya, who stood dusting his hands as he gazed out over the courtyard of Apeny's tomb.

Hani nodded. "And how he knew there would be an attempt tonight. But it puzzles me that he let us continue in our watch."

"I guess he didn't care if we caught the robbers, knowing that nothing would happen to them in the end. It confirmed his association with the great and powerful, which is what he lives for," Lord Ptah-mes said scornfully.

"Or perhaps he fully intended to have them put to death himself, to silence them." Hani couldn't keep the disgust out of his voice.

Maya turned to them, his face flushed with excitement. "That was quite a fight, Lord Hani. What a scene this will make in my *Tales*!"

Glad for the distraction from his dark thoughts, Hani threw back his head and laughed. "Get these men down to the River. It'll take several trips, and I'd like to catch an early boat across to Waset. The sooner these birds are locked up, the better I'll like it."

"Who is going to lock them up, Hani?" said Lord Ptah-mes dryly. "The police? The army?"

"The army. But it will be the infantry. Menna's company. And then I'm going to see the vizier."

＊

Hani and Maya sailed back down to the capital before the holidays were ended. Hani wanted to update the vizier on developments and ask how Aper-el wanted him to proceed—or whether he should proceed at all. And he needed to talk to Keliya to see if he was aware of Pirissi's moonlight career as a tomb robber. *Although perhaps it no longer matters; he's gone home now.*

After the glorious hustle-bustle of the Great Jubilee, Akhet-aten seemed deserted. Faded garlands still wreathed the neck of a king-headed lion here and there, where cleanup crews had overlooked them. The dusty streets were hotter than ever in this season of preparing for the Flood, and Hani's shirt was soaked by the time they'd trudged from the embarcadero to the Hall of Royal Correspondence.

They entered the reception hall of Aper-el's offices and found it empty, their footsteps echoing on the gypsum floor. *I guess they're all still at home for the holidays*, he thought. But something didn't seem quite right. A scribe came striding through the room, oblivious to the newcomers' presence. He had a mourning scarf around his head. Hani stared after him, his heart in his mouth, as the man entered a chancery hall and pulled the door shut behind him.

"What's going on?" Hani murmured uneasily. Maya's eyes had grown round as plates.

They followed the man and knocked on the door where he'd disappeared. Someone else, also marked as being in mourning, stuck a head out. Hani's hair rose on the back of his neck.

"What do you want? We're busy," the man said brusquely.

"I am Hani son of Mery-ra. I have a report to give the vizier."

"You'll have to deliver it to the Field of Reeds, then. Lord Aper-el is among us no longer." The scribe looked more annoyed than sorrowful that his superior had died.

Hani sucked in his breath in horror. "When? How?"

"A few days ago. The plague." The man smiled bitterly as if to disarm his fear. "Lady Sekhmet doesn't spare high rank. They say one of the king's little daughters has died too."

"Who has been named in his place?" This was a question Hani hardly dared ask.

"We don't know yet."

Hani drifted back through the reception room in a state of shock, his secretary in his wake, murmuring, "I can't believe this."

His protector was no more. Who would replace him? What would this mean for the investigation—and after? In the courtyard, he knelt and strewed his head with dust in a decent gesture of condolence, forcing himself to remember that Aper-el was a human being, no doubt with a family who would now be suffering and a soul in need of prayer. But selfishly, the thought kept floating back: *My protector is gone.*

Lord Ptah-mes had returned to the capital on his fast yacht, at last daring to leave his wife's tomb now that the robbers had been apprehended. Perhaps he already knew about Aper-el and perhaps not. Hani and Maya crossed the court to the building occupied by the foreign service and made his way gratefully into the cool interior. The secretary at work in the reception room looked up from the floor with a haughty lift of the eyebrows. "May I help you?"

"Is Lord Ptah-mes in? It's Hani to see him," Hani said, trying to make his voice level and polite despite the turmoil that raged within.

The secretary got to his feet and disappeared into Ptah-mes's office then returned a moment later. "He will receive you, my lord." Maya took a seat in the corner of the reception hall, and Hani approached the high commissioner's door.

Ptah-mes was sitting in his chair when Hani entered. He looked up with a vacant smile. "Hani."

He, too, was wearing a mourning scarf. It had become a far too frequent occurrence.

"I see that you've heard about Aper-el, my lord," Hani said. Fear fluttered in his belly but also anger at the injustice of things.

Ptah-mes's mouth cracked in a humorless smile, and he replied, as if he could read Hani's thoughts, "Yes. We're unprotected now. Our heads are sticking up above the shield."

"Mahu must be laughing." Hani gave a sarcastic snort.

They sat in grim silence, then Ptah-mes said, "Here's some good news for you, though. Your friend Mane is on his way back from Naharin—Tulubri and Pirissi must have reached Wasshukanni. Although..."

Hani felt a thrill of fear. "Although?"

"I fear Tushratta's days on the throne are numbered. Mane sent a courier before he left. Things are unraveling fast. This Prince Artatama seems to have picked up support and, more to the point, gold enough to buy troops."

Hani shook his head sorrowfully. "I'm glad Mane got out in time. But what will happen to Lady Kiya if her uncle takes the throne?"

Ptah-mes shrugged and raised his eyebrows. "I'd say she has been thrown into the fire as an offering." He added, as if to soften his words, "Perhaps he'll marry her to legitimate himself."

"We'll never know what Pirissi's role was in all this," Hani said reluctantly. He had to admit that regime change was messy business, and while he wished the Crocodiles success, he didn't want to see such costly fratricidal strife overwhelming the Two Lands. Somehow, the chaos now swallowing up Naharin made that possibility real to him in a way it had not been before. He felt torn in two.

"Will I enjoy the pleasure of your company this evening, Hani, or are you planning to start back to Waset this afternoon?"

"I think I'll wait, my lord. I'd like to talk to Keliya before I leave."

Ptah-mes tipped his head. Then he said a little shyly, "Thank you, my friend, for all that you've done. I'm aware that it's your job, but know that it means a lot to me that you saved Apeny from the indignity of having her grave goods stolen and our *ka* house violated."

"It was the least I could try to do, my lord, and the gods were kind enough to grant us success." Hani looked his superior in the eye warmly and saw Ptah-mes's stiff face reflect some of that warmth. "I'm off to the Mitannian embassy, then."

"Until this evening, Hani."

✦

At Lord Hani's reappearance, Maya popped up from his seat on the floor where he was jotting notes on a potsherd. "Was he aware, my lord?"

"Yes. In fact, he said one of the king's daughters has been stricken as well."

They strode through the doorway and into the blinding glare of the court. Hani looked around then started out with purposeful strides toward the south.

"Where are we going, my lord?" Maya asked breathlessly as he scrambled to stay abreast of his father-in-law.

"First, to pick up Neferet to take her home for the holidays. Then, to see Keliya. There are some things he needs to know."

They set out on the now-familiar route to the villa of Lord Pentju, and after they'd traversed the luxurious garden, the doorman admitted them to the vestibule. "Did you want to speak to Lord Pentju or Lady Djefat-nebty, my lord?" he asked Hani.

"Neither. I'm just here to pick up the lady's two young apprentices."

Hani and Maya waited for a long space of time in the cool silence of the vestibule. Maya's thoughts were churning—there were so many questions yet to be answered, and the most pressing one was, *Why?* Ay's involvement made that all the more puzzling—unless, of course, he had his eye on the throne of the Two Lands. The more Maya thought about it, the more likely that seemed.

At last, a clatter of sandals and the giggling conversation

of adolescent girls broke the silence. Neferet came galloping in with Bener-ib in tow. Hani's daughter rushed to him and threw herself on him joyously. "Papa! Guess what we did today?"

"Drained pus? Pulled out worms? I can't think why else you'd be so cheerful," Hani said with a grin.

Maya tried not to stare at Neferet's head, shaved smooth. It gave her a kind of old-fashioned chic, like a woman from a very old tomb painting. She was wearing earrings too. Perhaps this new style consciousness was the result of Bener-ib's influence. Or maybe it meant that Neferet was simply growing up—and doing it in her own eccentric way.

"No-o-o, Papa." Her voice dropped. "We went with Lord Pentju to treat the crown prince, the Haru in the nest."

"Is he sick?" Hani cried uneasily.

"Yes, but it wasn't plague, Lord Pentju said. It was sweating fever."

People can die of that too, Maya thought. *What then? More chaos over the succession? Poor half-witted Prince Smenkh-ka-ra succeeding to the throne?* "How is he now?"

"He's recovering," Bener-ib said in the first statement she'd ever volunteered, to Hani's recollection.

"And do you know why?" Neferet demanded excitedly. "Lord Pentju gave him some of the medicine that Ibet and I made! Lady Djefat-nebty told him how good it was!"

Hani squeezed the girl proudly. "That's wonderful. You two are really becoming first-rank *sunet*s. I suppose the queen was there with… her son."

"Yes, Papa. Her son," Neferet said, exchanging an all-too-transparent knowing look with her father.

What's that about? Maya wondered.

"She's so beautiful, isn't she?" Neferet added lightly, as if to cover for the understanding that she and her father had shared.

Hani said, with a clap of his hands, "Let's get going, girls. I have another stop to make before we catch a ferry. You can wait outside the office."

Maya could have sworn he was deliberately changing the subject.

Before they reached the battlemented white wall of the smaller Aten temple, Hani turned east, his little troop following, and then stopped at a featureless building on the outskirts of the clerical district. Within, a lone scribe in a long woolen tunic sat writing clay tablets at a table. He looked up at their entrance. "Ah, Lord Hani, if I'm not mistaken. Do you want to speak to Lord Keliya?"

"Yes, please. If he's in."

The secretary rose and disappeared into the ambassador's private office. Hani and Maya stood looking at one another. The girls stared at them both, Neferet's curiosity written clearly across her face.

"Ah, Hani, my friend. Maya. How good to see you." Keliya emerged from the office and embraced Hani then led the two scribes inside. The girls drifted to a corner and took a seat. "Our men made it back safely with Lady Kiya, and Mane has been released. He should be home within the month."

"So I've heard, Keliya. We just talked with Ptah-mes.

He said…" Hani's voice dropped discreetly. "He said things were looking bad for Tushratta."

"Alas, that's true. My whole mission expects to be recalled to make way for Artatama's officials." Keliya was putting on a bland face, but the lines in his forehead revealed how worried he was.

Maya wondered what such a recall meant for a career diplomat like Keliya. Surely, it would be a simple formality, as Hani's and Maya's had been when Nefer-khepru-ra had come to the throne alone. But perhaps Keliya would refuse to serve a usurper.

Lord Hani took his Mitannian friend by the arm and led him into the center of the room, as if the very walls themselves might be listening. "As you know, we cleared young Tulubri of any involvement with the tomb robbers, Keliya, but now it's come out that there seems to have been some collusion on the part of Pirissi."

Keliya glanced sharply at Hani, although he replied in his easygoing voice, "Oh, I wouldn't worry about it, Hani. He's gone now anyway."

Hani caught his eye uncertainly. "You've dealt with it?"

"His masters have taken him back."

Hani stared at him a moment longer then said with a shrug, "That's your business, my friend. I just thought you might want to know."

Keliya smiled, his lugubrious face creasing. "You're a good man, Hani. But much as I love you, you're not a member of my mission."

Maya took that to mean there were internal things Keliya couldn't tell an Egyptian.

Hani nodded. "Understood. Were you ever able to get an audience to protest the seizure of your two aides?"

Keliya smiled thinly. "No. I put in my request, but I'm still waiting. And now, of course, it makes no difference. I guess the message is pretty clear."

Maya sneered inwardly. *Only too clear.* The three men stood for a space in awkward silence.

"How long will you be here, my friend?" Hani asked finally.

"I don't know." Keliya scratched his beard. "But in any case, I'll stay until Mane gets back."

"Come see us, my friend. Once you've gone, who knows when we'll see one another again?" Hani clapped him on the shoulder, and then, as if his words had just sunk in, the two men embraced once more. Maya saw Hani swallowing hard as they made their way out. A pang pierced his own heart, not so much because of Keliya's departure but because a sudden doubt had descended upon Maya. *Was Keliya himself involved somehow? He seemed to be covering for Pirissi. We spoke so freely to him, told him of our suspicions. Was he the one to hustle Talpu-sharri to safety before he could be arrested?*

As they strode down the baked street toward Lord Ptah-mes's villa, the chattering girls trailing behind them, Maya blurted, "What do we do now, my lord?" He felt he couldn't expose to Hani how suspicious he had suddenly become of Hani's friend.

Hani smiled, but the expression held an edge. "I think our situation is very much like Keliya's. Until we know who our new master is, we hardly dare take an action. Nonetheless..." As his words trailed off, a considering look took possession of his face. His mouth quirked, and one eyebrow cocked. Something had clearly just come into his mind.

"What is it?" Maya cried eagerly.

"I'm not sure yet." Hani laughed, scrubbing the top of his head with his knuckles. "When it has wings, it will fly from the nest."

CHAPTER 12

W HEN HANI AND MAYA AND the girls reached Waset at last, Maya peeled off for home, and Hani entered his own gate with his daughter and her friend. As the young women headed off into the house, chattering, Hani saw Mery-ra crouched in the garden, staring into the plants.

"What is it, Father? Did you lose something?"

Mery-ra hauled himself to his feet with a grunt. "Ah, Hani, my boy. You're back. Neferet, too, eh? No, no. There was a movement in the bushes, and when I looked closer, I saw it was Ta-miu's kittens playing. As Neferet would say, they're ado-o-orable."

Hani laughed. "Somehow, that word sounds better in the mouth of an adolescent girl than that of a crusty old scribe like yourself." He slapped his father on the back, and the two men made their way into the house, where Hani dumped his baggage for the servants to take away. "And speaking of adolescent girls, the house is again officially full of them."

"So I see," Mery-ra said.

"Don't Bener-ib's family ever get to see her?" Hani pulled off his wig and tossed it onto a stool.

Mery-ra said thoughtfully, "I get the feeling there's a problem there, don't you? We seem to scare her."

"I'm sure Neferet knows all and will gladly tell all." Hani chuckled. "Where is Nub-nefer?"

"Back down at the farm with Baket." Mery-ra dropped with a thud into his chair and stretched out his legs.

So Neferet has managed to time her visit so that she avoids her mother yet again. That was another strange business. Different as they were, Neferet and her mother had always been close. Hani sat next to his father. "Tushratta's government is about to fall in Naharin. It may have already. Keliya expects to be recalled any day, but Mane is on his way back, and we should get the full story from him."

"Civil war is a terrible thing." Mery-ra shot his son a sharp glance. "I hope your friends the Crocodiles are giving that plenty of thought."

Hani had no answer for that. The high priests were prudent men, even if his incendiary brother-in-law wasn't. Nor had Lady Apeny been especially careful—she'd been a real firebrand.

"Firebrand," said Hani aloud, musing. Suddenly, it came to him why that word had resonated. "'I have witnessed the acclaim in Fenkhu.' What did they give you? 'A firebrand and a faience column.'"

Mery-ra looked at him in amazement. "You've memorized the *Book of Going Forth*?"

Hani laughed. "No, only those verses. They keep popping up in my life lately. If Apeny was the firebrand, then Ptah-mes must be the faience column."

Mery-ra nodded, a sad but humorous spark in his eye. "Yes, that fits him—beautiful and brittle. And the high commissioner of foreign affairs over Fenkhu, among other places."

Hani found this deeply disturbing. He knew he was floundering in a case where two truths seemed to exist at once, but it spooked him to see so much of the reality around him acted out again in the Duat. *Is life really just a rehearsal for the trial in the otherworld, as I've so often thought?* It wouldn't have surprised him to see in the *Book* a line like, *Hani, you'd better watch your step; you think you're righteous, but you're full of prejudices.* Musing aloud, he said, "Who is the scepter of flint?"

"Scepters are the symbol of power. It must be the king." Mery-ra added mischievously, "Life, prosperity, and health to him, of course."

"Maybe he's more involved in these tomb robberies than I thought. Maybe Ay isn't plotting behind his back but doing his bidding."

Mery-ra laughed and punched his son in the arm. "Because a scepter of flint is mentioned in the *Book of Going Forth by Day*? Maybe a seven-headed demon or one with a head of flames is the culprit. Come, come, Hani. Is this where your famous powers of deduction come from—magic texts?"

Hani was aware of heat rising up his cheeks, and he said, more than a little embarrassed, "Ideas come from all sorts of places, Father. The only thing that keeps me from accepting this one is the lack of motive. Why would Nefer-khepru-ra want a regime change?"

"And why would he rob his own father's tomb? And

why would he have you assigned to investigate the plot? I'm afraid it doesn't hold together, no matter what the *Book of Going Forth* says." Mery-ra smiled tolerantly at his son's folly.

"But they haven't robbed Neb-ma'at-ra's tomb. Maybe that was something our mysterious Mitannian made up to lure the workmen in with the promise of unimaginable riches."

Mery-ra shrugged with an eloquent lift of his shaggy eyebrows. After a moment, he clapped his son on the shoulder and headed off, leaving Hani wrapped deep in his thoughts. He was trying to force anything to make some sense when increasingly loud laughter and feminine voices told him Nub-nefer and her friend were approaching.

He heard Bener-ib cry, "Oh! I left the oil of cedar upstairs. Go on and start. I'll be right down." A patter of rapid footsteps mounted the stairs.

A moment later, Neferet entered, and seeing Hani, she came bouncing over to him.

"We're going to make more of that special medicine since it's worked so well." She beamed proudly and seated herself in Hani's lap.

"That's wonderful. You're getting to be a real *sunet*." A thought suddenly came to Hani. "My duckling, if you can put a drug together, can you also take one apart? Can you look at something and tell what it is?"

"Maybe, Papa. Sometimes it has a smell or a color that gives it away. Why?"

"I'd like to show you a little cup that we found in the room of a man who died mysteriously of apoplexy. I'd like to know if it's some kind of poison that might have made him sick." Hani strode to the kitchen and reached up to the high shelf for the leather bag with the small cup his father had found in Lord Pa-ren-nefer's house. He brought it back to Neferet.

She took it gingerly between her finger and thumb and looked into it, her mouth crooked into a dubious moue. "Well, I can certainly tell you if it's poison. We'll try it on something."

Hani cringed, imagining that some innocent creature was going to die to confirm his suspicions. For the first time, he hoped he was wrong. "Very well, my dear. Find the smallest thing you can, please."

"We'll put honey in the cup and then wait for the ants to find it," she said with the self-assurance of one who was long accustomed to poisoning things.

"You say *we*—do you mean you and Bener-ib will work together? I'm not sure her parents would like her touching poison." *And what kind of father am I who lets his daughter do such a thing?*

But Neferet pooh-poohed the danger enthusiastically. "We always work together. She's fa-a-abulous at diagnosis, Papa. And I like to treat the symptoms. So we're perfect together. We've thought of opening a practice together someday."

"Ah," said Hani noncommittally. "My love, your friend seems so sad around us, almost afraid, and yet I hear her laughing like a normal girl with you. Doesn't she like us?"

Neferet's face dropped into lines of sorrowful pity. She said under her breath in an earnest voice, "Oh, Papa, her childhood was so terrible. Her mother died when she was young, and her father remarried this awful woman who was really mean to her. Ibet thinks her father sent her to Djefat-nebty to get rid of her as much as anything. She dreads having to go home. That's why I invite her here. She'll warm up to you all when she sees you're not like her family."

Hani's heart clenched for the poor girl. "She's certainly welcome here. But Neferet, are you trying to avoid your mama?"

Her eyes grew shifty. "I'm afraid Ibet might be scared by a mother, Papa."

Hani considered this and found it wanting as an explanation. "I would think she would *want* to have a mother figure in her life who was kind and loving, little duckling. Are you... are you sure there's nothing else?" He almost hoped she would deny it.

Neferet dropped her head and heaved a sigh before she said unconvincingly, "Of course there isn't."

Hani didn't know if he should probe her or not. The last thing he wanted to do was scare his daughter away. He gazed at her in compassion, willing her to trust him.

She raised her eyes to him guiltily and put her arms around him. "Mama can be... she gets mad sometimes, and I don't want to have to fight her."

Hani drew out his arms and enveloped her in turn. "Your mother has a fiery nature, my love, but more than anything in the world, she loves you. She wants only what will make you happy. Give her a chance."

Neferet pressed her lips together in reflection then said determinedly, "You're right, Papa."

"So why don't you pay a short visit to the farm, show

Bener-ib what it's like? You may find medicinal herbs growing in the fields."

Neferet buried her face in Hani's chest and squeezed him with all her considerable strength. She drew back and beamed at him. After a moment, she said, "How do you like my shaved head?"

"It's very striking, my love. A lot of women do it, actually. It doesn't even show under a wig."

"The princesses all do it, even without a wig. It's becoming very fashionable." She grinned mischievously, and Hani understood, with amusement, that that was not her real motive. Neferet was certainly not one to let fashions or expectations rule her.

Bener-ib entered the salon, and Neferet slid off her father's knees and ran to her. "Papa has given us an experiment, Ibet. You see this cup? We have to find out if it has poison in it."

The two girls went hand in hand toward the door, and as they disappeared into the garden, Hani heard Neferet say enthusiastically, "Why don't we go to the farm this afternoon? You'll love it there. And you can meet my mother."

Their departure left Hani sitting alone, his heart full of tenderness for them both and for all young people in search of themselves and in need of their parents' approval.

⸙

The next morning, Hani sat in his garden long after he'd finished his breakfast and watched a *seshemty*, a blue-green rock pigeon, strutting along the top of the wall and then descending on heavy whistling wings to the ground to forage. He tried to imitate its soft, throaty, fluttering call to lure its mate down as well, but apparently, he didn't have the come-hither accent of a native speaker. The name of the bird, which meant turquoise colored, made him stop and reflect yet again on the unresolved case before him.

Could the striking garment in the baggage he'd assumed was Tulubri's have been Pirissi's after all? He hadn't noticed the size. "I wish I knew how common those tunics were in Naharin," he said to himself. Did Talpu-sharri have one as well, or had witnesses actually seen Pirissi and conflated him with his confrere? He was a considerably bigger man than the chamberlain, and no one had mentioned that the mystery foreigner was heavyset. Perhaps he'd played a more secretive, behind-the-scenes role than Talpu-sharri, who seemed to have interacted directly with the robbers. Hani would have given a lot to know what that closed meeting at the Osir Sa-tau's house had been about—he doubted it was music—but without knowing the other participants, he couldn't trace anything any further.

❦

The night before, Neferet had shared with him the results of her tests on the cup. After eating the honey mixed into its contents, the ants had died. Bener-ib had suggested testing it next on a mouse—who also died, in convulsions resembling those of an apoplectic fit. That was one question answered.

A crunch of footsteps in the gravel made Hani look up. "Good morning, son," said Mery-ra, as he emerged from around the bushes. "Enjoying a little idleness this morning?"

"Afraid not, Father. I've been trying to put together in my head all the loose ends of what we know about the tomb robberies before Maya gets here. Or should I say murders? I had Neferet test the contents of that cup on ants. And a mouse. The results could pass for apoplexy."

"You're not satisfied that Ay is behind it?" Mery-ra dropped into a chair with a plop.

"He's involved, I'm convinced. But in what? And why? Surely, this plan to put the 'right person' on the throne is more significant than the way in which he's tried to fund it." He emitted a bark of frustrated laughter. "I just keep having the same thoughts over and over again. We need more evidence." Then Hani remembered that people had lost their lives to the tomb-robbing scheme, and he regretted that his priority was to investigate the robbery rather than the murders.

That evening, Hani was standing in the gate, seeing Maya off after their workday. He'd just turned to go back inside when a small voice hissed, "My lord."

He turned to see a naked, knobby-kneed little boy of about eight pressed against the outside of the wall, staring up at him with big eyes. Expecting him to be a beggar, Hani turned to the lad and bent over him kindly. "Do you want food, son? I'll have to go inside to get you a bowl of porridge."

"Are you Lord Hani?"

Hani rose in surprise. Instinctively, he looked around, half expecting to see footpads closing in on him. But the boy continued to stare at him earnestly.

"Yes, I am," said Hani more quietly. "What is it you want?"

"I have a message from my father, my lord." The lad was polite and very grown-up. His accent was middle-class. He was no beggar.

Intrigued, Hani asked, "And who is your father, my boy?"

"Khnum-baf, the color man." The boy scratched at the roots of his sidelock then clasped his hands, as if his mother had warned him not to do that. "From the Place of Truth."

Hani recognized the name as one he had heard, but he couldn't remember the context. "Speak his message, then."

The boy cleared his throat and drew himself up with endearing solemnity. He said in a singsong voice that suggested he had memorized the words, "My father said that he was the man who fled the robbers. He said he has some information for you if you promise him im... im..."

"Immunity?" Hani finished.

"That's it, my lord. If you promise, he said I could bring you to him."

It occurred to Hani that Mahu might well be watching his gate. "Come in here, son. We'll leave through the service door." Hani drew him into the gateway and carefully closed the leaves behind him. Together, they walked through the garden and into the barnyard, past the geese, who greeted them in outrage, and past the curious donkey. Hani stuck his head out the little door in the wall and looked around. Twilight was well upon them; it wouldn't be easy to see them, and the alley seemed deserted.

"But promise first," the boy reminded him.

Hani said gravely, "I swear on my mother's *ka* that if your father gives me useful information, I will see to it he has immunity."

The lad nodded and set out ahead of Hani, walking, very straight and businesslike, on his little heron legs. Hani followed him down the alley and into a warren of small streets that were mostly lined with service buildings for larger houses, now abandoned. The crickets were throbbing as loudly as an orchestra of sistra. *I could be walking into a trap*, Hani thought uncomfortably. *And no one knows where I've gone. They'll never find me.*

The boy led him to the door of a featureless cube of a house with a door hanging cockeyed on its pivot pole. He looked up at Hani with wide eyes. "He's in there, my lord."

Lurking behind the door with a club, no doubt, Hani thought, his pulse starting to throb in his throat. *I'm probably going to get the same treatment as the other man who knew too much, Djau.*

But the little boy preceded him into the dark house, and Hani followed, his stomach clenched in expectation of the worst. Standing in a corner was a slight, good-looking young man with close-cropped, unwigged hair and a furtive expression on his face. He flinched at their footsteps then drew himself up. "Lord Hani?" he asked nervously.

"You're Khnum-baf?"

"Yes, my lord," said the man, stepping forward out of the shadows. "Thank you for coming. I didn't dare risk approaching you myself until I knew you wouldn't arrest me."

"Prudent," Hani acknowledged, finally relaxing. "How did you know who I was and where to find me?"

"I've talked to Bebi-ankh."

Hani grinned. "He wasn't very happy with you. He thought you had betrayed them all."

"That's not true, though. And I was the one who warned him what the punishment for tomb robbing was, my lord." The man spoke rapidly and softly. "After I explained things to him, he was grateful. He told me how good you'd been to him, how you'd sprung him out of jail."

Even in the darkness, Hani perceived that the man was none too clean. *He must have been in hiding for nearly a year.* "I'm glad you've resolved your differences. What news have you for me, Khnum-baf?"

The artist looked around him uneasily and said in a voice barely above a whisper, "I've... I've seen the foreigner again."

A frisson of excitement traveled up Hani's back. "Where? When?"

"In Waset. I'd sneaked back to the city because my father was ill, and I saw the man crossing the street. This was yesterday. I dodged out of sight, as you may imagine. He's the person I want most in the world to avoid. He knows I know who he is."

"Where exactly was this, Khnum-baf?"

"In the northeast part of town, my lord. My parents have a workshop where they paint coffins and *shabti*s and such."

"And that's all you saw?" Hani pressed. "You didn't see where he went?"

"I did. He went into the house next to my parents'. I was scared he'd come to do harm to them or my children—they've been living with my parents while I've been in hiding." He looked pleadingly at Hani as if he were afraid Hani would judge him. "I haven't been able to work, you know. The children had to eat somehow."

So Talpu-sharri is in Waset, is he? Hani said, "Who lives in that house?"

"No one. They were bronze workers, but they moved down to Akhet-aten, where most of their clientele had gone."

"Can your son show me where the house is?" Hani smiled at the boy, who stood pressed up against his father.

"He can." Khnum-baf licked his lips. "Will you hide us, my lord? Bebi-ankh said you hid him."

"I'll find a safe place for you, you may be sure," Hani said, not knowing exactly how he was going to fulfill that promise. If Mahu had him under observation, he could hardly bring them to his home without disguising them somehow. "Now, can this brave lad lead me to his grandparents' house?"

Khnum-baf took his son gravely by the shoulders and, leaning over him, said, "Take this man to Grandfather's house, Huy. Then stay there. I'll come back after sundown."

The boy nodded seriously and set off with Hani at his heels once more. They stayed well inland from the River and made their way through narrow streets totally unknown to Hani, even though he was a native of the City of the Scepter. Night had almost fallen, and the houses shadowed the alleyways into complete darkness. Overhead, Hani glimpsed a sliver of silver moon. *I'll never be able to find my way back*, he thought in annoyance.

At last, the boy stopped and drew Hani into the deeper shadows along the walls of a house. "It's that one, there." Huy pointed to a featureless stretch of whitewashed mud brick punctuated by a door. "Grandma and Grandpa live there." His finger shifted to the left, to another door. There were no windows at all on either.

They must be centered on courtyards, since both have housed workshops. Hani tried to fix the facade in his memory, but it was without any distinguishing marks. He counted up four doors from the far intersection and hoped that would be sufficient to guide him.

"Thank you, Huy," he murmured to the boy. "Could you take me back to the River by the straightest route?"

"Yes, my lord."

For an inhabitant of the Place of Truth, the boy seems to have a good sense of directions in Waset, Hani thought. *But then, he must have lived with his grandparents for the better part of a year, ever since his father had fled.*

In fact, the way to the River wasn't long and involved few turns except those made by the street they followed. At the water's edge, Hani thanked the boy and pressed into his hand a faience ring that might feed the family for several days. "My thanks to you, young man. Tell your father I'll be back in touch with him through a servant. May the Lord Bes watch over you."

Huy's eyes grew huge at the sight of the ring. He mumbled his gratitude and took off running into the dusk.

Hani stood staring pensively out over the River, where a mist had begun to gather, pearly in the weak light of the new moon rising behind him. In the darkness, boats lay rocking at anchor, the water clapping at their hulls. The call of frogs pulsed. Not far away, a heron cried hoarsely, and from across the River, a roar proclaimed the presence of a hippopotamus.

With a sigh, he turned and made his way south toward home. *Nub-nefer is probably worried about me.*

◈

The next morning, Maya showed up ready to write, but Hani was already in the vestibule with his sandals on, and he steered his secretary directly back out into the street. "We need to pay our friend Menna a visit."

Maya's ears pricked up. "Another stakeout, Lord Hani?" The last one, with his flying leap onto the back of a tomb robber, had been a particularly successful chapter in his tale. Sat-hut-haru and the children had shown a gratifying range of emotions—horror, nail-biting fear, admiration. It had set a hard standard to match.

"Not for us. I've found Talpu-sharri. He's right here in Waset."

"*Yahya!*" Maya cried eagerly. "He must be planning another break-in. Are we going to lie in wait for him?"

"In a way. I think I know the house where he's holed up. I want some of Menna's men to watch it day and night and catch him the moment he steps outside." Hani recounted for Maya the message sent by Khnum-baf and the visit to the empty house. "I think I'll send the man to the farm. He can stay in the servants' quarters with his children."

"At last, a new clue. If only we can catch that accursed Mitannian, we'll get some answers." Maya swung along at Hani's side, a spring in his step.

But Hani didn't answer. Instead, his eyebrows knit in concentration.

The two men strode down the processional way until they were in sight of the Ipet of the South—or rather, the *former* temple. It stood derelict these days, its flagpoles naked, its jeweled cult statue smashed. The very sight of it was a pain in the heart for any loyal Egyptian. Maya remembered all the times he'd stood between two of the ram-headed lions that rhythmed the road. Along with the crowd, he'd cheered in a delirium of joyful piety as the golden cabinet that held the statue of Amen-Ra passed by, held high on the shoulders of *wab* priests. He thought of all the times he'd seen the king enter the sanctuary and emerge divine under the transfiguring power of the Hidden One.

So much for all that, Maya thought, his good humor curdling. *Will those days ever come back? Will the king of the gods ever take his rightful place again in our Two Lands as he has remained in our hearts?*

They'd reached the army barracks, and Hani gave his credentials to the soldier at the gate. "Could we speak to Menna? King's business. Unless he's on maneuvers elsewhere…"

"He should be someplace in the garrison, my lord. Wait here, please." The guard hurried off into the broad court.

Hani exchanged a look with Maya. "Why all these precautions suddenly, I wonder? We used to be able to enter on our own."

Maya lifted his eyebrows in question. "Strange, isn't it, my lord?"

A long time passed before Menna came loping up, his face wreathed in smiles at the sight of his savior. "My lord! What brings you here?" He stepped back and gestured the men to pass inside the court.

"I need some of your men, Menna. We've located the

foreign leader of the tomb robberies, and I'd like you to arrest him before he slips away again."

But Menna shifted uncomfortably, his eyes avoiding Hani's. "Oh, uh... I don't think the men are available for that anymore, my lord. Since the death of the vizier, there have been some changes in our standing orders."

Hani fixed him with a stare. "You've been told not to take part in this investigation?"

"Not in so many words, Lord Hani, but... your authority has been revoked."

"What!" Hani cried, shocked. "They told *you* this and not me? By whose orders?"

"It was transmitted to us by General Ra-mes, my lord. He said because you had mission papers from Lord Aper-el, they were all revoked now."

"He specifically singled me out?" Hani's tone was incredulous, and Maya could see the scarlet of anger creeping up his cheeks.

Menna looked miserable. "I wish it weren't so, my lord. You know how I want to help you. But I can't go against orders."

"No, no, of course not, Menna. Thank you for being frank with me. I need to check into this." Hani flashed Maya a grim look, and the two men turned to leave. Before they'd walked away, however, he turned back to Menna and said, "What about those prisoners I gave you, my friend?"

"I had to turn them over to the cavalry, my lord. I'm sorry." The young officer looked mortally embarrassed.

Hani nodded, and the two men made their way out into the street.

"What's that all about, Lord Hani?" cried Maya in

outrage once they were out of hearing range. "They don't even want to catch this bastard who has deprived people of the food and goods they'll need in the afterlife?"

"From what I understand of the king's religion, there is no afterlife. The dead just hang around the altars of the Aten and bask in Nefer-khepru-ra's glow." Hani's lips were compressed, his tone bitter.

"I'm sure Lady Apeny is enjoying herself." Maya muttered a curse under his breath. "I'll bet they're going to let that dog turd Mahu get the glory of the arrest."

"You may be right. There seems no longer to be a place for *ma'at* in the Two Lands. Mane may regret that the Mitannians have sent him home."

Maya had never seen Hani so deeply angry—not with a superficial yelling-out-loud anger but with one that saturated his very bones. He was walking faster and faster until Maya had to surrender all dignity to keep up with him. "My lord!" he called plaintively as Hani drew farther and farther ahead.

Hani stopped and turned around, and Maya glimpsed his thunderous face before Hani broke into an apologetic smile, baring the winsome space between his front teeth. "Sorry, son. I'm letting this get under my skin, which does no good at all. 'Choose silence for yourself. Submit to what your attacker does.' I'd do well to listen to my own words, eh?"

He waited till Maya had caught up to him then, as they moved ahead, said, "I need to talk to Ptah-mes. And if we can't find him, I'm going to put my litter bearers on this ambush. We mustn't let Talpu-sharri get away. We owe it to those people he killed."

"What if Lord Ptah-mes is in Akhet-aten, my lord? Which is likely."

"Then we act without a commission."

Maya swallowed hard. He could feel his face flaming with something he hoped was not fear.

They strode on down to the southern part of the city, where Ptah-mes's ancestral mansion stood. Trepidation and excitement fizzed in a hot brew inside Maya. They would have no protection from on high from now on. Mahu would eat them alive.

The liveried gatekeeper admitted them and asked them to wait in the vestibule. Before long, brisk footsteps approached, clacking on the painted gypsum floors. Ptah-mes emerged from the salon.

"Hani," he said, eyeing Hani's face. "What's wrong?"

"The army has received orders not to help us anymore, my lord. Apparently, the death of the Osir Aper-el has invalidated our commission."

Ptah-mes said nothing, but his face grew harder and harder until it took on an edge like flint. His black eyes burned with a cold flame. "I'm going to see the king. And if he refuses to permit me to pursue this case, I'm resigning."

"Oh, my lord, be careful," Hani said uncertainly.

Maya could remember Ptah-mes saying that very thing to Hani a few years before. In fact, that had been Ptah-mes's advice all along: "Be temperate, stay under the notice of your superiors. Think whatever you think, but say nothing." The death of his wife had changed him. He no longer had anything to lose.

"Don't get into trouble for my sake," Hani pleaded.

"It won't be for your sake, my friend, but for mine."

Ptah-mes turned brusquely on his heel and headed back inside the salon. Over his shoulder, he called, "I'm leaving immediately. Come along if you want."

Hani hurried in his wake. "My lord, what I never got around to telling you is that we've located Talpu-sharri here in Waset. We must go after him tonight, or he may get away. I'm willing to put my own men on the capture. But what do we do with him afterward? Will anyone sentence him? Will anyone punish him? The army had to let their other prisoners go."

Ptah-mes stopped, his face concentrated with thought. "I'll lend you some men and wait to see how this turns out. Take him, Hani. Keep him here if you need to. After all"—a dangerous smile spread his lips thin—"no one has ever officially informed us that we're removed from the case."

"You're right, my lord." Hani turned to Maya with a dark grin. "He's absolutely right."

⁂

As night fell that evening, Hani's four litter bearers and a pair of Ptah-mes's servants stood guard over the house where Talpu-sharri had been seen. Hani had planted them in the neighbor's recessed doorway, at either end of the block, and even against the wall of the house, squatting with their heads lowered, like beggars. The building had no service door, Hani had assured himself, nor did any of the modest residences along the street. At his signal, the men would swarm the malefactor as he came out of the door. If he should manage to break away, they would stop him no matter which direction he ran. Hani himself waited beside the door, flattened against the whitewashed wall, his tallow lantern covered.

Time passed. The street grew darker and darker. The men blocking the entrances to the street lit their torches as Hani had instructed; it wouldn't do to lose Talpu-sharri in the night. Maya waited there as well because he'd pleaded to participate. *I wish he hadn't insisted on coming. How can I face Sat-hut-haru if anything happens to him?*

The crescent moon rose overhead. No one emerged from the house. Hani had seen a light through the small high windows of the place, so he felt confident that the Mitannian was within. He heard a cough and a rustle as one of his "beggars" shifted position, but still, no one came out.

It must have been near midnight when Hani heard a faint rasp as of a door being unbarred. A blacker crack appeared along the edge of the panel, which widened until a man emerged silently and drew the door shut behind him with scarcely a sound. He was wearing dark clothes, but Hani could see his legs and face, ghostly pale in the faint moonlight.

"Now!" Hani shouted. The two beggars surged up and grabbed the man's arms. Others came flying from their posts and fell upon him as he struggled.

"What under heaven is this?" Talpu-sharri spluttered as the men bore him to the ground.

"Tie him up." Hani stood over him. "We've got him," he cried to the torchbearers and Maya, who came running from the ends of the block. Here and there, a curious head appeared from a rooftop terrace.

The six stalwarts bound their captive's wrists behind his

back and shackled his feet so that he could hobble but not run. Hani leaned over and pulled the man up by the front of his tunic with more force than was strictly necessary. "Well, well, if it isn't Lady Kiya's chamberlain. How is it you didn't go back to Naharin with her like a good servant?"

Talpu-sharri had suffered some pretty brutal scrapes and bruises as the men had fallen upon him, and his thick hair was in wild disarray. But although he was panting, he faced Hani with haughty dignity. "I demand to know the meaning of this outrage."

"Why didn't you call for the watchmen when someone attacked you, my fine fellow? Perhaps you didn't want the authorities to find you. Just like you didn't want the authorities to find you on Lady Kiya's boat." Hani eyed him up and down by the fitful light of the torches. "Got anything on your conscience?"

"No. And I'm offended that you should imply such a thing. I want to see my ambassador."

"You'll see him; don't worry." From the corner of his eye, Hani observed that Maya had come to stand at his side, his face hard and threatening. "Not wearing your blue-green tunic tonight? It's a shame. Everybody loved it."

"What are you talking about?" Talpu-sharri cried, swelling with indignation.

"Why did you jump ship? Did the soldier warn you that troops were coming to arrest you?"

Hani could have sworn that the man paled, but it might have been a trick of the light.

"You must have me confused with someone else," the Mitannian blustered. "I demand to be released."

"You look like Talpu-sharri to me—unless he has an

identical twin. I arrest you for tomb robbing and murder."
Hani was relentless, but although he wanted very badly to
do violence to this impious specimen, he dared not. He was
already operating outside the law.

"Who are you?" cried Talpu-sharri, his voice rising.
"You're not policemen."

"No. You would have recognized your friend Mahu,
wouldn't you?" Hani said contemptuously. "I'm from
the foreign service. Because you're a foreigner who has
committed heinous crimes on Egyptian soil."

"You can't do that. I have immunity," Talpu-sharri
protested wildly.

A doubt began to simmer in Hani's gut, but he
said, "The servants of royal wives don't have immunity,
Talpu-sharri."

"I'm no man's servant!" the captive cried hotly. "I
demand to see your king."

In fact, anyone accused of a crime could request the
king's personal judgment, but a Mitannian was unlikely to
know that. This was arrogant bravado. Hani said, "We'll
start by visiting the high commissioner. Since you murdered
his wife and tried to rob her tomb, he may or may not be
inclined to mercy." He turned to the men who held the
prisoner between them. "Take him to Lord Ptah-mes."

"I want my ambassador!"

"You'll see him." Hani reached out and grabbed Talpu-
sharri by the upper arm. His hand closed on metal. "What's
this, an armlet? In this country, my friend, we usually wear
our jewelry outside our clothes." He turned to one of the
servants. "Cut off his sleeve."

The man pulled out his knife and hacked the fine wool

off at the shoulder. A handsome gold armlet was revealed. It looked suspiciously like one of the pieces of the gold of honor.

Hani ripped it from around Talpu-sharri's arm.

"I protest! You can't rob me like that!" cried the Mitannian, trying to grab it with his shackled hands.

But Hani pulled it out of reach and stared at it, a smile growing on his face. "You don't read our language, do you? Or else you would have known that this has the name of the owner inscribed on it. It was an honorific gift of Neb-ma'at-ra to a certain Ah-mes." He turned, and he and Maya led the way in a torchlit procession through the streets. Hani earnestly hoped that the police wouldn't show up, although it was likely that the local *medjay* knew nothing about Mahu's grievances against him. Hani had a suspicion that the orders to Menna had come from outside the official channels anyway—perhaps Hani wasn't quite the pariah he had feared.

It was nearing the approach of dawn when Hani knocked on Ptah-mes's gate. A sleepy-eyed porter admitted them and asked them to wait. After a longer stretch of time than usual, Ptah-mes himself appeared, immaculately shaved and dressed in full court splendor, as if he'd spent the night in his best clothes, awaiting the arrival of the miscreant. Hani suspected that he had jumped into his garments as soon as his servant awoke him, not being the sort to receive people shirtless and wigless.

"I see you have him, Hani," said the commissioner in a carefully neutral voice. He was easily as tall as Talpu-sharri and exuded authority from every pore.

Hani grinned with savage satisfaction. "Yes, my lord.

And here is the proof of his crimes—an armlet from the tomb of Ah-mes."

"This is an outrage," the Mitannian cried. "How dare you abduct me like this? My ambassador will hear of it." He tried to shrug off the grip of the two servants, but they kept him in control.

"He will indeed." Ptah-mes strolled around Talpu-sharri as if to consider him from every angle. "What was the purpose of your crimes, Talpu-sharri? Why was a chamberlain of the Beloved Royal Wife interested in murdering then robbing the tombs of Egyptian officials? Was it mere greed or something more sinister?"

"I refuse to answer," said the chamberlain disdainfully.

So quickly that Hani hardly saw it coming, Ptah-mes backhanded his captive hard across the face. Talpu-sharri staggered back at the unexpected blow. Cool and graceful as ever, Ptah-mes stepped away. His expression was blank, but Hani saw the muscles in his jaw jumping.

"That's no way to answer a magistrate of the Two Lands, Talpu-sharri," Ptah-mes said calmly. "What was the purpose of your crimes?"

"I have committed no crimes. My whole life has been devoted to the good of the kingdom." His cheek was bleeding from where Ptah-mes's rings had torn the skin.

"Which kingdom?" Hani snorted skeptically.

"Naharin. And Kemet too."

Hani turned to Maya and said under his breath, "Go get Keliya, if he's in town."

Maya melted away into the dark vestibule.

Ptah-mes ordered his men to throw Talpu-sharri into an unlit bedroom and guard the door, adding, "If he needs to urinate, let him do it on the floor like the jackal he is." They hustled the Mitannian off to his prison with much scuffling and loud cries of outrage. As the noise died away, Ptah-mes turned to Hani. "Who is he, Hani?"

"My father has said from the start that the man wasn't a mere servant. I think his instinct was correct. But who Talpu-sharri really is, I couldn't tell you, my lord. Yet."

A commotion at the door made them look up. Maya entered, followed by Keliya, whose long face looked worried. His recently abandoned pillow had left creases on the side of his cheek. "My lord Ptah-mes. Hani. What's going on?"

"We've arrested a countryman of yours, my lord," said Ptah-mes. "For five murders and tomb robbing. He claims immunity. Can you identify him? Is he a member of your mission?"

Keliya's eyes grew wide, and he shot Hani a look. "Let me see him."

Hani escorted him to the door of Talpu-sharri's prison, and the two servants on duty opened the door for him to look in. Keliya stood on the threshold for a space of time. Hani heard the man inside say, "Who are you?"

"I am King Tushratta's ambassador. You apparently wanted to see me. Do I know you?" Keliya replied.

Talpu-sharri gave a bark of laughter. "Tushratta? He's no longer king of anything. You have no authority."

Keliya considered him thoughtfully. "Then why did you ask to see me?"

"I thought—" Talpu-sharri began, but then he broke off. After another length of time, when Talpu-sharri had failed to complete his sentence, the ambassador turned back to the salon, and the guards shut the door behind him.

"Well?" Ptah-mes asked once Keliya had returned to their midst.

"I have no idea who he is—certainly no part of my mission. I can't imagine what he means by having immunity. Hani had told me earlier that he was the chamberlain of Lady Kiya, but apart from that, I know nothing. However"—he looked at Ptah-mes and Hani in turn—"from his words, I suspect he's a supporter of Artatama."

"Was what he said about Tushratta true? Has he been overthrown?" Hani asked.

"I've received no word of that, but it was certainly imminent. It may well be true by now."

The three men stood staring at each other. At last, Ptah-mes said contemptuously, "Are all Artatama's followers impious, murdering dogs, Lord Keliya?"

"In my opinion, yes." Keliya's droopy face twitched in a sarcastic smile. "I wash my hands of this man, Ptah-mes. If you want to impale him, you have my blessing." Ptah-mes and Hani thanked him for turning out so early, and Keliya made his way to the door. He turned briefly to say in a low voice to Hani, "Let's get together one more time before I go, eh, friend?" Then he stepped out onto the dark porch, and Hani heard his shoes scuffling away into the garden.

Hani heaved a sigh. "It sounds like Keliya has lost his protector too."

"Unstable times," murmured Ptah-mes cryptically. "I'm going to Akhet-aten to speak to the king. I need to have an authoritative word on what's happening."

"If you give me time to go home and pack a bag, I'll join you, my lord."

Ptah-mes nodded, saying, "Meet me at the boat," and Hani and Maya took their leave.

Once in the street, Hani said, "You don't have to come, Maya. I don't really have any role to play in this audience—I just want to know the outcome as soon as possible."

"But I want to come, my lord." Maya looked stricken at the idea of not being part of the grim adventure.

Hani's heart warmed with tenderness for the little man, with his courage and his youthful idealism. As for himself, Hani felt very old and cynical. He suppressed a sigh and tried to sound upbeat.

"The king will surely put all this straight. I still wonder if Ay isn't doing things behind his back."

"I'll go pack a bag and join you, Lord Hani."

CHAPTER 13

ONCE HE WAS IN AKHET-ATEN, Hani decided to kill the morning by saying hello to his brother. Aha was traveling, and his family was away in the country, but Pipi would still be around. So while Ptah-mes set off for the Great House and Maya went to see his mother, Hani headed in the other direction. Hani and Ptah-mes were to rendezvous at lunch, unless Ptah-mes was still in his audience.

Pipi's new home had about it the rawness of a house that hadn't been lived in long, with its sharp-cornered mud-brick walls and eye-assaulting whitewash. The modest garden was all newly planted and spindly, but Hani had a sense that Pipi's large, boisterous family would soften it up rather quickly. Nedjem-ib greeted him at the door with loud cries of pleasure, and she shouted inside, "Pipi, it's Hani!"

She escorted him into the salon. The paintings of water lilies and reeds around the top of the red dado weren't even complete, and the wooden columns were unpainted altogether. "I'm so tired of having to keep the children away from wet paint," she complained breezily, pulling off her wig and running her hands through her bushy hair.

"It's a very nice place, my sister. Whose good taste is all this, yours or Pipi's?"

She laughed heartily. "Pipi is as tone-deaf with his eyes as he is with his ears. But we love him anyway."

Pipi bounded into the salon with outstretched arms. "Hani! Welcome to my house. How do you like it?"

"It's beautiful," Hani replied as he and his brother embraced. "You've done an excellent job." He grinned wryly at Pipi. "You're turning into a conventional householder."

"Well, you know," Pipi said, ducking his head in pleasure and embarrassment. "A new job, a new life."

"Listen to him!" crowed Nedjem-ib. "Next he'll want a new wife, young and slim." She was as plump as Pipi. But they seemed to enjoy one another inordinately, always doubling over with laughter at each other's jokes, and Hani had a hard time imagining Pipi as a man with a roving eye.

"What brings you to the capital, Hani?" Pipi pressed as they took stools under the ventilator. His face was still red and beaming with the pleasure of receiving Hani in his handsome new house.

Hani suppressed a smile of tenderness for his little brother and said more seriously, "We're here while Lord Ptah-mes has an audience with the king. That is, if Nefer-khepru-ra will receive him."

"The thing is," said Pipi earnestly, "why would Lord Ay want to kill people and rob their tombs?"

"I'm sure I don't know." Hani was tempted to tell Pipi about the arrest of Talpu-sharri, but it was too sensitive a matter. Hani and Ptah-mes might be outlaws by now, and nothing revealed to Pipi would be secret for long. "Why are you not at work today?" he said to change the subject.

"It's another holiday. The king is going to bestow the gold of honor on some people, so everything shuts down. Half the scribes will be there, anyway, to watch with envy while their colleagues are honored."

Hani wondered how the king would grant Ptah-mes an audience if he were occupied all day with ceremonies, but he said nothing about it and asked his brother to show him around his new place. As they strolled through the garden of saplings, Hani said, "Are you still wanting to become a farmer?"

"Maybe," Pipi said indifferently. "I've been thinking it might be nice to be an investigator."

Here goes the competition again, thought Hani with an inward sad smile. He said carefully, "That's not really a career, Pipi. It's just something a superior may ask you to do from time to time."

"Oh, I know I don't speak all kinds of languages like you, brother," Pipi said, sounding disappointed.

"That has nothing to do with it. You just have to be asked—or told. It's a task, not a job."

"But I've worked with you on this case, Hani."

"True, and perhaps your overseer will remember that when he looks for someone to investigate for him," Hani said kindly.

"Who exactly does an archivist investigate?" said Pipi, not mollified.

Hani laughed in spite of himself and gave his brother a quick squeeze. "You're doing well for yourself, Pipi. This house is beautiful." He turned to go and called over his shoulder, "Make my goodbyes to Nedjem-ib, will you?"

His stomach told him lunchtime was approaching, so he set out for Ptah-mes's villa on the off chance that the commissioner might already have obtained an audience, though it was more likely that the audience had been put off till some time in the future. He took a seat in the garden pavilion and stretched out his legs. The day was hot, and Hani found himself sliding imperceptibly toward sleep.

"Ah, Hani. Here you are." Ptah-mes's voice brought him quickly to consciousness. Hani rose, flustered.

"Where is Maya?" said Ptah-mes with a smile.

"I'm not sure, my lord. He went to visit his mother, and he may or may not still be there. Perhaps he's taking a siesta. As you see, I found the same occupation very tempting."

Ptah-mes made a noise resembling a laugh, but his face had resumed its somber lines.

Hani asked hesitantly, "Did you have your audience, my lord?"

"I did, Hani, before the good god went off to bestow the *shebyu* collar on several men. Among them, our friend Mahu."

Hani's stomach did a flop, like the final throes of a fish in the mouth of a gull. "Does that foreshadow what I think you're going to say?"

Ptah-mes seated himself, straightening his skirts, then he crossed his legs, clasped his hands around his knee, and nodded slowly. "Let me start at the beginning. I commenced by telling Nefer-khepru-ra that I was pleased to announce that you had apprehended the culprit in the crimes he had commissioned us to investigate."

"And how did he react?"

"He commended you for your skills, Hani. He said, 'We can always trust our dear Hani to pursue his quest to the end.' The tone I found... ambiguous. But then, our king is a master of ambiguity."

"He said that?" Hani cried, a wave of uneasiness breaking over him. He'd hoped more than anything not to attract the king's notice.

"And then he said that the death of the lamented Aper-el had put a brake on things in the Hall of Correspondence, that some affairs were going to have to be dropped to make way for the new vizier's agenda." Ptah-mes smiled bleakly. "Can you see where this is going?"

Hani felt rage rising like hot steam up his face; it vented itself in a loud snort. "Only too well, my lord. They're stopping the case."

"Oh, no. *Ma'at* must come to light. But the vizier and the foreign service will no longer have charge of it."

"And Mahu and his *medjay* will?" Hani could no longer control the sarcasm in his voice. He threw up his hands. "That's like saying the investigation will stop. I don't doubt that he intervened at Lady Apeny's tomb to take the robbers to safety, not to arrest them."

Ptah-mes's face flickered with hatred then settled into blankness. "I told Our Sun God that there was some evidence that Lord Ay might be involved in working for a regime change." He curled his lip in a bleak simulacrum of a smile. "He said, 'Oh, no. He's completely loyal, have no fear.'"

"Frankly, that makes me fear the more," Hani said

grimly. "That suggests the king himself is aware of the collusion of the cavalry in this sordid business."

Ptah-mes rose and walked to the edge of the porch as if he could no longer restrain his nerves. "I told him that my wife had been one of the victims, Hani. He said first, 'Our condolences,' and then he said, 'Can you prove they were murdered?' Needless to say, I admitted that we could not. And he said, 'Well, then. This remains an improbable theory.'" He reseated himself.

"Well, I now have evidence that at least some of the deaths were murders." Hani told Ptah-mes briefly about Neferet's experiment on the contents of the cup from Sa-tau's house.

"I think no one is much concerned with evidence in this case, my friend. For your daughter's safety, say nothing of this."

Hani was so full of disgust and hopelessness he could hardly speak. He groaned and put his hand over his eyes. "I suppose the fact that we found some of Ah-mes's jewelry on Talpu-sharri's arm is nothing more than an improbable theory too."

Ptah-mes sneered. "The king also told me that Artatama is now on the throne of Naharin."

"No surprise there. No surprise in any of this, in fact. Our government is a pigsty of corruption, starting with—" Hani stopped himself in time.

"Life, prosperity, and health to him," finished Ptah-mes with a caustic smile.

"And what becomes of Talpu-sharri now?"

"We are to turn him over to Mahu."

Overcome with frustrated rage, Hani slammed his

palm down on the stool at his side. He sat there, his breath sawing in his nose. Then he said in a tight voice, "I hope you'll forgive me for not staying for lunch, my lord, but I feel I can't spend another hour in this city of the damned. As soon as I find Maya, we'll be gone."

But instead of replying, Ptah-mes, staring into space, concluded the recital of his audience as he said in self-contempt, "And then I said, 'I thank my Sun God for bestowing upon me the breath of life.'"

☥

Maya was not in his room. He'd said something about using the morning wait to visit his mother's workshop, so Hani was preparing to go look for him there when the secretary came barreling into the house. Before Hani could even tell him about their imminent departure, Maya blurted, "Oh, my lord. Get out! Get out! I passed a whole troop of policemen on their way here. It can mean nothing good."

Hani said dryly, "I can tell you exactly what it means. Mahu has been given the case, by the king's orders."

Maya stared at him, speechless, then he tore his wig from his head and hurled it to the floor in the same impotent fury as Hani had felt earlier. "How can he? We did all the work."

"That's the problem. Even though he assigned us the case initially, we uncovered things the Good God Nefer-khepru-ra doesn't want uncovered. Mahu will quietly undo it all for him."

"Leaving five people's souls unavenged…"

"He doesn't believe in the Duat, Maya. In his mind, he has done no harm." Hani smiled unhappily.

"Since when is killing someone—and by a horrible death. Plague, no less!—doing them no harm?" Maya's face was red with anger.

"Kings have people put to death every day."

"Are you defending him, my lord?" cried Maya in horror.

Hani shook his head gloomily. "No, son. I'm just trying to understand how such things happen in the world. The person who does them never thinks he's done anything bad. Or even if it's bad, his goal justified it." He shot Maya a wry look. "After all, those four people weren't supporters of the true god."

"And Djau? What evil was he guilty of?" Maya was implacable.

"A man of his class probably doesn't even exist for Nefer-khepru-ra. I've known plain grandees who weren't much better."

Maya made a noise of disgust and picked up his wig. "Let's get out of here before the storm hits, my lord."

Hani was on his way to the room to collect his baggage when a thought occurred to him. "Maybe I shouldn't leave Lord Ptah-mes alone to face this…"

Maya snorted. "He seems like a man who can take care of himself. Come on."

"But he's not himself these days. He might say or do something regrettable. You know how he and Mahu react with each other."

"And can you stop him, Lord Hani?"

"Probably not." *You can't solve everybody's problems*, Hani reminded himself. But it was hard to head for the door.

The two men were crossing through Ptah-mes's garden rapidly when they heard a hammering on the gate ahead. They stopped in their tracks, uncertain. The gatekeeper had barely pulled back the heavy panels of the outer gate when Hani realized, with a prickling of fear and antipathy, that Mahu and his men had already arrived. They stood in a menacing block of four medjay and a baboon, with Mahu at their head. His eyebrows rose in icy recognition at the sight of Hani and Maya. "Well, well. We keep finding you at the scene of the crime, Hani. I think I made a mistake in not apprehending you sooner."

"And what crime is this the scene of, Mahu? Surely you don't think Lord Ptah-mes is one of the tomb robbers?" *By all that's holy, Hani, control your temper*, Hani told himself. But Mahu was a burr in his sandal; every time they were around each other, he felt anger and aggression mount within him. Mahu apparently felt the same—and made no effort to keep it in check.

The chief of police smirked. "Insubordination. You both have been told that the case is no longer yours, yet here you still are."

"Two points here, Mahu," Hani said acidly. "One, the fact that I am visiting my superior, who also happens to be a bereaved friend, has nothing to do with the case and is hardly a crime. And two, it was only this morning that the high commissioner was told that the case had been handed over to you. I can assure you, he has done absolutely nothing since then."

"Handsome of you to defend the commissioner so zealously. Why don't you just step back inside while we listen to him defend himself?" Mahu pushed Maya aside roughly and strode past Hani into the garden.

Hani was dimly aware of the gatekeeper scuttling off toward the house. It occurred to Hani that it might be a good thing to occupy Mahu a little longer. "Here!" he cried. "I object. This young man has done nothing. You have no right to shove him."

At Hani's side, Maya bristled, brushing himself down as if to shake off the contamination of Mahu's touch, and glared at the policeman with loathing. Mahu whipped around, and rocking back on his heels, he eyed Maya up and down. "What if one of my men just heaved him out into the street, Hani? He was obstructing justice."

"He was only standing there. And even if he had obstructed *you*, it would hardly have been justice he was obstructing." Hani's teeth were clenched with the effort not to do something irreversible.

But Mahu had heard the contempt in his voice. The chief of the *medjay* reached out and snatched Hani's shirt, jerking him toward himself. "Watch your tongue there, my friend," he snarled. "Your protector is in the Duat."

Hani wasn't sure he could control the tidal wave of fury that surged up though his veins. *Keep your mouth shut. Do not answer him back. They could take it out on Maya or Ptah-mes.* Instead, he silently wrenched his shirt out of Mahu's grasp, giving him the most scornful stare he could muster. He hoped the gateman had warned his master by now of the police visit.

His face crimson, Mahu pushed Hani aside and stumped up the path, his henchmen in close formation behind him. The baboon shot Hani a contemptuous look as he passed.

Let Ptah-mes be ready for this. Let him have hidden Talpu-sharri.

The little band made its way through the extensive gardens, past shady trees and refreshing pools—the setting for a life of culture and repose, the very opposite of Mahu and his troubled, violent spirit. Hani and Maya trailed them, exchanging an uneasy glance.

A doorkeeper met them at the entrance of the house. "How may I help you?" He spoke levelly, but his eyes cut back and forth in anxiety.

"Where is your master?" Mahu growled.

From the interior of the vestibule, Ptah-mes stepped forward, as tall and elegant as a figure from a tomb painting, his arms crossed. "His master is here, Mahu. What brings you to my property again?"

"Rumor has it that you still have a witness in your custody—after you were told that the case was no longer yours."

"Then you'd better tell Rumor he's wrong." Ptah-mes's black kohl-rimmed eyes glittered dangerously.

Mahu's heavy jowls were almost purple with rage. "You have Talpu-sharri, don't you? I want him now."

"I do not have Talpu-sharri. *I* want you off my property, Mahu."

"We'll see about that." Mahu made a savage gesture, and his men surged toward the door. Ptah-mes stepped coolly back to let them pass.

"Have you no decency?" Hani cried. "This is a house of mourning."

Mahu turned on him. "And so will yours be, *Lord* Hani, unless you shut your mouth."

N. L. HOLMES

Biting his tongue, Hani watched the backs of the troops as they passed into the cool darkness of the vestibule, their feet reflected on the polished gypsum as if it were water. Ptah-mes stood frostily but calmly to the side while they swarmed into his house. He caught Hani's eye, but no expression gave away what he was thinking. In the vestibule, the three men stood side by side as the policemen ransacked room after room, Mahu storming around among them, snarling orders. Hani saw with a wince that they were slicing curtains and ripping the stuffing out of cushions—as if a man could have been concealed inside. The servants huddled, terrified. But Ptah-mes watched with no reaction, his arms still crossed.

At last, Mahu came to Ptah-mes's household shrine, where a beautiful statue of gold and ebony depicting the King of the Gods reigned, flowers wilting at its feet. The police chief turned back to the door, his face lit with malice. "Oh dear, Ptah-mes. Where is your stele of the Aten and his one priest?"

"I had it removed," said Ptah-mes icily.

"This doesn't look very loyal for a servant of the king." Mahu knocked over the statue with the back of his hand.

"I will serve the king's foreign policy with all my soul, Mahu, but my religious loyalty goes only so far as the limits of my conscience."

Hani heard Maya draw in his breath, and a sparkle of fear caught in his own throat. This was very dangerous talk directed toward a man who already hated Ptah-mes and would seize upon any excuse to humiliate him.

A triumphant smile curled Mahu's lip, but he yelled, "You! Men! Have you found the prisoner?"

"Nowhere, my lord," one of them called back.

"Keep looking. Look in his granary. Look in his barns." He turned and thrust his face into that of the commissioner. "I hear you have nice horses, Ptah-mes. Maybe we'll have to slit them open to see if Talpu-sharri is hiding inside."

Hani felt rage boiling up in him again. *How did this unworthy man ever climb so high?* For his part, Path-mes showed no emotion by so much as the slightest flutter of his eyelashes—not when heavy crashing sounded from outside that might well have been his granaries suffering assault. Not when animals screamed.

At last, the policemen came trooping back in, leaving a trail of destruction behind them. Some of the horrified servants were weeping helplessly. Mahu drew near to Ptah-mes once more. "Where is he?"

"I have no idea."

"Perhaps he's at Hani's, eh?" Mahu said slyly, turning to Hani.

"He is not," Hani said, defiant but fearful. He didn't need Mahu bullying Nub-nefer again and frightening Baket-iset.

"Does it occur to you that I may have let the man go when I learned that the foreign service no longer had jurisdiction over his case?" Ptah-mes said.

Mahu laughed scornfully. "You wouldn't have thought to have turned him over to me, would you?"

"Oh. You didn't get him? How awkward."

Hani cringed. Mahu wouldn't take much of this sarcasm. Hani was beginning to fear for Ptah-mes's physical safety.

But abruptly, Mahu pulled away, still simmering,

and called to his troops, "Come on, boys. We'll deal with this inbred scum later." They stormed out the front door, baboon and all, and Hani heard their footsteps thundering down the path and out of hearing.

Hani held his breath for a moment longer then finally let it out in relief. Ptah-mes looked icy. Maya stared from one to the other.

With tears in his eyes, Ptah-mes's steward rushed in and fell at his master's feet. "Oh, my lord, forgive me. I couldn't stop them. They've smashed everything, killed the cattle, knocked holes in the silos—"

"It's all right," Ptah-mes said neutrally. "Where did you take the prisoner?"

"To my brother's house, my lord."

"Good man." Ptah-mes turned to Hani. "Well, my friend," he said with a bleak smile. "We've declared war."

⁂

"If it's the last thing I do—and it may well be—I want to find out what is going on here. The idea of that brute imposing his so-called justice on anybody he takes against is contrary to every principle of *ma'at*. Something very shady is going on," Hani told his father after he'd described the events at Ptah-mes's. Even at the remove of six days, his blood was boiling at the memory.

Mery-ra shook his head heavily. "I want to say, 'Good for you,' son, but something tells me you're swimming in very dangerous waters by antagonizing this man. If he's just an envious cur acting out of his own malice, that's bad enough. But if his actions are really at the behest of a higher power…"

"I was pleased to see Ptah-mes stand up to him."

"Did you doubt that he would? You didn't see him in action when we went to rescue you from the police barracks two years ago." Mery-ra chuckled at the memory. "I can still picture him with those gloves in his hand."

Hani smiled, but his heart was heavy. "He's been blaming himself for everything for so long…"

He changed the subject. "I guess I'd better get Khnumbaf off my property before Mahu comes sniffing around."

"Who's that?"

"My witness—the one of the robbers who escaped arrest. He's at the farm. I don't know how an artist feels about working in the lettuce patch." He had to smile at the thought of the slightly built Khnum-baf, with his fine hands, kneeling in the dirt. "But he asked to work so he could earn a little something."

"Is he really in danger from Mahu?" Mery-ra leaned back and stretched out his legs, his arms above his head to cool his armpits. Hani and he were sitting in the garden pavilion, seeking whatever trifling breeze Flood season could waft at them, and they almost had to shout over the deafening cicadas. "I thought you said Djau didn't tell Mahu about Bebi-ankh, and he was the one who knew all the other conspirators."

"You may be right. But the other workmen heard me call his name. He might be a sort of pariah in the Place of Truth for a while."

Mery-ra grunted noncommittally.

"I need to talk to that Talpu-sharri before he slips out of our hands. I also want to say goodbye to Keliya."

"He's finally been recalled, has he?"

"It seems so. He's invited me to dinner at Mane's. He says he has a surprise for me."

"A turquoise tunic from Naharin, for old times' sake?" Mery-ra flashed an evil grin.

Hani laughed. They sat in companionable silence for a while. Hani, gazing into the bushes, found himself missing the silent grace of Qenyt.

A'a came around the bushes and bowed. "My lord, there's a boy here to see you."

Hani and his father exchanged a curious glance. *Is it Huy again?* "Send him to us, my friend," Hani said, straightening up.

Mery-ra put down his arms. "Do you want me to leave, son?"

"No, no. This can't be anything too personal."

A'a disappeared then reappeared momentarily with a sturdy adolescent still in his Haru-lock, a covered basket in his hand. He looked frightened at the upper-class magnificence around him, and made a deep hesitant bow.

"Khawy!" cried Hani in delight. "How is life for you, my lad?"

The boy managed a smile, but his face was drawn with uncertainty. "My lord, I thought you'd want to know that my grandmother has died. And my sister is married. So I don't have any responsibilities to the family anymore. If my lord is still offering to teach me to write, I... I can come."

Hani exchanged a look with Mery-ra. "This is your decision, Father."

"Why, no decision is needed, son. I made the offer, and I stand by my word." Mery-ra beamed at Khawy. "By all indications, young Khawy is a smart, well-spoken lad, and we know he has artistic skills. It will be a pleasure."

Hani added kindly, "You can live with us if you have no relatives in Waset. I'm sure one boy won't disrupt too much. Nub-nefer is used to much worse."

The boy fell on his face before the two scribes, and in a voice trembling with tears, he cried, "Oh, my lords, how can I thank you? I want to be a draftsman like Uncle, and you've fulfilled my prayer." He fumbled at Hani's bare foot to kiss it.

"None of that is necessary, Khawy. We know you're grateful. But it seems like the least of favors we owe your uncle for his brave testimony," Hani said, lifting him to his feet.

A moment later, Nub-nefer emerged from the house with a tray in her hands. She set it down on a little folding table between the men. "I thought you gentlemen might like some fresh fruit," she said, holding up a wedge of pomegranate to her husband. He bit it out of her hands and began to crunch it down, seeds and all, the juice dripping from his chin.

"I can see we brought you up right," commented Mery-ra as he served himself a fig.

Nub-nefer noticed the boy standing in shy discomfort to one side. "And who are you, my dear?" she asked with a smile. She held the fruit out to him and encouraged him to take some.

"This is Khawy. He's going to be a resident pupil of Father for a few years."

Her eyes widened, and she caught Hani's glance. "Oh. How nice." She turned toward the house and called for one of the servants then addressed Khawy once more. "She'll take you to your room, dear."

But the boy cried out, "I have something for you first, Lord Hani." He stopped to pick up his basket and, laying back the cloth that covered it, offered it to Hani. Inside, Hani saw, nestled in a swirl of dry grass, a large bluish-gray egg.

"What's this, Khawy?" said Hani, looking up at him in surprise.

"It's just an egg I found. I thought it was pretty and thought you might like to have it. It's nothing, I know..." The boy's voice trailed away, and his face grew red with embarrassment. "I hated to come empty-handed."

It was a heron egg. Hani took the basket from him and stared at the egg, moved almost to tears. "Why, it's the nicest present I've ever received." He reached out and cuffed the boy's head affectionately.

Khawy made a deep bow and followed the servant girl out.

"Who is he?" Nub-nefer asked once Khawy had disappeared from sight. "He's young to leave home like this. What do his parents say about it?"

"He's an orphan, my dove. His uncle was the draftsman who was murdered."

Compassion melted her smile. "Poor child."

"And how are *our* children? Neferet's been down at the farm with you at last."

Nub-nefer smiled. "Neferet and her friend enjoyed their stay, I think. Bener-ib seemed to be coming out of her shell before they finally left." She pulled up a stool and seated herself. "The unfortunate girl. Did Neferet tell you about her awful stepmother?"

"In general." He helped himself to another wedge of fruit. "So she isn't so strange after all?"

Nub-nefer exchanged with him a knowing look. "No. She's sweet. She got on very well with Amen-em-hut's children. And what's more, Baket-iset likes her."

"That's the best test," Hani said, squeezing his wife's hand. When Nub-nefer rallied, she rallied.

"I should prepare you for the fact that Neferet has had her head shaved."

Hani chuckled. "I saw it. Did you object and try to talk her out of it?"

"Not at all. It's very fashionable with young people right now because of the princesses. She can always wear a wig for dressy occasions." Nub-nefer delicately lifted a fig from the tray. "She said it would obviate questions about why she had her maiden braids when she was fifty years old and still unmarried."

You are a gem among women, Hani told his wife silently. *Love won, just as I knew it would.* He got to his feet. "I need to get some work done before the dinner at Keliya's this evening. I told Maya to come over. Let's see if he's inside."

He leaned over to kiss Nub-nefer on the top of her head as he passed. With the egg in its basket cradled against his chest, he moved into the shadowy depths of the house. It was cooler inside than out. Sure enough, Maya sat on the floor with his writing tools spread around him, waiting.

"Sorry I'm late, son. Nub-nefer brought out fruit, and I couldn't resist staying for a piece or two."

"That's all right, my lord," said the secretary. "I was

363

going over a few stanzas of my tale in my head. The confrontation at Lord Ptah-mes's will be an asset, I think—conflict is a favorite."

Hani shook his head and laughed as he seated himself next to Maya. "I have a dinner tonight with Keliya. He promised me a surprise."

Maya's face grew suddenly grave and uneasy. "My lord, please don't think I'm acting out of place, but I feel I must warn you. I have doubts about Lord Keliya."

Hani stared at him in surprise. "Whatever for? I've known the man for years."

Maya's voice dropped conspiratorially. "Remember how shifty he was when you asked him about Pirissi? He's concealing something."

"Undoubtedly. He can't reveal Naharin's secrets to a couple of foreigners."

"But, Lord Hani, think about it. He pretended Pirissi was a bona fide diplomat, and he kept deflecting your suspicions. But it turned out Pirissi was as guilty as anything." Maya's eyes were wide and avid. "I've been thinking a lot about this. Do we know for sure that the soldier was the one who warned Talpu-sharri that we were coming? We were pretty uncensored in telling Keliya all our thinking. Who better than he to hide a Mitannian? He could pass him off as a member of the embassy—"

"But he didn't, Maya. He turned him over to us and said, 'Impale him for all I care.'" *Of course, that could have been bravado. Or perhaps he'd finished with the man and was disposing of him.* But Hani found himself more than a little defensive. This was Keliya they were talking about, a man who was like a brother to him. "Can you possibly think Keliya was a party to murder and tomb robbing?"

"My lord, I don't know him as well as you do, but perhaps that makes me less prejudiced. All I'm saying is, be careful. If he's part of this, he's ruthless, and he's able to conceal his real thoughts like a master."

Hani was deeply disturbed by this speculation because, in fact, he didn't—and couldn't—know what Keliya might be up to. The ambassador's loyalties necessarily lay with Naharin, after all. *Are the Mitannians somehow working to replace Nefer-khepru-ra with a less hostile king?* Hani chewed his lip, wanting to cry, "You're crazy, Maya." But perhaps Maya was perceptive and he, Hani, was just naive. Perhaps he'd let his affection for the man of Naharin blind him to things he should have seen. Perhaps there were two truths even here—Keliya was a kind, charming man, and Keliya was involved in some nefarious scheme.

He said somberly, "I hope before all the gods you're wrong, Maya, but I'll keep my eyes open."

They set to work then, but Hani was distracted by his tumultuous thoughts. His strained loyalties. His fears.

❖

Shortly before dusk that evening, having shaved and donned fresh linen, a handsome collar of beads, and his best wig, Hani mounted his litter and set out for Mane's house at the edge of the same neighborhood. It was not so much that he didn't want to walk but that he felt safer with a few men of his own around. Maya had infected him with suspicions. *That's what we've come to*, he thought with a grim sigh. *Friend has been severed from friend. The king has sliced the bond between people who loved and trusted one another. Between Ptah-mes and his wife. Between me and Keliya. Between some of the servants in the Place of Truth and their neighbors. He is like a blade of flint.*

A scepter of flint. Who bestows the breath of life.

Hani's hair stood up on the back of his neck. There was that passage again. This was what he had found by the pool of Two Truths.

Still chilled by his fears, Hani crunched up the garden walk of Mane's charming villa. The doorkeeper admitted him, but instead of Mane's wife in the vestibule, there stood Mane, his arms wide, his grin just as wide.

"Hani, old friend! Come embrace your surprise!" The two men hugged one another with joy.

"So you're back, you old rogue—and just a jump ahead of the fall of Tushratta, from what I understand."

"Yes," Mane said, giving Hani a meaningful look. "Everything has changed. I've learned quite a lot that will interest you. And so has Keliya."

Hani made an interested noise, but within, he didn't know how to react.

Keliya stood in the inner door, his droopy face beaming. "How do you like your surprise, Hani, my friend?"

He wore a handsome tunic of wool dyed the color of turquoise.

A shiver ran up Hani's spine. *How do I act toward him?* But nothing had been proven against the ambassador. Hani let friendship guide him. "Keliya, my friend. Where did you get that beautiful garment?"

Keliya smiled; he had to remember that Hani had found such an incriminating tunic in the baggage of his aides. "Mane brought it back for me. He said they've been all the rage in Wasshukanni ever since some dyer figured out how to get that color."

Hani felt he could breathe for the first time in several moments. He laughed in relief and clapped Keliya on the shoulder.

The three men headed into the salon. Mane laid an arm across Hani's back and guided him with exuberant affection. "We'll eat on the porch, my friends. My wife has supervised a wonderful dinner for us. And we can talk politics, eh?" He winked at Hani.

Servants came out with little tables and set them up before the guests. Others with basins and pitchers washed their feet and faces.

"That feels good on a hot night, doesn't it?" Mane beamed.

"How was your experience as a hostage?" Hani asked him. "I hope you weren't mistreated."

"Not at all. They just wouldn't let me go. Tushratta was very depressed toward the end. Then he was angry. I think it relieved him to be able to make a gesture of hostility toward our kingdom, even though he and I are cordial personally. Then, once he was dethroned, his own son murdered him."

"Murdered, eh?" Hani gave a cynical snort. "He had good reason to be angry at Kemet. We abandoned him shamelessly."

Mane's cheerful face grew sober. "That's truer than you know, Hani. You remember I told you I was being sent to Naharin to feel out which side we should support—Tushratta or Artatama."

367

Hani nodded. At his side, Keliya listened with lowered eyes.

"I'm sorry to say, Our Sun God had already made up his mind. He was actively working with Artatama to overthrow his brother."

"You mean *we* were the foreign power behind his increased activity?" Hani cried incredulously. "Of all the double-crossing—"

"My sentiments exactly," said Mane. "And do you know exactly where the funds came from?"

Hani's heart was in his throat. "Don't tell me—tomb robbery." He put his face in his hands. "It makes me ashamed for our kingdom, Mane. To turn on an ally like that…"

Keliya spoke up in his easygoing way. "That's how kings are, Hani. All of them. It's always about their own best interests. Honor and justice mean nothing."

"Can anyone explain to me why they took such devious means of coming up with funds? Surely, the treasury could have footed the bill."

"They tried, but the treasurer was having none of it. Needless to say, none of this could go through the ordinary chain of command, which would have been too public. It was all under the table. He couldn't know that the king himself had instigated such a request."

"Sa-tau," Hani said. Everything was starting to come together now. "His was the first tomb robbed, after they had killed him."

"Then they approached a judge, thinking he could arrange a judgment against the treasury in court, but he refused to be part of it."

"So that's why Ah-mes was targeted. And Pa-ren-nefer?"

"The king's steward and his father's friend from childhood. They must have thought he could exert some influence to make the king cough up directly. And of course, once they'd approached these men and been refused, they had to get rid of them because they knew too much."

"And Lady Apeny?"

"They were hoping the group of disgruntled priests, of which she was a vocal part, might be interested in earning some favor with the new king Artatama. Imagine—the present administration dealing with those it knew to be its enemies in order to betray a faithful friend."

Hani was speechless with disgust. He shook his head as if to shake out these disillusioning images. "You mean the king promised Artatama support but didn't want to pay him?"

Mane and Keliya exchanged a steaming look. "Oh, he intended from the first to do it this way, I think," Mane said. "Because an alliance works two ways. Nefer-khepru-ra funded Artatama's insurrection, and Artatama got rid of some major foes of the king, while *his* hands stayed clean."

"Their own king assassinated these people." Hani shook his head in disgust. "He robbed them of the food and goods they would need in the afterworld. Our worst enemy could have done nothing more heinous."

Keliya said sadly, "I told you that, Hani. That's the way kings are."

Mane continued, "You've probably figured out by now how Talpu-sharri was involved. He was the agent of Artatama."

"And Pirissi was part of this?"

"Oh, no, Hani," Keliya assured him. "Pirissi was Tushratta's man. A spy, if you will, sent down here to try to stop Talpu-sharri or at least undo what he'd done. That's why he kept showing up at the houses of the victims. He wanted to know what Talpu-sharri was up to and change the minds of any potential target who might have yielded. I think he must have been surprised by the lethal ruthlessness of our countryman."

Hani's face was burning with shame. How could he have suspected Keliya? "Did you know about this all the while, Keliya? While I was trying to convince you that Tulubri was somehow involved?"

"No, no," said the ambassador. "I only found out recently. As far as I knew, they were simply what I had been told—young diplomats come to second me at the embassy until they took Lady Kiya home. I suppose Tulubri really was."

Hani's thoughts tumbled around in his head, struggling to take some shape. "So when Talpu-sharri spoke of putting the real king on the throne, he meant the throne of Naharin. He meant Artatama in place of Tushratta. That was what confused me. I couldn't understand why Nefer-khepru-ra would want to see a new king in his place on the throne of Kemet."

"Right," Mane said. "Nefer-khepru-ra told Ay to do what he needed to do to help the effort, even to the point of involving cavalry personnel in the robberies."

"And Mahu's task was to undo everything I did to figure the situation out," Hani said bitterly. He sat in pensive silence for a moment. "But why did the king even put me on the case at all? He must have known that if anyone investigated, they would expose something. Why is Mahu still looking for Talpu-sharri? Why did he have the workmen who carried out the robberies in custody?"

Mane sighed. "That I can't answer, Hani. Perhaps he wanted to make a show of tracking the criminals to deflect suspicion from himself."

"All this happened during the Great Jubilee, when foreign diplomats were everywhere. He probably didn't want any scandal," Keliya reminded Hani.

"Regarding your other questions, maybe the king wants to protect Talpu-sharri from you until he can hustle him out of the country safely. He knows that you could get a confession out of a stone. As for the poor workmen, I wouldn't be surprised if he administers the maximum penalty to keep them from ever figuring out what happened—or telling someone who could figure it out." Mane stared Hani frankly in the eye as if to confirm that this was the pitiless world they lived in.

"And I suppose when Talpu-sharri kept demanding to see his ambassador, he thought Artatama had already installed his new man," Hani said.

Keliya smiled dryly. "One assumes so. He certainly wasn't happy to see me."

Hani sat, speechless with outrage, until he finally said, "I feel used, my friends. Once again."

"We all do, Hani," said Mane, more serious than usual. "We all are."

"But both of you—what happens now? Keliya, will you be missioned back here by the new government in Wasshukanni? You've had years of experience in our kingdom; you know Kemet better than anyone."

"I don't know," said Keliya. "I'm not sure I would serve Prince Artatama. I may just call my wife to join me here in permanence."

"You'd be more than welcome my friend," Hani assured him with a broad grin. "I wish *I* had a place to flee to. And you, Mane?" He turned to the tubby little man at his side.

Mane heaved a sigh. "I'll go wherever I'm sent. Probably back to Artatama's court. Although knowing what I know about his tactics…" He raised his eyebrows then grinned. "But as Keliya would say, 'That's the way kings are.'"

The next morning, as he and his son tore chunks off a pot-shaped loaf of bread and washed it down with milk, Mery-ra asked, "How was your party last night, my boy? Seems like you got home pretty late." They were seated in the garden pavilion, catching the fresh breeze of early morning. Hani had put the heron's egg under one of the broody geese. Any day now, the Flood would begin, and new life would spring up along the River. It was the one thing that could be counted on, the one sure thing. That and death.

"Very illuminating. I can't wait for Ptah-mes to hear about it. It may pitch him right over the edge of cynicism," Hani said, although, upon reflection, he wasn't sure that would be much of a kindness to him. His superior already lived in a dark, sharp-edged world.

Mery-ra raised his bushy eyebrows. "Sounds interesting. Anything you can repeat?"

In a low voice, Hani told his father what Mane and Keliya had revealed to him the night before.

Mery-ra's little eyes grew wide, and he pursed his lips in

a whistle. "So that's the way the land lies. I'm shocked but not surprised." He shook his head then said more loudly, "My favorite part of all this is that you seem to have gotten out of it alive. You have your answers, and the king has his way, and you need have nothing else to do with that abominable excuse for a man, Mahu."

"But has *ma'at* been served, Father? Can I say before the Judge of Souls that I have preserved *ma'at*?" asked Hani. Contemplation of this whole sordid affair made him feel downright unclean.

"You've done all you could, Hani. The rest of it is on the consciences of others." Mery-ra rose and stretched. "Does Ptah-mes still have that Talpu-sharri hidden someplace?"

"As far as I know. I suppose he might as well turn him loose now. And that's what makes me angriest. Artatama gets his throne by insurrection and murder. Talpu-sharri, that foreign dog turd of a man, kills five of our people and starves the souls of three, and he'll walk away with praise instead of punishment. No wonder the gods have sent plague upon us."

"Speaking of the Judgment, I think I'll work a little on my *Book of Going Forth by Day*."

"How was Khawy's first lesson?"

"He's a natural because of his artistic background. Plus, he's very mature. We didn't make a mistake when we accepted him." Mery-ra looked satisfied with himself. "I'm going to pay him to finish the pictures in my *Book*."

"I think we should read it every day to remind us how to live," Hani said fervently. He heaved himself from his stool and followed his father into the salon. "I'm going to

Ptah-mes to tell him what I've found out. Consider it my last official report on the case."

Hani was calmer by the time he'd walked to the southern edge of the city, where Ptah-mes's ancestral villa stood. Hani was cheerful by nature, after all, and while his idealism had been tarnished by its brush with corruption, his basic conviction was that the world the gods had made was a beautiful place. The day was hot but with a little of night's freshness still lingering. Any hour now, the priests of Hapy, farther up the River, would send fast couriers to tell the Two Lands the joyous news: "The Inundation has begun."

He breathed in a deep draft of air and cast his eyes lovingly over the pure pale-blue sky, where a heron winged its way along the banks of the River, that generous mother. *Someday, my egg will know the ecstasy of flight like that,* Hani told himself hopefully. *I'll call her Qenyt-ta-sherit, Qenyt the younger.* At least one small sorrow would be set right.

Ptah-mes was home, looking almost cheerful himself, although his smile had a carnivorous edge. Before Hani could even tell him the news from Mane, Ptah-mes said neutrally, "There has been an unfortunate accident, Hani. Talpu-sharri fell on a knife and slit his throat. His body found its way into the River, where crocodiles are known to gather."

Hani gaped at him for a moment, then a kind of grim pleasure seeped into him. He struggled not to grin. "Then justice has been done after all, my lord. Let me tell you what Mane brought back from Naharin." As Hani told him all he had learned, Ptah-mes listened without any interruption, his face concentrated, until Hani concluded, "You've bilked Mahu of his prey—or rather, his colleague in deception."

Ptah-mes looked both satisfied and reflective. "The death of a man is never a light thing," he mused. "Only a high good can justify it."

Like avenging your wife, Hani thought. "He was a danger to our kingdom, my lord."

"Yes."

"So I suppose our case is closed."

"Our case is indeed closed. A new vizier of the Lower Kingdom has been appointed, Hani. He has declined to renew my office."

"Oh, Lord Ptah-mes!" cried Hani, struck to the soul by the injustice. *Gods know what kind of truckling sycophant I'll have over me now.* "Are you being punished for standing up to Mahu?"

"Punished? I'm not so sure. I'll be taking up residence in Azzati as commissioner of the northern vassals. The appointment is a step down, so I presume it's intended to be a punishment. But it has in its favor that Azzati is very far away."

Hani sat there, stunned. That post had remained unfilled since the death of Yanakh-amu some years before. He tried to think of something positive to say. "You'll still be my immediate superior, then, at least. Who is replacing you in the high commission?"

"I don't know," said Ptah-mes lightly. "Some Aten-worshipping toady, I don't doubt. He's welcome to it. I will quietly do my little job far from the rays of the Dazzling Sun Disk. With any luck, my name will be forgotten."

Hani flinched. Ptah-mes wasn't over his painful self-contempt after all, despite his insouciant air. But at least he was out of danger. And the vassals had gained an honest and skillful advocate. Ptah-mes rose, and Hani followed suit.

"Goodbye, my friend," said Ptah-mes, his smile warming. "I thank you for everything."

"And I you, my lord. For your support and your extreme generosity. I wish it could have been better rewarded." Hani grasped the hand his superior extended and clasped it hard for an instant. Then, finding his throat starting to tighten with tears, he made a profound bow, fingers to mouth, and his respect was genuine.

When he rose, Ptah-mes was already walking away into the dark salon. Hani gazed at his straight, elegant back. Then he turned and made his way to the door and out through the garden.

When he emerged onto the sun-washed street, he looked up. A hawk was circling overhead on strong, graceful wings, for all the world like a painted image of Haru, the One on High. *Honest men still have a protector,* Hani thought with a smile.

Did you enjoy this book? Here is a sample of
The North Wind Descends, the next volume
in the Lord Hani Mysteries series:

H ANI STOOD IN THE RECEPTION room of the vizier of the Lower Kingdom and wiped the sweat off his face with his arm. The dim, high-ceilinged hall was blessedly cool after the withering heat of the courtyard. At his side, his secretary, Maya, said uneasily, "What do you suppose the vizier wants to see you for, my lord?"

"I have no idea, my friend. I've had precious little contact with Lord Ra-nefer since he took office except to send written reports. I think I've sort of slipped through the cracks of his notice, since I've been working locally." Hani thought gratefully of his former direct superior, Lord Ptah-mes, who had managed to get him off the rolls of foreign postings. Alas, Ptah-mes himself, in disfavor with the king, was now stationed abroad at Azzati in Djahy.

"Maybe he wants to give you the gold of honor, eh, my lord?" Maya said sarcastically. The two of them knew Hani was no more in favor than his superior, after he had only too successfully uncovered the mastermind of a series of tomb robberies two years before.

"More likely, he needs me to take the blame for some botch-up." Hani grinned.

Their conversation was interrupted by the appearance of Lord Ra-nefer's secretary at the vizier's door. He tipped his head and said loftily, "The vizier of the Lower Kingdom will see you now."

Hani took a deep breath and strode forward through the shadowy reception room and into the office, luminous with the buffered glow from its high windows. The vizier sat on a fine chair on a dais. He was a rotund figure in his long kilt knotted across the chest, his thick neck full of gold that doubled his chins up. There was a sheen of sweat on his face.

Hani folded in a formal bow, hands on his knees, and when he rose, Lord Ra-nefer said in a high-pitched, weary voice, "The famous Hani. I thought I'd never meet you."

"I'm honored by the summons, my lord." Hani was unsettled. *Famous?* This hyperbole augured nothing good. He had tried hard to stay below the notice of the court.

"Well, Ptah-mes isn't around to intercede for you for the moment, so we'll be seeing more of one another, I daresay—at least, until a new high commissioner of foreign affairs in the north is named." Ra-hotep crossed his arms, which rested on the mound of his belly, and leaned back in his chair, while Hani waited, curious, to be told why he was here.

Ra-nefer eyed Hani up and down for a moment with a considering expression on his jowly face. That face was a strange color, as of a pallid green laid over the copper of his Theban complexion.

Does he know about my resistance to orders? Is he wondering if he can trust me? Hani asked himself.

After the two men had sized each other up for a heartbeat, the vizier resumed, "Two reasons why you're here, my friend. One is, I have a commission for you in Djahy, or maybe Kharu—I forget which it is—but Ptah-mes will fill you in on the details. See him in Azzati. And the other..."

He trailed off, and an ominous ripple of apprehension crawled up Hani's spine.

"Our Sun God Nefer-khepru-ra Wa-en-ra—life, prosperity, and health be his—wants to recognize you. You're to be named a Master of the King's Stable and receive the gold of honor."

It was as if the floor had dropped out from under Hani. Of all the events in the world he had never expected to happen, this was surely the most improbable. *May the Hidden One protect me. Is this a sarcastic joke?* He had been a thorn in the king's flesh for years—criticizing the foreign policy of the Two Lands, uncovering a shady bit of political intrigue that Nefer-khepru-ra would probably have preferred to keep hidden...and now he was to be honored? Suspicion smoldered like a banked fire in Hani's middle, but he said only, "The king's favor is the breath of life in my nostrils, my lord. I fear I am unworthy."

"Well, if by that you mean you know nothing about horses, that's not an obstacle," Ra-nefer said dryly, as if Hani's protestations were an imposition. "The association with the cavalry is purely honorific. But some pompous title will give you more clout when you deal with our vassals in

Kharu. Or was it Djahy?" He suppressed a belch and patted himself on the chest with a fist. "Damned cucumbers."

Hani groped unsuccessfully for words for a moment and finally managed, "I'm speechless, my lord."

Ra-nefer emitted a burble that might have been amusement, although his put-upon expression never brightened. "Don't be too speechless. We're counting on your eloquence in Djahy."

Or is it Kharu? Hani thought, with the kind of giddy interior laughter of a man who has had his world overturned. "And when is this honor to be bestowed, if I may make so bold, my lord?"

"Two weeks. That gives you time to get your people down here. Any questions, Hani? If not, that's all." Ra-nefer rose, none too tall even on his feet. He hitched at the knot of his long kilt as if afraid it might all come sliding down, although Hani suspected the man's belly should hold it comfortably. Quite a difference from his late predecessor, the lean, hawk-faced Aper-el.

Hani bowed, glad the prostration hid his expression. He should be wildly honored, but this was all too strange, and he couldn't help but wonder what lay behind it. By the time he rose, the vizier had disappeared through his inner door, and Hani was left to totter, like a man in shock, out to the reception hall once more.

ACKNOWLEDGMENT

THE AUTHOR GRATEFULLY ACKNOWLEDGES ALL those who have helped her in the production of this book. To the wonderful women of my writers' group, for their critique and encouragement, my thanks.

To Lynn McNamee and her editorial team at Red Adept—Jessica, Sarah, and Laura—profound gratitude (and Lynn, for so many other forms of help). To the flexible and talented gang at Streetlight Graphics for the cover and map. To my cousin and her husband, my technology guru: thanks, guys. To Enid, who urged me forward by her support, I can't thank you sufficiently. And most of all, to my husband, Ippokratis, who put up with the months of fixation it takes to write a novel, many, many thanks.

ABOUT THE AUTHOR

N.L. Holmes is the pen name of a professional archaeologist who received her doctorate from Bryn Mawr College. She has excavated in Greece and in Israel, and taught ancient history and humanities at the university level for many years. She has always had a passion for books, and in childhood, she and her cousin (also a writer today) used to write stories for fun.

Today, since their son is grown, she lives with her husband and three cats. They split their time between Florida and northern France, where she gardens, weaves, plays the violin, dances, and occasionally drives a jog-cart. And reads, of course.